Praise for *Unrest*

"Dark secrets seeded in Ireland burst into full and furious bloom in Gwen Tuinman's *Unrest*. With sharply-seen details of 1830s Ottawa, *Unrest* parallels personal and political peril in the gritty world of Bytown's Irish poor. Tender, brutal, heartbreaking and true, this is historical fiction at its best." —Beth Powning, author of *The Sister's Tale*

"In her stunningly beautiful story *Unrest*, Gwen Tuinman's memorable antiheroes—the transcendent and mesmerizing Mariah, and the dazzlingly rebellious young Thomas—navigate the wilds alongside a gang of unforgettably diverse eccentrics in the lawless Ottawa Valley of 1836. The writing is a triumph—unflinchingly powerful and at the same time a meditation on motherhood, love, and what we must do to become our true selves. Tuinman's prose is as remarkable and exquisite as its setting, saturated with period detail and heart. I couldn't put it down." —Maia Caron, author of *Song of Batoche*

"Meticulously researched and exquisitely written, *Unrest* is unapologetic in its starkly vivid depiction of Upper Canada's frozen wilderness and the people who survived within it. A marvellous adventure." —Genevieve Graham, author of *The Forgotten Home Child*

"I could not rest until I turned the last, thoroughly satisfying page of *Unrest*, a mesmerizing tale that drew me in from the first gorgeously lyrical page. With unforgettable characters and meticulous detail, the author immerses readers in the cold, hard-scrabble existence of Upper Canada and the soul of the oppressed Irish . . . A compelling story of deception and truth, terror and courage, subjugation and transformation, *Unrest* makes history both vividly particular and timeless in its incisive depiction of human passions." —Lilian Nattel, author of *Only Sisters*

"Gwen Tuinman's *Unrest* depicts a little-known aspect of 19th century Canadian history. Her portrayal of the lives of Irish immigrants to Ottawa is expertly drawn in remarkable detail, from political gatherings in taverns to encounters with the harsh winter landscape. . . . An important story that opens a window on what it means to fight for your place here." —Suzanne Desrochers, author of *Bride of New France*

"Set in frontier Ottawa and the frozen wilderness of Upper Canada, *Unrest* offers a unique, vibrant account of the Irish poor as they navigate a society awash in hardship, corruption, and prejudice. Tough-as-nails Mariah and her rash, willful son Thomas come to vivid, aching life as they rise up against the oppressive forces that restrain them. A skillfully researched, compelling tale of resilience, love and the relentless pursuit of one's dreams." —Cathy Marie Buchanan, author of *The Painted Girls*

"*Unrest* is a wild ride through a bygone world bristling with life. Tuinman's flawed and feisty mother-son duo hold on tight through it all, losing and finding their way amid poverty and longing, violence and lies. An unforgettable portrait of human cruelty and its only possible conqueror, love." —Alissa York, author of *Far Cry*

"Lively, many-voiced, and replete with detail, *Unrest* is a great adventure and an impressive portrait of little-known settler life around Ottawa. Its characters will live on in your mind." —Alix Hawley, author of *My Name Is a Knife*

UNREST

GWEN TUINMAN

VINTAGE CANADA

Published in 2025 by Vintage Canada
Previously published in hardcover by Random House Canada in 2024

Vintage Canada, an imprint of Penguin Random House Canada Limited
320 Front Street West, Suite 1400,
Toronto, Ontario, M5V 3B6, Canada
penguinrandomhouse.ca

Vintage Canada and colophon are registered trademarks of
Penguin Random House LLC.

The authorized representative in the EU for product safety and compliance is
Penguin Random House Ireland, Morrison Chambers, 32 Nassau Street,
Dublin, D02 YH68, Ireland, https://eu-contact.penguin.ie

Library and Archives Canada Cataloguing in Publication
Title: Unrest / Gwen Tuinman.
Names: Tuinman, Gwen, author.
Identifiers: Canadiana 20250113481 | ISBN 9781039011489 (softcover)
Subjects: LCGFT: Historical fiction. | LCGFT: Novels.
Classification: LCC PS8639.U52 U57 2025 | DDC C813/.6—dc23

Cover, interior, and map designs by Talia Abramson
Cover images: (frame) Sharmin, (ornaments) sakedon, (landscape) Serghei V/
Adobe Stock; (texture) MILO TEXTURES/Pexels; (figure) Anna Gorin, (sky)
Florian Blondeau/500px/Getty
Typeset by Erin Cooper

Printed in the United States of America

2 4 6 8 9 7 5 3 1

Penguin
Random House
VINTAGE CANADA

For Eric,
River, Carly and Zach

But were I loved, as I desire to be,
What is there in the greatest sphere of the earth,
And range of evil between death and birth,
That I should fear,—if I were loved by thee?

Lord Tennyson, "But Were I Loved" (1832)

Fear is a fine spur; so is anger.

Irish proverb

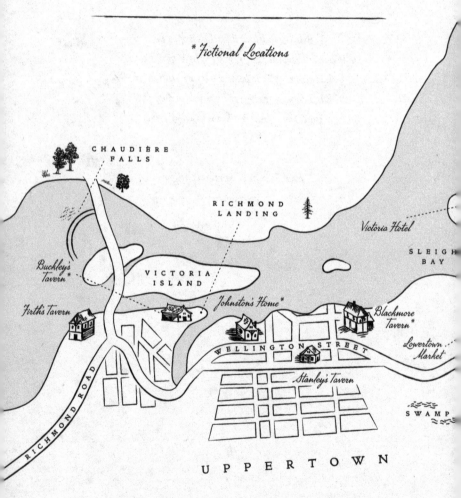

BYTOWN, 1836

* Fictional Locations

CHAUDIÈRE
FALLS

RICHMOND
LANDING

Victoria Hotel

SLEIGH
BAY

Buckley's
Tavern *

VICTORIA
ISLAND

Johnston's Home *

Blackmore
Tavern *

Firth's Tavern

Lowertown
Market

WELLINGTON STREET

Stanley's Tavern

SWAMP

RICHMOND ROAD

UPPERTOWN

OTTAWA RIVER

RIDEAU RIVER

LOWERTOWN

RIDEAU RIVER

Bytown Coffeehouse
Christie's Tavern*
Notre Dame Church
Peg's Shanty*
Home for Friendless Women*
Edwards Mercantile*

SUSSEX STREET

RIDEAU STREET

Sappers Bridge
Mueller's Blacksmith Shop*
Mueller's Home*
Newell's Home*

LAY-BY

RIDEAU CANAL

Corktown

1

MARIAH

September 1836

My fear is a black dog crouched and snarling in the middle of a road. It follows me everywhere. So it's been all my life. Menace lurks high and low in the snake pit known as Bytown. If money fell from the clouds tomorrow, I'd be on my way out of here as soon as I could fill my basket with the stuff.

Bytown's no place for a son to learn about being a man—at least not a good man. Alas, it's my boy, Thomas, I'm walking there to see, at the blacksmith shop where he apprentices for a German, Mr. Mueller. Thomas prefers the song of Mueller's hammer against the anvil to the dull thwack of his da's axe chopping white pine. With the first hairs sprouting from his chin, he fancies himself a man. Although he speaks too freely, the boy knows his own mind. In this way, he has surpassed me.

Darkness began to lift soon after I left the homestead, but already the sun inches above the crimson tops of the maple groves. If I don't reach Thomas before the forge is hot enough for working iron, he'll be too busy to talk. Time is running out. Not even the tip of a cobbler's nail jabbing at my right heel will slow my pace.

Four miles to go. My boots crunch dried leaves and pine needles against the forest floor and my mind drifts toward disheartening thoughts about Thomas's future. His appetite for freedom and Bytown's flurry of lawless mayhem have ensnared him. He forgets about his mother and looks restlessly to the horizon.

Geese honk overhead. Even they wish to fly far away.

Another sound rises so faintly from behind me that I nearly miss it. My shoulders tighten and for a few seconds I hold my breath until it resolves into hooves clomping an uneven rhythm against the dirt road. As the horse draws nearer, I recognize the underlying rattle of a cart.

Men are approaching.

"Keep walking, Mariah," I whisper to myself. Dew wets the hem of my skirt when I veer from the road, and the leather soles of my boots slide down the grassy embankment so that I barely keep my balance. My knuckles turn white from squeezing the handle of the basket I'm carrying. The taunts of Diarmait Flynn and his sons travel across a decade and a half from behind their stone fence in County Cork to terrorize me anew.

As the cart begins to overtake me, my breathing quickens.

Through the tunnel formed by the brim of my bonnet, the horse's whiskered muzzle comes into view. A glance downward reveals his limp. It's plain to see he needs reshoeing.

The driver is a square-shouldered man with a hat pulled low on his forehead. He glances back at me for only a split second as the cart rolls past, but my chest constricts all the same. He resembles one of the Flynns.

Except for Seamus and Thomas, all men do.

Thoughts of my son push me onward.

Since he started boarding with the Muellers a year ago, Thomas has not come home. Today he must accept our invitation to return at least to share a meal with us. I wish for his homecoming so hard, it cannot be otherwise. The entire family—Seamus, my sister, Biddy, and their children—misses my son. But I miss him more than anyone. His lengthy absence makes it even more difficult to endure my sister's resentments.

Her impatience is at the root of our undoing. On the afternoon of Thomas's conception, Biddy's pestering had driven me from Mam and Da's cottage. If not for her, I would have never braved crossing our road, making my way through the nearby copse of oak and chestnut trees and down to the river, where I found Seamus stricken with grief and bawling over the fresh news of his da's death. Had Biddy been content to let me grieve quietly over the ruination of my face, Seamus would never have laid his head upon my shoulder. I'd have never rested a hand on his back or kissed his hair.

I was only sixteen. He was twenty-two. Weeks previous, he'd carried me home after beating away the Flynns' dog, whose teeth were tearing at my flesh. When a man saves your life, you save him back. You pick up his burden and bear it as your own.

I know it was a sin to lie with my sister's betrothed. But with a face as scarred as mine, you don't pause to weigh moral implications. A thin white line like a crack in spring ice begins in the centre of my forehead, then opens wide and slices southeast through my brow. The deep split continues across the bone ridge beneath my eye and ends suddenly where the rounded flesh of my cheek should begin. Across the outside corner of that same eye, a crest of bunched scarlet tissue, measuring three fingers, dips over my cheekbone, then narrows and cuts downward through my upper lip.

Our union was a sweaty and frenzied event that finished before I'd recovered from the wonder of its beginning. There is a tarnished place in my heart where I lock away fragments of memory—his ragged breath, the scent of damp earth, the bed of moss cushioning my tailbone. It is difficult to unsee the look of mortification that darkened Seamus O'Dougherty's face when he crawled from between my legs afterwards and took measure of my disarray. Remorse still swims in his grey eyes sometimes when he looks at me, and floods me with shame, although not as much as in the early days after our union. I'd say that I regretted my sin, but then I'd be regretting our creation of the one good thing to come of my life—Thomas.

It wasn't until a few years after we'd all immigrated to Upper Canada that the pieces fell in place and Biddy realized Thomas's da is Seamus, not a stranger on the road as I'd claimed.

Since that day, Biddy has claimed the domestic realm. I mostly work outside. A line of hurt divides us as clearly as the Rideau Canal cleaves Bytown in two, with the English and gentry of Uppertown to the west and the poor Irish and French of Lowertown hunkered along the opposite bank.

We don't discuss our situation. What can be done? Biddy swore an oath to Mam and Da before we stepped off the dock at Cork all those years ago. She promised to take me in and make sure no harm befell me, and to raise my unborn child as her own in this new land of fresh beginnings where no one knew us.

The stillness of Uppertown is a reprieve of sorts. Not a single painted carriage yet stirs. At this hour, rich women wrapped in flowered silk robes lounge by their fires and order poor Irish girls in mended dresses to pour more tea. Along the hard-packed dirt of Wellington Street, stone-built houses stand two storeys high, with sturdy chimneys, proper glass windows, and polished oak doors hung with pairs of brass lanterns. The drawing of lace curtains as I pass by reminds me that I don't belong on this side of the Rideau Canal. The British have a way of letting their inferiors know where they stand. They don't mind venturing to the poor side of the canal to hire a blacksmith or to fetch incoming guests from ships docked at Sleigh Bay. But they don't want us mincing past their houses.

The buildings are strung farther apart as I continue east toward Lowertown's narrow streets, clustered hovels and outhouse reek. But before I can reach Sappers Bridge to cross the canal, the sprawl of two dead strumpets in front of a tavern grinds me to a halt. I should continue on my way, but something in their sordid condition compels me to linger. There must be someone else in the street who might help to cover them up or summon the authorities, like the man smoking his pipe in the doorway of a neighbouring house. But when he sees me looking, he promptly backs inside, then shuts the door.

I suppose we're on our own.

The first body is propped up on a rough bench and leaning against the wall. Her head lolls to one side and her wide, bloodshot eyes are rolled upward to meet the sky. Her mouth gapes, the rotted and missing teeth telling me that she was no stranger to the feeling of an empty stomach resting against her spine. From a length of blonde hair that's tumbled over her shoulder, a red bow hangs like an autumn leaf trapped in a tangle of branches. Her shift is peeled downward to her waist, leaving her breasts exposed to the world. A necklace of finger-shaped bruises circles her throat. Some brute has done this to her. She's been arranged with her bare feet set far apart, her skirt hiked high, and her knees wide to shock the gentry passing by in their upholstered carriages.

The sight of corpses rarely startles me. In Ireland, Mam was a healer but the healing didn't always take. People died. Sometimes they starved. I saw them. Death followed us across the ocean and slid bodies over the ship rails. Shrouds splashed into the briny waters. Men, women and children die here too from all manner of illness. But the ones taken by violence unnerve me. It's the terror locked in their eyes that does it.

One of the dead women's hands clutches the neck of an empty whiskey bottle. The other hangs over the shoulder of the second woman, lying on the bench with her head of raven-black curls resting on her companion's thigh and her lily-white backside facing the street. Except for her scuffed boots and the stockings pooled around her ankles, she's naked as the day she was born.

When the dark-haired woman shivers, a strangled cry escapes me. She's alive, so now what? I've spent hours walking so that I can have a word with Thomas and sell this basketful of my sister's curatives. To help this tarnished woman will draw attention to me when all I want is to move unnoticed through the streets—to finish my business and return to the refuge of our cabin in the southwestern woods.

Morning smoke has begun curling from Lowertown's chimneys. Thomas will no doubt be stoking his master's forge. Soon he'll be hard at work and my chance to speak with him will be lost. It's unlikely that Biddy will spare me for a second day. If not for my selling her wares, she would have argued against this day's trip.

My decision is made. I'm leaving.

A thread of guilt tugs at me as I rush toward the canal. "Half given is better than full refusal," Mam often said. Even a bit of help is better than none at all. But these women are the tavern owner's problem. If he entertains the likes of murderous men for the sake of coin, he can deal with the calamity left in their wake. My anger flares. This town is filled with the mad-dog rabble of my countrymen. Until the winter timber season calls them back to the woods, they pass their nights drinking whiskey, fighting and releasing new havoc on the well-to-do of Uppertown, including those rich Britain-loving Irish turned Orangemen. They don't lift a finger to help fellow Protestants like us.

Remembering these words from a Methodist circuit rider of my girlhood brings hot tears to my eyes. *The blackest sin can be forgiven in the face of good works. Good begets good.* I'm in need of both clemency and good fortune, so I turn back to the tavern.

Two scrappy boys, no more than ten years old, stand staring at the women while a third kneels and pokes at the inside of the dead woman's thigh with a stick.

"For shame," I yell. Caught off guard, they scrabble backward when I stride past them to pull the woman's skirt down over her knees. The fabric is caked with vomit and smells of dried urine. When I wheel around, the curious boy drops his stick.

"Whoa," he says, gawking at my face.

A second boy whistles. "It looks like something tried to eat you!"

The sleeping woman stirs on the bench and draws the boys' attention away from me. When they giggle, I turn and fan my skirt to block their view of her bottom.

"Go on home!" I say over my shoulder, but when I look back at them, they haven't budged. "Where's your da or your mam?"

The boy who so far has been silent answers me. "Da's clearing skid roads at a camp near Perth, and none of your business about where Mam's at."

The waking woman pushes herself upright on the bench and is instantly confronted with the blank stare of her benchmate. "The tree-chopping bastards! This is the second time in a month they offed a girl who owed me money." She searches the vicinity of the bench and adds, "And they took my one good dress." With an arm hugging her breasts, she peers up at me. She's a slip of a girl, no more than eighteen years old. The endearing gap between her front teeth eases my twinge of nerves over the anger sparking in her eyes.

The only thing I have with which to conceal her vulnerable state is my mother's shawl, but I'll not be giving that up. It's one of the two things of Mam's I own. She wore it so often, it was part of her.

"Give me your shawl," the girl says. "I can't walk home like this."

I bite the inside of my lip and say nothing.

"For God's sake, I'll return it." Her hand stretches toward me and flutters with an impatience that makes my mind go blank. My hands do her bidding and pass the shawl. I'm not sure if I want to slap the girl or hug her.

She tucks one end under her chin and clamps it against her chest while she raises herself off the bench to gird her hips with the remaining length.

"Show us your bubbies again," shouts one of the rascals waiting behind me.

She nudges me aside and stands with a hand on her hip. "Come back when your balls have dropped and there's coin in your pocket."

"Whore!" the boy yells. The others laugh as they tear off in the direction of the canal.

I want to run with them. Time is wasting. When I look back at the girl, she mistakes my expression.

"Name-calling don't bother me. I am a whore—but I'm a whore with a plan. This is just the beginning for me." She yanks the bow from the dead woman's hair and pins it to her own. "Once I got enough money, I'm taking myself somewhere real quiet where no one knows me. I'm gonna start a new life. And I'll live it on my own terms."

"That's a nice dream," I reply and begin to walk away. I'm surprised she hasn't learned yet that dreams are dangerous. When unfulfilled, they hollow you out until you feel worthless.

"Oh, it's not a dream," she says. "I'm going to make it happen." As I turn around again to face her, she scratches her ear while studying me. "I've seen you near my shanty off Sussex, close to the market."

"I deliver medicinal herbs to families in Lowertown."

"Got anything to stop a man's sap from rising?"

I nod. Her direct manner amuses me. In the O'Dougherty home, people seldom speak their minds.

"Eh, I knew there was a smile in there somewhere. You should use it more often," she says. "Can you fix me up with some of *that* medicine?"

"I could."

"Grand. I'll be dropping that into some fellas' whiskey," the girl says. "I'd like to dose up Bess's customers. Drive her fellas to my door instead. You know how it is."

I don't. There's been no one since Seamus.

She glances at the woman on the bench. "Once the girls hear this one is dead, they'll be going through her things and there'll be nothing good left for me. I've had my eyes on her green dress so I best hurry over to her shanty if I'm going to have a crack at it."

"I'll want my shawl back," I tell her, though my voice shakes as if I'm asking a favour.

She eyes me with amusement. "What are you called?"

"Mariah."

"Finish your business in town and come find me. Everyone knows me as Peg." And with that, she turns away and struts toward the Rideau Canal in my shawl, with all the dignity of a gentrified Uppertown lady.

The tolling of a church bell alerts me to the hour. If I'm to reach Thomas before his work day starts in earnest, I must run for all I'm worth. My damned luck, the cobbler's nail stabs my left heel with every rushed stride and the wild swinging of my basket threatens to toss its contents onto the road. Can something not go right for a change? The sound of Peg's laughter rings behind me until the labour of my breath takes its place.

2

THOMAS

B y God, I love town life. Every hour of the day and night, something is happening. My head still aches from the ale I drank at the public house last night. But it was worth it. When three raftsmen from Burritts Rapids sang our Irish ballads, I pictured the emerald fields even though I've never set foot outside this county. A true Dubliner with ale sloshing from his cup performed a ballad from atop the bar and a lump rose in my throat. Around the room, moist-eyed men pressed hats to their hearts and listened.

This morning it's the black cloud billowing from the forge that has my own eyes watering. It's always worse before the fire burns clean and the smoke is drawn through the roof vent and into the sky. I reach a coal shovel over the kindling mounded like a haystack at the centre of the forge and rake the coke closer to the flames. The music of metal scraping across the bricks matches the singers' pitch from the night before and I'm visited by a sense of pride—for my people and my vocation.

A few local lads wait outside the shop doors each morning, hoping to be hired as day labour. We'll need the extra hands today if we're to finish our work for the wheelwright. When I turn to see which one Mr. Mueller is hiring on, the corner of my eye catches sight of her. All at once I'm thrust back into Mam and Da's cabin and that shite feeling that comes from sucking hind tit all the time.

Aunt Mariah's presence across the road is a sliver trapped under my skin. Nothing inspires me to claim her—not the threadbare bonnet she wears nor the frizzed red hair jutting from beneath it like something the birds have teased out for nesting material. The basket over her arm tells me she's been sent into Bytown to do Mam's bidding. Nothing changes.

Rory Whelan slips in next to me. He reaches overhead and, under the pretense of being helpful, pulls downward on the handle of the bellows. He's an apprentice too, but he'll never be as good as I am. "Yer girlfriend's back, Tommy," he says, smirking over one shoulder.

"You know full well she's my aunt. And stop calling me *Tommy*. I hate that." My elbow connects with his ribs. He lets go of the bellows and grabs his side.

"My aunt never fawns over *me* like a lovesick puppy."

The fire is dying down so I pump the bellows and reposition the glowing coals with a shovel. From behind me, I hear kissing sounds. Someday I'll knock Rory on his arse. We'll see what kind of noises he makes then.

"She's coming," he whispers but I pretend not to hear. Maybe if I wish hard enough, Aunt Mariah will turn and leave.

"You gotta tell me, man," Rory says. "What happened to her face?"

I answer him with silence.

"You best be telling me or I'll ask her myself."

I take two steps toward him before Mr. Mueller calls out sharply, "O'Dougherty!"

"Sir?"

"You've got a caller." Mr. Mueller holds up two fingers. Two minutes, he's telling me. He's no happier with Aunt Mariah being here than I am.

Rory sniggers. He's worse than my sister.

My spinster aunt is so pathetic standing there in the doorway, stoop-shouldered, as if trying to disguise her imposing height. She's a good head taller than Mr. Mueller, but not nearly so thick in the chest and arms.

"Good morning, Mr. Hobbs!" Mueller greets a newly arrived farmer. The man excuses himself and squeezes past Aunt Mariah, holding his young daughter's hand tightly.

There she goes admiring me again, all dewy-eyed and smiling. Rory is right about one thing. That's not natural for an old aunt. What does she want from me?

"Auntie Mariah, you've got to stop showing up like this." The words come out more hateful than I intend. She squints, the way folks do when they think their ears are playing tricks on them, then turns her head to watch a driver steer his horse and cart toward the smithy stable. She's always treated me a notch better than my sisters. I don't know what stops me from being kinder to her.

"G'day, ma'am," Rory says, coming up behind me. "Fine day for a walk, don't you know. Lovely dress you're wearing." He's staring at her scarred-up face and planning the yarns he'll spin about her later at the public house. I've heard what he says about Mr. Mueller's plump wife. Anything he relays about my aunt will be ruthless.

Aunt Mariah's no fool. She knows what he's about.

Rory's not the first mean-spirited rapscallion to examine her like a sideshow exhibit. "I've come to have a word with my nephew," she says evenly. "Alone."

"Well then," he says, backing away awkwardly. "I'll leave you to it. Good to see you, Auntie." He doffs an imaginary cap and returns to the forge.

Something stirs in Aunt Mariah's eyes. Not shame, but something I can't name. "You have a message from Mam?" I ask.

Her gaze darts over my shoulder when a hammer strikes the anvil. It's Mr. Mueller's one-pound ball-peen. I can tell by the note it sings. Just when I think my aunt's about to answer me, her lips press together and water fills her eyes. Talking to her is like walking across a single strand of yarn stretched tight between two trees. I don't know where to step next for fear of falling.

"Dinner on the sabbath," she finally says. "Please, Thomas . . ."

All I can do is sigh. It's the same question each time she comes by.

"Your da and I are butchering hogs this week," she offers. That means pork roast with Mam's rosemary and potatoes baked alongside. I can smell it already.

"When's Da going off for the winter?" I ask.

"In a few weeks," she says, looking at the floor. We both know he'll remain at the timber camp until the spring thaw. There'll be no one to soften Mam and it will be Aunt Mariah who suffers most. Her eyes search mine while she waits for my answer.

"I'll come," I say, "but—"

"Thomas!" Mr. Mueller points toward the fire lagging on the forge. A sharp nod to Mr. Mueller, then I turn back to Aunt Mariah.

"—but I must return home that same evening."

"Home?" she repeats.

"Home to the smithy. I'm needed here in the morning." Truth be told, I could plead my case with Mr. Mueller, insist that my family needs me to stay overnight. But I don't want to be away from the excitement of this town for that long.

"My two minutes are up," I announce. Without waiting for her response, I hurry back to the forge. Partway there, I hear her voice calling after me, "Wonderful, Thomas. I'm much pleased."

Mr. Mueller frowns as I pass him. Muscles flex as he raises and lowers the hammer. His wrists and forearms are thick from years of work. He's a God-fearing Methodist with high expectations for himself and anyone under his roof—which is why Mam has allowed me to apprentice here.

I am glad to see the back of Aunt Mariah. When I was younger, she often took me exploring in the woods or fishing along our creek. I think she still sees me as that boy. If I lived at home, she'd never let me be a man. She's kin but her attention annoys me to the point where I sometimes hate her for it, which I know causes her hurt. But I also suffer when she so clearly favours me. My mam hates it, though I'm not sure why.

But I've no time to think on that now. The wheelwright has arrived with a load of wheels in need of metal tyres. He hops down from his wagon and tethers his horse to a post next to the water trough at the front corner of the shop.

"Look lively," Mr. Mueller tells Rory. "Money is about to walk through the door. Get the young lad to pump water and fill the slack tub outside. And you, O'Dougherty . . ."

I'm in for it now.

"Today I will show you how to rim a wheel!" Deep laughter escapes from beneath his bushy moustache as he teases me, and I brace myself against the force of his beefy hand thumping between my shoulder blades. I needn't look at Rory to see his raised brow.

It takes a moment to absorb the good news. Only a year into my apprenticeship and I'm being trained to do work for the wheelwright. I told Da that blacksmithing *is* the best line of work for me. I won't be like him, freezing my fingers off chopping trees all winter, spending the remainder of the year farming or hunched up alone in his old shed making chairs. This sabbath, I will tell him how right I was to not follow him to the timber camps.

I am my own man now.

🌿

At noon, Mrs. Mueller bustles through the side door of the smithy with a basket over one arm. In the opposite hand hangs a wrought-iron pot whose wire handle is wrapped with a rag. The Muellers' daughter, a shy blonde-haired child of six years, walks next to her cradling a glass jar of apple cider in her arms. While I bank the coals on the forge, Rory clears tools from the butcher-block worktable and hoists the pot onto it for Mrs. Mueller. After doling a watery beef and cabbage stew into tin bowls for us hungry men, she unfolds a square of cloth and offers us each a small portion of bread and cheese.

Outdoors, the air is crisp but the wind is low, so I take my meal to a bench in front of the smithy. My stomach has been talking to me since breakfast so I wolf down spoonfuls of stew right away and tear into the bread. I crave a greater portion of the loaf. With so many people in Lowertown hungry on account of food shortages from the summer drought, I should try harder to be grateful, but what would that get me? When I lean my back against the clapboard wall and close my eyes, the bench suddenly wobbles beneath me. Rory has plopped next to me and my disappointment is immediate.

"So," he says around a mouthful of food, "your aunt looks like someone threw her into a bucket of knives face-first."

"Watch your mouth."

"Just tell me what happened," he urges. "Then I'll leave you alone, I swear."

I burn to grab his shirt front and bang his head against the wall, but Mr. Mueller would send me packing. I look straight ahead and continue chewing.

Aunt Mariah never speaks on the subject. I've asked her myself on several occasions only to be met with a pained smile and silence. It was Da who told me that a dog had attacked her. If I tell Rory the whole story, he'll hammer the details into a cruel comedic performance to share with anyone who'll listen—men in the saloon, the day-labour boys. Before you know it, riffraff will be following Aunt Mariah along the street barking at her.

"I'll only tell you that my da saved her. A hero, he is."

Rory grins, his mouth stuffed with bread. This offering of information appears to satisfy him, at least for now.

Da *is* a hero. I dragged the story from him of how that hateful lot, the Flynns, sicced their mangy dog on my aunt. Bunch of lousy drunks, Da said. The old man and his sons would taunt her as she passed their cottage each afternoon carrying food to my granda at the estate stables where he worked. My da was driving the master's donkey cart along the same road. From a long way off he could hear the screams. When he came upon them, the beast had Aunt Mariah pinned to the road, its great head shaking as it ripped her face. Da leapt off the cart and smashed the dog's skull with a rake handle until it fled, then picked her up from the dirt. She couldn't see him for the blood streaming down her face and at first resisted, striking him in the chest with her fists, thinking he was one of the Flynns.

When I look at Da now, it's hard to reconcile him with the man he must have been that day. He never talks about the crossing from Ireland or his days on the Deep Cut digging the Rideau Canal. His rescuing Aunt Mariah from the jaws of that mad dog may be the last brave and decisive act he ever commits.

"Hey," Rory says, wiping the back of one hand across his mouth. "What d'ya say we mosey over to the public house tonight? We could sneak out again."

I want to go, but I shrug.

"Oh, is that how it is? I'm hammering out feckin' nails all the live-long day while you're working with Laird Mueller outside. You're too good for me now?"

UNREST

"Might be," I tell him. "We'll see."

He finishes his cider and nudges my shoulder. We both know I'll go. There's a current of possibility that runs through Bytown and it's most powerful after dark. While docile men sleep at night, forward-thinking Irishmen gather to discuss the ills of this world and how to fix them.

I'll never be like my father. It's these men of action I take after.

3

MARIAH

The cabin walls push in on us during the cold months. Some-one is always underfoot and privacy is non-existent. There are days when I dislike my sister's children—particularly eleven-year-old Elizabeth. She understands her good looks are a currency to purchase her mam's attention. In a few years she'll blossom into womanhood. I suspect her arrogance will be insufferable. This morn-ing, she sits across the table from Biddy while they prepare apples for drying. Biddy smiles like a rich banker each time she glances up at Elizabeth, who pretends not to notice.

Each of my three nieces take after Biddy, who in turn resembles our mam—in the physical sense at least. They share the same wil-lowy build, silvery eyes and wavy blonde hair. Although I am Biddy's younger sister, I tower over her by a head. I'm more like Da, big-boned and ham-fisted, which makes me resent my sister and niece all the more.

From the end of the table where I'm measuring flour into a wooden bowl, I can't help but witness the way Biddy dotes over her daughters.

Her gaze travels over the girls each time she reaches for a new apple from the basket resting at her feet.

The younger girls—Annie, who is seven, and Katherine, only two—play in front of the crackling fireplace. On days like this when I'm overtired from lack of sleep and my nerves are worked raw, their tussling over wooden blocks wears on me. The pair of them are innocent enough, but I worry they'll one day reject my kindness, as Elizabeth has done. Already they know to ignore me in their mam's presence.

Katherine's cheeks are rosy and she's begun rubbing her eyes. If she's coming down with fever, Biddy will brew a cure from some combination of herbs hanging in bunches along the rafters. But if the child is restless for more than a night, Biddy will be short on sleep and even more of a misery to live with.

Bitterness floods me upon seeing Katherine toddle toward Biddy. She burrows her face against her mother's thigh for a moment before returning to play in front of the hearth. I've been robbed of my own child seeking comfort from me. Since visiting Thomas days earlier, I've thought of little else. When he sits at this very table on the sabbath, Biddy will bask in the glow of his attention. He'll acknowledge me but there'll be no warmth in it.

After a few minutes of threading Biddy's apple rings onto strings, Elizabeth is fidgeting. She plunks an unfinished garland on the table and then, with the tip of her index finger, pushes some peels toward where I'm making bread. At the start, I think her arrangement is haphazard, but the concentration on her face convinces me otherwise. I roll up my sleeves to begin kneading the bread and try to make sense of what she's doing.

Elizabeth curls the first strip of apple skin into an incomplete circle, with a gap on one side. Next is a closed circle pushed against a vertical peel. The last two peels intersect each other like the lines of the two wooden crosses which stand by the pine windbreak, marking the wee graves of Biddy's lost babes.

"Bet you can't read what that says." She smiles at me triumphantly.

I'd rather button my wool coat up to my chin and brave the damp outside than give her the satisfaction of my answer. It's humiliating to be shown up by a child.

If only I could wipe that know-it-all grin off her face. If not for our old neighbour Roweena Newell's eldest daughter passing along what she learns from her mistress in town, Elizabeth wouldn't know how to make words either. Why does she target me for mockery when Biddy can't make sense of those curves and lines either? When I don't answer, Elizabeth grins in her mother's direction. "C-A-T spells *cat*!"

Biddy lays her knife among the skinned apples on the table and opens both arms wide. "Come kiss your mam. Such a smart girl you are."

Elizabeth traipses coyly around the far end of the table to collect her mother's embrace. Then she faces me and asks, "Auntie, why can't you read?"

To my surprise, Biddy answers. "Mariah and I were too poor for school." She carries on with peeling apples and adds, "That, and our mam and da were too daft to see the value in girls being able to read."

"They weren't daft," I mumble, pushing harder against the dough.
"What's that?" Biddy says sharply.

"I said I'd like to learn how—to read, that is."

"You? Learn how to read?" Biddy's tone is incredulous. "You're a bit long in the tooth for that, don't you think? A sharp mind is required for book learning. It's all you can do to pick apples worth preserving."

A giggle erupts from Elizabeth.

It's true that some of the apples are scabbed and wormy, but even had they been flawless Biddy would find fault since it was I who foraged them from the forest and not Seamus who'd bartered for them at the market.

It's unwise to ruffle Biddy's feathers any further, so I push my feelings down and think of what I'll do once I'm free to leave this kitchen. While the bread rises, I can escape outdoors to add new night-pail waste to the saltpetre beds behind Seamus's carpentry shed. If Seamus has replaced the handle on the pitchfork, I'll turn over the layers of straw and grass as well.

My most recent batch of salt crystals is waiting in a sack and ready for selling to his boss at the timber camp. Seamus is proud that my salt sprinkled on the horses' oats renders them docile in the woods. Next year, I'll double my production. The hard work will be worth it just to see the approval in his eyes. I've withheld a pouchful of saltpetre to sell Peg as I promised. It'll be a happy day when she drops the coins into my hand. I'll buy something for Thomas. And nerves won't stop me from collecting Mam's shawl, not like last time.

Thoughts of Peg resurrect an image of the dead woman on Wellington Street. Her violent end is burned into my mind. Among us, her murderer roams free and unpunished. More and more often, I'm plagued with worry over Thomas. He's proud and too young to see around corners. And Bytown is rife with temptation of every sort. The safest place for my son is away from there and with his mother.

His true mother. Me. Not Biddy.

The loaf is sticky, so I scoop a bit of flour for sprinkling the tabletop. No sooner have I withdrawn my hand from the flour tin than Elizabeth darts hers inside. With eyes rolled toward the upstairs loft, she roots around the bottom of the tin. My jaw tightens. In a moment, she'll taunt me—yet again—by removing the treasure I keep buried in the flour.

Thank God my son is nothing like her.

Elizabeth opens the cloth packet she pulls from the tin. Although I huff, a smile lights her face as she removes one of my pearl earbobs—the set bequeathed to me by Mam—and holds it next to her face. She cocks her head like a fine lady modeling her purchase in a shop mirror. Is there nothing that's just mine?

"How do I look, Mam?"

"Like a proper lady," Biddy answers, so clever with her insults, telling me without saying it that I'll never measure up to her daughter's beauty.

"Katherine is playing too close to the fire," I warn Elizabeth. "Fetch her back. If she touches the kettle—"

Without looking up, Elizabeth orders, "You do it, Annie!" She proceeds to rub an index finger over the gold filigreed that holds in place a pearl, equal in size to a Juneberry. From loops of gold, thin as a thread, a second pearl is suspended beneath the first, like cream dripping from a pitcher.

Biddy smirks, an acknowledgement that my ploy to distract Elizabeth from the earbobs has failed. This screws the lid tighter on my silence. I've learned to make myself small and of seemingly little consequence. Biddy is happiest when I take up the least space in her world.

I fold the dusted oval of dough over on itself and try to think of other things as I bear down with the heel of both hands. Is Thomas looking forward to the visit? Does he feel any remnant of fondness for me? At the smithy, he appeared eager to be rid of me. He's forgotten that it was I who taught him to tread silent through the woods to observe deer unseen. I was the one to instill in him an interest in the forge through the telling of tales about his granda blacksmithing in Ireland.

Mr. Mueller's other apprentice is sharp-eyed and looking for trouble. I hope he doesn't drag Thomas into some mischief he can't get out of. In Bytown, a boy bent on devilment needn't look far to find it.

"Where's Da?" Elizabeth leans over the water bowl, hoping to catch her reflection there. "I want him to see how pretty I look with Gran's pearls."

"He's out doing heaven knows what," Biddy says. Before she finishes speaking, Elizabeth flings the door open to look outside.

As if I'm not listening, I busy myself returning leftover flour to the tin. Seamus is making himself scarce in the shed again. For hours, he sits in deep concentration astride the shaving horse, pulling the sharp blade of his father's drawknife along lengths of birch.

I wish I was with him now. I live for Seamus's looks of approval when I anticipate his needs—passing him a tool before he reaches for it, returning home with a rabbit on a day he's been busy making chairs, or discovering a sapling perfect for chair spindles.

"Close the door and keep the heat in," Biddy calls out to Elizabeth, but the girl stands stock-still.

"Mam, there's a strange man," she finally says.

Biddy's eyes widen. I forget to breathe. Every week, new stories surface about thieving and ne'er-do-wells spreading violence in broad daylight.

Annie bounds to Elizabeth's side. "Where is he at?"

"Across the road, close to the treeline," Elizabeth says.

"Walking away from us or toward us?" Biddy asks as Katherine climbs onto her lap. I edge behind Elizabeth to see where she's pointing. A man is crossing the stretch of meadow that lies northwest of us. With a hand pressed to my chest, I tell Biddy, "He's not coming here." Just then, two other men step out from among the trees. My nieces and I watch intently. *Please don't come this way*, I pray.

"What's happening?" Biddy demands.

"There's others joining him, Mam," Elizabeth tells her.

Annie adds, "I think they're friends. They've stopped to chat. They look happy."

"What do you know?" Elizabeth scoffs. "They could be troublemakers, Frenchmen even."

"Come inside and close the door before they spot you," Biddy says. She flicks a glance at the small window next to the door and I understand she wants me to keep watch. Katherine slides from her mother's knee and follows Annie back to their game at the hearth, but Elizabeth, eyes full of worry, sits next to her mother.

"I should get Seamus," I say. My mouth is dry. I've seen what bad men can do. What if they come here? Seamus could be caught unawares in the shed.

"Leave him be," Biddy warns. "You'll draw more attention."

It's only when, moments later, the men adjust their packs and disappear into the woods that I breathe easy again. A nod to my sister tells her as much.

"Katherine, come away from the fire," Biddy says with an edge of impatience. The child pouts and backs closer to the centre of the floor, where Annie is galloping a carved horse across her knees and playing with her cornhusk dolls.

One day, Biddy won't need me anymore. I can see it coming in the way she sizes me up when she thinks I'm preoccupied and beyond noticing. Thomas has struck out on his own. With me gone, there'll be one less mouth to feed. Soon it will be Annie's job to watch after Katherine, and Elizabeth will take over doing the tasks that make me necessary in the house. I'll become a dried-up thing with nothing of value to call my own except my most cherished remembrance of Mam—a pair of earbobs I'll never part with.

Biddy smiles at Elizabeth. "Are you conjuring a wealthy husband, leanbh?"

"I am, Mam. He'll buy me horses and plant roses in my garden."

"That pretty face will take you far," Biddy says. "A man appreciates beauty in a wife."

Elizabeth's eyes flash in my direction to see if her mother's slight has drawn my tears. She's still fiddling with the earrings, which makes my jaw clench.

"Tell me again how Lady Harris gave them to Gran," Elizabeth asks her mother.

"Gran and Granda were tenant farmers on the Harris estate. Lord Harris's baby son took ill while the village doctor was away, so the kitchen women passed on a word about Gran being a healer."

"Gran taught you about doctoring herbs, right, Mam?"

Biddy nods. "His lordship sent for Gran, and her know-how brought the fever right down. Lady Harris gave her the earbobs by way of thanks."

"And Gran should have given them to you, Mam—not Auntie Mariah. You're the first-born," Elizabeth says. "That's how it's done."

My eyes cut to Biddy. There's an expression on her face I can't quite read, and it worries me. I dust my hands off over the table. "That's enough, Elizabeth. Put Gran's pearls back into the flour tin." My voice is firm, with nary a waver. But when I present my upturned palm, she doesn't comply.

"Give them to me now!" I say, but still she ignores me. Annie's gone quiet, watching to see what unfolds. Elizabeth is showing her who rules the roost.

Just then, Katherine begins to bawl in earnest and runs to Biddy. When my sister leans sideways to pick the child up, I stride toward Elizabeth. Her eyes widen, her lips press together tightly and her nostrils flare. I reach for her arm.

Biddy shouts at me, "Do not touch that child."

Suddenly, Elizabeth squeezes her eyes shut. Bringing the earbobs to her lips, she opens her mouth and makes a show of swallowing, then opens her eyes again.

I stop where I am and it's all I can do not to unravel completely.

Biddy lurches to her feet with Katherine howling astride her hip. "Look what you've made her do. Charging at her like that. You're twice her size."

"I only wanted my earbobs."

"*Your* earbobs," she snaps, then turns her attention to Elizabeth.

"And you, missy, will be returning Gran's pearls no matter how unpleasant the process!"

At first, Elizabeth appears stricken. But then a twinkle lights her eyes and a second later she convulses with laughter. She spits the earbobs into her hand, holding them out for us to see.

"Elizabeth Margaret O'Dougherty," Biddy says. "You scared the devil out of me." There will be no further scolding or consequence for Elizabeth's sass. I know this from experience, and it pleases me not.

I thrust a flour-coated palm forward. Instead of returning the earbobs to me, Elizabeth snatches up the scrap of cloth from the table and wraps it around them. She takes her time tying a strand of wool around the precious bundle.

Mam gave the pearls to me out of pity, I think, because I'm apt to die a spinster. I've never done anything more than hold them and think of Mam. Through the hardest years, when we were living in the squalor of a six-by-ten-foot Corktown shack along the canal banks south of Lowertown or squatting on land reserved for clergy, I never entertained thoughts of selling them. But now it occurs to me that I should sell them, if only to get them out of this house. And if I sold them, the money could help me move to a peaceful bit of country with Thomas. When his apprenticeship ends, we could buy a little house with a shed that'll accommodate a forge. My son would be proprietor of his very own blacksmith shop, and I'd plant my own garden. We'd be a real family.

Elizabeth theatrically shoves the packet of pearl earbobs into the flour tin, then replaces the lid and gives the tin a shake. She's about to take a seat and return to slicing apples when Biddy speaks up.

"Elizabeth, fetch Gran's shawl. I'm feeling the chill."

Usually, I leave Mam's shawl hanging from a wooden peg above my jack bed at the far end of the cabin. I won't be telling my sister that it's currently warming the shoulders of a prostitute in a Bytown brothel.

"I can't find it, Mam," Elizabeth says from behind me.

"Look harder."

Finally, I tell them, "The shawl's not here."

"Where, in the name of blessed Jesus, is it?" Biddy asks.

"I've lent it to a friend."

"What are you on about?"

I won't answer. Biddy will find the pebble of untruth in any story I try to spin, then she'll exaggerate it into boulder size and use it to crush me. My hands smooth the loaf while I brace for her interrogation.

"You have no friends around here." Biddy stops peeling and her eyes narrow. "Oh," she says with a sigh. "It must be someone in Bytown. Mam's shawl is gone for good, then. It's clear you can't be trusted with anything of value. You've no sense at all."

"She's good for it," I tell her.

Biddy snorts. "I'll believe you when I see that shawl coming through the door—"

The latch rattles, and the door creaks open. Dear God, have the men returned? But it's Seamus, thankfully, who steps inside. Annie runs toward him and wraps her arms around his waist. "Da, men were by the road!"

"You'll be seeing lots more of them. Men are heading to the camps earlier than usual this year to secure work," he says.

More men on the road. The thought chills me.

My sister ignores my stricken state. "Mariah, Roweena Newell will need a new delivery of feverfew to keep her headaches at bay. You can take it to her in Bytown next week but not before. There's too much work to be done here." She begins peeling another apple and adds, "And get Mam's shawl back too."

"Wouldn't it be better if you went, Biddy?" The request sounds weak even to my own ears.

My sister shoots me a look of disbelief.

"I should be splitting firewood and rechinking the walls," I offer weakly. "The nights are getting colder."

"It's not safe for a woman the likes of me to walk alone to Bytown," Biddy says. What she means is that a pretty woman like her won't be safe. But a woman with my looks is undesirable, even to the debased standards of drunks and criminals.

Seamus's eyes close slowly as his head drops forward. "Biddy," he scolds.

"Plus, I'm required here with my children," my sister continues. "Any dog can have puppies. Not everyone can be a mother."

Another dig. Biddy latches onto my gaze and holds tight. She's never let go of my past sins and never will. The fifteen years ahead of me will be as shame-filled and miserable as the fifteen behind me. I must do something to change the course of my life. In my mind, I hear Biddy laughing at me. *You're not smart enough for that.* The scar at the corner of my eye begins to tingle.

We'll see.

4

MARIAH

It's a good morning to slaughter hogs. The sky is appropriately bleak and there is no wind to hamper the fire burning under Biddy's largest cauldron. Over the past two days, I've hauled countless buckets of water from the nearby stream to fill it within inches of the rim. Although my shoulders are broad and well muscled for a woman, the wooden yoke has left them tender. Steam rises from the surface in white puffs, then twists into thin strands as it is drawn horizontal by the wind. The roiling water is now hot enough for scalding the carcasses.

Long before the sun rose, I lit the fire. Thoughts of my son had woken me in the wee hours of the morning. I'd lain on my narrow bed, eyes wide open in the darkness, brooding. Thomas deserves to know where he comes from and I yearn to be a proper mother, not relegated to the role of aunt. He is *my* son, and the only thing I can lay claim to in the world—except for the pearl earbobs.

From where I wait beneath the oak tree at the front edge of the field, I can see Seamus leaning over the hog pen with his forearms resting on the top rail. At moments like these, I pretend it's me who's married to him, and the flesh of *my* body his weight will press upon in the still of night, not the bird bones of my sister.

As we prepare, we barely speak to each other. There's no need. Our butchering and salting of pork resembles the dance of an old married couple. We each know where to step next according to the slightest signal given by the other. Even so, Seamus is particularly quiet this morning. He takes no pleasure in the killing—he can't bear to hear a thing cry out. A morning spent casting into the stream and hauling trout from the current is more to his liking. If fish made noise, he'd wince at that bloodiness too. When we hunt deer together, it's often me who takes the shot. Seamus hesitates too long before pulling the trigger on a creature so beautiful.

Seamus rounded the five hogs up from the woods a few days ago. From them, we'll butcher one for the timber camp and two for ourselves. They've fattened up nicely from foraging acorns and chestnuts, their bellies skimming the ground. Biddy's upset that their fat will be no good for rendering, not like the plentiful years when Seamus penned the hogs a month before slaughter and fed them corn. Dread of starvation changes everything. This year, we'll grind all our corn into meal to help sustain us over the winter. We've barely enough grain and there's no money to buy more. Coin is scarce everywhere.

The idea of revealing the truth to Thomas has me by the collar and won't let go. I must seize upon the right moment to discuss my intentions with Seamus. He won't like that I dredge up our past. But I would say that the past lives with us every day like a sickness. The secrecy is killing me and I can no longer tolerate being half of who I am. It's only my fear of being ousted from my sister's cabin that's kept me from blurting it out until now.

Biddy likes to remind me of my indebtedness to her. She stood by her promise to our parents and kept a roof over my head. "What would you do without me?" she asks routinely.

But there's more to my hesitation. To be the cause of my separation from Seamus would be like sewing my own lips shut and denying myself sustenance. Not seeing him each day—his thoughtful eyes, or the way his hands rest on his knees when he's pondering something— would mean starvation to me.

What if Seamus also feels imprisoned by obligations to Biddy? Their bed rarely squeaks as of late. Perhaps he thinks of me too. Maybe it *is* time for Thomas to learn that I am his real mother. We could be a family—Thomas, Seamus and me. But then, what of Biddy, Elizabeth and the other children, little Annie and wee Katherine?

It's a tiresome business suffering in silence for other people's happiness.

5

SEAMUS

Strange how animals sense approaching doom. The hogs are restless inside their pen this morning. The trio jam their snouts between the rails in hopes of busting out. Perhaps they foresee my cudgel striking sharply against the back of their skulls. That same foreboding rises in me this morning, as if I'm the one waiting to be bludgeoned.

Something is brewing in our cabin. I can't put a finger on it just yet, but the ground is shifting and it gives me an uneasy feeling. The news that Thomas is coming to dinner on Sunday has stretched Biddy's and Mariah's nerves thin. One of the women is going to snap and my money is on Biddy. The woman's a pistol. I only wish she wasn't aimed at me so often.

But then, who could blame her for that, raising my bastard as her own, with his mother under her roof? I wanted him to come work in the timber camps with me, but the more I pushed, the more mule-headed he became about going his own way. Biddy seems glad the boy is in Bytown, gone but not too far away.

Although she resents the boy's very existence, she demonstrates a mystifying possessiveness over him.

In a few weeks I'll be heading north along the Gatineau River to the same timber camp I've wintered at for the past three years. I'll miss Biddy, in a fashion, and our children, but I'll be damned happy to escape this powder keg. It's a devilish thing to live with your wife under the same roof as the woman you've done wrong with. Still, I can only leave because I know they'll all be warm and fed over the winter. The few potatoes we produced this year have been harvested and the fields turned over. Biddy dries or pickles any fruit or vegetable she can barter for medicinal herbs. Two years of drought have been hard on everyone. With any luck, there'll be a bit of milk for the children through my absence. It's unlikely our cow will survive the winter by foraging tree shoots from the forest floor and eating the dried grasses that Mariah and I gathered from the nearby meadow, but we can't spare any corn for feed. If the beast weakens, she'll walk it to Bytown to have it butchered by someone willing to accept the hide as payment. Mariah takes on my duties while I'm away. She's dependable that way and can chop firewood as well as any man I know of.

From over my shoulder, I can see her standing next to the scalding pot. Something weighs on her mind. I can tell by the way her hands are folded behind her back the way her old man used to do when he was mulling over a problem. Whatever's bubbling in her head, I hope it doesn't spill over to me. I don't need any more troubles than the ones I already have.

Thirty feet behind her, Biddy lingers inside the back door of our cabin, arms crossed. Our wee Katherine tugs at her mother's apron but Biddy seems not to notice. Instead, she glowers at Mariah then turns her face toward me. When I force a smile, she wheels inside and closes the door.

6

MARIAH

As Seamus leads the first hog toward me, I try to gauge his mood but it's impossible. His eyes refuse to meet mine as he passes the end of the rope into my hands. The hog jerks its head away and the rope rips across my palms. The burn is immediate. Seamus curses softly in Gaelic. He seizes the rope close to the knot and yanks upward so the noose tightens around the hog's neck. He straddles the animal and squeezes its writhing body between his knees, but the hog only squeals and fights harder. Seamus raises the oak cudgel above his head and pauses for a grim moment. I know he waits for the heartbeat of time when the hog's stillness aligns with his own mind and might in perfect union, so his strike will land with deadly precision.

As he's poised motionless, my eyes trace the line of his jaw above the turned-up collar of his wool coat. What if Seamus spurns me for wanting to tell Thomas the truth? It could happen. The thought is unbearable. The jute bites into my palms as I grip the rope tighter. I focus on the pain. When the hog settles for only a second, Seamus's cudgel descends with lightning speed and strikes the back of its head—once, twice, three times. There is a crunch of bone, then air whistles through the hog's snout and the animal wilts to the ground.

When I remove a small knife from my skirt pocket and squat next to the carcass, Seamus steps aside. I slit open the artery running along the left side of the hog's neck. Blood overshoots the collection pail and speckles the grass like red dew.

I douse rags in the boiling water, then layer the body with them to loosen the bristles. We crouch over the hog carcass, flicking our knife blades in tandem. Bristles soon lie in prickly mounds on the pink skin. Every few minutes, I reposition the rags and ladle more scalding water over them. By the time the hog is nearly cleaned, we're on bended knees, our faces mere inches apart. I'm breathing the air his lungs had warmed seconds earlier.

The moment is perfect to tell Seamus how I feel.

He wipes his knife blade clean on a rag and looks up at me, his blue eyes so earnest and unsuspecting. His raised brow is meant as an invitation for me to speak. He probably thinks I have some small grievance to voice, that he'll let me tell it and the trouble will be over. But it's not so. I'm struck dumb by the enormity of what I'm about to set in motion. Lives will be upended to right this wrong done against me and Thomas. For that's what it is—a wrong.

"All right, then," Seamus says when I remain silent and rocks onto his feet. I watch him walk toward the shed, but only for a minute. Biddy could be spying from the window. If she thinks I'm pining over her husband, I'll suffer the cold front of her belligerence for days.

I rinse the carcass with a bucket of cold water. Just as Seamus returns with a coil of rope slung over one shoulder, I slice open the back of the hog's hind legs above each hoof and slide the sharp ends of the gambling stick through hamstrings that lie exposed like a pair of belt loops. Seamus lays the rope on the ground under the oak tree and flings one end over a horizontal limb, then ties it securely around the centre of the stick skewering the hog's hind legs. He passes a pair of old gloves to me. It's these caring gestures that make life bearable and give me hope.

We stand together below the limb—me in front and him directly behind me. With feet braced, we commence hoisting the carcass into the air. The hog slides a few feet across the grass and stops. On our next pull, the hind legs lift off. A few more tugs and only the head and forelegs are left resting on the ground. When I lose my footing, the body doesn't drop. I thought I was making a difference, but turns out it's Seamus's brawn that raises the weight.

The hog's snout now hovers a few inches above the ground. "I've got it," Seamus says.

That's my cue. Twice I wind the tail end of the rope around the tree trunk and secure it with a knot.

"Okay," I tell him when I've finished. It occurs to me then that the O'Doughertys need me as much as I need them. Without a son at home to help with outdoor tasks or a second pair of hands to help Biddy over the winter months, they couldn't survive. But still, they have everything—a home, children and each other.

I've got Thomas. I want him for my own.

Seamus wipes his hands on his pant legs and picks up a clean knife. He punctures the hide and draws a shallow cut from the crotch to the chin along the underside. With the toe of my boot, I push a metal tub under the body to catch the intestines that will drop out of the gut cavity after the next pass of the knife. Seamus repeats the cut, this time sinking the knife deeper. The belly opens like a new flower, gleaming and pink above the descending blade. Suddenly, Seamus's head jerks back and he curses. The razor-sharp stench of hog shit assaults me. He's mistakenly cut the intestinal membrane. It's unlike him to miscalculate. Guts roll from inside the rib cage with a sucking sound and slosh into the bucket. We both jump back to avoid being splashed by putrid juices.

Without so much as looking at me, Seamus barks, "Clear that mess."

I'd expect this tone from Biddy, but not from him. In a flash of anger, I tip the bucket toward him. Shit and guts cover his boots before he can yell out in surprise. I steam past him and set off across the field. I can think of nothing else to do but march deep into the woods.

"Mariah!" he hollers. "Come back."

But I continue tromping along the muddy furrows. He tries again, this time yelling, "I'm sorry."

I turn to discover him with shoulders lifted and palms up. His bewilderment pricks me. "Have I done something? What's wrong?"

I whirl toward the forest. After I've taken a few long strides, he calls out again. "You're behaving like a child!"

Hands shaking and teeth gritted, I wheel around.

"Come on, Mariah. We've two more hogs that need slaughtering. I'm leaving for the Gatineau camp soon. That pork needs to be salted in the barrels before I go." Impatience melts from his face and his voice softens. "Biddy is all set up for making sausages. You know how she gets when she's kept waiting." As I walk toward him, the corners of his mouth relax in a hopeful smile. He figures I'll fall in line and not make a fuss. He's wrong.

"I'm telling Thomas!" There. I've said it.

Seamus understands immediately. His mouth tightens and his eyes cloud over. For what seems like an eternity, he stands there with his arms hanging at his sides. Me speaking my mind is a turn of events he's unprepared for.

He shakes his head. "Don't do it, Mariah."

"You've all had your way long enough," I counter. "He deserves to know the truth."

Seamus takes a step toward me, then stops when Elizabeth calls out. "What are you all doing?" She comes toward us wearing the same expression that lights her face when she reports on the misdeeds of the other children.

"Go inside," Seamus tells her.

"But Mam sent me to find out what's taking so—"

"Inside now!" Seamus's voice is stern.

Elizabeth bursts into tears and sobs all the way to the cabin. Her carrying on brings her mother to the back door. While Biddy hugs her and strokes her blonde curls, Elizabeth peers sideways in our direction. She's an actress, that one.

"You can't tell Thomas," Seamus pleads softly. "It will ruin us."

As I turn away and walk toward the woods, I realize that by *us* he means him and Biddy. My mind is made up.

7

BIDDY

Our bed is cold without Seamus lying next to me. I've turned in early, feigning exhaustion. Truth be told, my nerves are crackling and I'm wide awake. I wait in the flickering candlelight for him to follow my lead and trundle up the loft stairs, but he lingers downstairs in hushed conversation with my sister. The sporadic hum of their voices below my girls' chatter frustrates me. I cannot decipher the words they're speaking.

When he comes to bed, I will ask him what they discussed. He will tell me everything.

Have they had a falling out? Perhaps they are hatching a secret plan. I don't know whether to take heart or sink into a dither.

There's always been an easiness between my husband and sister that at times leaves me seething. They labour in the field side by side and have even raised outbuildings together. The pair of them tramp deep into the forest to hunt—deer, rabbits, pheasants—then return home to clean and dress them.

I am left to tend my husband's home, preserve food for winter, and

GWEN TUINMAN

raise the children—Elizabeth, Annie and our little Katherine. And Thomas, when he was still here. I care for my plot of medicine plants, but beyond that the outdoors holds no interest for me. Inside the four walls of the cabin, I control the elements of hearth and home.

I refuse to slog through the forest like those grubby Indian women Mariah natters about. She meets them at the Lowertown Market even though I tell her to stay away from their kind. Drink a tea brewed from ground hemlock to relieve rheumatism, they told her. Ridiculous! They'd love nothing better than to see me poison my customers with some horrid concoction brewed with leavings scavenged from the forest floor.

The forest is Mariah's realm, not mine. It's a filthy and unpredictable place, rampant with the swamp fever that killed so many of our Irish men while they dug the canal in the early days.

Those of us who lived in Corktown's shacks and dug-out caves along the Deep Cut suffered it too. My fear of the illness kept me indoors. Only the Bytown gentry could afford the quinine cure. My wormwood tea made little difference to those whose bowels had turned to water in the final stages. When Seamus's chills turned into a raging fever, I was beside myself. How could I tolerate being left to mourn him alongside Mariah, with her pitiful face drawn long from grief? And her with a son of my husband's and me with no son of my own. Seamus couldn't die. He owed me, and I wouldn't let him die with that debt outstanding.

If there is a chasm forming between Mariah and my husband, I will drive a wedge into it with such force that nothing she does can repair it. A new baby could be the very thing. A few months ago, I stopped taking wild carrot seeds for the week after each coupling with Seamus. His seed may have already taken. My sworn oath to Mam and Da must be honoured, but if Mariah should determine to leave of her own accord, I won't have broken my promise.

My daughters' banter at the bottom of the ladder continues to confound my attempts to overhear words spoken between Seamus and my sister. Chair legs scrape against the floor and Mariah tells the girls it's time for bed. Their bedrolls will be dragged from beneath her bed, in the corner of the cabin, and spread across the floor. While I can't make out Elizabeth's response, her tone tells me that she is giving Mariah grief over something. Just as achy joints foretell stormy weather, children perceive household tensions. My Elizabeth knows whose side she's on.

I've loved Seamus since we were children in Ireland. Although the flame has settled to a steadily glowing ember, my commitment to him has not faltered. We've always needed each other and it must remain so. Our children bind us.

I've tried to give him the sons he needs to work our land. I remember the excitement and relief of having conceived our first child. "A son of our own," I told Seamus. "*Your* son, with O'Dougherty blood flowing through his veins." What a fool I was! We buried his tiny ill-formed body thirteen years ago under a flat rock at the edge of the Ottawa River. Now, two more crosses mark tiny graves at the end of the windbreak outside our cabin. One of the children was a girl, born too early, and the second a boy. The seed takes, but it's keeping it that's the trouble.

And then there's Thomas. He's mine but not mine. People always say he has his father's looks. They know not how their words humiliate me.

I had my first inkling of Seamus's role in siring Thomas only after we'd emigrated. For two years we'd been living at the edge of Corktown—Seamus and me, Mariah and Thomas—crammed into a rundown shanty. One afternoon following our son's death, Seamus returned home for dinner and hung his hat on a peg. I watched from our bed in the corner while he ate broth next to Mariah at our crude table. When he'd nearly finished, Thomas climbed onto his knee. He ruffled the boy's hair and kissed the top of his head.

I remember Seamus flashing Mariah a smile, followed by a look of guilt. My sister's blush sent a jolt of knowing through my heart. I suddenly awoke to what I'd missed seeing. Thomas's eyes were Seamus's eyes. Their hair lit auburn when the sun shone upon it, and their mouths were similarly shaped.

Thomas began to squirm. As Seamus passed the boy to Mariah, his hands brushed hers. It was more than I could take.

"Give him to me!" I'll never forget the way Seamus's eyes widened and my sister's face went pale. They knew they were caught.

"I'm his mother!" The cords of my neck strained as I spoke. Tears blurred my vision. "Give him to me. He is mine."

My sister slid the child from her lap, but he only clamoured to return.

"Tell Thomas to come to his mam," I yelled at her. The boy began to squall. Mariah's chin trembled and the red of her scars deepened. I felt nothing for her but anger. "Tell him!" I cannot adequately describe the satisfaction of seeing my sister flinch.

"Thomas, go to your mam," she finally whispered and nudged him lightly. He toddled toward me, whimpering all the way.

Seamus opened his mouth as if to speak, but thought better of it, and instead pushed away from the table. He returned the hat to his head and ducked out through the door.

Had I known of Mariah's treachery before I'd sworn an oath to Mam and Da, I would have left her behind. Still, I've never challenged Seamus or demanded an explanation. None of us has ever said out loud that Thomas is his son. To do so would make the facts all too real. I'll not risk what might happen then.

Downstairs, voices go still. When the ladder rungs creak under Seamus's weight, I arrange my hair on the pillow. I finish smoothing the sheets across my body just as his head and shoulders crest the loft floor. His eyes show mild disappointment that I'm still awake. He's definitely hiding something.

"The children are settled," he tells me and sits on the edge of the straw mattress with his back toward me. The bed jiggles beneath us as he tugs a sock from one foot.

"Tell me what's going on between you and Mariah."

He removes the other sock and lays the pair over a stool as I've taught him to do. "I don't know what you're talking about."

"She needs to go, Seamus."

"For the love of God, Biddy . . ."

"It's only for Thomas's sake that we've kept her with us this long. Now that he's struck out on his own, our obligation is met. Surely my parents didn't intend for us to bear this burden forever." My husband's shoulders drop slightly as he unbuttons his shirt. I know he's considering my words. "She'll never marry and leave this home of her own accord. No man will want her with a face like that. My sister is a millstone around our necks, Seamus, and we need to put her out."

Seamus stands and unbuttons his pants. "She depends on us," he answers quietly.

"Why do you so doggedly defend her?"

"She's needed here while I'm away at the camp."

"Then don't go to the camp. Stay home with us for the winter," I tell him. "Build more chairs and sell them. Cut timber from new settlers' allotments. Get yourself hired on with a road crew."

"We need the kind of money a timber camp pays." He lays his pants on the stool and eases into bed. After he blows out the candle, we lie silent for several minutes.

A married woman knows well how to wear down her husband's mulishness. And if we make a baby in the process, all the better. I roll toward him and slide my free hand along the inside of his leg. "With one less mouth to feed we won't need as much money," I whisper. Before I can cup his manhood, Seamus catches my wrist and pushes my hand against the mattress. He turns away from me without so much as word.

I plant a kiss between his shoulder blades and reach an arm over his hip. The matter is not closed until I've won.

8

THOMAS

Darkness is falling, but Mr. Mueller has yet to perform his final check of the building before going to bed. Although the streets of Bytown are coming alive, we apprentices must delay sneaking off to the taverns until his nightly ritual is complete. In our room above the smithy, I have nothing to do but wait. And think. Someday, when I have my own blacksmith shop, I'll befriend my apprentices, let them have a bit of fun now and then. That's the smart way of things.

From our second-storey window, I look across the cedar shakes on Mr. Mueller's rooftop to the street below. Men dressed in tall boots and upturned collars rush along the dirt street like whiskey streaming from a spigot. I count five men in one passing group. Their deep, rolling laughter tugs at me. If my sisters had been brothers, things might have been different for me growing up. I might have felt stronger ties to my family. I might have belonged.

Others move through Bytown freely and do as they wish. Yet here I am pent up in this tiny box of a room to satisfy my master's standard of a good man: God-fearing, early to bed, early to rise—and no whiskey. Who can blame the revellers, most likely timbermen, for seeking their fun before heading off to the snowbound isolation of the lumber camps? A wave of men, my da among them, will leave soon to prepare the shanties and skid roads for the winter work. When the rest leave in October, I'll miss the excitement their antics provide.

A carriage pulled by a team of matching bays hurries past, bouncing over the ruts and rocks of our Lowertown street. The passengers, no doubt, are anxious to reach Uppertown before the unruliness of their French and Irish lessers can disrupt their evening. Those rich English bastards should be grateful to Lowertown folk. It's our labours that make their way of living possible.

Michael slouches on a straw mattress and angles his paper toward the candlelight while he sketches with his charcoals. On the bunk above him, Rory sits with his back against the wall and practises shuffling cards.

"'Tain't fair," I say.

"What's that?" Rory asks without looking up.

"Those rich buggers from across the canal have never known a hard day's labour, yet they live like kings. There's no justice in it."

"Still, it'd be nice to have some of what they got," Rory replies, rolling his eyes.

"I hear they sleep on goose-down mattresses," Michael adds in a voice barely above a whisper.

"And without fleas, I'd wager." Rory scratches his arm at the thought.

To wish for their finery is disloyal to those of us with nothing. Besides, if I had all I wished for, I'd be like them, which is worse than being like us.

"Here's a quick tip for you, boys," Rory says with a sly grin. "Bed a girl from one of those grand houses. She marries you, then you're in like flint. When her old man kicks off, it'll be you with a hand in the money pot."

"I'll make my own way," I reply.

Rory lays down a few more cards and says, "You're visiting kin tomorrow?"

"Don't remind me."

When the dull rattling of a side door interrupts us, I lean close to the glass and peer downward to see the top of Mueller's hat in the glow of his lantern. He tugs at the door one last time to be sure we've properly barricaded the smithy against overnight thievery. A moment later, we hear more of the same rattle as he tests the door on the south side. Rory grins and gathers his playing cards. After that, Mr. Mueller trudges back to his shanty and disappears inside.

"All right, boys. It's time," I say, reaching for my hat.

"Thank Christ!" Rory blows out his candle and tucks the cards into his shirt pocket. "Took him long enough." He grabs his jacket from its hook on the wall.

Michael continues drawing.

"You comin'?" I ask him. If I'd had a brother, I'd have liked him to be like Michael. He's a man of few words who keeps to himself.

"Oh, I don't know," he says slowly. "Aren't you worried about Mr. Mueller finding out?"

"Mueller hasn't caught us yet, has he? Tommy and I know what we're doing, mamma's boy," Rory scoffs.

"Leave him be," I snap.

Rory freezes with one arm shoved through a coat sleeve and his eyes narrow with uncertainty. I like that I've unbalanced him, if only for a second.

His face relaxes into a lopsided grin. "More girls for me." I know he's trying to bring me around. He doesn't like it when we fall out.

"You'd piss yourself if a girl so much as said hello," I tell him.

"Would not," he protests.

I shove Rory into the door frame as I pass by him on my way to the landing.

"Wait up," he calls out when I reach the top step. I glide my calloused hand along the well-worn banister as I lead the way down to the smithy. Moonlight through the south-facing windows stripes the wood floor. It's this side of the shop from which we prepare to make our escape.

The butcher-block worktable laden with hammers and tongs sits beneath a window held shut by a slide bolt. Rory and I each lift one end of the table and shuffle it over a few feet.

Rory laughs. "If Mueller could see us now, he'd shit a brick."

"Knock it off before he hears us." I jimmy the vertical slide bolt free of the sill and the bottom edge of the window swings open on its hinges. The reek of piss immediately wafts inside on the damp air, from the drunks who prop themselves against the walls of the darkened building to relieve themselves.

"Sveep da shope an' nooo dreenk'n!" Rory mimics, with a chortle. He never shuts up.

"Quiet," I hiss, then push the window open wider so he can boost himself over the sill. He lands outside with a stumble. I climb through after him. I'm taller than Rory, so the drop is easy. From my pants pocket, I pull an inch-wide strip of metal bent at a right angle on one end. I tuck it against the inside of the window frame and hold it in place while Rory gently lowers the window. The metal sticks out past the glass panes by two inches, a nice handle with which to open the window when we return later tonight.

Rory begins whistling his rendition of "Roddy McCorley." When I punch his shoulder, his eyes cut to mine, suddenly dead serious. For a moment I think he might wail on me, but his grin soon returns, and with a shrug, he starts walking.

We edge past the stable, then along the back of the building where we dodge mounds of horseshit. Once past the smithy outhouse, we continue along the back of the cooper's shop next door, checking over our shoulders to be sure no one is trailing us. In the nick of time, we sidestep to avoid a basinful of water dumped from an upstairs window. Rory curses mildly and I smile.

This time of year at Mam and Da's, the darkness is so dense right after dinner you can't see a hand in front of your face. The air smells like decaying leaves, and except for the odd howling of a wolf or the crackling of the fire, it's dead quiet. I'll take Bytown over the homestead any day of the week. Here, the streets are alive all night and spotted with lantern light, and there's always a fiddle playing somewhere.

As Rory and I broach Rideau Street, my shins bang against something that produces a reverberating clatter. Some damned idiot left a metal washtub in the middle of the alley. In the time it takes to rub the pain away, Rory shoots past me to the street. I glance back toward the Muellers' shanty, hoping our master hasn't heard the clatter and come out to see what made it. He sacked an apprentice last year for tipping back pints at the Bytown Coffeehouse.

As I catch up with Rory, a metal clang rings out behind us, and our heads crank toward the alley. Someone else has collided with the washtub. I suppress the urge to run and raise my fists in case we're about to be set upon by ruffians. I won't give up the few coins tucked in my pocket to anyone. Then I recognize the figure emerging from the shadows.

"Hey," says Michael, stepping toward us. "I changed my mind." He smiles like a dog that's recovered a stick and is now waiting for his pat on the head.

"You daft bastard," I hiss. His eyes widen in confusion.

"Never sneak up on a man unless you mean him harm." Rory aims his index finger at Michael like it's a pistol.

Rory and I set off along the street. Seconds later, Michael is at my elbow. "Where are we going?" he asks us.

"How about the tavern near the old wharf?" Rory says.

"A waggoneer was gunned down in that one just last Wednesday," Michael replies with an edge of worry in his voice.

"They've got women there!" Rory answers with exasperation.

I raise my collar against the wind. "Old *whores*, you mean."

"They're not that old," he protests. "Where do you want to go—Blackmore Tavern, I suppose?" He means to mock me by naming an Uppertown establishment, but that's exactly where I want to go.

"What's wrong with that?" Michael asks.

Rory says, "I hear it's full of rich merchants and half-pay soldiers. Not to mention the feckin' Orangemen who side with them."

"And what of it?" I say.

"Ha!" Rory cries out. "You want to tip a pint with the same lot who've been starvin' out the Irish for centuries?"

"At Blackmore's, men talk about two things that interest me: politics and the future."

If I'm going to be someone, I need to rub shoulders with men who've achieved the success I dream of—owning my own land and business. The rabble who drink at the waterfront taverns think no further ahead than their next mug of rotgut.

"I thought you hated the English," Michael says.

"True enough. But there's no sense in cutting my nose off to spite my face, is there?"

"Fine, but for only one ale." Rory turns his head to spit on the dirt street. "I don't want to be late getting to the tavern on the wharf in case that crowd has scooped up all the girls."

"You wouldn't know what to do with a girl anyhow," I say.

"I've had lots of girls," Rory protests.

"What's it like?" Michael asks in wonderment.

Rory laughs. "Imagine the horse you wagered a week's pay on is first across the finish line," he says. "It's like that, then your eyes roll back in your head."

"You're full of shite," I tell him.

As we near the Rideau Canal, a scrappy-looking mutt lies on the roadside. It turns its head as we approach. Rory picks a few rocks from the ground and pitches them one by one at the dog. As the third rock sails through the air, the dog leaps to its feet and growls, teeth bared. Rory smirks at me.

After we walk a wide circle around the mutt, Rory scoops a handful of gravel and pitches it back. When a spray of stones bounces off its back, the dog sinks into a crouch, its ears laid back. The growling makes my heart beat faster but I maintain my pace.

"Cut it out, Rory," I say.

"You worry too much," he says, then turns back to the dog to shout, "Woof, woof!"

The dog coils and launches at us. We all bolt. At first, I'm in the lead, but Rory's legs are pumping hard and soon he's at least three yards ahead of me. From somewhere behind me, Michael screams like Elizabeth did the time I left dead mice in her boots. The dog must have caught him. I steal a quick glance over my shoulder to see Michael scrambling up a tree. My heart lurches when the snarling dog sets its sights on me. A jolt surges through me and I fly along the road toward Uppertown. My muscles burn and water fills my eyes. The teeth will rip into my calves at any second.

A sharp whistle cuts through the air as the dog tries for a bite at my ankles. Onlookers blur together along the sidewalk. My breath is ragged, and I fear my pace is slowing before I reach the bridge. Again, I hear the whistle. After a few more strides I realize the dog is no longer chasing me. Men cheer from either side of the road while I'm bent forward sucking air into my lungs with both hands braced against my knees. As he trots away, the dog barks sporadically, like an old man muttering to himself.

Michael catches up to me. "Are you all right?" he asks, panting and out of breath. I cannot form an answer yet.

Rory joins us too. He can barely speak for laughing so hard. "Tommy-boy, the look of fright on your face—"

In a blind rage, I charge and knock him to the ground. The high emotions of the past few minutes ignite something in me. My fists swing at his laughing face over and over. "Shut up," I yell. "Shut up!"

Suddenly it's me pinned against the ground and he's trying to grasp my wrists as I'm grabbing at the front of his coat. I buck him off and again, it's me pushing Rory's shoulders against the road. Still he's hooting with laughter.

"Attaboy! Ged 'im," a gravelly voiced Brit shouts.

"Ya scrawny bugger, stop yer gigglin' and fight back, li' a man!" another says.

A third chimes in. "My money is on the big scrapper." He's talking about me.

Rory's brows lift, urging me on, but I suck my teeth in disgust. I won't lower myself for the crowd's entertainment. One last shove against his shoulders and I scramble to my feet. The embers of a few lit pipes glow against the darkness. Weathered men wandering the streets have moseyed closer for a better view. They shout after me as I stalk off.

With Michael in tow, Rory reappears next to me. When his shoulder bumps against my arm, I turn on him. "If you ever pull a stunt like that again, I'll knock you clear into tomorrow. You hear me?"

In mock surrender, he raises his palms to the sky. "You should thank me, brother. Don't you feel alive? Isn't your heart poundin' like a bodhrán?" He's right on that account. There is a rush of something I'm feeling. A smirk lights his face and he hooks an arm around Michael's neck. "When the dog came at us, I heard a lass screaming as if she'd been caught in the outhouse with her knickers down. Turns out—it was this one!"

Michael's face reddens. Serious as a judge he says, "I nearly pissed myself." At that, Rory howls with laughter. My anger melts away and I join in. "Hey, that's not funny," Michael grumbles.

One of Rory's arms slips around my shoulders and the other sweeps a wide gesture in the direction of Blackmore Tavern. "Let's go have some fun, boys!"

It's a rarity for Irishmen to be strolling Uppertown streets if not carrying out a master's bidding. To be walking so close to the granite-faced buildings, two and three storeys tall, is like journeying through another world. Soon after crossing the canal bridge onto Wellington Street, I'm dumbstruck. There's not a shanty or even a timber-framed building to be seen, save for the impressive stables we glimpse through alleyways.

"By jeez," Rory says. "Even the horses here live better than we do." Michael drinks in the view, his jaw gone slack in awe.

The glow of kerosene lamps filtering through the curtained windows makes me wonder what's inside these houses. I hate my own curiosity. The rich hid here while hundreds of us lay dying of cholera not four years ago, their money sheltering them.

One day I'll start my own blacksmith business far from Bytown and my family. The men I hire will boast about my fairness and work hard for me. People will hear of this and do business with—

"That's Blackmore's, I think," Rory says, and points to an establishment ahead. A sign overhangs the street, but none of us can read.

A pair of blinkered roans pull a closed carriage past us as we cross the street. A woman's laughter and the smell of burning pipe tobacco trail from the carriage windows. Even the rich seek lively entertainment this evening.

Michael releases a slow whistle. "This place is too grand for the likes of us," he says, looking upward at the two-storey stone-faced building with brass lanterns burning on either side of its oak front door.

"I've only got a few shillings in my pocket," Rory says sourly. "I'll be broke after one drink."

I'm going in with or without him.

It takes a bit of muscle to heft the door open. Michael and Rory hesitate behind me, but new arrivals crowd us and we're shoved inside before we know it. We're met by warm air rife with tobacco smoke and bustling chatter. I stop short. Never have I seen an establishment so fancy or so large. Rory shoves next to me. For once, he's speechless. Michael peeks over my shoulder. "Oh shit," he whispers.

The tavern is filled with men much older than the three of us and many of them finely dressed—tall hats, tailcoats, and narrow scarves knotted under their clean-shaven chins. The room is jammed with tables, each circled by patrons who are eating, talking and debating, or playing cards in the glow of kerosene lamps. A polished wood counter, at least three times longer than the one at the Bytown Coffeehouse, stretches the length of the barroom. Patrons lean against it while they wait to be served by the square-shouldered bartender. He wears a white shirt with a black vest and his moustache is trimmed in the style of a gentleman. Even as he's pouring drinks, he watches the goings-on at the tables. Above him hangs an enormous framed mirror in which I can see the reflection of the fiddler playing tunes next to the fireplace at the far end of the room. When my gaze returns to the bartender, he lances me with a steely look.

I stand my ground and take a deep breath. I wouldn't want to tangle with him, but neither will he scare me off. "Follow me, lads," I say and head toward the last vacant table. Distracted momentarily by a swell of roaring laughter from the centre of the barroom, I nearly collide with a man dressed like the bartender. As if he hadn't noticed the close call, he continues on his way carrying two plates of potatoes and meat swimming in rich gravy. My stomach growls in answer to the aroma.

When we reach the table, we discover we're a chair short. A pair of stocky old-timers each nurses a full glass of whiskey next to us. Their well-fed bellies test the shiny buttons straining to hold their vests closed. When I reach for their spare chair, the balder of the two men says, "It's taken." His voice is low, his tone full of warning. We both know that no one is using the chair, but he looks like a man who could flatten me so I back away. Rory is already seated and Michael stands uncertainly, his gaze darting around the room.

"Thomas, you take the chair," he says. "I'm too nervous to sit." The old-timers finish scrutinizing us, then return to their conversation.

I sit as the balder man flattens his palms against the tabletop. I hear him say, "One Irishman dies and ten more pop up in his place. They breed like rabbits."

"All the same," his friend replies, "I don't miss pointing my musket at the women and children when the rent's overdue. A landowner instructed me to flatten a cottage once so the tenants couldn't creep back."

"You're telling me your heart bleeds for those filthy bog-jumpers coming off the ships, spreading their diseases among us clean folk? Have you forgotten the cholera epidemic?" The first man mops his forehead with a handkerchief. "Those Shiner hooligans are the worst sort of anarchists. They won't be happy until they've squashed every aspect of British civility."

British civility, my arse. I squeeze my hands together so tightly my fingers go numb.

"I hear tell it's worse back home," his friend replies. "The lower class has been rising up against the landlords same as the Whiteboys done twenty-five years ago. If maiming livestock catches on here, our farms could be next."

Rory elbows me at the mention of the Whiteboys and I give him a warning glance.

The balder man takes a swig and thumps his glass on the table. "All the more reason to knock the Irish down a peg. We can start by retaking control of the Bathurst District Agricultural Society. Our man Johnston should never have let that pissant Peter Aylen scheme his way into being president. He mocks the Empire. Someone needs to cut the pegs from under Aylen and teach his lackeys what's what."

I'm on the edge of my seat trying to overhear their plans when a newcomer joins their party. I guess their chair was indeed taken. They raise their glasses to him as he removes his hat and coat.

"Gentlemen!" he calls out to the crowd. He reminds me of Mam's rooster, puffed up and eager to crow. The fiddle music halts and conversations tail off as everyone turns toward the source of interruption.

"Gentlemen, the Shiners must be stopped," the rooster shouts, and the old men clap for him. "These barbarous Irish villains terrorize our streets. The answer is—and always has been—more police."

"Hear, hear!" his audience cries, and the rooster basks as they applaud.

Mr. Mueller would be much pleased to hear this, as he worries constantly about Peter Aylen and his Shiners stealing horses from his livery.

"I agree," another voice hollers. "Our twelve constables can't control the gangs that will flood Bytown when the spring river drive ends. We must prepare!"

"Yes," the rooster cheers. "There must be five more men out there willing to protect us. You're captain of the Bytown Rifles, George Baker. What say you?"

A dark-haired man leaps to his feet. "I put out the rallying cry in June, but not a soul answered! You'll remember that Constable Dixon was kicked to death this past summer by Shiners, in broad daylight, while able-bodied men stood by and watched." A pall falls over the room. "For shame!" he says, dropping onto his chair.

The bartender shouts over the crowd, "Retaliation is the problem. The Shiners have men everywhere and their memory is long if you cross them. They're organized like an army, with that Irish rat bastard Aylen leading them." Voices rumble in agreement.

Michael leans over my shoulder. "Let's get out of here."

"Why? We aren't part of the Shiner gang," I tell him. "I want to hear what this is all about."

He regards me with doubt and presses back against the wall.

"What good are more police when we can't get criminals to trial?" a Scotsman calls out from a table by the fireplace. "Last summer, the Shiners rescued that bunch who were convicted of raping the Indian woman before their transport made Perth jail. Another lot broke out of their cells and fled to the United States."

Still standing, the dark-haired man adds, "The military refused us use of garrison cells on Barrack Hill to detain men."

"If they get hauled to court when Magistrate O'Connor is on the bench, the Irish get a slap on the wrist and set free," the Scotsman hollers again. "So what's the point?"

"Then we must appeal to the government again and request military intervention to run the Shiners out of town," the rooster says. He smiles at the hum of conversation his comment has sparked.

"The Tories withhold any support. They're reserving the military in case the Reformers uprise," someone yells.

Rory leans toward me. "What are *Reformers*?" I raise a hand to silence him.

A portly fellow with wire-rimmed glasses chips in. "I don't like the Shiners either, but a lot of us who profit from the money they spend at our shops would feel less coin in our pockets if they left town."

The rooster appears flustered. "We'll all be losing business if the Shiners continue to harass travellers crossing Union Bridge. You can't get across the Ottawa River from Wrightsville without Shiners bullying you for money." The crowd murmurs in agreement.

"Keep the Shiners on their own side of the canal," the Scotsman says. "They've been undercutting the wages of the French workers. If we wait long enough, maybe the French will solve the problem for us." He draws an index finger across his throat and the other men laugh.

The bald man at the next table struggles to his feet and raises a glass. "Think on it, gentlemen. There must be a way to bring the Shiners to heel. I was a commander in the King's army. We routed Napoleon and we can rout these low-born Irish rapscallions too!"

"Huzzah!" his friend yells, and all around, cheers raise up and glasses pound against the tables.

Low-born. The words light a fuse in me. I will not be defined by an accident of birth that limits my future.

The rooster grins smugly. "Gentlemen, send out the call for able-bodied men interested in defending us against Shiner anarchy. I'll draft a petition for your signatures. We must press our government for assistance." He bows to the cheering crowd and takes his seat.

Rory rests his elbows on our table and leans forward, staring intently at the bartender, who continues wiping glasses with a rag. "Thank God that's bloody well over," he murmurs. He's about to shout his order when I grab his arm.

"Hold on," I tell him. "This is a fancy establishment. Wait for him to serve us." I resent the man's dallying as well but I've come here to learn how to get ahead in the world of men with money. I'll not be leaving until I've gathered something useful.

In the time it takes for the fiddler to reel off three more songs, the old-timers finish another round of drinks but we're still waiting for ours.

Enough is enough. When I loose a sharp whistle, the bartender presses his palms flat against the counter, then leans forward. "What'll it be?" he asks.

"Three ales," I call.

His expression shifts instantly from disinterest to contempt. "We don't serve Irish scum."

His words are a stinging slap. "Since when?" Rory counters.

"Since your lot put a torch to the tavern stable two summers ago."

"Fine! We'll take our business elsewhere," Rory says, pushing away from the table. "Come on, Tommy."

Coming here was my idea. If I allow us to be thrown out, I'll never hear the end of it. Beneath the table, my knees are shaking with fear and anger.

"I'm not leaving," I announce loudly. "My friends and I have caused no trouble. We're not with the Shiners. England's tyranny over the Irish is over and my money is as good as the next man's."

Sniggers and guffaws sound from the crowd.

"I'll wait outside," Michael whispers.

"First off, shut your mouth about England!" the bartender yells, thrusting a finger in my direction. His gaze drills me as he walks to the end of the bar closest to our table. "And second, I'm giving you one more warning to leave like your friend just did. All you Irish should crawl back to the bog you slithered from."

The faces of the men seated at neighbouring tables are tense with anticipation. It occurs to me that they've seen Irish turned out before and look forward to the entertainment of watching Rory and me being soundly thrashed. My heart pounds in my ears with such fury, I can barely speak. For the first time, I understand how men are driven to murder.

"I wipe my arse with England."

The bartender is upon me before I've fully stood up. His fist, which seems twice the size of an anvil, bashes into my left eye. Pain explodes like shattering glass and the back of my head thuds against the wall before I slide to the floor. Rory loses his usual bravado, crying out, "We're going!" He lifts me to my feet amid the cheers of the crowd and whiskey glasses pounding against the tabletops. I'm humiliated that I can't fight back, but my head feels queer and I want to vomit.

Rory hustles me toward the door. As we leave, the bartender's voice booms, "Snot-nosed Irish whelps. That'll show 'em, eh, gentlemen?"

Once outside, Michael comes rushing to my aid. He and Rory jump back as I double over and splatter the ground with chunks of Mrs. Mueller's beef stew and cornbread dinner.

I'm still hunched over when a giant pair of scuffed boots steps into view. "You must learn to hold your liquor better," a voice rumbles in an Irish brogue.

I wipe a sleeve across my mouth and straighten. Before me towers the tallest man I've ever seen. His face hides behind a thick beard, dark as tar, and his eyes are topped by shaggy brows.

"You've had trouble, looks like," he says, studying my left eye.

I look toward the tavern, then back at the stranger. "They won't serve our kind."

"The bartender bashed him in the face," Rory pipes up.

"Really," the man says and nods slowly. He draws back his coat to reveal the pistol tucked into the waistband of his britches. "Wait here and don't move."

As he turns to walk away, I press a hand to my eye and pain shoots through my head again. "Who the hell is that?" I ask.

"Dunno," Rory says. "But I'm staying put all the same."

"He has a gun," Michael hisses in disbelief.

The pistol worries me too. I wish for justice but not at the cost of seriously harming someone.

A short time later, the stranger returns with a gang of seven rough-looking strangers. They walk bunched together and their eyes comb the street warily. A few of them are carrying cudgels. My breath sticks in my throat when I see the glint of a knife blade among them. Without slowing at all, the black-bearded man grabs my coat sleeve and says, "Let's go."

Rory scrambles to keep pace with us, but the man shoves him aside.

When our motley crew presses through the door, the tavern hushes and the fiddler lowers his instrument. The big man nudges me forward. "Which one of these bastards struck you?"

The bartender's eyes spark with worry and I hesitate to single him out. I don't want the man's blood on my hands or my conscience. Again, I feel a push against the back of my shoulder.

"Come on, man," he urges. "Which one of these English sons of bitches treated you like scum?"

I think of all the stories Da has told about the English landowners turning our cousins out to starve and the injustices done to our people at the stroke of an English pen or sword. My finger shoots up and points to the bartender. Colour drains from his face.

"I'm Gleeson," the big man tells him. "And who might you be?"

"John Blackmore, proprietor. My tavern, my rules," he says. His lips purse and his gaze leaps like a frightened rabbit from face to face.

Gleeson laughs, then turns deadly serious. "Tell this man you're sorry." My shoulders straighten. He called me a *man*.

Blackmore stands silent, his hands hidden beneath the counter.

Gleeson turns to his gang in amusement. "I don't think he takes me seriously." While his head is turned, Blackmore reaches under the counter and pulls out a rifle. Before he can level it at Gleeson, two Irishmen draw their pistols on him. Gleeson casually faces the bartender, who makes a show of laying the rifle on the counter and raising his hands.

"You shouldn't have done that, Mr. Blackmore," Gleeson says calmly as he pulls his own pistol. "Step out here where we can see you." The bartender reluctantly leaves his refuge behind the counter. "All right, then," Gleeson says. "Now, give this man the apology he's owed."

The bartender regards me with belligerence. "I'm sorry."

I look from Blackmore to Gleeson. "Okay," I say with a shrug.

Gleeson points to the bar and tells me, "Go back there and help yourself to a bottle of whatever you like. Come to think of it, fetch two." When I hesitate, he says, "Go on, man, it's free!"

Blackmore deserves his comeuppance, but not this way. Nothing is truly free. That I know for sure. The gleam in Gleeson's eyes begins to dull and a look of impatience takes its place. I wish for more time to decide what to do, but there is none.

"Have at it, lads," Gleeson tells his gang.

Men blaze past me to claim bottles for themselves. Rory is suddenly among them. He grabs my arm and pulls me along. Grabbing a bottle in either hand, he shrieks with laughter and jostles past me to wait behind Gleeson. One bottle remains. Whether I take it or not, an enemy will be made of either Blackmore or Gleeson. I'd best ingratiate myself with the man posing the greatest danger. I take a deep breath, reach for a bottle and rejoin Gleeson's men.

Through the door, I notice Michael pacing with his hands tucked in his pockets. He sees me and waves for me to come out. I know it would be wise to leave now, with or without Rory, but it feels wrong to abandon Gleeson, who defended me, after all. So I wait.

With his men safely gathered behind him, Gleeson raises his pistol and fires at the portrait of King William IV hanging behind the bar. Now there's a singed hole where the face should be. Gleeson's men swipe cudgels across tabletops. Glass smashes against the floor and shards glitter everywhere. Flames from a kerosene lamp spread across the floor and someone calls for water. Patrons cower beneath their tables, some with hats held over their faces.

Gleeson bellows, "You sell to Irishmen now."

"Yes!" Blackmore cries. His chin quivers and tears stream down his face as he measures the damage.

Gleeson winks at his men. They chuckle in return and I wonder what sort of joke I'm missing. He flips his pistol mid-air and catches the barrel, then lifts his arm and slams the butt downward against Blackmore's temple with full force. The man crumples to the floor in an unconscious heap.

A collective groan rises from the patrons.

"Don't think of leaving this fine establishment or following us,"

Gleeson shouts. "Our man is posted at the door. He'll blow your head clean off if you do."

The Irishmen funnel out to the street. Rory's face glows with excitement. "We're heading down to the waterfront to see the whores! Come on!" He races after Gleeson's men with nary a backward glance for me.

It's hard to know how to feel about the mayhem I've just been witness to. I'm troubled but exhilarated by it at the same time. I search the street for Michael, but he's nowhere to be seen. My head is spinning and my stomach remains queasy. Perhaps it would be wisest to go home, and yet . . .

Gleeson suddenly appears next to me and clamps a hand on my shoulder. "You haven't told me your name."

"Thomas O'Dougherty," I say. The pressure of his grip is disarming. Finally, I manage to stammer, "About what happened in there . . ."

"No need to thank me. You're under the care of the Shiners now, protectors of the Irish. Let's celebrate, Thomas O'Dougherty. Your world is about to change, providing you're man enough to reach for what is yours."

I look up at him with an uneasy smile as he locks an arm around my shoulders and sweeps me along the street.

9

MARIAH

A soft chorus of breathing rises from the children's pallets on the floor next to my bed. They have found sleep, but I am wide awake. The argument with Seamus plays over and over in my mind. Have I been too forceful? For the past two evenings, he busied himself with sharpening his axe before the fire and scarcely turned away from the hearth. Biddy seized upon the opportunity to pull her chair next to his while she knitted. Their backs presented a formidable wall, reminding me that I am the *other*. And when she'd tilt her head toward Seamus to whisper in his ear, my heart was further crushed.

Before he leaves for the timber season, this rift between us must be worked out or the winter with Biddy will flatten me. I do not know how to bring about a truce without agreeing to continue to keep our secret from Thomas. Seamus may be right to fear that the truth will turn their worlds—his, Biddy's and their children's—upside down.

But Thomas surely knows something is off-kilter in this family. Biddy treats him as a second-class citizen, while Seamus sits by without protest as if a show of too much caring toward our son would rub salt in her wounds. Once Thomas knows the truth, he'll stop running from them and begin running toward me. I hope.

Thomas will come home later this morning. What if he shuns me upon hearing that I am his mother? For certain, Biddy will turn me out with neither money nor prospects to sustain me. Peg springs to mind, the poor lass. Poverty forces her and so many others to sell themselves. The tickle of a tear feathers along my cheek. With this scarred-up face, it's doubtful I could save myself from starving were I in her shoes. No one would buy me, not looking the way I do. Biddy is right. What would I do without her?

Again, I think of Seamus.

I'm an idiot to have said unsettling things to him. I want to go deep into the woods where no one will hear me and scream at the top of my lungs, *I am the woman who loves you truest. Don't look past me. See me and love me the way I love you.*

A low moan breaks the silence. The bed begins to creak upstairs. The rhythm of lust gathers speed. Dust mites and grains of sand sift from between ceiling boards. They glimmer snowlike inside a shaft of moonlight and sprinkle onto my bed. I'm crying in earnest now.

The high winds gusting outside the cabin roused me from a fitful sleep well before the cock crowed. I've long since stoked the fire so it burns steadily in the hearth. Leftover potato soup is simmering for our breakfast and I've hung a kettle of water for brewing coffee from the dried corn grown by the Algonquin women I met at the Lowertown Market. The smell of breakfast will greet Seamus when he wakes and he'll be happy again. The warmth between us will return. It must.

Everything needs to be as perfect as I can manage to make it— and that includes me. I've taken care to wear a clean dress with all the wrinkles pressed out. There's a mended tear near the hem where the skirt got snagged on a branch while Seamus and I were hunting partridge deep in the bush. My leg was badly gouged too, but I said nothing. Seamus would have insisted we return to the cabin had he known, and our time alone would have ended too soon.

For now, my hair is smooth on the top, with a fringe of ringlets that cluster on either side of my face. The rest I braided and pinned at the nape of my neck. I've tried to copy a style worn by the ladies of Uppertown, but I fear my attempt has missed the mark. I ought to avoid lingering over steaming kettles and venturing outdoors today or I'll resemble an overworked scullery maid again instead of a woman my son would wish to claim as his mother.

I hear stirrings from the loft overhead as I begin to set plates on the table. It's Seamus who climbs down the ladder first. On the floor between my trundle bed and the bottom of the ladder, Elizabeth and Annie are fast asleep on their pallets with Katherine wedged between them. Seamus treads lightly so as to not wake them.

What a fine figure of a man he is. In a moment he'll look up to see me standing by the table. My stomach flutters in anticipation. His reaction will be a gem I turn over in my mind again and again throughout his winter absence.

But he fails to notice me. Deep in thought, he crosses to the door with his head down and pulls on his boots. It's not until he's fastening the buttons of his coat that his attention finds me and his fingers stop their work. He appears startled in a way that pleases me. I want to say something, anything. But my mouth opens just as the loft ladder creaks again. Biddy is on her way down.

Seamus snatches his hat from another peg and lifts the bar on the door. For a moment, he pauses with his thumb on the latch. "The animals need tending," he whispers. Cold air blows through the open door and he is gone.

Biddy steps into the circle of light cast by the fire. Her slender back is straight, her chin slightly lifted. Even in her greying nightdress and with a simple braid of hair lying across her breast, she is beautiful. I can feel her judgment sweeping over me, head to toe. She needn't speak a word for my mind to hear her sniping.

I wish she'd die.

"It's too early in the day to be gussied up," Biddy says. "There's much to be done before my son returns home." She repositions a plate I'd set at Seamus's spot.

If Biddy died, Seamus would be free to marry me. The bed would creak with the rocking of my hips, not hers. Two winters ago, one of Biddy's customers died in childbirth. The woman's first cousin lived with her family. The cousin married the dead woman's husband and now his brood of children call the new wife Mother. It's as if the first wife never existed.

"Mariah!"

"Huh?"

"You're daydreaming again. Wipe that ridiculous grin from your face and fetch more butter from the spring house." Biddy scrunches her nose. "And don't be letting Annie fiddle with your hair anymore. You look foolish."

My face burns as if she'd slapped me.

"Butter. Bring it in now so it will soften before Thomas arrives."

The wind will dash my hair. "I'll ask Seamus to go back for the butter crock when he comes up for breakfast."

"My husband may be lacking the energy for a trip to the spring house." Biddy lances me with a smirk and I feel sick.

"But I think it's begun to rain," I say, touching the plaits at the nape of my neck.

My sister snorts. "You never could follow a simple instruction. I thought you'd have learned your lesson by now."

Another painful reference to the past. On the morning of the dog attack, Mam had warned me to steer clear of the Flynns' place when I set off to visit Da at the estate where he shod horses. "Take the footpath through the woods south of their meadow," she'd told me. "The shortest distance between two points is a straight line," I replied. I thought I knew it all back then, just as Thomas does now. I was only a child then, but my sister doesn't understand and how could she? Biddy was born old.

She stirs the soup and taps the ladle against the edge of the kettle. "Don't let your vanity get in the way of what needs doing. A silk purse can't be made from a sow's ear, you know."

"That's cruel, even for you, Biddy."

I brace for backlash, but she continues as if I've said nothing.

"When you head for the spring house for the butter, take back the pork roast you brought in last night. Fetch a smaller one, a shoulder cut. That'll do."

"I will not. A visit home from Thomas is a special occasion. He deserves—"

Biddy's voice is venomous. "You forget yourself, Mariah Margaret Lindsay."

"What's going on?" Elizabeth says with a yawn. She's sitting up cross-legged on her pallet.

"You could wear Mam's shawl pulled over your head." In a theatrical tone, Biddy adds, "Oh, you can't! A friend has it." She huffs. "A friend! I'm the closest thing you have to a friend. And the provider of the roof above your head. You'd do well to remember that."

How could I possibly forget?

"Fill that up too," she mutters. A wooden bucket rolls toward me from across the floor. The sound startles Katherine from her sleep and she begins to bawl.

I turn and smoulder at Biddy.

It's difficult to fathom that we came from the same mother. A quick glance sideways reveals Elizabeth smiling wickedly.

I fling the door open and head into the rain bare-headed and empty-handed. Biddy can take back her own damn roast and haul her own damn water.

Where is Thomas? He's hours late and I imagine all sorts of trouble that could be delaying him. My nerves are as frayed as my hair.

The aroma of rosemary and roasted pork has set my stomach to grumbling. Annie begs her mother for something to eat while Katherine whines and rubs her eyes, both sure signs that she's ready for a nap. Biddy and Elizabeth's jabs about Thomas's tardiness exhaust me. From where I sit at the foot of my bed mending Seamus's torn shirt pocket, I can at least pretend not to hear them.

This wait is excruciating. I know Seamus must feel it too. He's outside in the shed preparing for his departure to the timber camp. When preoccupied or vexed, he putters. In a few short days, men from neighbouring farms will come by with a wagon to pick up Seamus and his barrels of salt pork. They'll head to a camp, three days' ride north along the Gatineau, and there they'll remain until the spring thaw. Although the men are peaceful, their presence always unnerves me. I must find the opportunity to say my farewell to Seamus in advance of their arrival and avoid them altogether.

His shirt rests across my knees as I stitch, albeit clumsily with hands not so dainty as most women's. If only he was wearing the shirt while I worked and watching me mend the hole torn over his heart—my needle and thread would sew memory and longing along the jagged edges of cloth. I am in every stitch. This winter, he will feel my yearning in spite of our separation.

I may be a lovesick fool, but without this dream my world would shrink so small I'd disappear.

At the sound of a horse nickering, I lay Seamus's shirt on the bed and get up to peer out the window again. Strangers are approaching on horseback. One man rides slightly ahead of the other. A rock drops to the bottom of my stomach and I crane my face closer to the wavy glass. The broad square shoulders and black beard stretching upward to meet the ridge of his cheekbones send a cold shiver along my spine. If not for the ocean separating me from Ireland, I'd swear it was a Flynn brother. This man sits high in the saddle, like someone accustomed to giving orders. Men who demand compliance don't understand that loyalty is a two-sided coin. They are the most dangerous type. True loyalty is won with love—not instilled with fear.

The stranger's coat is wide open, and I squint to see if I can make out a pistol in his belt but he's too far away to tell. Though I do notice that someone is riding on the saddle behind him, mostly blocked from view by his hulking form.

The other horseman wears a hat pulled low on his head and a scarf around his neck. He scans from side to side as they ride, like he's on the lookout for trouble. As they draw nearer, I see that he travels with one hand on the reins and his other balancing a musket laid across his lap.

I say nothing so as to not alarm the children now playing games near where Biddy is sitting by the hearth. I can only pray that my Thomas hasn't encountered them on the road. I hope they'll ride on past. No trouble, dear God.

When I bring a hand to the hollow of my throat, Elizabeth asks, "What's wrong, Auntie?"

"Not a thing."

"I don't believe you," she says and runs to the other window.

Seamus appears out of nowhere and stops a few yards in front of my window. The horsemen veer from the road and onto the stretch of grass between us and them. My heart leaps. Seamus is unarmed.

I reach up to grab the loaded musket from where it lies across pegs by the door. "What on earth are you doing?" Biddy asks.

There's no time to answer as I race back to the window. I take careful aim at the rider carrying the musket. Seamus's rifle is always loaded. I'll have one shot if anything goes awry. But in the time it would take me to reload, the bearded man will be upon us. My heart is pounding like a drum. Dear God, make my aim true.

Elizabeth gives a small gasp and cries, "Mam!"

"Empty your da's leather bag on the floor next to the door," I tell her without looking. Biddy flies to the window and gasps. "Jesus, Mary, and Joseph!"

"Like this?" Elizabeth asks shakily. She's laid out neat piles of packing and lead balls next to an open tin of gunpowder.

"Good girl," I tell her. "Take Katherine and Annie under the ladder and hide behind the flour barrel." She looks at me worriedly but gathers her sisters.

Seamus walks to meet the men thirty yards away from the cabin. He draws himself to his full height and stands waiting. The horses stop. The second rider looks in my direction and my blood runs cold.

Elizabeth leaves her sisters and returns to the window, but Biddy pulls her away. "Mam, I want to see what's going on," she cries.

I stand fast with the musket tucked under my arm. My index finger is hooked around the trigger. I'm ready.

The bearded man speaks to Seamus, then leans forward so his companion can slip from the horse. The passenger's hat brim conceals his face and his coat is unfamiliar to me.

"Biddy," I say calmly without looking from the window. "Get ready. On my say-so, open that door as fast as you can." At the first sign of trouble, I'll burst outside and take my shot.

Biddy's voice is tight with fear. "I can't raise five children on my own."

People either shine or fall to pieces under pressure. Still, it strikes me as odd that Biddy would miscount her children.

The bearded man speaks once more to Seamus, then pulls sideways on the reins and urges his horse to move. The second rider follows suit, and the horses head toward the road.

But what of the dismounted man? Seamus steps toward him and snatches the hat from his head.

"It's Thomas!" Elizabeth cries out. She makes to run for the door, but Biddy holds an arm out to stop her.

I relax my hold on the rifle. The men are riding away and I should feel relieved. But Seamus's voice is raised and Thomas's face is still lowered as they walk toward us. At one point, Seamus throws the hat on the ground and walks away rubbing his jaw, but then he wheels back and thrusts his finger at our son's chest. I've never seen him so angry. Seamus finally stalks off in the direction of his shed. Thomas lifts his chin and looks up at the cabin. That's when I notice the ring of black around his left eye.

Oh, Thomas, what's happened to you?

10

BIDDY

God may have ordained Seamus O'Dougherty as head of this family, but it is me who holds us together or pushes us apart as needs doing. It's a task that requires vigilance, a delicate hand, and blunt speech. Calling upon Seamus to exert authority only leaves him addled. The man can see his way through any problem to do with fields and four-legged creatures, but trouble of the human kind stymies him.

He sits in a chair of his making at the head of our table, with Thomas and myself occupying the bench seat on his left. To his right, Elizabeth, Mariah and Annie sit in a row. Katherine is napping on a folded quilt next to the hearth. Her eyelids flicker in her sleep and she occasionally smiles, as if she's dreaming something pleasant.

Seamus and Thomas shovel pork roast and potatoes into their mouths to avoid talking about the black eye. The rest of us pick at our food and wait for the father to rain his judgment upon the son. My nerves crackle with impatience. Were I the man of this family, how different things would be. There'd be no need to speculate what was on my mind. I'd state my opinion on every matter and pry open every secret. But I am not the man, and so I must allow my husband to issue the first words of rebuke about Thomas's tardiness and the condition in which he arrived, not to mention the men who brought him home.

When I look across the table at Mariah, I see shadows of our da. If Mariah cut that mop of hair and put on a shirt and pants, she could pass for Da's younger self. This brings up no nostalgia for me. Da was a weak man given to drink. To make up for his spending all our money at the pub, Mam worked herself to the bone. And I worked alongside her—cooking, tending house and looking out for Mariah. I've been carrying the burden of my sister for as long as I can remember. Mariah slouches around like a victim, making everyone feel sorry for her. Pity is her power and she uses it to cut away chunks of my flesh each day. I steal them back and stitch myself together again so I can carry on.

Elizabeth, sitting next to Mariah, reaches for another chunk of bread and regards Thomas thoughtfully.

"Did you really get that black eye from helping to shoe a horse?" Elizabeth says, with her elbows resting on the table. "Does it hurt?"

"Yes and no," Thomas replies between forkfuls. His tone is surly.

Elizabeth stands and reaches across the table to touch his swollen cheek, but his left forearm shoots up to deflect her. "Thought you said it doesn't hurt," she says victoriously and drops back onto the bench. "I think you're lying about the horse. You got walloped in a fist fight."

Thomas guzzles apple cider from a tin cup and fumes at her over the rim.

His reaction confirms my worst fears. "Those men, Thomas. How do you know them?"

He sets the cup down and studies the remaining bits of wild garlic and pork on his plate.

"Are you cavorting in the taverns?" I ask him. "You'll lose your position at the smithy."

He looks up at me. "I wouldn't risk my place at Mueller's."

Finally, Seamus speaks up. "The men you rode in with—are they part of Peter Aylen's gang?"

"Who the devil is Peter Aylen?" I cry out.

Thomas shoves his plate away and bangs Seamus's cup. Cider sloshes onto the table.

Now more than I ever have, I see that Thomas is cut from the same cloth as Mariah. Must I bear the stain of his behaviour too?

I cannot let go of this notion that my son will repeat the sins of my da. "Thomas O'Dougherty, I smelled the drink on you the moment you stepped inside. It's enough to knock a horse over," I tell him. "Have you been falling down scuttered in the streets?"

Thomas raises his right hand. "I promise not to tarnish the good O'Dougherty name."

"Don't be smart with your mam," Seamus says, then glances at my sister.

Red splotches climb Mariah's throat and her gaze falls to her lap, but too late. I've glimpsed tears. Already, Seamus has resumed pulling at his bread and shoving pieces into his mouth. Neither of them will look at me, and my temper flares.

I turn on Thomas. "I won't have you becoming a wastrel like your granda."

"Biddy . . ." Seamus says with a heavy sigh.

"Da was nothing of the sort!" Mariah fires across the table.

Her left eye widens while the other remains bound half-shut by her scars. The effect, paired with the erratic frizz of hair jutting from her temples, catches me off guard. When a laugh escapes me, Seamus's expression turns dark. Mirth drains from me. Once again, Mariah is the focus of his empathy.

"Da was a nice man," she insists.

"You have a convenient memory, but then, so did he." I let that remark sink in before adding, "He had neither the good sense to be humbled by his sins, nor to regret hurting those he was supposed to care for."

Mariah regards me with naked loathing,

Annie has been quiet since we sat down, and her food remains untouched. Finally, she peers sharply upward at Thomas and says, "You smell bad."

From the mouths of babes! I can no longer hold my tongue. "Don't think I overlooked the leavings of your last meal splashed across your shins. And how did you come by that tear on your trousers' cuff!"

"The tear is not my fault. There was a dog."

Mariah emits a small cry and clamps a hand over her mouth, and he gives her a shrug. "It was nothing, Auntie."

Elizabeth pipes up. "Those are store-bought trousers he's ruined. He's bought a new coat and hat too while I'm here stuck with this." She plucks at her sleeves, which end well above her wrists.

"How I spend my hard-earned money is up to me!" Thomas says.

Elizabeth's eyes narrow. "You're supposed to be saving for your future."

"Although no decent girl will want a boy who frequents the taverns at night," I add.

He's about to protest when Seamus interrupts. "How well do you know those men who brought you here?"

Thomas sets his fists on either side of his plate. "Well enough."

Seamus leans toward his son. "Thomas, listen to me. You'd best come away with me to the camp. Day after tomorrow I'm heading up with Patrick Newell. The wagon will be tight for space, but you can ride on top of the pork barrels."

"The timber camp's your life. Not mine. Someday, I'll have my own blacksmith shop and a fine house. No man will be my better. I won't live like an off-the-boat Irishman, like you, Da."

Elizabeth sucks her breath in loudly.

"Seamus, don't let him speak to you like this!" I tell him.

My husband's expression remains placid as he doggedly tries to persuade his son.

"I can get you hired on as a skidder. You'd be working a team of horses, pulling felled timber out of the bush. It's an honest living. Steer clear of that bad lot, son. They'll have you thieving in no time."

"It's not like that," Thomas replies.

"For goodness' sake," I say. "Someone tell me who those men are."

When Thomas stays silent, Seamus explains. "They're Shiners."

"Oh dear Lord! And you brought them here?" I cry. "It was Shiners who raped that old woman. She was an Indian, but still . . ."

Mariah cranes her head forward and squints. "Biddy, she's a woman same as you and I."

I don't waste my breath on a response. She's pitifully naive.

"What's Shiners?" Annie asks.

"Very bad men," Elizabeth whispers with an edge of excitement. "They shoot people."

Thomas points the tines of his fork at her forehead. Elizabeth goes quiet and studies this new and deeply angry version of Thomas who has returned to us. His gesture silences us all.

"Annie," Thomas says as he lowers his arm. "The Shiners are friends of the Irish."

"Not of *all* Irish," Seamus cuts in. "They clubbed an Irish merchant to death and left him under the Union Bridge."

"Seamus, such talk," I say. "The children . . ."

"Thomas has brought murderers and thieves to our doorstep. The girls saw them. It bears open discussion."

"I agree," Mariah says. "No secrets." Her chin trembles slightly.

A stricken look passes across Seamus's face and his eyes cut to mine. Whatever is brewing between them, I don't like it.

"Last winter, they chased a French raftsman through Bytown after dark," Seamus tells us. "He jumped from the bridge to escape them and sank chest-deep into the snow. The Shiners brained him with an oak club. Split his skull wide open and let his blood drain into the snow."

Thomas's mouth drops open. "That's not true! Someone from Uppertown did that and—"

"Someone's been filling your head with lies," I say, grabbing his arm. "Is it the Shiners?"

"Let him talk!" Mariah says.

"You'd best mind yourself, Mariah Margaret Lindsay. This is none of your affair. Thomas is our son, mine and Seamus's."

"Biddy . . ." Seamus cautions.

"I can speak for myself," Thomas shouts and yanks his arm free.

"And you should," Mariah interjects loudly.

"You always stick up for him, Auntie," Elizabeth says.

"No she doesn't," I say.

"Yes, actually, I do."

Thomas, his eyes full of questions, is staring at Mariah now. Her eyes beg him to speak. Suddenly, I understand what's afoot. Mariah wants to tell Thomas that I've been lying about being his mother. The idea pops in my mind like green wood on a fire. Seamus has known it all along.

"Why is she always nicer to Thomas than the rest of us?" Annie says. "And, Mam, you're nicer to us than to Thomas."

The children are all staring at me. "That's simply not true," I sputter. "I love you all the same." Tears trickle from the corners of my eyes. Still, the children regard me with suspicion, hearing the false note in my voice. In desperation, I turn to Seamus. "Tell them!"

"It is so," he says.

The creases between the children's brows relax. How is it that they trust him above me?

Mariah stares at Thomas as if in a trance, then a smile bunches her godawful scars. "I remember everything about the day you were born," she says. "Below deck. I was with some women from Carrigaline."

"Were you afraid, Mam?" Elizabeth asks me.

I don't answer straight away. I didn't witness Thomas's birth and know nothing of it. The women attending her all knew she was birthing a bastard. Even among strangers on a ship, I had my good Methodist name to uphold.

Finally, I choke out the words. "I can't recall."

"Your mother was very brave," Seamus says. "She uttered not a sound."

Elizabeth's head cocks sideways when she studies me. I know she's reconciling her father's account against the sounds of childbirth she's come to know. My growls and cries shook cobwebs from the rafters when Annie and Katherine were born. There's nothing soundless about me when I'm pushing new life into the world.

"Not a sound . . ." Mariah says, her voice trailing off.

"Well, that's enough of that," I tell her. "Women's talk is unsuitable for the dinner table, and not fit for mixed company."

But Mariah goes on. "Thomas, you were the most beautiful thing I'd ever seen," she says. Thomas squints at his father in confusion.

"Mariah!" Seamus says. His tone is stern. When Mariah's head jerks toward him, the spell is broken. "Let's not embarrass the boy."

"I'm no boy," Thomas protests. "I'm a man, earning a proper wage and making his way in the world."

Seamus leans back in his chair and rolls his eyes toward the rafters.

Now that Seamus has brought Mariah in line again, she dips her head forward, like a dog beat into submission, and stares silently into her lap. My relief is met with a fleeting wooziness. When I brace myself against the bench, my right hand grazes Thomas's thigh.

He turns his face, full of concern, toward mine. I smile overbrightly and he goes back to arguing with his father.

"And it's I who'll choose my path and the friends I'll meet along it," he says.

"Your youth blinds you," Seamus warns. "These men aren't friends—they're foxes pulling you into their lair. You'll be taken advantage of and turned out once you're no longer of use."

"Da, you give me no credit for having a mind of my own," Thomas shouts, seething. "Why do I bother to come home? This family drives me mad."

Mariah lifts her face then. Her eyes bear an intensity that raises panic in me. The white dots speckle my vision in greater numbers than before.

"Thomas . . ." Mariah smiles, reaching a shaking hand toward him. She begins to weep.

"What?" my son says angrily.

"I must tell you something," she says. "I'm—"

The world slips sideways. And everything turns dark.

As I begin to rouse, the muffle of voices becomes clearer.

"Biddy, wake up." It's Seamus speaking. Hands are patting my cheeks. Slowly, I open my eyes to find him kneeling over me. His face hovers close to mine.

"Annie, you're in my way," Elizabeth says and passes a cup over Seamus's shoulder. "Here, Da, give her a drink." It takes a moment to register Katherine balanced on her sister's hip.

Seamus raises my head from the floor and touches the cup to my lips, but I wave it away. "Mam! Say something!" Thomas pleads.

He's calling me Mam. Mariah hasn't finished what she began. "Biddy, what's wrong?" Seamus asks.

All my family—except Mariah—is gathered by my side. Their worry makes clear now how much they need me. I matter in their lives. The moment is perfect. I rope them in with my prolonged silence. And then I announce the news I was unsure of until this moment.

"I'm with child."

Instead of the outpouring of excitement I expect, Seamus is struck dumb. He recovers himself and kneels forward to kiss my forehead. I accept his offering, but it's too late. He's let slip his true feeling. Elizabeth digests the news with a frown, while Annie claps her hands together and giggles. Behind her, Thomas is rising to his feet, his jaw clenched.

Seamus winces at the sound of the cabin door slamming shut. Mariah has stormed off to brood, no doubt. The reminder of how loved I am, and news of the baby, has bought me time to straighten her out. As if he's read my mind, Seamus refuses to look me in the eye while rising to his feet. He walks away from me, with Thomas at his heels.

"Sit up, Mam," Annie says, tugging my hand.

"I'll lie here a while longer until the dizziness passes," I say and pull her close to me. "Did anything happen after I fainted?"

Annie returns a blank look.

"Did Auntie Mariah say anything?" I whisper.

"No—nothing."

"Good girl, Annie. Mam's going to rest now."

The moment I close my eyes, I hear Thomas arguing with his father. "Who are you to question my judgment," he says. "Look at you!"

"Be careful what you say," Seamus replies, low and even.

"You couldn't just leave her alone? Especially after what happened the last time."

"Let's take this outside," Seamus says. Shame leaks from his voice.

"I'll say what I want to right here!"

There's a skirmish. Boots scuffle against the floor.

"Get your hands off me," Thomas shouts. "I'm going back to Bytown."

Annie's bawling now. "Don't go."

"See what you've done?" Elizabeth says angrily. Right on cue, Katherine joins her sister with a chorus of howls.

"Thomas," I call out as I struggle to sit. "You can't leave now, not in this poor weather."

"I'd rather be wet and cold than stuck here." With that, he heads out the door, jacket and hat in hand.

Seamus raises a finger to his lips and I clamp down on all the words I want to say.

11

THOMAS

For much of my return journey to Bytown, rain pisses down, leaving me drenched and miserable. The wind whips up on occasion and drives the chill deeper into my bones. In an hour or so night will drop like a hammer. I cannot risk being caught out by myself on the road—although the experience couldn't be worse than feeling alone among my family.

Last night, when I slopped my pilfered whiskey into the glasses of my new friends down at Richmond Landing, they patted my back and raised their drinks to me for busting up Blackmore Tavern. It's rare for anything finer than home-brewed poteen to pass their lips. They welcomed me at their tables and offered up bawdy timber camp humour, and I laughed with them despite the pain it caused where Blackmore struck me. When they cheered me, my chest burst with pride, but still I told them, "It was Mr. Gleeson's doing."

"No! 'Tis you we must thank," Gleeson said. "You stood up to that limey bastard, Blackmore. 'My money's as good as any man's, Irish or otherwise.'" Gleeson raised his glass then and bellowed above the cheers, "To Thomas O'Dougherty, procurer of fine whiskey and champion of his people. Sláinte!"

Shouts of my name sounded throughout the log cabin. Glass bottles clinked together.

When I think back on it, I suppose what Mr. Gleeson said is true. Had I not spoken up, the true chain of events leading to the whiskey liberation would never have taken place. Mr. Gleeson sees the man I am. Perhaps I'm more like him than my own da. Mr. Gleeson commands respect and takes what he wants. He makes things happen. Not like Da.

By the time the rain slows to a light drizzle, a clearing ahead on the trail and a patch of grey sky signal that I'm about to meet up with the main road. My fingers are stiff with cold, so I cup my hands together and breathe warm air into them. As I'm walking, a gnarled root catches my boot and I pitch forward, but somehow I recover my footing and avoid the fall.

A vision of Mam's face returns to me. Just before toppling, she turned jittery as a cornered rabbit. Blood drained from her face and down she went, sliding from the bench before my brain caught up with what was happening.

Pregnant! Huh! How could Da put Mam through that again? Damn him. She nearly died bringing Katherine into the world. Another baby may finish her. Thank God when this one comes I won't be trapped in the cabin for another twenty-one hours of her screeching and begging for Christ's mercy.

All of a sudden, a dull thud of hooves races toward me. I scramble to flatten myself against a massive white pine. Has Blackmore rallied men to arrest me? Shit! Maybe he's sent volunteers from the Bytown Rifles to comb the woods. The hoofbeats are nearly upon me now. Pine branches lie wind-scattered across the forest floor. None within reach are large enough to swing at a man. My heart bangs inside my chest. If I've only fists with which to defend myself, I'm doomed.

Quick as a blink, a burst of tan and grey fires past me. The deer's white tail is raised in alarm as it streaks through a cluster of sumacs with a slate-coloured wolf in hot pursuit. Their flight takes them over a crest of land that dips into a shallow gully on the other side. As suddenly as they appeared, they disappear, and I exhale long and slow, feeling foolish for not distinguishing between the sound of deer and horse hooves. Aunt Mariah taught me better than that. At the height of fear, it's difficult to perceive those subtle details. More so for a deer, of course. As they say, eat or be eaten.

I turn back to the footpath just in time to detect a fleeting motion— the back of a dark coat slipping behind my pine tree. Someone is lurking. I suck in my breath and ease ahead with both fists raised. This is it. Be ready. I lean forward and peer behind the trunk. No one is there. Am I losing my mind?

Just as something lightly skims the hollow behind my right ear, another twig snaps. Ready to throw the first punch, I spin around.

"Don't hit me, Tommy!" Rory says with hands raised to the sky, a willow switch in his right fist.

"What in hell are you doing here?"

"Hairy Barney sent me to fetch you," Rory says. "Said to wait by the road until you showed up."

"Hairy Barney?"

"Yeah, Gleeson's fellow from last night. He's the dynamite man, blows things up for Aylen. You remember," Rory says with a grin. We both know I don't. I was too drunk. "He told me Gleeson wants us at Richmond Landing by dusk. He'll be waiting at Buckley's Tavern, where we ended up last night."

I nod slowly. It's an honour to be called upon, but what can the man possibly want with a pair of blacksmith apprentices? "Mr. Gleeson and I parted ways a few hours ago. Why didn't he tell me then?"

"No idea. But Hairy Barney doesn't look like the type of man you want to disappoint."

"Right."

Rory laughs and tosses his stick aside. "I got you good. I was skimming your neck with that switch and you kept swatting it away like it was a bug."

"Yeah," I say. "Like a mosquito, you sneaky little shit."

His eyes deaden. "Mosquitoes are clever, brother. They light on a man without his knowing it and siphon off his blood. He won't know they were there until he feels the itch they've left behind. Or the malaria. That's what took my da. He was mosquito-bit while draining the Corktown swamp along the Deep Cut."

"Him and hundreds of others. It's a damned shame," I feel like shit for having reminded him. A sombre mood is rare for Rory. Nothing lifts his spirits like a bit of trouble, so I shift the subject. "How did Mr. Mueller react when I was missing for breakfast?"

"No worries. I told the Muellers you hopped a wagon last night after dinner and went home early. The missus will be relieved to see you're still alive. She's convinced you'll be discovered face down in a creek bed."

This makes me smile. I can picture Mrs. Mueller's round face, pinched with worry. Once darkness falls, upstanding folks barricade themselves in their houses to keep out all manner of evildoers—man, animal or otherwise—that lurk in the dead of night. Rory's lie was a small stretch of true events. I did get a ride home that involved a horse. What the Muellers don't know won't hurt me.

Rory regards me with one brow lifted. "You're here earlier than I expected. What? Yer mam or yer auntie didn't like your black eye much?"

I don't bother with an answer. My family is behind me and my future lies ahead. I try to imagine what knowing a man like Mr. Gleeson might do for my prospects.

It's late afternoon when the familiar landmarks of Richmond Landing come into view. In the distance ahead of Rory and me, a closed carriage jostles across the end of Union Bridge, which spans the Ottawa River. To our left, water courses mightily with a restrained roar. The carriage continues along the short stretch of Richmond Road leading to Firth's Tavern. One day, I'll own a pair of roans and a carriage. But not today. I must first pull myself up the ladder of influence.

"Do you figure Gleeson is rich?" Rory says.

"How should I know?" I do my best to maintain a tone of disinterest, even though I've been wondering the same thing. Mr. Gleeson dresses like a labourer, but a certain quality I can't yet name sets him apart from the others.

"He owns a pistol and a horse," Rory says.

"That doesn't mean anything."

A group of travellers, pulling a small cart, advances in our direction. I suspect at the pace they're keeping, we'll meet up with them at the junction ahead.

"You think he stole them?"

Something in Rory's eagerness stops me from answering truthfully, so I shrug. "He likes you well enough," Rory says.

"No more than the others," I reply.

We step onto the road a few yards ahead of the ragtag group, who, by the droop of their shoulders, I judge to be down on their luck. A craggy-faced man roughly Da's age and a girl close to my own are pulling the two-wheeled cart. A thin shawl is knotted around the girl's shoulders and the bottom edge of her dress is torn. Some of her hair—auburn, I think—has come loose from its tie and hangs wet against her face. Even so, her presence is angelic.

The procession comes to a halt and two young boys step away from the back of the cart.

They're both shoeless and neither of them wears a coat. A woman, their mother I suppose, gathers them to her side while the man studies us at a distance. When we come closer, I hear moans rising from beneath the pile of blankets inside the cart.

"We're lookin' for help. My wife's mam is sufferin' terrible," the man says.

Rory pipes up. "Try the hospital off Sussex down by the river."

"They help Irish there?" The man looks doubtful.

I clear my throat. "No sir," I tell him. "Try inquiring at Mrs. Edwards's mercantile. She'll know someone who can help your mam."

He nods without speaking, and my eyes stray from his face to the girl's collarbone, visible above the frayed neckline of her dress. She notices me looking and casts her gaze downward as she adjusts her shawl to cover herself.

The man steps in front of his daughter and his eyes narrow. He then asks Rory, not me, for directions to the mercantile. So focused am I on the bit of the girl's shoulder not hidden by her father that I don't follow the conversation.

When it's over, the man tells us, "Guh rev mah a-gut."

"You're welcome," I say in response.

He and the girl pick up the tongue of the cart and lean their weight forward. Just as the wheels budge and the cart squeaks into motion, a thought leaps into my mind.

"My mam is a healer," I call out. No one turns around, so I try again. "Come see me at Mueller's Blacksmith Shop. I can get medicine for your gran." The girl looks over her shoulder. "I'm Thomas O'Dougherty," I shout. My eyes strain against the shadows to read the expression on her face, but her head turns sharply toward her da and then back to the road ahead.

"She's pretty," Rory says, elbowing my ribs.

I shrug. She's beautiful, but I won't be telling Rory I think so.

"But she's a bridget through and through, with her knees locked together and her da holding the key. Too much work, Tommy. Best to go for the low-hanging fruit, eh? Plenty of girls will spread their legs as quick as you can say 'How do you do?' Find yourself one of them."

"With a gun to my head, I wouldn't take advice on girls from you," I say, pushing past him.

Without another word between us, we press toward Buckley's Tavern to wait for Mr. Gleeson.

Inside, men sit on all four sides of plank tables, not caring that their shoulders press against those of their neighbour. Lumbermen's shanty life has them used to packing together tightly on benches. Others lean in clusters along the walls. Rory and I stand among them. The air is thick with smoke and my eyes have been burning since shortly after we arrived. They water up when I stifle a yawn. But it's not raining in here, at least.

The room smells of damp woollens and stale sweat. As we all begin to dry out, a liveliness returns. Men laugh and toast one another. Some play card games by candlelight and a few old men are content to smoke their clay pipes and watch the fiddler and fife player. The barman is doing a brisk business, selling glasses of poteen and bowls of hot broth, one of which I lapped up as soon as we arrived.

In the centre of the room, four men laze on wooden chairs gathered around the firepit in the dirt floor. These men must be Shiners to be hogging such warmth unchallenged. Two of them balance grimy-clothed women on their laps. A third nuzzles a black-haired girl wearing a green dress. He hooks a finger inside her bodice, pulls it away from her chest, and peers inside. Mock-scolding him, she pushes his forehead away and they both laugh.

Behind them, a mountain of a man—whose beard is as dense as an uncut forest—stands guard with an oak cudgel gripped in one anvil-sized fist. This, Rory reminded me earlier, is Hairy Barney. With vigilance, his eyes sweep across the packed room and frequently come to rest on a table of Frenchmen seated next to the tavern entrance. One of them wears the telltale red knit hat, the tassel of which hangs behind his right ear, and soon gets up and marches over to Hairy Barney, raising his glass with a broad smile. I can't understand the foreign gibberish he spouts, but by the gestures he makes toward the Shiners, it's something insulting. His friends whoop and lift their glasses high.

Hairy Barney steps closer, his grip tightening on the cudgel. His eyes are slits beneath the line of his thick brows. The music trails off and the crowd quiets. "Say that again—in English this time."

The Frenchman's eyes twinkle. He shrugs and says, "I wish you long life and de good healt'." His companions keep their eyes on the Shiners until their friend is back in his chair. The fiddle and fife music resume playing above the revived thrum of conversation.

That was close—too close.

Rory tips his glass of poteen back and scowls. "It's not Blackmore's whiskey, but it'll do." He wipes his mouth with the back of his free hand. "I'll front you the coin for another drink."

I shake my head and pan the room.

It's been hours since I last ate; hunger gnaws at my stomach. Resentment hastens me to the conclusion that I've been strung along for someone's entertainment.

"Mr. Gleeson isn't coming," I say.

"He'll be here. There's others waiting for him too." Rory tips his head in Hairy Barney's direction. "And stop calling him Mister. He's just Gleeson to us. We're Shiners now—in the family, so to speak."

No sooner does Rory utter those words than the tavern door swings open. Gleeson steps inside and pauses to take measure of the crowd.

Men nearest the entrance back away to clear a path to the fire. Hairy Barney taps the shoulder of one of the Shiners, whose face brightens when he spots Gleeson. The two slovenly women slide from his friends' laps and loop their arms through Gleeson's when he steps in front of the fire and make a show of pressing kisses to his cheeks before he pushes them away. The youngest of the four men nudges the black-haired girl from his lap and motions for Gleeson to take his chair, but he declines. The men return hats to their heads and rise to gather around their leader.

I glance at Rory to gauge his reaction, but his gaze is following the girl in the green dress. When she finds a new lap to occupy, he frowns. My elbow connects with his ribs and he shoots me a startled look. "Something's happening," I tell him.

The four Shiners head for the door, and a dozen other men gulp the remainder of their drinks and follow them outside.

"Let's go," Rory says excitedly. I grab his arm. "Wait."

Gleeson and Hairy Barney are still talking. Surely, they'll wave us over to join them. Or maybe they no longer have need of us? When Gleeson falls silent, they make for the door—without us.

"Come on or we're going to miss out," Rory says. He's halfway across the tavern before I react. The Shiners step into the night with my friend at their heels. What can I do but follow?

Rory and I walk briskly to keep pace with the long strides of Gleeson and his men, none of whom have acknowledged us. Pale moonlight shows the road unfolding ahead, but we are mostly guided by lights flickering from the windows of the cabins peppered along Richmond Road, all of us heading for Uppertown.

Within minutes, we're surging past fine stone houses. The point men lead us across grassy lots and along a number of dirt alleyways until I'm disoriented. Stray mutts growl at us with hackles raised. Tension climbs into my head and spreads to the muscles squeezing my chest. I'm swept along in a strong current with no means of escape.

We stalk along the side lane where we stop at the rear of a two-storey stone house. A large dog leaps to its feet next to the back door and barks wildly, straining against its rope. Firelight glows through the curtain of an upstairs window. Whoever lives here—a damned Englishman or Scot—is wealthy beyond anything these Shiners or I can ever hope for.

Gleeson draws his pistol. He steps ahead of the pack and signals for me to join him with a fierceness that jolts me into obedience. He holds the pistol out, clearly intending for me to take it from him. I don't want it. But it's in my hand before I can decline.

The pistol is heavier than I expected. And cold. I learned to fire Da's musket when I was ten years old, and then I only shot at mallard ducks and red squirrels. This closeness to a weapon with no other use than to harm people makes me wary but oddly excited at the same time.

"Fire it," he says.

My heart pounds in my ears and the pistol hangs limp in my right hand. A gunshot in the middle of the night is going to attract attention, and that means trouble.

"Do it." His voice is low and his tone commanding.

"What am I supposed to fire at?"

He grabs my wrist and raises the gun like a torch above my head. "Shoot," he says, glowering down at me.

My gaze fixes on his. The only way out is forward. There is a slight resistance as I squeeze the trigger, then it gives way.

Bang!

Whoa, that was . . . fun.

A figure appears in an upstairs window, then quickly backs away.

Wolfish faces of the Shiners watch as Gleeson continues to hold my wrist above my head. He's testing me. Not sure if I'm passing. I can't think straight. The barking doesn't help.

"Now shoot that son-of-a-bitch dog," Gleeson orders. Another of the Shiners passes his pistol to me in exchange for Gleeson's.

There is no question that I must impress Gleeson. Eyes burning, I raise the barrel and look down the sights. My safety hangs on one shot. The dog crouches and its lips roll back—so closely resembling the cur that tore at my heels the night before. A crust of ice forms over my heart and I pull the trigger. The dog yelps and drops to the ground like a sack of potatoes.

Before I've lowered the pistol, Rory sweeps forward with a few other men, each wielding clubs. They whoop and smash every window across the back of the house. The sound of shattering glass fills the night. A sash of a second-storey window rattles open just as I see Rory flee around the corner of the house.

Damn it! Instinct tells me to run away too.

As if reading my mind, Gleeson says, "Stand your ground."

A bald round-faced man dressed in a white nightshirt leans out through the window. "You Shiner bastards! I'm not afraid of you eejits."

"Us neither, Johnston, you Orangeman prick," Gleeson shouts back. "You're a traitor to your people."

My stomach knots. Surely this man will recognize our faces and report us to a magistrate. I've already been seen causing a ruckus at Blackmore Tavern last night. Mr. Mueller will sack me for sure if I'm hauled off to gaol in Perth.

"You people are a scourge. I'll see that you all meet the justice of the law—starting with your leader, Peter Aylen," Johnston bellows.

"I wonder if your house will burn as pretty as your shop did last year," Gleeson shouts back.

Johnston disappears from the window and returns a second later. Moonlight glints from his rifle barrel. I may fill my drawers.

"Don't move," Gleeson says to me. "He can't aim worth shite."

Blam!

I flinch as the thunder-like boom echoes into the night. The shot is wide.

"Let's go," Gleeson says. "Nice and easy. No running. Johnston's hands will be shaking. It'll take him close to a minute to reload." His men fall in line and follow us to the road.

I look over my shoulder to see if we're being trailed. "What about the neighbours? They'll be after us. Shouldn't we hide?"

"You're a Shiner, Thomas O'Dougherty," Gleeson says, staring straight ahead. "Men will look up to you now."

'Tis a fine thing to be appreciated. But why has he singled me out? Why not Rory, who is game for all kinds of mischief?

Again, he reads my mind. "You stood up to Blackmore with no weapon but your fierce Irish temper. I respect a man who knows himself."

Uncertainty slides from my shoulders and my stride lengthens to match Gleeson's.

12

SEAMUS

Love distracts from ugliness and hate breeds contempt. My feelings for Biddy swim somewhere between both those two shores. She watches me this morning from the pine windbreak alongside our cabin. Can she not see that I'm sinking? That her being with child again weighs my pockets with rocks? She's beautiful in the morning sun—a delight to look upon for any man who doesn't know her. But her bitterness exhausts me and I'm ready to be away from her.

Patrick Newell has come to fetch me. We've wintered together chopping timber at the camp ever since our work digging the canal ended. I dust my hands off once he finishes helping me heft the last barrel of salt pork into the back of his wagon. His two brothers slide it to the front of the wagon bed while I pile in the last of my gear—a long-handled axe, a sack containing a wool blanket along with a few changes of clothing, and a wooden crate of food Biddy packed for the trip.

Annie chatters sweetly to the horses and feeds them handfuls of grass, which they greedily accept. Breath steams from their nostrils and into the chill morning air. She'll be a hand taller when I return in the spring.

"Say your goodbyes, man," Patrick says, then walks to the far side of the wagon to help tether the barrels in place.

Biddy hugs herself and waits expectantly. She's smiling, even as she searches my face for reassurance. Last night, her voice was hopeful when she asked if I was excited about the child in her belly. She's certain it's a boy. If the birth is as horrific as the last, I'll be a widower come spring. We'd agreed—no more children. She must have stopped using the herb concoction that she assured me would prevent my seed from taking root. The situation feels more like a tightening snare than a blessing. Still, I regret my answer to her. I told her it's bad luck to count your chickens before they're hatched.

Biddy lifts her chin and strides toward me now. I swear the woman reads my mind, but it's no comfort. "You needn't worry your head, Seamus. Everything will be all right. I forbid it to be otherwise."

"Right."

Next to Biddy, Elizabeth stands sharp-eyed with Katherine in her arms. Since Thomas's fit of anger yesterday, my eldest daughter's sly looks have been jabbing at me. Her mother is in peril and it's my fault. Elizabeth has questions I cannot—will not—answer, so I've avoided being alone with her. Much like her mother, she won't rest until she's wrung the truth from me.

If Mariah reveals our deception to Thomas, Biddy will toss her out like diseased fruit. The boy will never speak to us again; our girls will never look at us the same way. In the upheaval, Biddy's apt to lose the baby like last time. Or worse, she'll die in agony delivering it and I'll be left to raise four children—half of them babies—alone. I'm not built for it and am sure to fail them all. If the worst of my imaginings come true, would Mariah stay on?

Annie wanders over to rest her head against Biddy's right hip and studies me. Even wee Katherine, sensing something is about to happen, turns her face in my direction. My wife and daughters wait for me to spin an affectionate phrase upon parting. But all I can say is, "I should check on the cow one last time." My words hit the ground with a thud, and I slink away from my family. I'm such a coward.

The cow is fine. It's the woman milking it that I need to see. Biddy's jealousy drills at my back as I set off to find her sister.

I follow the trail of Mariah's boot prints through the frost-tipped grass from the chicken coop to the cowshed. At first light, her axe rang out against the pine stump out back. Freshly split firewood was stacked against the front of the cabin when I stepped outside after breakfast. Her fear drives her to steer clear of the other men. But at the moment, I'm the one she most wishes to avoid. How to navigate our conundrum must confuse her as much as it does me.

On my way to the cowshed, I hear the swell of male voices behind me. Patrick's stands out above his brothers'. "Grand news, Biddy," he says.

I glance over my shoulder. Biddy's hand rests high on her belly. These men will tell others at the camp, and she knows it. On the winter evenings huddled around the camboose fire, the crew will drive home, over and over, the blessing of the new baby that awaits me come summer. She's recruiting them as unwitting accomplices in her campaign to oblige me to our family.

I step quietly into the doorway of the shed and pause. Mariah's back is turned toward me as she leans forward on the milking stool. She's wearing one of my cast-off coats with a wool scarf loosely wound around her neck. The cow twitches her tail and her massive head swings sideways, a low-pitched chime sounding from the bell around her neck. When she begins lowing, Mariah reaches up and rests her hand, fingers splayed, on the cow's bony flank.

"There, there, Esmerelda. There, there." And she begins to sing "Bonny Light Horseman": *Like the dove that does mourn when it loseth its mate, Will I for my love till I die for his sake.* A lump rises in my throat for reasons I don't fully understand. As she rounds into the chorus, I'm reminded of Thomas singing Biddy's Methodist hymns just before his voice broke. The cow stills and Mariah's hands deftly return to the udders.

"I'm going now," I say.

The pulling and squeezing continue, with no change in the quick tempo of milk spurting into the pail.

Praise will unlock her. It always does. "Thanks for the saltpetre you set next to the door for me this morning. There's three times the amount I need in that sack. S'pose you want me to sell some to the other skidders?" The cow blinks with disinterest and Mariah says nothing. "Should fetch a good price. The boys at camp are always telling me, 'Bring us yer sister-in-law's magic dust. It turns our randy stallions docile as ole dogs.' Sets a man's mind to ease knowing the day of pulling timber out of the bush will go so smoothly."

Her silence shouts at me. As I'm about to say more, a sharp whistle cuts my ears—Patrick signalling for me to come. I turn to him, raising a finger. One minute more.

"Mariah, if anything goes wrong while I'm away, send the Newells' eldest boy to come get me. I can be home in three or four days, depending on the weather." There's no need for me to name the thing that could go wrong.

She straightens and casts a withering look over her squared shoulder. Her jawline is mottled with red splotches and the scar at the corner of her left eye has turned a darker crimson. She turns back to the cow and resumes milking.

"Biddy doesn't act it," I continue. "But she's fragile. Anything that upsets her will bring about a bad end." I wait for Mariah to indicate her usual resignation to duty. None is forthcoming so I try again. "Your sister needs you. The children need you." Silence. Fearing defeat, I blurt out the first plea that comes to mind. "And I need you."

Mariah swivels on the stool. Her face opens up like a fresh bloom.

Until a few days ago, I could read Mariah. A kind word could appease her, steer her in a direction of my choosing. But now I can decipher nothing from her expression with any degree of certainty. I need someone on my side, for God's sake. Her eyes begin to search mine and I suddenly realize my gaff. I've mistakenly professed feelings for her.

"What I wanted to say is—"

Annie flings herself against me. She wraps her arms around my legs and tilts her face upward to beam a smile at me. "Mam says to come now."

I look back at the wagon. Patrick is seated on the front bench clutching the reins. Biddy shields her eyes from the sun to stare my way, her mouth set in a hard line.

All I can do is look at Mariah with an urgency that says *Don't tell*. Annie grabs my hand with both her small ones and begins tugging me away from the shed door.

I'm running away from a powder keg with no idea what I'll come home to.

13

MARIAH

What I most desire and what I must do are sisters at war inside my head. I waffle between determination for a better life and fear of losing what little comfort I do have. Mam always said, "You never miss the water until the well runs dry." She also told me, "Patience is a virtue that causes no shame," but mine has.

On the inside, I'm a fire throwing off sparks. Biddy infuriates me to the point that my thoughts turn dark; at times, I imagine my sister dying and me taking over her life. I'm filled with the Old Testament anger of Cain for Abel. While she rubs her belly this morning and smirks, I plunge a knife into pumpkins, one after the other, then hack their shells open and gut them. From the stringy innards, Annie picks the seeds to be dried for next year's crop and arranges them on the table in the shape of flowers and smiling faces. At least I can count on her agreeable nature. Elizabeth is supposed to be slicing the halves for hanging in the rafters to dry, but instead she's flitted off to stare at her reflection in the window again. She turns her head side to side while, against her earlobes, she holds my earbobs.

Since Seamus left a month ago, Biddy has been laid up by her pregnancy. At the first twinge, she assumed the habit of sitting on my bed with a blanket folded over her legs. This morning, she busies herself preparing a basket of herb bundles for market and doling out orders as if I don't have enough to do now that she's ailing. *The fire's gone down. Fetch more wood. Pick up that cauldron.* Everything is too far beneath Her Royal Highness Elizabeth to bother with, and Biddy won't risk lifting anything heavier than the cup she's sipping from.

If only God would take Biddy. I could be the mother to these children and a wife to Seamus.

As I prepare to carve into a new pumpkin, Annie wipes her hands clean on the front of her dress and joins her sister at the window. "I want a turn holding the earbobs."

"No," Elizabeth snaps. "They're mine."

My knife blade slips along the outside of the pumpkin shell and gashes my thumb. Blood wells from the cut and drips, dark and red, onto the pumpkin flesh while I look around for something with which to staunch the bleeding with.

"See that, girls? Always pay attention," Biddy says.

A few swift strides and I'm at her bedside snatching up one of her newly made sachets.

She protests, but it's too late. I fold the white cloth around my bloody thumb.

I glare at my sister, before turning to admonish Elizabeth. "Put Gran's earbobs back where they live and come slice these pumpkins."

With a saucy lift of her chin, Elizabeth turns back to the window. "I don't take orders from you."

Annie examines me as if seeing me clearly for the first time and quietly says, "You're not our mother."

Biddy folds her hands across her belly and says, "Back to work, sister. Leave my children to me. *All* of them."

Shrew! I storm across the room and yank my old coat from the hook. Blood pounds in my ears as I unbar the latch. With all my might, I push against the door so it flings wide and the outside handle smashes against the front of the cabin. A cluster of Biddy's hens part like the Red Sea as I charge toward Seamus's chair shed. They squawk and flap their wings to scramble away, but I manage to send one laggard flying with the toe of my boot.

Once inside the shed, my tears burst free and I pace like a cornered bear. To hell with my sister and her ungrateful whelps. It's my turn for happiness. I'm telling Thomas that I'm his mother.

Attempting to calm myself, I scoop some precious curls of bark and wood that remain on the ground beneath Seamus's shaving horse and pack them inside a pocket on my apron.

What did Seamus mean when he said *I need you*? Does he need me as I need him—like air? Or will this unveiling of our secret drive him farther from me? *Push it from your mind*, I tell myself. *Don't be soft*.

The secret is best revealed while he is at the winter camp and cut off from us. Then I will be the target of Biddy's wrath while her emotions are highest. By the time Seamus returns home in March or April, her anger will thaw like snow on a spring river. She'll replace Thomas with the boy she insists she's carrying and I'll be free of my sister's spite at last.

I sigh as I imagine Thomas's face when he learns that Seamus and I laid together after his father and Biddy were handfasted. And what about the girls? They'll know too. Not just about me, but their father. They'll hate me. Us. Will it matter?

After Thomas knows, I'll no longer be welcome at Biddy's house. Winter moves closer each day and I've nowhere to go. Maybe there are jobs in Bytown. For my son, I will endure the closeness of men and dogs. I could take in mending, although my fingers are clumsy with the needle. I'd much rather chop wood and hunt—but no one will hire a woman for that sort of work. Some well-to-do family must be in need of a servant. I'd despise the cooking and cleaning, but I'd have food and a roof over my head, plus I'd be closer to Thomas. A sensation spreads through my chest. Happiness, I think.

Once I'm standing in front of Thomas and looking into his eyes, I'll know what to do.

Biddy's eyes widen when I bound into the cabin with a smile lighting my face. She lowers her cup of bone broth to her lap after I snatch up the herb basket from the foot of my bed and announce that I'm leaving for Bytown.

"Edwards Mercantile doesn't expect you for two days," she says warily.

"Oh well," I reply. "You know what they say about the early bird."

Biddy wears the same expression as when we played hide-and-seek as children. She'd search the bushes, determined to find me, all the while braced for the dreaded moment when I'd jump out and yell *Boo!*

I warm with power. So this is how it feels.

The tired sun hangs overhead and a northerly wind cuts through my coat. How foolish I was to give up Mam's shawl to Peg, the forward lass. If she's run off, I may never see that bit of wool again. *Eejit*.

Determination propels me past Bytown's stray dogs and drunkards. It's odd to see so many seedy characters lingering about the streets in late October. Other years, most of their sort are deep in the woods where they belong, hard at work in camps at Maniwaki or as far away as Chicoutimi on the Saguenay River. Frenchmen from Lowertown keep a strong hold on timber jobs, but the Shiner violence pries loose some chances for our people. Aylen's thugs and displaced Frenchmen without work linger in Bytown.

Bearded, clean-shaven, labourers or men of letters—it matters not. They're all men and a reason for caution. A two-wheeled cart comes from behind and passes on my left. At the reins is a gaunt-faced man whose hat brim hides his eyes. Although I cannot gauge his nature, my fear doesn't stir. Two children, a boy and a girl, roughly the same ages as Elizabeth and Annie, sit among the scattering of mangy cabbages their father is hauling. The children's gangly legs hang over the end of the cart and jerk with each rut the wheels bump through. The boy looks at my face with curiosity, then turns and whispers to his sister.

Another wagon rattles up behind me and another, pulled by a single horse, approaches as I near the canal bridge. I squeeze closer to fine stone house fronts. The peak of my bonnet funnels my gaze to the toe of my boots kicking out from beneath my skirt with each stride. I strangle the basket handle. *Walk. Walk. Walk.*

A matronly voice calls out from ahead of me. "Clara."

"Coming, mistress." A delicate reply.

I look up to see a wire-thin servant girl, about the same age as Thomas, sweeping the top step of her master's grand stone house. Her smile doesn't falter at the sight of my scars. She has kind eyes and her hair is red like mine although not unruly. Before she turns away to heft the front door open and go inside, I thank her for that smile with a quick nod.

A furry head peers over the top edge of a wagon sitting idle in my path. *Dog!* My throat constricts as I leap sideways, tears burning my eyes. It's like this every time. My mind replays the searing pain of teeth ripping at my flesh. The growling. Blood in my eyes, my mouth.

In fervent whispers, I beg for God's protection and carry on. Soon I resort to counting the number of steps I take. *One. Two. Three. Four.* Men laughing to my left. *Five. Six.* The springs squeak as if heavy barrels or perhaps lumber is being loaded into the bed of a wagon. I can't look up to know for sure. Then I'm crossing over the canal. *Twenty.*

Twenty-one. The distinct scent of pipe tobacco. A deep-voiced shout followed by the beat of feet racing across the dirt road ahead of me, and a torrent of French curse words. I only raise my head when I hear the ring of a hammer against an anvil.

Mueller's Blacksmith Shop lies ahead. Thomas is nearby.

Oh Lord! I stop dead. A small group of shifty men have planted themselves at the entrance of the smithy. Thomas is with them, a lamb among wolves. I see one of the Shiner horsemen from that sabbath, the quiet one who carried the rifle, among them, smoking a pipe. Four more shady characters, two with oak cudgels dangling from beneath their coattails, stand alongside him. Inside the shop, I see that Mr. Mueller continues to work but he glances warily in their direction.

I startle when a man brushes past, leading his spirited chestnut mare across the front of the smithy, where he slows to take a look. Mr. Mueller looks up and, spotting him, waves him in. The man studies the Shiners and continues walking. On the opposite side of the Lowertown Market, there's another blacksmith shop, one without Irish gang members blocking its entrance, I wager. Mr. Mueller's smile fades and he rests a hand on either hip as he watches the man move on. After a long moment, he walks over to Thomas. My boy lowers his chin.

Oh no. Thomas, what are you doing?

The rifleman speaks out and then draws on his pipe while his armed henchmen step forward to separate Mr. Mueller from Thomas. Rory also shoulders in next to my son. Words are exchanged and, after one disappointed frown at his apprentices, Mr. Mueller returns to the forge.

Thomas is headed for certain disaster.

Now more than ever I see the wisdom of my plan. Thomas needs me, his *real* mother, to steer him away from harm.

I nearly jump out of my boots when a hand grabs my arm. A woman in a green dress has swooshed next to me. Then I see the gap-toothed smile and Mam's shawl draped over an arm—Peg.

"Jesus," she says. "I'm out of breath. I've been chasing after you and calling your name. I even whistled. You must be deaf."

"Been busy," I say, stealing another glance at Thomas.

"I'm still waiting on that potion you promised me over a month ago. The one to weaken a fella's cockstand." She thrusts a hand forward. "So let's have it."

"Not now," I tell her.

"But we had a deal!"

One of the hoodlums looks our way. When he sees Peg, he smirks and elbows his friend. Peg will ruin everything.

That's when Thomas notices me. His frown dashes my heart against the rocks, but still I wave at him feebly. One of the men nudges his shoulder and the group walks off, laughing.

That dark-haired shammer, Rory, waves with fervour but Thomas turns his back and stalks into the gloom of the smithy. A sour feeling settles in my stomach.

"I'd give him a deal, that shy one," Peg says. "Virgins ride for free."

When I scowl, she quirks her head. "You know him?" she asks.

"I do."

I tear blindly across the street and blast into the blacksmith shop like a woman possessed, thinking only of saving my son from the pull of these horrid people. By the time I come to my senses, I'm standing in front of the forge. Thomas, his apron dangling from his neck, gapes red-faced at me.

Rory laughs and says, "Top of the morning, missus."

"Shuddup, you right eejit," Thomas says.

Mr. Mueller shouts out, "O'Dougherty! Business first. Talk on your own time." When Thomas squints at him, cold and steely, his master adds uncertainly, "There are others looking for work who'd bring less trouble."

Thomas grabs my elbow tightly and ushers me around an upright beam draped in chains and toward the street. Once outside, he turns on me and says, "Thanks a lot."

"Thomas, I need to tell you something."

"Go home, Aunt Mariah."

"Thomas, I love you."

He snorts at that and turns his back on me, saying, "Don't come back here. Ever."

It's as though a donkey has hoofed me in the gut. I stumble backward, then whirl, stupefied, and begin walking in the direction of the market. My hands shake and I sink my teeth into my bottom lip to keep from crying. I'm done for.

Without Thomas, there is nothing.

"Well, you made a fine hash of that. Who is he?" Peg is at my elbow again.

"I can't talk about it."

"Sure you can. Just move your lips and the words will come out."

When I clamp a hand over my mouth to keep from sobbing, she tries a new tack. The woman is like a flea on a dog. She won't let go. "He's too young to be your sweetheart. So I'm guessin' he's kin. Which, take it from me, you're lucky to have."

"He's my nephew," I blubber. "But he hates me."

Raising both her hands as if shooshing birds away, she exclaims, "So what! A teenage boy is angry with you? They're all hot under the collar at that age 'cause their oats are wantin' to be sown. He'll get over himself. You just have to wait."

"You think so?" I wipe my eyes with a threadbare cuff.

"I know so. See it all the time," Peg replies.

Fifteen years I've waited. I can be patient, then try again once Thomas's temper cools.

"Here you are, and thanks for the loan." Peg thrusts Mam's shawl at me. "Now that's sorted, how about my potion?"

As I pull the bag of saltpetre from my coat pocket, she snatches it and hugs it under her arm.

"You want me to starve?" she says. "If men see ol' Peg taking a package from the healer's woman, I'll lose customers. They'll think I have the itch again."

"Two shillings," I tell her.

She goggles in disbelief. "Surely you don't think I'm daft enough to carry coin among this bunch of thievin' rascals. Maybe I would if I was a strapping lass like you, but my money is hidden far from town where no one will find it."

I'm struck by the urge to yank her dark hair out by the roots. "Pay up when I come to collect or the price doubles."

Peg recovers from the shock of my anger and crows with laughter. "It's a deal. If this powder does its job on my cribmate's customers, they'll be visiting me instead of her and my purse will overflow with coin." She sets off down the street and hops easily onto the back of flatbed cart.

"One week. I will find you," I call out.

"Make it two weeks. And bring more," Peg shouts back. "See you later, Red!"

Red. I smile in spite of myself and wad my stray hair inside my bonnet. Then I think of Thomas again, and it's all I can do not to head back to the homestead in defeat. Instead, I must distract myself for a few hours before the mercantile opens and I can complete my business.

Along the opposite side of the street, three Algonquin women lead five children, each of whom carries rolled blankets under their arms. I've seen these women before at the market. The one closest to me wears a tumpline stretched taut across her forehead by the load of baskets it supports against her lower back. Her hair is streaked with grey, but she moves with a youthful agility. Another brings a brace of rabbits to market and the third, a pair of wild turkeys. Not even when a staggering old man spits on their path do they hesitate.

In this moment, I feel more kinship with these strangers than I ever have with my own sister.

All manner of sellers hawk their goods in the market this day. Bundles of firewood and half-starved cows are to be had, plus baskets level with eggs and a few crates of live hens, but it's the produce I've got my eye on. The summer's drought left us with little for the root cellar.

A mother, still a child herself, sways back and forth to quiet the distressed youngster in a grimy nightshirt who straddles her hip. The boy looks to be about two years old. His cheeks are splotched with red and his chin quivers between bouts of wailing. She's tried her best to wrap him in a tattered blanket but he's kicked his wee legs free, and they're exposed to the cold breeze. A pitiful bunch of wrinkled carrots are lined up on the ground next to her feet, clad in men's boots, a ring of filth ground in around her ankles.

If not for Biddy's promise, that could well have been Thomas and me.

"How much?" I ask.

"A pence each," she replies. "Or a shilling for the whole lot."

"I've no coin."

For a moment neither of us speak. She frowns and openly sizes up my scars; I study the bruise circling her left eye.

"What's wrong with your baby?" I ask.

"His teeth are coming in."

"I have white yarrow in my basket. Use the flowers to make a tea for him. It relieved my—son." I've said it. *Son.* "I'll give you two sprigs for six carrots." The woman bites her bottom lip as she mulls my offer.

"No," she finally says, eyes watering. "It's coin I'm needing, missus. The rent is coming due on our place. The landlord will be at my door if I don't make good."

There must be something better for women than this. "Life is hardest on mothers and their children. Hope is the physician of each misery. Be strong, miss." The young woman weeps openly when I withdraw a sprig of yarrow and pass it to her.

"God bless you, missus," she says. "I hope so."

I look across the market, to where Mrs. Fran Edwards, the owner of Edwards Mercantile, stands with her round face pressed close to her shop's front window. She adjusts her glasses and cocks her grey head left, then right, assessing the busyness of the street. Many's the time I've seen her do so. I pause to make way for a team of horses pulling a wagon of sealed barrels into the market square. In the time it takes for them to pass by, Mrs. Edwards has disappeared from sight.

A clutch of giggling servant girls approaches from Uppertown, no doubt to pick through the offerings of the market. They're among the few with shillings in their pockets, albeit of their masters. With any luck the young mother will make her rent.

A wish for her luck is a wish for my own.

I turn the doorknob and push into Edwards Mercantile. The smell of woodsmoke rises from the fireplace at the far side of the room. Mrs. Edwards now stands behind the polished wood counter to my left.

"Morning, Miss Lindsay," she says, raising her gaze from her ledger book without lifting her head. Her black dress is ironed with precision and the row of perfectly aligned buttons ends where one pulls together her stand-up collar.

"Mrs. Edwards." I loose the ties knotted beneath my chin and let the bonnet slide from my head so it rests between my shoulder blades. A million times I've asked her to call me by my Christian name, but she refuses, insisting that we are businesswomen and should address each other with a formality befitting our duties. Suits me fine. The mercantile is the one place where I feel like I'm somebody. She's claimed that using surnames was an ounce of British civility she could add to this heathen town.

There's a strain of British in the world more godless than anyone I know of—the sort that would turn starving people out of their turf houses to shiver in a damp Irish bog with little more than rags to cover them. Fran Edwards is not that sort of English. She's a breed unto herself—a British woman who befriends the poorest of Lowertown, French and Irish alike. Da would call her a pistol if he were ever to meet her. She's blunt and shoots straight. I first met her back in the days when Seamus was digging the canal and busting rocks, and he, Biddy and I were living in a Corktown shack along the Deep Cut with Thomas newly born. She saw me looking peaked and wan, and gave me two rusty nails to boil. *Drink the water*, she told me. *Good for the blood.*

Mr. Edwards was still alive then. He yammered at her to charge me for the nails, but she refused. When he stormed out of the shop, she pushed ten more into my basket and told me to share with whoever else I saw fit to.

I browse the goods while I wait for her to finish her tallying. The mercantile stocks basic wares for woodsmen and the poor of Lowertown—tin ware, buckets and axes; cruiser lamps, oil and wicks. At the end of the counter are barrels of flour and cornmeal. Across the room bolts of linen and skeins of wool are piled on a table.

"That's that," Mrs. Edwards says and lays her quill alongside the book. "What have you got for me today?"

I cross to her counter. "It will soon be weather for catarrh, so my sister has sent horehound and wormwood. I have yarrow, and for women's complaints, there's lady's mantle and valerian."

Her head bobs as I sort herb bundles onto the counter. "Have you brought any of that ointment for blisters and bruises? It's a good seller with the men going off to the timber camps." With an eyeroll she adds, "God willing, the murderous rabble will soon empty out of town. They drive away nearly as much business as they bring in."

"I can deliver more arnica balm next week," I say, regretting instantly that I hadn't sent a tin with Seamus.

"Since the canal build ended, there's stiff competition for timber jobs. Peter Aylen's lot is trying to run the Canadiens out of the Ottawa Valley. What has your brother-in-law heard about work at the camps this winter?"

"Same as what you're saying. He's gone up a bit earlier than normal to make sure he gets hired on."

"There'll be more Shiner trouble, to be sure. Everyone knows that Aylen's crew were burning other lumbermen's timbers and stealing rafts during the spring drive. Is your sister's husband the sort to join in undercutting the French loggers for the sake of work?"

"No," I tell her, although I've no idea. What won't a man do for the survival of his family?

Mrs. Edwards appears to realize she's gone too far. Her tone is softer as she changes the subject. "The little garden out back may see me through the winter, but just barely."

"My sister's garden has not fared so well." In truth, the drought took its toll and deer grazed on the earliest greens.

"Your sister's garden . . . ." Mrs. Edwards repeats. "Miss Lindsay, do you have anything set aside for yourself? Money is power, especially for a woman. If you've got savings, it matters not that you're a member of the fairer sex."

"A little." Fifteen years in Upper Canada and all I have to show for it is a tin of keepsakes I've stashed inside the hollow of a tree in our woods.

"If you'd been born a man, what would you dream for yourself?"

The question stymies me, never having considered such a thing. My eyes travel to the floor as if the answer is lying there and waiting to be picked up. Hopefully, if I'm quiet long enough, her mind will turn back to the business at hand. But when I glance upward, she adjusts her spectacles and says, "Well, you must have some idea."

My mind is blank. I've never been asked what *I* want. At home I'm told, *Fetch this. Wash that. You're always underfoot.*

"Horses. I'd shoe horses," I blurt, just to have something to say.

"You'd become a farrier?" Mrs. Edwards looks amused, then adds, "Why not!"

"My da was a farrier at the Harris estate in County Cork. I watched him work every day after I delivered his lunch. I had the makings of a farrier, he always told me. Shame I wasn't a boy. Sometimes Da let me remove a shoe, put on a new one. I cleaned around the horses' frogs, filed their hooves. He showed me how to adjust a shoe for a horse that had gone lame, talked me through every step of the way. Mam used to say I hammered nails in my sleep."

"Your nephew is a blacksmith apprentice, is he not? Perhaps a family business one day."

"I'm talking foolishness," I say. But still, there's something in the idea that lights a fire in me.

"Your world is what you make it, Miss Lindsay. You must stake your claim. No one will hand you anything. Mine is the only woman-run mercantile in Bytown."

"I'm a spinster," I tell her. "Without a man to back me up . . ."

"You're a handy woman," Mrs. Edwards says. "Find yourself a farrier, preferably one with a weakness for tall women. Play the game, Miss Lindsay. If you're the wrong age and sex to be an apprentice, marry the teacher."

My eyes water up, and I duck my chin to hide it. She's wrong. Although he and I are a shamble, I've loved only one man my entire life—the one who picked me up from the road where death nearly took me. There's room in my heart for no other, even if only a business arrangement.

The mercantile door suddenly flings open and a fierce-looking stranger barges toward us. A gasp catches in my throat. He flops a brace of furs on the counter between Mrs. Edwards and me without a care for my horrified expression or whether he's interrupted us. Greasy hair juts from beneath his red woollen cap and a striped sash is knotted at his waist. He smells of sweat and wild things. I edge away from him, but it's too late. The odour carries me back to the dirt road in front of the Flynn cottage and triggers a feeling of dread.

The man fans the pelts across the counter in an agitated fashion. "Qu'est-ce que tu vas me donner?"

"Again, in English," Mrs. Edwards says. She's all business now.

"How much?" He jabs a grubby finger at each fur in turn. "Marten, mink, rabbit . . ."

If I didn't have to wait on payment for Biddy's herbs, I'd leave. My hands have begun to tingle and my lips are numbing, a sure sign that my past is rising to meet the present. I lean my hip bones against the front of the counter to steady myself and wish I'd kept my bonnet on. Summoning the courage to remain standing next to any man would be much easier if I was blinkered.

Mrs. Edwards runs a thumb along a smaller brownish-grey pelt, then flips it over to examine the skin. "I'll give you six pence for the rabbits."

"And the others?" he demands loudly. The man is a tight coil of sinew, craning over the counter, meaning to intimidate Mrs. Edwards. In doing so, his hands splay against the oak. The ring finger of his right hand ends in a blunt line at the top of his second knuckle. Skin stretches in rope folds over the bone.

"My customers will buy rabbit to line mittens and gloves. The rest they can't afford."

"What you lookin' at?" He's caught me staring at his missing finger and slams me with all the force of his attention.

Fear ratchets tight around my chest. I look away from his hand.

"Eh, I'm talkin' to you!"

Startled, I turn to face him. He jerks back, but then he processes what he's seeing and begins to laugh. His breath reeks of decay and two bottom teeth are black to their cores.

He thrusts his half finger close to my face. "This you gawk at when you have a visage like sliced ham?" He edges closer. I back up and still he comes at me. The heat of the fireplace is so close behind me I fear my skirt will catch flame.

I squeeze my eyes shut as his rancid breath sets the blood to thrumming in my ears. My shoulders press against the fireplace mantel while the wood crackles in the fire. The searing heat gives way to the snapping teeth of the Flynns' black dog.

Click.

I open my eyes to find the man staring at the muzzle of the musket now levelled at his forehead. Mrs. Edwards squints along the length of the barrel, the stock braced against her right shoulder. His damaged hand slowly makes for the hilt of the hunting knife visible above his sash.

"Hands over your head and back slowly toward the same door that let you in. Our business here is finished," she orders.

He pauses as if considering her willingness to shoot him. His gaze never leaves her face.

Mrs. Edwards steps closer and jams the muzzle against his forehead. Finally, he laces his fingers over the top of his wool hat and takes a step back. She's a tiny woman but as his soft leather moccasins move soundless against the floor she matches every step with the muted click of her boot heels. If not for the gun between them, they might be accused of dancing.

"I ain't leavin' without them pelts," he threatens.

"Miss Lindsay, kindly return the gentleman's goods. All but the two rabbit hides. And bring the loaded pistol from under the counter." Mrs. Edwards does not lower her rifle. "You keep backing up," she tells the man. "I'll tell you when to stop."

"The price of those rabbits just doubled," he shouts.

"You'll get nothing for the rabbits, but I'll let you leave with your head intact. Consider we're even for the disruption."

I steal a glance over my shoulder. It appears that he'll argue even as he reaches the door, but instead his jaw muscles flex and his eyes narrow at me. "You caused me this trouble. I won't forget it."

The leather thong is difficult to untie, my hands are shaking so. Once I've separated two rabbit furs from the other pelts, with knees quaking I grab the pistol and follow Mrs. Edwards outside. Curious passersby walk a wide berth around the man.

"Lindsay . . ." the Frenchman says, then turns his head and spits as if ridding himself of a foul taste. "Someday, you're gonna pay for this."

So much hatred is squeezed into the space of my name that those fifteen-year-old girl feelings flood me again. But this time a friend's stubbornness fortifies me. With Mrs. Edwards at my side, his words have no teeth; they are just air.

I toss the furs on the ground. The weak knot gives way and the pelts land in a loose heap.

Let him kneel. Let him feel the humiliation of gathering dead things while his knees grind into the dirt.

I can see by the way he glares at me that he knows what I'm thinking. Still, he is at my feet. And for a moment I am victorious because I put him there. He squats and deftly reties the sinew. On his feet again, he turns to walk away, hissing over his shoulder, "Ugly Irish bitch!"

Sparks flash from Mrs. Edwards's flintlock and my free hand flies to my ear. Chunks of fur explode from the man's brace of pelts. He leaps sideways.

"Hey!" he yelps. There follows a string of indecipherable French words as he examines the remains of his wares. He looks up at us with an incredulity that soon switches to rage. He comes at us, fist raised and spewing curse words.

I level the pistol at him and he halts immediately. If I had to shoot, I could.

He laughs to save face, then turns on his heel and walks away. I only lower the pistol once he's veered onto Sussex in the direction of the Ottawa River.

A youthful glow flushes Mrs. Edwards's cheeks as she says, "That was positively exhilarating!"

I smile so hard I feel a tug on the bunching of scar tissue at the corner of my eye. Suddenly I see my way through to Thomas.

The sun melts into the horizon as I sweep, full of optimism, into the darkening cabin. Biddy has taken Katherine up to bed with her. Elizabeth lights a candle with a burning splinter of wood that she casts back into the hearth. "You were gone a long time," she says. "The fire is dying."

"So it is." My light mood disarms her.

Annie, hauling her sleeping mat by one corner, pauses halfway up the loft ladder. "We're all sleeping upstairs with Mam," she tells me, then continues climbing.

The bottom half of Elizabeth's face glows in the candlelight as she crosses to the ladder.

She soon reaches the top rung and disappears into the loft.

I drink some broth and devour an apple. After I put another log on the fire, I fall, fully clothed, onto my bed and wait for them all to sleep.

In the small hours of the morning, I tiptoe to the worktable and take the flour tin from Biddy's shelf. I push my coat sleeve up and wiggle my fingers through flour until I find the folded cloth that holds the earbobs. I draw it out and return the tin to the shelf, careful not to make a sound. I latch the door quietly behind me as I leave the cabin.

Darkness lifts just enough for me to find my way through the forest beyond the windbreak to my treasure tree. Once there, I strain my ears for any sound, human or animal, and scan the spaces between the trees. No one is here but me. I rise on my toes and reach inside the hollow far up the trunk. My fingertips grasp at the tin and pull it down. I pry off the lid and look inside—a lock of Thomas's baby hair tied in a piece of wool, a strip of lace and a blue ribbon, a nail taken from the pocket of Da's farrier apron, and a flower I pressed, a gesture of kindness from Seamus following my rescue. Before I nestle the cloth-wrapped earbobs in the tin and return it to the tree, I kiss the pearls, my heart overflowing with hope.

I hang a couple inches more than usual of blue ribbon over the lip of the hollow so I can find the tree again. Too much? I'm about to tuck the ribbon further inside when a wolf howl cuts through the air. I dash back to the cabin with my heart pounding from fear and excitement.

When Thomas's temper settles, I'll tell him that I am his mother. And I'll also tell him of the future the pearl earbobs will secure for us. Mam told me ten years of Da's wages couldn't match their value. She held off selling them, even in tough times. *Things are bad, but tomorrow could be worse,* she'd say. Tomorrow has come. I'll sell the earbobs and buy a smithy. We can hire men to apprentice with us. Imagine that—me and Thomas working side by side as farrier and blacksmith.

14

THOMAS

I used to dread the monotony of Sunday, my one day free of the blacksmith shop, with all those hours to fill. There's a limit to how many streams a man can fish or the number of times he can listen to Rory's stories without losing his mind. All that's changed now. On Sundays, I tag along on the fringes of Gleeson's crew, trying to make sense of where I fit in and how I might benefit. The influence of Peter Aylen's relentless ambition is a whetstone sharpening my view of the future and holds as much value as any apprenticeship I'll get from Mr. Mueller. Still, if I am to have my own business one day, I have to mind that the frenzy of this rabble doesn't grab my ankles and pull me under, like it almost did the night we went after that prosperous Orangeman.

Tonight, I've gone along to a tavern on Sleigh Bay, just east of where the canal empties into the Ottawa River. A crew from the *Alexander* has come ashore for an evening of drink and women. Earlier today they delivered a batch of Montreal whores to the dock for further transport to Peter Aylen's house somewhere on the road between Bytown and

Perth. He brings them in to entertain his men at regular gatherings he hosts. Rumour has it these women will prance naked through his house and perform all manner of acts on a man's pecker. Everyone here's talking about it and hopes to be invited, myself included. I'd do some looking at those naked women, but I'd never bed a whore. I'll wait for a chaste girl, like the red-haired colleen I passed on the road. We only met for a moment, but I'm powerfully disappointed she hasn't dropped by the smithy to see me yet.

The tavern is a seething mass of torsos and limbs. Rory and I take turns standing on the end of a crowded bench—stooped forward, with the backs of our heads pressed against the rafters—and report in to each other about what we see.

Gleeson sits alone smoking his pipe at a table by the fireplace, while a few feet away Hairy Barney challenges men to contests of strength. Gleeson watches with a serious expression that reflects his wariness. Not even the pulsing beat of the bodhrán and fiddle music lifts a smile.

"Is he winning again?" Rory yells up at me.

I barely hear him over the clamour of men urging on Hairy Barney and the sea captain he's arm-wrestling. A pair of women shout encouragements so loudly their necks strain. Without tearing my gaze from the action, I give Rory the thumbs-up. He looses a whistle and jostles me in celebration. What a fool he is to idolize a muscle-bound Shiner who barely speaks to him.

Hairy Barney calmly regards his opponent, then ratchets the man's hand a few inches lower. The sea captain's wrestling arm begins to shake and his face draws nearer to their strained fists. Hairy Barney's smile grows broader so his eyes are reduced to a squint and he barks out a laugh, and then he growls like a mad man and slams the sea captain's hand against the table. A whiskey bottle crashes to the floor.

Arms reach through the forest of bodies to congratulate him, but he shakes them off and raises his own fist in victory as he surges to his feet.

He turns to the nearest woman and grabs her buttocks with his bear paws, lifting her off the ground. She wraps her legs around his waist and whoops as he spins her in circles. And again, the room goes wild with cheering.

Rory, wanting his turn on the bench, pulls at my jacket. But I refuse to give away my view.

Something new has caught my attention. Gleeson is speaking to one of his men and pointing a finger in my direction. Now I swear both men are staring at me.

"Let me up there! Something's going on," Rory says. "I can feel it."

"Hold your horses," I tell him.

Gleeson settles back in his chair and his man begins worming his way through the crowd.

As he closes in, I hop from the bench and Rory takes my place.

"It's over. I've missed everything," he says and knocks my hat forward over my eyes. I adjust the brim and elbow his shins just as Gleeson's man draws up.

"Gleeson wants ye."

Rory hops back down. "Let's not keep him waiting." He steps ahead of me, but the man plants a hand against his chest.

"Just him." His head jerks toward me.

Rory's mouth falls open and his eyebrows bunch together. I am wanted. He is not. Before he can taint the moment, I begin pushing my way through the crowd to where Gleeson waits—for me.

When he gestures to an empty chair, I waste no time sitting down. "Get him a whiskey," he tells his man. "Not that rotgut they're pouring for everyone else. The good stuff from under the counter."

I sit quiet as he draws on his pipe and continues to look out over the crowd. Aunt Mariah says a wise man rests as comfortably with silence as he does with talking. So I wait in tortured curiosity until Gleeson's ready to speak.

When Hairy Barney, glassy-eyed and reeking of sweat, drops into the chair across from mine, Gleeson removes the clay pipe from his mouth and gives the order.

"Start watching Johnston's house," he tells me.

Hairy Barney takes a swig from his full glass, but his gaze never leaves my face. Unsure how to respond, I look from him to Gleeson again. Hairy Barney slams his glass against our table and whiskey splashes my face. "Say you'll do it," he roars.

"Yes—I'll do it," I say with conviction, even though I'm not clear as to what he's asking of me yet. Hadn't they already done their best to intimidate the Orangeman?

Gleeson nods slowly. "Tell me who comes and goes, and when. And keep your mouth shut if anyone else starts asking you questions."

"What's Mr. Aylen planning?"

"Johnston printed upsetting comments about the Shiners in his newspaper. So we burned his last house and the press to the ground. The next move is his. All you need to know is that Aylen wants him watched." Embers burn orange inside the bowl of Gleeson's pipe as he draws on it.

"Should I report to you here?" I ask.

He exhales a stream of smoke. "I'll find you in a few weeks, maybe a month. We're taking the men to the timber camp on Aylen Lake."

Hairy Barney's face lightens. "We're going to raise a little hell along the Mattawa River."

The two women who'd been cheering for him earlier slide onto either side of his lap and plant kisses in his beard. He looks squarely at me and says, "But first, I raise a little hell at Mr. Aylen's house with the Montreal whores. I plow two at once, boy!" Laughter thunders from his throat.

I chuckle as if I understand the jest. When Gleeson's man finally arrives with my whiskey, I'm still trying to figure out the mechanics of two women on one man.

"You do good for Gleeson, and I take you to Mr. Aylen's," Hairy Barney promises. "You get French girls too, like me."

When my jaw drops, he reaches across the table and punches my shoulder. He thinks I'm hooked by the promise of women and dreams of dominating men by brute strength as he does. He's wrong. That's Rory's dream. It's the possibility of meeting the Shiners' mastermind, Peter Aylen, that lights my imagination.

※

The next morning, a wall of silence stands between me and Rory. For the entire day, neither of us tries to bust through it. The absence of chatter pleases Mueller, who takes it as a sign that we're focused on our work. I know better. I can tell by the way Rory drops the flat jaw tongs and then mislays Mueller's favourite square punch that he's as distracted by his thoughts as I am.

He's angry that I've told him nothing in spite of the grilling he gave me when we walked back to the smithy last night. *What did Gleeson want? Why won't you tell me?* Rory's the sort who needs to know everything before it happens. Even if I could tell him, I wouldn't. Instinct tells me to keep the assignment to myself.

One thing I know for sure is that if I disappoint Gleeson, there will be consequences. He gives orders quietly, but men are swift to obey him. It's not purely out of admiration that a dozen men, and sometimes as many as thirty, follow Gleeson as he moves along the streets. I've heard stories about bloated bodies found face down along the banks of the Ottawa River. His men kill to please him, even if it means eliminating each other.

When people see the Shiners coming, mothers avert their eyes and drag their children to the opposite side of the street. Times I've been with Gleeson, the Wesleyan minister and even hardened lumbermen clear a path on the sidewalk to let us pass. Without consequence, we pluck apples from merchants' bins or nick goods—harmonicas, playing cards, straight razors—from their shops. They turn a blind eye and chalk their loss up to a donation that exempts them from harassment and future beatings. Every Shiner man, high or low, follows orders from above, but he is also free to wreak his own brand of havoc on whoever he pleases.

Any Irish who don't appreciate the battle Shiners fight to advance them do so at their own risk. Those non-Irish who look down on us deserve what they get. Many is the tavern or shop reduced to smouldering ashes after its owner crossed a Shiner.

And that is why I will keep an eye on Johnston. It's not the only reason, but still . . .

There's something else to be said for Gleeson. Unlike that Orangeman bastard Johnston, I believe he truly has the interests of the poor Irish at heart. He's a Redmond O'Hanlon to his people, a regular Irish Robin Hood. I've seen him hold a gun on a pair of cheap Scots who tried to short-pay working girls outside Firth's Tavern. "Even Irish whores have a right to what they're owed," Gleeson told me.

Early on, I thought it always wrong to inflict violence on a man. But now I see it as a tool, an instrument to help achieve equality for my people so they needn't worry about losing the roof over their head or how to feed their families. The Shiners are in a war against anyone who's not for the Irish working people—the gentry, Orangemen, the French and even the church. And every eejit knows, all's fair in war.

From what I can tell, the Shiners are run like an army but better. Peter Aylen is at the top. He's a self-made man—a thinking man. Word is he landed here when he was the same age as I am now and without a penny to his name. He somehow got money to buy timber limits along the Gatineau and Mattawa Rivers. Once he made his fortune, he built that fancy house on Richmond Road. I'll bet he can even read.

Without Rory pestering me today, I've been free to do some thinking of my own. Gleeson, and the likes of him, gather the rabble to carry out Mr. Aylen's schemes. But it's the man who can feed Mr. Aylen information so he can make those schemes who'll be thanked in big ways. I aim to be that man.

I'll watch Johnston's place, as instructed, to see who comes and goes. In fact, I will go beyond what's been asked of me and deliver secrets so magnificent that I can't be lumped in with the other lackeys. Soon, I'll be in the same room as the greatest Irishman to live on this side of the ocean. Yes sir, the Shiner King will owe a debt of gratitude to Thomas O'Dougherty.

After dinner, the fire burns low in the pot-belly stove that squats in the corner of our room. Against the wall next to it leans a single stick of wood—not nearly enough to burn throughout the night. In the morning, the cold of the floor will stab through our socks. Rory and Michael will suffer chattering teeth by midnight despite sleeping fully clothed beneath the blankets. Still, they'll be warmer than me.

While I lace my boots, Rory lies on his belly across the top bunk and watches with his chin resting on his crossed wrists. "Tommy's keeping a secret," he says. "Something do to with Gleeson, isn't it? C'mon," he says to me. "Two heads are better than one. We should make a deal: one of us never does any Shiner business without the other."

I glower at him, then pull my laces tight. "I told you before, stop calling me *Tommy*."

Michael lowers his pencil from the drawing he's been working on. "Both of you should be careful," he says. "Mr. Mueller's losing respectable Uppertown business now that the Shiners are coming around here. If he finds out you've been sneaking out at night to go around with them . . ."

"Ah, he won't catch us. We're too sharp for that, aren't we, Tommy?" Rory says. His face is lit with the same mad excitement as the night he helped bust Johnston's windows. It's a look that makes me leery to tell him anything I don't want half the world to know.

"For the next two days, you can help the cause by bringing the night's firewood upstairs," I tell him.

His expression darkens. "But it's Michael's turn tomorrow and yours the next."

After winding a scarf around my neck, I pull my hat low over my ears and square my shoulders. I stare into his eyes as if to set him ablaze with the intensity of my determination. It's how Gleeson subdues his men.

"Who made you the boss?" Rory asks, his dark eyes dulled coal under the onslaught.

There's no need to answer. We all know the score. Gleeson has trusted me with a job; I'm moving up in this world.

🌿

The first seven nights of my spying on Johnston have been frigid as a witch's teat. This one is by far the coldest. A few flakes of snow skitter through the sky. What I wouldn't give to be inside rubbing my hands together over a blazing fire. I need to find a way into Johnston's stable or risk losing my toes.

Since the Shiners busted up his place, Johnston has replaced the windows, and lanterns now hang on either side of the kitchen door. I expected to see a man posted outside keeping watch, but Johnston has taken no extra precautions except for a new dog chained there. The wiry-haired crossbreed, tan with a dark patch on his back, appears fully grown, but he's playful as a puppy. I've taken to calling him Patch. His affections have been easily bought with Mrs. Mueller's biscuits.

On the west side of the house stands a tall cedar hedge blocking the Johnstons' view of their outhouse, which backs onto a forested lot.

About fifty feet from the rear of the house, the stable—which houses two horses plus an open carriage and a closed one for winter—is locked up tighter than a drum. I've been looking through the windows—even climbed onto the roof of the chicken coop in back of it—but have yet to find a way inside without riling the horses or otherwise alerting Johnston to my presence.

As far as I can tell, Johnston and his wife are predictable to the point that they're boring me to death. Each night, light glows through their bedroom curtains soon after I arrive. One night when Patch yelped for want of more biscuits, Mr. Johnston jerked the curtains open and I suffered a clear view of his wife's lily-white knockers hanging nearly to her waist. It was the only irregular occurrence so far and I hope never to witness it again.

Tonight, as every other night just before bed, Johnston—with his musket in one hand and a lantern in the other—escorts the missus to the outhouse. After she's done and it's his turn to piss, she stands outside holding the gun at arm's length as if it were a snake. When he comes out, he trades the lantern for his gun and they begin their return to the house. Patch whines for attention, but Johnston pushes him aside with one foot and pulls the kitchen door closed behind him. A moment later, the kitchen goes dark and the glow of a candle moves from window to window as the Johnstons proceed upstairs to bed. Above the kitchen door there's a second-storey window with a view into a hallway separating a pair of rooms on either side. I can see the Johnstons approaching their bedroom door now.

When Gleeson returns from Aylen Lake, I must have something more than an outhouse and bedtime schedule to report. I'm not going to freeze my arse for nothing but a pat on the head and an *attaboy*. A man creates his own destiny.

The Muellers' rooster crows soon after my head hits the pillow. As the nights have gone on, it's gotten tougher to rise after so few hours of sleep. My head pounds as if I'd been out drinking last night. I'd best get up and stoke the forge. My feet barely touch the floor when I hear Rory's voice floating up from the workshop.

"'Tis a fine morning, Mr. Mueller." The metal rake scrapes across the brick surface of the forge.

"Where's O'Dougherty?"

"Still in bed, sir."

That little weasel . . .

"That's the second time this week," Mr. Mueller replies.

"I don't mind readying the forge. Again," Rory says. The handle of the large bellows creaks and a whoosh of air follows.

In a flash, my boots are laced and I'm splashing my face with icy water from the wash basin. My feet bang against the wooden steps so quickly it sounds as though I'm tumbling down the stairs. When Mueller and Rory pause their conversation to look up at me, I force a wide smile.

"I apologize for spending too long on my prayers this morning." Mueller is stone-faced.

"I'll ready us for the wainwright's work," I say.

As I set off to gather a sledgehammer and a tyre dog for prising heated bands of iron onto wooden wheels, Mr. Mueller says, "Don't bother."

Rory smirks as he and Michael drag a tub of water to the centre of the smithy floor. "You'll make nails today," Mueller tells me.

"But that's a first-year apprentice job," I say. Rory rolls the first wheel out and lays it down next to the tub.

"Yes. You work with Michael."

I'm about to protest—remind him that I'll soon be a third-year apprentice and nail making is beneath me—but he raises a massive hand to silence me. His patience with me dissolves like snow on a hot skillet. "Where are your friends now, eh?" he says, and turns and walks away.

"A fair warning to you, Mueller," I shout.

He turns sharply to face me.

"My friends will come back. And when they see I'm not happy here, there's no telling how they might try to cheer me up."

Mueller says nothing as he soaks in my meaning, but I see his fists tighten as he heads outside.

Rory, with eyes gleaming, leans in close and says, "So, Tommy— where's Gleeson's crew at?"

"Hairy Barney didn't tell you?" My sarcasm drains the smile from his face.

For the rest of the day neither Rory nor Michael speak to me. Although Mueller relents and we finish eight wheels together, he says little. The silence allows me to plan how I'll climb the next rung of this new ladder. I decide to risk sneaking into Johnston's house so I can steal some information Aylen can use to plot against him.

Even as I resolve to pursue this course, my stomach ties itself in knots, and sweat dampens my back. What if Johnston catches me? His Brown Bess will fire a hole through me. But then, Johnston's aim is poor and the musket is a relic from nigh twenty years ago, so how true can she shoot? My mind is made up. I'll break in.

※

This night I conceal myself behind the row of shrubs and bramble on the east side of Johnston's place. The dim light of the new moon keeps me safe me from anyone who might be looking this way from the neighbouring property. From here, I'll have a full view of Johnston and his wife the moment they step outside to visit the outhouse. As usual,

Patch is staked outside the kitchen door. With both ears perked, he sits on his haunches and whines in anticipation of the biscuits I bring to buy his silence.

While I'm blowing warmth into my cupped hands, Johnston's bulk crosses the softly lit window. I can just make out the rifle stock jutting from under his arm. Every nerve in my body crackles and my ears strain against the wind. I crane forward to see Mrs. Johnston pass in front of her husband with a lantern in her hand. A moment later, the door opens and they both set off for the privy.

I break from the shrubs and dart toward the back corner of the house. Patch sits and wags his tail the moment he sees me. I reach into my pocket for a chunk of biscuit and toss it to him as I pass by. The other half is for the way out.

The fanciness of the Johnstons' kitchen takes me by surprise. On the left wall is a fireplace nearly triple the size of Mam's and grander than anything I've ever seen. The toasty fire casts light along the wall, but the corners fall into deep shadows. I walk the length of the table that stretches through the centre of the room. On either side are fine chairs, the sort Da makes. At the far end is a tin cup and a plate of buttered bread. My mouth waters. Next to the cup sits a brass bell mounted on a wooden handle. It's for raising the alert in case of Shiners, I suspect. I'm still smiling about it when the panic sets in. I've lost track of how long I've been inside.

Breathe.

I calculate that there's just enough time to search the front room, snatch something of value. I could leave through the front door. In the morning, the Johnstons will blame each other for leaving it unlocked.

When I wheel around, my blood runs cold. A girl, pale and round-eyed, stands on the other side of the table. Her gaze shifts to the bell. She lunges for it, but I am faster. A win for me. But she's blocking my path to the front door. A win for her.

Her eyes are now full of tears.

"I'm new here. You can't steal anything," she pleads. She's Irish, but from which county I can't decide. "They'll blame me for whatever goes missing and I'll be out on my ear with no money to send my family." She studies my face and her brow furrows. "I know you," she says.

My heart thumps so hard it's like the front of my jacket moves with every beat. All I can think of is a musket firing at my head, or me being carted off to the Perth Gaol.

"On the road that night we brought Gran for help. Your mam's a healer," she says. My mouth opens but no sound comes out.

Just then Patch yips. The Johnstons are returning.

My eyes beg the girl's help. She flicks a glance through the back window at the approaching lantern light. "Quick, in here." She opens the door to a nook at the front of the kitchen and I lunge inside. The latch clicks shut behind me.

Wood scrapes across the floor. Through a crack between two boards, I see the girl has seated herself at the table and is sipping from the cup. Johnston comes inside first and leans his rifle against the wall behind the kitchen door. His wife follows close behind. When she continues across the kitchen to set the lantern on the end of the table, I inch deeper into the nook.

"Clara, have you turned the bed down?" Mrs. Johnston asks.

"Yes, ma'am, and I've added a log to your fire as well."

Heavy-footed strides pass from the room.

"My husband will take his coffee at sunrise. Don't be late. He has a busy day tomorrow. And he'd like porridge again." There is a slight pause as the stairs begin to groan under her husband's weight. "More milk this time," Mrs. Johnston continues. "He complained that this morning's was too thick."

"What would you like with your tea at breakfast, missus?"

"A thin slice of toast and marmalade. No butter." Floorboards squeak along the centre hallway. "And Clara?"

"Yes, missus?"

"Is something troubling you?"

My body tenses. "No, missus. I'm fine."

"Good. Keep your troubles out of this house. Mr. Johnston has no patience for sentimentality."

"Of course," the girl says quietly. The mistress must have noticed the remnants of the girl's tears.

After a patch of silence, the staircase groans, followed by footsteps on the floor above. A latch clicks shut upstairs. I sag and brace a hand against one wall. It's cold and smooth to the touch. I can just make out the pattern painted there. Only a wealthy Orangeman would fancy up a bit of hidden wall while his countrymen go hungry. I hate him even more. I wish I could sneak out of here and be on my way without seeing Clara again. I'm at her mercy now. All I can do is wait for her cue that it's safe to leave.

Minutes tick by like hours. Soon, the dark nook feels more like a trap than a haven. I'm failing my first mission. How will I impress Peter Aylen now?

A live-in servant! I should have known the Johnstons would have one. Clara is a poor girl who loves her family. They probably rely on her earnings.

What kind of man would I be if I stole from Johnston and left her to take the fall? But if I fail to impress Aylen, I'll be a small man forever.

Through the gap between the door and the frame, I can see Clara sitting, elbows on the table and her thin fingers laced together over her plate of bread. She stares into the fireplace, her face glowing soft like apple blossoms in moonlight. *Clara.* I like that she doesn't appear flustered anymore. She's careful, a thinker like me. For a moment, my mind pitches back to that night on the road, and how her dress had fallen open and her skin . . .

The girl cranks her head toward my door as if she senses me staring at her. I jerk back, certain she's read my thoughts. Surely she'll ring the bell now. I'm done for. How long will it take before Johnston makes it downstairs to his gun?

Then the door eases open to reveal the girl, one index finger raised to her lips. She leads me across the kitchen without question. My heart sinks when I notice the sleeping pallet and threadbare quilt spread in front of the hearthstone. She's protecting me at great risk to herself. And her family. Would I do the same if our situations were reversed?

Once we're outside, she looks up at me. The dying lantern light washes over her face—the tip of her nose, her mouth, her chin, her shimmering silver eyes.

I want to relieve the worry I sense at the edges of her composure, but what comes out of my mouth sounds weak and apologetic. "Clara . . ."

Patch, tail wagging, crams his head between us to demand the remaining half biscuit that's owed him. He licks my hand. As I pat his head, my heart squeezes in my chest. The dog's affections betray that I've been here before.

Clara steps close to me. Her voice is gentle. "Don't let me down, Thomas O'Dougherty."

She remembers my name.

15

MARIAH

Peg's door rattles when I knock. Wind gusts along her narrow snow-filled street and lifts a corner of the cloth laid over my basket. I lean over the tip of my snowshoes and knock once more for good measure, then back away and wait for her to answer.

Her shanty is smaller than the one I used to live in with Seamus and Biddy, but at least Peg has a window.

Again, I knock, but this time a bit harder. Peg owes me money, and I mean to collect.

How long must I wait?

"I'll be right there," Peg finally calls out, her voice gravelly from sleep. But minutes pass and still no sign of her.

A man steps out of a neighbouring shanty. He pulls a wool hat down over his ears, then regards me with curiosity as he rubs his hands together briskly. I press so close to Peg's door that the brim of my bonnet crushes against it. After he sets off, I bang the heel of my hand against the door until at last a flurry of movement is visible through a gap between the splintered planks.

"Yes?" Peg says with false brightness. The door opens halfway and there she is wearing only her shift and pushing back her dishevelled hair. When she recognizes me, her eyes roll to the right. "You can come out now," she calls over her shoulder, then lets out a sigh of relief.

A man steps from behind the door with a pair of well-polished boots tucked under his right arm. He rifles through his pants pockets.

"Geez, Red. You gave us a scare," Peg says to me as he drops a coin on her table. "We thought his wife had found him out. Again."

The man gives a lopsided smile and adjusts his glasses before checking his pocket watch. He appears harmless enough, but still I give him a wide berth when he finally leaves and watch the snowy ground until he is safely away.

"You gonna stand there until we both freeze or are you comin' in?" Peg asks.

I unlace my snowshoes and kick the snow from my boots. Once my eyes adjust to the dimness inside, I see little clue of the existence Peg leads. The room is tidy and small. Six steps separate the east and west walls and there is double that number between the door and the back wall. The pallet rolled out in front of the hearth surprises me. I presumed Peg's bed was hidden behind the hanging blanket.

"I'd offer you a tea, but Princess Adelaide just dropped by and finished off the last of it." Peg laughs at this and stoops over her makeshift bed. As I lower myself onto a stump seat at the table, she picks up her pillow—a dark folded square—and fluffs it out to become a green dress. Something about the intimacy of watching her pull it over her head makes me look away. That's the moment I notice the black dog lying with its back against the right side of the fireplace.

"Ohhh!" I shriek, leaping up from my seat.

Braiding her hair, Peg turns to follow my wide-eyed gaze. "Sit down, Red. He's harmless."

From behind the blanket curtain steps a young woman with a shawl hugged tightly around her shoulders and large unlaced boots on her bare feet.

"This is my roommate. I lost the coin toss, so she got the bed last night. Didn't you, lass?"

The woman yawns and clomps past the table to fling the door open. A dull brightness streams inside and it's then that I notice—through the gap between the hanging blanket and the wall—the pair of wool-socked feet, unmistakably male, overhanging the end of the bed. Toes point toward the floor and a hole stretches over one heel. After a heavy sigh, the man rolls over and begins to snore. Now a big toe leers out through a second hole.

My body tenses even more, like a deer that's heard a twig snap.

"Don't worry. He's too hungover to be a problem," Peg says slowly.

It's all too much—a dog, strange men. Fear urges me to run for the door and straight back to the homestead. But I grip a fistful of bunched-up skirt in both hands instead and press on.

"I want my money," I tell Peg. We both look at the single shilling her customer left on the table. "That won't cover it."

Peg lifts a finger to her lips to shush me, then reaches into the woodpile next to the fireplace and pulls out a cloth bag tied with string. She plops herself onto the stump seat next to me, thankfully blocking my view of the man's feet.

"Two shillings," I tell her.

"Whatcha got in that basket?" she asks, undoing the knot.

"Fennel seed and slippery elm. For—"

"—girls in a family way. I know." Peg leans in and whispers, "How about some more of that saltpetre? I'm drivin' raggedy Bess out of business. Been sprinkling your magic powder in her customers' whiskeys! Softens 'em right up." She grabs a dried apple slice from a bowl at the centre of the table and bites off one end. "Her customers come to see me now 'cause she can no longer raise the general." Peg laughs.

The snoring pauses, then the bed frame creaks and a muffled blast trumpets from behind the blanket curtain.

"Ach. You rotten devil!" Peg scrunches her nose. "Get outside if you're going to do that."

A pins-and-needles sensation spreads in my hands when a balding head appears above the top edge of the blanket curtain. "Give me a minute to put my boots on, woman," he says.

"That's two shillings and I'll be on my way." I can't help the quaver in my voice.

"Red," Peg says sharply. Her expression relaxes into one of compassion when our eyes meet. "I don't know what happened to you, but no one's going to hurt you here."

I want to believe her. I take a ragged breath and whisper, "How do you do it?"

Peg looks puzzled until I flick a glance at the hanging blanket.

"Cozying up to fellas like him?" she says. "I throw a leg over 'em and get on with it. The whole time I dream-travel."

"What do you mean?"

"While this carcass does the work that feeds me, I tell my thoughts to carry me back to Kilcullen, where I walk the banks of the River Liffey with my two brothers. The peat smoke and smell of bread baking in Mam's hearth is so real, it's like I'm really there. Just like that, the customer's done. There's coin in my hand and I'm closer to my new life away from this shithole." She rests her elbows on the table and squints at me. "Was it men that did that to your face?"

I let myself sit again but thrust out my hand. "The shillings, Peg."

"They aren't all bad, you know." Peg slides coins across the table to me, then grasps my hand the way Mam used to. I'm discomfited but calmed all at once. "Close your eyes," she says.

"No, I—"

"Close 'em," she urges, so I do. "Now imagine a time and place far away from here." I conjure Ireland.

"The sun is warm on your face," Peg whispers. "And you're happy."

I'm sitting in the grass along the stream that flows through the Harris estate. Seamus stands next to me. We're watching Thomas chase a dragonfly. He's a baby again, apple-cheeked and stumbling along on chubby legs. He laughs when Seamus swings him high in the air, then pretends to fall and lands next to me. We all lie tangled together in the grass.

Surprised by how calm I now feel, I return myself to Peg's shanty. I no longer grip my skirts, and even my pulse has stopped galloping.

"He's gone," Peg says. "Left with the dog while you were travelling." When I laugh, she says, "See, Red? Your mind is always your own. You just gotta figure out how to work it."

On the walk home, I feel like a different woman. Me, who for fifteen years has quaked at the presence of men or dogs, had been capable of spending several minutes confined with both. Maybe I'm braver than I think. Who could have predicted that a girl like Peg would open my eyes by telling me to close them?

Biddy's herb basket swings on my arm in time with my strides. Inside is a skein of red yarn from Fran's mercantile. I need new mittens, so why not! I can scarcely believe I treated myself and neither could Fran. She beamed when I used her Christian name, then refused to accept full price for the wool. As I wind through the woods, I bring the skein to my nose and breath in the lanolin. Best smell in the world, next to a baby's head.

Everything about this day cheers me. Snow buntings sing out as they flit through the tree branches, and rabbit tracks criss-cross the snow alongside my path.

With coins jingling in the pocket inside my skirt, I feel like Lady

Harris herself on the estate back home. Granted, most of the money is owed to Biddy for her herbs. But some of it is mine, so I'm on the way to hide my share inside the treasure tree. There've been times lately when I've sensed that, few as they are, my possessions in the cabin loft where I now sleep have been rifled through. Biddy refuses to strain herself by climbing the ladder so I suspect it's Elizabeth who snoops for her.

My tree waits in a section of maple grove nestled just beyond a knoll. I'm approaching the crest marked with two massive tree trunks lying one over the other. For the past mile I've put up with an aching bladder, but now the urge to make water is too strong to ignore. Off the path's edge is a dense screen of low pine boughs, so I shuffle behind them. I hike up my skirt, unlace my knickers and squat. The relief is immediate.

Just as my stream ends, a quiet sound reaches my ears. I hold my breath and listen hard. A crow caws. And then all is quiet. I'm about to stand and reorder my underthings when robust laughter announces men on the other side of the knoll.

They'll pass, I tell myself. One voice speaks. Another answers. The entire valley will hear the thunder of my heartbeat if I don't calm down. Still hidden, I force my eyes to close and picture Thomas heating a band of metal on the forge. His eyes are warm and his smile wide. But then something behind me captures his attention and his jaw hangs slack.

My eyes pop open and return me to the snowy forest. The voices grow more distinct, a sure sign the men are closer.

My earbobs! Hairs stand up on the back of my neck. What if the blue ribbon I left to mark the hollow of my treasure tree leads these men to discover my keepsakes? If they're stolen both my future and Thomas's will be gone in a blink. We'll be trapped.

Directly overhead, the sun glows dull through the cover of bleak sky. The voices linger—these men must be stopping for a midday meal.

I decide I need to see their faces. Still squatting, I manage to hike up my knickers and retie the string at my waist. I lower myself onto one hip without kicking off the snowshoes, and twist at the waist so my belly and forearms press into the snow. Inch by inch, I use my elbows to pull myself forward.

Ridges of frozen earth grind into my forearms and ribs as I drag myself toward the cover of fallen trees at the crest of the knoll. Despite the pain, I continue on with the same stealth and focus Seamus taught me to use on turkey hunts.

Finally, I'm in position. Hidden behind the downed trunks, I peer below. Two men, each with his back facing me, are crouched over an old firepit. A small tin pot hangs from a propped-up branch over a meagre fire. The red sashes tied around the waists of their coats reveal they are French. Two pairs of snowshoes are thrust upright into the snow, one with a dead rabbit flopped over its top edge. A broadaxe handle juts from the snow and leans against the second pair. Closer to the fire, the long, curved handle of a felling axe hovers at an angle above the stump in which its blade is buried.

One of the men stands and turns toward me. His black fur hat matches the unruly mange of beard hiding much of his face. He reaches both arms above his head and yawns loudly. The second man looks up with a hand raised in warning and calls out, "Benoît!" He begins to scan the forest.

Benoît topples him with a shove and begins making his way up the knoll. My hands shake as he approaches my position. Any move on my part will draw his attention. The man Benoît knocked over springs to his feet and looses a string of French words, some of which I recognize from living among the French Catholics in the days of the Deep Cut. *Arrêt*, stop. *Frère*, brother.

Benoît grumbles and, to my relief, tromps back through the snow past the other man. A few yards away from the fire, he lets down the front of his britches to piddle. "Maurice, mon frère," he says over one shoulder. The rest I cannot understand. He gives a low laugh, then tucks himself back into his britches and pats his coat pocket as he comes back to the fire. In a thick accent, he says, "My woman, she will be so happy."

I clap a hand over my mouth. The Frenchman has my earbobs in his pocket! I know it.

Maurice doesn't laugh. He sets two tin mugs on the stump, grabs the pot handle with the cuff of his sleeve, and pours. "If it doesn't snow too much, we can make Bonnechere River in three days. And Sinclair's camp two days after that."

Benoît lifts a mug and slurps loudly. He responds in French, but I hear him mention Round Lake.

I commit these names to memory—Bonnechere River, Round Lake, Sinclair.

Maurice tosses him a half loaf of bread, then continues watching the fire. "Brother, if you hadn't had that trouble in Perth, we'd have been there by now."

"They put me in that Perth gaol, and I broke out like I told you I would." Benoît slaps his knee. "There's no gaol strong enough to hold the likes of me."

Benoît rocks to his feet and tosses his mug onto the snow, and laughter shakes his towering frame. While he laces up his snow-shoes, Maurice puts out the fire and gathers their possessions up after them. Although Benoît is well ahead before Maurice secures his snowshoes, the gap between them narrows quickly and they disappear into the woods.

Silence screams in my ears. When I can wait no more, I get to my feet and bolt from behind the fallen trees. My skirt wraps around my legs and nearly trips me as I bound past the Frenchmen's smouldering firepit and farther into the woods. What I find knocks the wind from me, sure as any blow. At the foot of the tree my blue ribbon lies on the snow, along with all my worldly treasures—except for the flowered cloth packet that contained my earbobs.

"No, no, no!"

I lean forward, with hands on knees, and labour to suck in gulps of air. The snow is tamped down by the men's snowshoe prints. Perhaps the earbobs are here, buried. Dig! I root through the snow, sifting through icy flakes and breaking them apart with my fingertips.

My numb fingertips scrabble across something smooth and hard. An earbob! The other must be nearby. I brush the snow away from the pearly finish, but there's no gold wire to grasp. It's one of Thomas's baby teeth. My hand wraps around it and squeezes shut.

Back and forth I pace, not bothering to wipe the tears and snot from my face. I'd dared for the space of a couple of hours to hope for love and a life of my own. *Is it so wrong, God, for wanting things you've so freely given to my spiteful sister?*

I rush at the tree, going up on tiptoes to feel inside the hollow. I search every surface and cranny, but the earbobs aren't there. Hopeless, I drop to my knees and sob until I'm exhausted.

My treasure gone and with it, my future and my son's.

It's dusk when I reach the homestead. Seamus's two hogs crowd into a corner of the pen when they hear the squeak of my snowshoes. A pair of bristled snouts push between the rails of the pen and sniff at the air. Elizabeth should have locked them in the pig shed by now. She's even left the coop door open, though the chickens will have roosted for the night.

If not for the wolf tracks and fox droppings I recently discovered near the edge of our woods, I'd leave these chores undone. But we can ill afford to lose the meat, and so I trudge through the drifts to do what my niece should have done already.

Firelight glows through the cabin windows. Neither Elizabeth nor Annie have seen fit to close the shutters yet, though Biddy likes them closed at an early hour—especially with Seamus away.

I stand bone-weary and fretting in front of the cabin. Why does Biddy get to have my life? It should have been me married to Seamus. She had other suitors. She could have married one of them and stayed in Ireland. Instead, we're all miserable here for the sake of my reputation back home. I thought my tears spent, but they're flowing again.

Through the window, I see the back of Elizabeth's head. Her hair's been plaited. No wonder the girl thinks she's someone. As if she hasn't a care in the world, she turns and smiles brightly in the direction of my bed, where Biddy now rests. I pitch Biddy's basket at the log wall and heave one snowshoe after the other toward the cabin. When I slam the first shutter, it bounces open. Elizabeth cowers and wheels around to face me through the window. Her eyes are wide with fear, which stokes my grim satisfaction. If she hadn't kept taking my earbobs, I'd have never hid them. They'd never have been stolen.

I close both shutters and turn the block of wood to latch them tight. Annie waits for me inside the next window. "It's Auntie!" she calls out. When the last set of shutters bang shut, Katherine begins wailing.

Before going inside, I lean against the cabin, looking out at the forest edge. I wonder what danger lurks this night. I'd rather be pitched out there in a tent than face my sister. Biddy is on the other side of this wall. She'll be filled with questions and mad as a hornet that I'm so late. She's been sick with catarrh and drinking a tea brewed with hyssop for the past week, but the wracking cough has settled in her lungs. None of her usual herbal concoctions seem to help. On top of that, there's the baby in her belly. A fact she never lets me forget.

When at last I try to pull the door open, it's barred shut from the inside.

"Open up!"

"Wait," Biddy shouts. A coughing fit follows.

The bar scrapes as it lifts and the door eases open. Elizabeth jumps aside when I shove past her.

"Where in God's name have you been?" Biddy says in a strangled voice, then hacks again.

"You scared me half to death. I thought you were an angry ghost," Elizabeth adds.

Wee Katherine, still red-faced and whining, patters to the foot of the bed, where Annie sits round-eyed, a cornhusk doll laid across her lap.

How long will it take for my sister and her brood to realize the earbobs are gone? Biddy was right about me. I can't be trusted with anything. Already, I can hear her gloating and playing the wounded martyr. My legs are shaking to the point that my knees may buckle. I wish a bolt of lightning would strike her dead.

Biddy's eyes narrow. "Where's my money?"

"Stop riding me!" Hot tears sting my eyes.

My sister's head jerks back. "You'll not use that tone with me! I don't know what kind of shenanigans you were up to, but you were needed here."

"I'm hungry, Auntie," Annie says, hugging her doll tightly. Katherine tries to stand on the bed, but she tumbles backward and knocks her head against the log wall. Her cry is ear-splitting.

"Come take her," Biddy says. "She needs feeding."

"Elizabeth can do it," I tell her, and I head for the loft ladder.

"But I've done all the work today," Elizabeth says.

"Come back here, Mariah Margaret," Biddy shouts.

I'm halfway to the loft when above her coughing fit I hear Elizabeth shout, "Who will look after the fire?"

I stop climbing. "You do it."

"I don't know how."

"It's time you came off your high horse," I tell her. "You're a poor Irish girl, a bridget. Pull your weight and quit acting like lady of the manor. Plenty of girls your age are already hired out and bringing money home to their families."

Elizabeth's bottom lip quivers. For once, she's speechless.

"Do not speak to my child that way," Biddy hisses.

I hook one arm around the next rung and swing out from the ladder to face her. "Shut up, Biddy!"

"Well, you ungrateful—"

My arm shoots toward her and I look along it as if it were the barrel of Seamus's musket.

Years of resentment and frustration funnel through my index finger now aiming between her eyes.

16

THOMAS

I smell like horseshit. When I first broke into Johnston's stable,
I tripped over an apple crate in the dark and fell into a pile of
fresh manure. The odour clings to my coat. I don't mind the
smell, but even if I did, it beats hiding in Johnston's shrubs like a
right eejit waiting for nothing to happen. Again. Even the watchdog
has become listless from boredom.

Johnston feeds a chain through the door handles of his stable and
fastens them with a padlock. It was my lucky day when Rory fell in
with drinking friends well versed in opening locks without the use of
a key. He couldn't wait to show me his new talent. Even hammered
out a pick for me, which I now put to good use. Turns out Rory's good
for something.

If Gleeson had supplied me with the name of someone or something
specific to look out for, I'd go out in search of information instead of
waiting around here. But I've no idea. My dream of impressing Peter
Aylen may be just that. A dream. But with certainty, Gleeson will
return in a few weeks, maybe sooner, expecting my report. I can well

imagine the consequences of my having nothing to tell him—a solid clout to the back of the head and my blood darkening a snow-filled gully where no one will find me.

Because it's a Sunday, I've come as soon as it got dark. I look over my shoulder as one of the horses shifts its weight to rub a haunch against a post inside its stall. At the south end of the stable, beyond the horse stalls, is a heavy blackness I can't see into. Two small windows on the north end face the rear of Johnston's house. Beneath them is a workbench, something to prop me up when my eyelids grow heavy.

From this vantage point, I have a clear view of the house about fifty feet away. People come in and out of sight as they pass by windows. Tonight, the Johnstons linger in the dining room. It's late and Clara has yet to serve their sabbath dinner. Mam would have a conniption to see how these people waste the precious candles burning in wall sconces and at the centre of their table too.

Johnston stands and checks his pocket watch, then slips on the suit jacket hanging from the back of his chair. As he sits again, Clara leaves the kitchen to stoke the fireplace in the Johnstons' bedchamber like she does each night while the couple eats. She will have added a new log by the time I count to twenty-two. The soft glow through their window soon gains the brightness of a hearty blaze. "Well done, Clara," I say out loud.

How would she look in a nightdress, standing in front of the fire with her hair untied and hanging loose over her shoulders? At work I've been trying to make a wee metal heart for Clara to wear around her neck on a ribbon. So far, I've made nothing worthy of her, but Christmas is two weeks away, so there's time to get it right. Her shoulders must be as flawless and smooth as her neck. The light would shine through the cloth and I'd be able to see—

Clara flashes across the window and rushes in the direction of the landing. What's happened?

In the dining room, Johnston blocks his wife's arm when she reaches out as if to pick something from the sleeve of his jacket. Her hands drop to her lap and she averts her gaze. Without speaking to each other, they wait.

Something is afoot.

Seconds later Clara delivers a dark-suited man to the dining room, then vanishes. Johnston rises from his seat at the head of the table to shake his guest's hand. When the man turns toward Mrs. Johnston, my excitement dies. It's only a minister I've seen on the steps of the Anglican church. Nothing to be gleaned here. He bows to the missus, takes a seat opposite her, and dinner service begins.

They bore me in their gluttony and piety. I'd rather watch Clara toil by candlelight at the kitchen window. Once every so often, she peers up at the night sky. It's unlikely she thinks of me. Since that night she saved me, I've seen her, but she hasn't seen me. I close one eye and touch a fingertip to the glass of the stable window, as if I'm touching her cheek.

When did I go soft in the head? Diligence, I remind myself. Focus on Johnston.

A section of shrubs jostles back and forth, left of the window where Clara is standing. Patch lifts his head and his ears perk for a second, but he quickly lays his muzzle across his paws again. I strain my eyes against the darkness and discover nothing to alarm me.

With a yawn I allow myself a last look at the kitchen window, where the hearth fire gives off an inviting glow. Clara pauses for a moment and stands with her nose pressed to the glass. She's looking in my direction, and although I know it's impossible, it's as if she looks right through me. My heart gives a pang and I step back from the window.

She'd be let down if she knew I'd broken into the stable or that I'd been spying on her master with plans to betray him. But more than that, I've been watching her too, stealing private moments. I should be feeling guilty, but instead I'm wishing I could be closer to her. Clara is unlike other Bytown girls flitting about in silliness. She's a serious girl, a thinker like me. And there's a sadness in the set of her brow that makes me want to take care of her so she can smile again.

Just then, Clara's face turns sharply toward the dining room as if her name's been called. She stands tall and tucks her hair behind one ear before darting deeper into the kitchen. In a blink, she reappears in the dining room with a glass pitcher and begins refilling everyone's cups.

A minute later, she's back at the window, drying dishes. She reaches for another plate, but it slips from her hand. Her shoulders hitch. She ducks down and I know she must be cleaning up the pieces.

My eyes cut to Mrs. Johnston shoving away from the table. Her husband and the minister rise halfway to their feet, then drop onto their chairs again as she wheels toward the kitchen.

Poor Clara.

I scramble to the leftmost corner of the stable window for a better view of what's about to happen and frighten the horses. They whinny as they back deeper into their stalls in search of escape. "Shhh!" I soothe, then check to see if Johnston has heard them. To my relief, he and his guest remain deep in conversation.

In the kitchen, Clara stands at attention with her head bowed in front of Mrs. Johnston. When the woman leaves, Clara returns to the window and leans against the sill. This time when her gaze lifts, there's no question—she's looking directly at me.

Red-faced, I step away from the window. When I dare to peer outside again, she's slipping out through the back door carrying a lantern. I'm certain she's coming to deliver a good telling-off. If not for me, she wouldn't have dropped the dish. But she scoots left along the same path the Johnstons take each evening to the outhouse.

For a moment I lose sight of her, so I squeeze between some barrels at the east corner of the stable to a spot where the chinking between the logs is missing. Through the gap I can see her holding her shawl closed against her chest. Her skirts lift slightly on the wind as she closes the outhouse door behind her. Lantern light seeps through gaps between the boards.

I wait for Clara to return to the house. And wait. The dining room is empty now. The Johnstons must be bidding the reverend a good night. Clara best not be occupying the privy when the Johnstons trot out for their last piss of the night or she'll get more of the missus's sharp words.

Worry scurries across my skin like mice through the hayloft. Barn boards creak against the push of the wind.

Suddenly, Patch leaps to his feet and stands rigid next to the kitchen door with his ears flattened, while his gaze drills the hedge. Again the shrubs ruffle to the left of the kitchen window. This time I can make out a sleeve and the pale white of a hand. No! This can't be happening. Has Gleeson asked a second Shiner to watch Johnston?

The dog barks his warning, and the horses nicker and push against their stall gates in response. I lean over the workbench, searching for the intruder. I won't sit by waiting for some up-and-comer to outdo me. This new fella has gotta shove off. Gleeson assigned me first. Johnston is mine. Then I remember Clara. If I leave the stable, she may see me. So what if she does? I don't know. My thoughts are in a jumble. I run back to the east corner to peer between the logs again. The outhouse is still lit. If the man out there so much as lays a hand on her, I'll—

The chain thunks against the outside of the stable door. I snatch up a pitchfork and wheel toward it. As the hinges begin to creak, I brace myself and aim the sharp tines of the fork at chest height. The door swings wider and my heart plummets.

Clara pauses for a second inside a shaft of moonlight. No words need be spoken to voice her disappointment. When I let down Da or

Mam, anger floods my veins—but failing Clara squeezes at my heart. She breaks the stalemate by turning away to pull the stable door shut.

"You can't be out here, Clara. The Johnstons will be calling, and how will you explain your whereabouts?"

She stares at me. "Thomas O'Dougherty, what are you playing at?"

"It's not what you think," I answer.

"And what might that be?"

"That I'm planning to rob the place."

"Well, that's what it looks like to me, you out here skulking around in the shadows armed with . . . that?"

Shamed, I lower the tines until they rest on the ground. My mind reaches for a story that will convince her not to report me to the Johnstons.

"I work here at night," I blurt. Clara looks as surprised to hear it as I am to have said it.

"For Mr. Johnston?" she asks with a smirk. When I don't come up with the next lie fast enough, her mouth opens slightly and her eyes widen. "For Mrs. Johnston?"

"Yes," I answer too loudly.

"I don't believe it. Why didn't you tell me that the other night?"

"Since the Shiner trouble a while back, the missus hired me to keep an eye on the place through the small hours." I'm on a roll now. "I took an oath of secrecy. No one is supposed to know, especially not Mr. Johnston. She says he's too proud, thinks he can do just fine himself."

Clara takes measure of me. "Well, it's true he is a stubborn man. The last lot who showed up made a right mess of things. One scoundrel even shot the dog, if you can imagine."

My face heats. Thank goodness it's dark. "'Tis a terrible thing he did."

"You're very kind to say so. Poor mutt was all chained up and couldn't escape. The heartless devil just pulled the trigger." She's close enough now that I can see her eyes welling up with tears.

I take no pride in what comes next. But I see my opening and I must take it.

"Join me at the window," I tell her. And she does. "You see those bushes over there? I've been watching a man there all evening. A tall brute," I lie. "He's gone now but there's no telling when he'll be back."

"You pursued him?"

"I couldn't risk alerting Mr. Johnston to my presence."

Her eyes search mine and I focus with all my might to reflect her earnest gaze. Still I sense she's undecided as to whether or not to trust what I say, so I push the story further. "Mrs. Johnston told me that your master keeps an old Brown Bess musket in their bedchamber, but he can't hit the broadside of a barn with it. I couldn't know that without the missus telling me, right?"

"No, I suppose not." The hint of a smile rises to Clara's eyes. "Still, you've a thing or two to learn about hiding, Thomas O'Dougherty. You can start by rubbing some dirt on that pale Irish face of yours. I could see it glowing like a full moon from the kitchen window. I'm guessing you've never hidden from a Kinsale landlord back in County Cork, then. Not with all the footsteps you're leaving in the snow."

By God, she's stellar.

"Now, I must go before the missus starts searching for me," Clara says. "She's already vexed that I broke a plate." She pushes the door open and looks back at me. "It's good that you're here, Thomas."

Happiness punches me in the gut as the door moans shut. I could be losing my mind, but this is the girl I'm going to marry.

Long after she's returned to the house, I ponder the lies I've told her. They're only for a short time, and if what I learn by being here puts me in good stead with Peter Aylen, he'll return the favour and move me closer to owning my own smithy. 'Tis a small deception for the greater good— mine and Clara's, if she'll have me one day. Still, I wonder who that eejit was, hiding in the bushes. Should I worry about him coming back?

Monday night, I return to the stable and discover a gift from Clara waiting on the workbench—an apple pie slice wrapped in cloth. She's a true talent. On Tuesday, the cotton square holds oatmeal cakes and tonight, buttery cookies melt on my tongue. I take small bites to make them last and watch her at the kitchen window.

I gave up on making her metal heart. From my pocket, I pull out a bit of wire I've twisted into the shape of a daisy. It's simple but I'm given to believe that girls like this sort of thing. I wrap it in her kitchen cloth and tuck it under a rusted tin sitting in the window where it will draw Clara's eye.

The following day close to noon, Rory and I are rolling two wagon wheels over the packed-down snow of Rideau Street toward Sappers Bridge to a wainwright at the west edge of Uppertown. The air nips the inside of my nose with every inhale. It'll be cold in Johnston's stable tonight. Less so with Clara's inviting lips upturned to mine . . .

After a stretch of silent pushing, Rory asks, "Tommy, where are you off to every night after dinner?"

"Never you mind." One edge of my wheel rolls over a fist-sized chunk of ice and I must step lively to prevent it from wobbling out of control.

"Still holding out on me, eh?" Rory says. "What? Did you find yourself a woman to poke?"

My eyes cut to his face. He laughs at me and I want to take a swing at him. "I got things to do, is all."

"What sorts of things, Tommy?"

"Things!"

"Geez, you're testy," Rory tells me. "I think you're a wee bit jealous?"

"Of what?"

The moment I ask, Johnston's sleek cutter turns onto the road ahead from a side street, and heads for Uppertown. Johnston is at the reins and a slightly taller man wearing a fur coat and a tall hat sits next to him.

I roll the wagon wheel faster until Rory must break into a lope to keep up. When the carriage halts in front of Blackmore Tavern, I slow my pace.

"I think you're jealous of Mueller now treating me, not you, like the number-one apprentice," Rory says between breaths. His boastful tone wears on me.

Johnston raises his hand in greeting to another man waiting in a wagon across the road and climbs down stiffly to tie his reins around Blackmore's hitching post.

The wagon driver hops from the side runner and strides toward Johnston to pump his hand with vigour. Johnston's passenger jumps down too and the three men are about to go inside when they're joined by a fourth I recognize from the night Gleeson busted up Blackmore's. It's Baker, the Englishman who heads up the Bytown Rifles.

It's all I can do to conceal my interest from Rory. This could be the moment I've been waiting for, so I can ill afford to tip my hand to the likes of him.

"I'm getting the silent treatment now. Is that how it is?" Rory says.

I don't respond to him, just pull my hat low and raise my collar for fear of being recognized by either Baker or Johnston. Rory snorts and keeps walking.

As we roll the wheels past the tavern, I look over my right shoulder to see the door shut behind the last of the men. What I wouldn't give to know what they're up to.

"Don't worry about Johnston coming after us. The Shiners protect us now. We're untouchable," Rory says.

He's mistaken my curiosity for fear. I don't tell him otherwise.

The rest of the afternoon is more of a torture than most. My mind is a stone wheel grinding out reasons why Johnston and Baker might be meeting and how the other two men might be connected. Clara may be the key. She must know something that can help me piece together the purpose of their meeting. I pray—and I never pray—that I uncover a conspiracy worthy of Peter Aylen's interest.

It's then I realize that to impress Aylen, I must bypass Gleeson altogether and take my report directly to the leader. Gleeson will be angry that I've skipped over him, but he won't dare retaliate, not once Aylen takes me under his wing.

After dinner, the moon lights my sprint to Johnston's stable. I barely wait for him and his wife to climb the stairs to their bedroom before leaning over the workbench to wave my arms to attract Clara's attention. She waggles her fingers. When I continue waving, she checks over her shoulder and leaves the kitchen window. A moment later, she comes out through the back door. Wrapped in a cloak, she walks to the outhouse, then circles around the back of it and scampers to the stable.

"Hello," she says, gathering her collar around her neck with hands that are red and chapped. I remove my gloves and hold them out for her to take.

"Thank you," she says. When I pass them into her hands, the backs of my fingers brush against her skin. For a moment I forget I intend to further abuse her trust. She puts them on and we both smile at how oversized they are.

"But now your hands will be chilled," she says with concern.

"No matter," I say.

"Cold hands, warm heart." Her eyes gleam. "I treasure your daisy."

It's difficult to maintain my smile. I'm such a shit.

Her gaze lights on the workbench and the cloth bundle resting there. "You don't like the spiced cake?" she says with a frown.

"I'm saving it," I tell her. She's just reminded me of what's in my pocket. "This is for you, Clara." I pull out a length of green silk ribbon and hold it out to her in the shaft of moonlight that falls between us.

"Oh, it's beautiful!" Clara steps forward. I know she means only to kiss my cheek. She's a good Irish Catholic girl. But I can't help myself—I'm a bad Irish lad. I turn my head so that our lips touch. We spring away from each other, surprised that we're kissing. But then, we look into each other's eyes and draw together again, and this time our lips linger. My heart races; I'm butter melting on a hot pan. When she pulls away, too soon in my opinion, Clara's lashes flutter like the wings of a small bird.

"I must be going," she says breathlessly. "The missus . . ."

I come to my senses and remember my purpose. "Clara, I saw Mr. Johnston meeting with some men in town today."

"Ah yes, I overheard him telling the missus he was joining friends today to discuss the council election for Nepean Township."

"Do you think these men have Mr. Johnston's best interest at heart?" I hope my tone is edged with enough worry to pry her open.

"Why would you ask that?" A tiny crease appears between her brows.

"I feel responsible for his safety."

"Of course. But hasn't the missus told you about Mr. Hobbs and the two Georges—as she calls them?"

"You know them?"

Clara nods. "Mr. Hobbs has been here for the noontime meal twice this month along with Mr. George Baker and Mr. George Patterson."

"What do they discuss?"

"Thomas, it wouldn't be proper for me to repeat such talk. I don't know why you're—"

"I'm just trying to do my job."

"She's told you, then, about Mr. Johnston hoping for a spot on the council," she says. I nod and she keeps going. "And about the two Georges, and the farmer, Mr. Hobbs?"

"When's the election? I should be there to watch over him."

"I don't know when, just that the vote is to take place at Stanley's Tavern."

I'm afraid to speak again for fear of laughing out loud. Mr. Aylen will conjure a way to strike out at Johnston using this information and I'll reap a reward. All I need now is the date of the vote.

My cheeks begin to cramp from smiling so hard. "You're a wonder," I blurt. Clara's eyes light, then quick as a blink, she slips out the stable door and back into the night.

Before she's safely returned to the house, the spice cake is in my pocket, the stable door is padlocked, and I'm sneaking onto the road that will take me to Stanley's Tavern.

A short while later, I'm standing in front of the establishment with my chest heaving from the slog along the snow-filled road. A notice is posted by the door but damned if I can make sense of it. I recognize a two and a seven, but that is all.

"Excuse me, sirs," I say to a couple of men about to go in, removing my hat. "I've left my spectacles at home. What does this say?"

The first man snorts with laughter. "Stinking bog-jumper can't read," he says and steps past me.

His companion stands in front of the sign and exhales a cloud of smoke from his pipe, then reads aloud. "Nepean Township, Election of Councillors, January second at seven o'clock."

I quirk my brows and nod, all business-like.

"Members only," he says. "They're voting in three new councilmen to represent Nepean."

I try to stifle my triumphant laughter. When at last I can hold it back no longer, the man looks at me as if I've gone mad, which only makes me laugh harder. In one celebratory bite, I devour Clara's spice cake. The night air is charged with excitement and so am I. Time for a drink.

☙

I find Rory and Michael at the first Sleigh Bay tavern I come upon with fiddle music and a roaring fire. These days, throngs of men crowd into every public house. It's the season when teamsters gather supplies for delivering to timber camps throughout the Ottawa Valley. Soon, caravans of horse-drawn sleds stacked with goods and men will proceed over the thick ice of the Ottawa River. Labourers travel with them, hoping to snag any jobs that have opened up because of loggers already injured or dead.

At the next table, a row is escalating over a card game gone wrong. The four men are firing insults across the table. Rory watches, in hungry anticipation of a brawl. He doesn't notice that I've squeezed onto the bench next to Michael and already finished half my drink. Michael is a different story: round-shouldered and forlorn until my arrival lifted his spirits.

Still, he regards the arguing men with concern. "We should be getting back to the smithy," he says. "I got a bad feeling."

The old-timers seated across from us share his sentiment. They slide empty glasses to the centre of the table, then turn up their collars and begin to leave. In pushing his arm through his coat sleeve, one man topples their bottle onto the glasses and, against all odds, breaks one. A triangular shard lands on the table between Michael and me.

His eyes widen at me as if to say he'd told me so.

I flick the shard so it spins like a child's toy. Then I give him three quick slaps on the back. "Ah, you worry like an old woman. Have a bit of fun."

The card players are all on their feet now. One of them takes exception to Rory's gawking and says, in a strong Scottish brogue, "You lookin' for trouble, boy?"

Michael leans away from Rory, bumping the glass in my hand.

Rory drops his grin and turns to Michael, muttering, "Piece of shit—" When he sees me, his eyes narrow and, for a few seconds, his anger sears me. Then his good humour suddenly reappears. "To what do we owe the honour, your lordship?"

His wild shift in mood strikes unease in me.

"Hey!" The three of us look up to see the towering Scot is there with his hand cocked. "Does the Irish whelp want to say something to me?"

Michael keeps his gaze on the table. I can feel him trembling.

Rory spreads both palms flat on the table as if he's about to move, but remains where he is.

The Scot braces a hand on the table and leans in. "Just as I thought. A boy playing at being a man."

"Your mother had no complaint," Rory sneers.

The Scot's free hands goes to his pocket and comes out with a knife. He lunges across the table and slashes at Rory, who manages to lean back just far enough to avoid the blade. While the man recovers his balance, Rory pulls an oak cudgel from beneath the table and stands. He takes a wild swing that misses. The man grabs the cudgel and yanks so hard that Rory falls forward and bangs his chin against the table. Michael lurches to haul Rory out of harm's way. When the Scot raises the knife blade above his head, I launch from the bench to seize his wrist. In the scuffle, we both fall on top of Michael. I try to separate the Scot from his knife, but in the melee, an elbow smashes into my eye. Pain stuns me for a split second.

"Stay down, Michael," I shout as the Scot and I continue to tussle. But I'm no match for this man's brawn. If his friend jumps in, I'm finished. "Rory!"

Suddenly, the Scot shakes me off and stands there looking around for Rory, who's nowhere to be seen.

"My fight is not with you," he growls, and walks away.

I nod, sucking in air, and collapse onto the bench. "Michael, we're in the clear, brother."

He struggles to sit up and turns to face me. His eyes are confused, like they are at the smithy when he's been given instructions he can't follow. I can't make sense of what's happening, but then he gurgles red and touches his neck. And I see the glass shard slick with blood and jutting out from between his fingers. A pool of blood spreads to the edge of the table and drizzles steadily to the floor.

Michael is a dead man.

❧

I run along snow-filled Rideau Street, slipping and falling more times than I can count, heading for the smithy. Rory, the coward. He's sure to be hiding there behind locked doors. I'll beat him to a pulp. His smarting off and running away killed Michael. He was fourteen but the closer he came to the end, the younger he appeared. He breathed his last word, *Mam*, as a round-eyed boy of six. Tears freeze on my cheeks and snot streams from my nose. I should have taken him home when he asked.

Just before the smithy, I cut through the neighbour's alleyway and around the back of Mueller's stable, intending to crawl in through the smithy window. But our metal strip has been removed so I can't hook the window frame and pull it open. Rory! The window ledge is cleared of snow from where he climbed in before me, and he made sure I couldn't follow. I try repeatedly to hook my fingernails on the window frame to pull toward me. Each time, it refuses to budge. I'm soon shaking with cold and angrier than ever. Maybe I can pick the lock on the front door. I'm about to set off when a light appears behind the frosty window. The glow of a candle, small at first, widens as it nears the window. I brace myself to see Rory's face. The window eases open and I grab the bottom of the sash and launch myself through the opening to grab his collar. "You son of a—"

"Thomas, you're safe—praise the Lord!" Rory shouts as if relieved, then looks squarely at me with an oily slyness.

I'm thrown off guard and stuck in the window now, with the sash weighing on my lower back.

"O'Dougherty!" Mueller steps out of the darkness. The candlelight glints off the barrel of his rifle, aimed straight at me. "You're finished here!"

17

BIDDY

M am and Da's fireplace is choked with peat smoke. A haze dulls the air. I understand it's a dream when the taste of scorched earth in the back of my throat floats me toward waking, the same way panic thrust me toward the surface of the river when as a child I'd been swimming too long underwater.

But then Seamus appears at Mam's table—and he is lovesick for me. I sit with him below the cottage window with its dim cast of morning sun. We talk about the future and warm our hands around steaming cups of gorse flower tea. His smile is sweet enough to make me weep.

Pangs of longing usher me toward waking again. Seamus begins to fade into the smoke. He calls out to me but the harder I try to stay in the dream, the farther away he drifts. *Heavenly Father, I beg of you, show me the depth of your mercy. Let me rest a bit longer in this place free from the worry about this baby not taking or my husband not loving me.*

This baby must be born. And it must be a son. I cannot bear the grief of another child driven from my womb, nor can my marriage. *I've been a faithful servant to you, Lord. Hear my prayers.*

God's attention must be occupied elsewhere. The vision of Seamus is replaced by a soft pulse of light through my eyelids. The strain of my rattling cough rouses me further. I press the arm of my coat against my mouth, but it doesn't do much to muffle the racket.

One of the girls is stirring on her mat on the floor next to my bed. Light dances in the corner of my eye and the fire crackles with too great a vigour. Something's awry.

"Mam!" Annie wails.

I bolt upright. *Jesus, Mary and Joseph. Fire!*

Flames have spread from the fireplace to the floor. The end wall of the cabin is fully ablaze. Sparks float upward to my herb bunches hanging along the rafters. A year's work will be lost!

"Elizabeth!" I cry.

She sits up and goggles at the flames. "Take Annie and Katherine to the windbreak!"

Elizabeth remains transfixed by the flames climbing the left wall of the cabin.

"Now!" She leaps into action while I push my socked feet into unlaced boots. Thank God we sleep fully dressed.

"Mam, come with us," Annie says, tears streaming from her eyes.

"I'll be along."

Elizabeth hoists Katherine onto her hip and makes for the door, but it's Annie who flings it open and leads them outside. The rush of cold night air is a momentary comfort before the fire grows threefold.

My knees quiver like jelly. Fire springs up along the back wall and the smoke thickens so I must hold a handkerchief over my mouth to breath. Everything Seamus and I have worked so hard for will be ash by daybreak. I must save things. It's what Seamus would do. Grey smoke clouds fill the cabin and my eyes burn. I lean against the foot of Mariah's bed and begin coughing. My head grows light. Cooking pots? The heat is unbearable, yet I'm frozen by fear.

Where is my sister? "Mariah!" I yell, but no answer comes.

I suddenly remember Mam's earbobs hiding at the bottom of my flour tin. The pearls will fetch enough money for us to start anew. They are the things I must rescue.

Dense smoke swallows me as I shuffle in the direction of the shelf where the flour tin sits. Pray God I reach it ahead of the flames. Still no Mariah. Perhaps she's been overcome by the smoke and has drifted into that deep and final sleep. A good Christian entrusts fate to God. He knows best. And if He should take my sister from this earthly realm, so be it.

Life would be easier without her.

18

MARIAH

I awake to the sound of my name. Moonlit clouds churn above my face as I make sense of the heat and loud crackling. The loft is choked with smoke. And so am I. Panic shakes me. *Fire!*

Biddy hollers for me, but I can't inhale enough to answer. My eyes burn and my heart feels about to explode. Fire races inches above my head to devour the shingles I helped Seamus to split. If I don't get out of here, I'll be left a charcoaled corpse, same as what happened to poor Mrs. McCord last winter.

Pressing Mam's shawl to my mouth and nose, I crawl to the foot of the bed and scramble to unlatch the small window below the roof peak. I desperately need fresh air. The window won't budge when I try to wrench it open. My boots! I'll smash the glass with a heel.

During the seconds I've spent battling the window, thick smoke has filled the loft from roof peak to floor. I blindly feel my way, coughing and gagging, to where I've left my boots. I grab them and smash the glass, then lean my head and shoulders through the opening. A billowing cloud pours past me and blows sharply to the right, then whisks toward the field behind the cabin. Against the glow of the snow, dark figures are wading toward the pine windbreak. Thank God Biddy and the girls are safe.

The ground is a fair ways down, but I'll have to risk the jump. The roar of the fire builds and the floor heats beneath my socked feet. I fear the room below me is ablaze. Soon fire will consume the loft and bring it crashing down. One way or another, I'll be falling. I take a last deep gulp of night air, then duck inside to push my feet into the boots.

I try to think if there's anything here I can save. Seamus's chair tucked up in the corner? There's no room for sentiment, only what's required to survive this night. Bedding is all I can manage.

I drag the quilt and sheets from the bed and shove them through the window. For a split second, I see Annie watching from the pines. But then thickening smoke tumbles past me to the outdoors and she disappears. Fire snaps and pops behind me and I turn to see a yellow glow in the centre of the loft.

I crane my head out the window, but smoke hides my view of the ground. The prospect of leaping blind terrifies me. I must not think. I must act. So I hike up my skirt and climb onto the sill. I teeter there for a moment, then *one, two, three*—I push off. The ground rushes up to meet me and a jolt of pain needles through my right ankle.

Annie struggles through the snow toward me, sobbing. "Mam's still in there!"

In an instant, I'm bounding around the cabin, ignoring my hurt ankle. Flames flicker behind the shutters. *Please, Biddy, be alive.*

Smoke surges out the open front door. I bend low and scream, "Biddy?"

And there—I spot her on her hands and knees, halfway across the room, head slung low. Fire sprouts from the floorboards all around her. "Biddy," I shout and she looks up. Her mournful expression turns to hope; she reaches a shaking hand toward me. At that moment, we are sisters again.

One flaming timber, then another, crashes to her left and Biddy's arms fly across her face. The roof has caught fire. A torrent of embers rains down inside the doorway. It's now or never.

I jam the hem of my skirt into my waistband and run to her. When I begin pulling her toward the door, she windmills her arms to fend me off.

"I dropped Mam's earbobs," she shouts, her cheek burned raw and singed hair jutting from her temple. She clutches her belly, then her panicked eyes direct me to the flour tin lying on its side close to the newly fallen timbers.

My insides twist. She's burned herself saving an empty tin. I can't tell her the truth—that the earbobs are gone. Overhead, the rafters crackle.

"There's no time!" I pull harder, but still she resists. "Please," she begs.

I snug Mam's shawl around my face and fold my left arm across nose and mouth as I scramble toward the tin. The metal burns my fingers when I grasp it, so I yank the shawl free and wrap it around the canister. I scoot back to Biddy with the sensation of a hundred bees stinging my calves and thrust the bundle at her.

She hugs it tightly. When I bend sideways to slide a hand around her waist, her arm hooks around my neck and we press forward together. I remember to snatch Seamus's rifle from where it hangs next to the door and sling the kit around my neck. Once in the fresh air, Biddy collapses into the snow and I double over, coughing the smoke from my lungs.

Annie rushes to meet us. After I recover myself, we carry her mother to the row of pines where Elizabeth waits with Katherine. Biddy crumples in a heap and the girls ply her with kisses and tears. Their anguish causes me more pain than the blaze. Elizabeth looks up at me like a hound awaiting the first blow, then buries her face against Biddy's chest.

The truth slaps me open-handed. Elizabeth banked the fire last night. She's made a mistake—perhaps left embers exposed—and thinks she caused the fire. But it's me who's to blame, thrusting the duty upon her. And there lies my sister, who I've wished dead on several occasions. Guilt is trampling any happiness I thought I might feel at the prospect of her death. When Seamus returns, he will be furious and forever lost to me. My Thomas will have no home to return to.

Orange flames on the cabin roof lap at the dark like a famished cat. What's been set in motion must be stopped. With blinding determination, I fling the kit and the rifle onto the snow next to Elizabeth and plow toward Seamus's axe, the blade of which is still buried in a chunk of pine on the nearby woodpile. I grab it and race to the water barrel at the corner of the cabin. Again and again, I bring the axe down on the layer of ice covering the water, trying to break open a hole big enough to fit a bucket through. What a fool's errand. Even if I was able to crack the ice, I might as well toss a thimble of water for all the good it would do.

The windowpanes shatter and flames shoot between the shutters. Dense smoke drives me around the corner of the cabin for a gasp of clearer air. A chunk of fiery debris smoulders in the centre of the bedding I'd dropped from the window. I smother it quickly with handfuls of snow and trudge back to the windbreak, dragging the sheet and quilt behind me.

Biddy is slouched against a tree and cradling the flour tin like an infant. Hair bristles like a worn broom above her right ear, which is burned as badly as her cheek. The rest of her face is black with soot and streaked with tears. She coughs violently, then cries out and tilts sideways, but Annie keeps her from tipping into the snow again. On Biddy's opposite side, Elizabeth sits bleary-eyed with Katherine asleep on her lap and watches the blaze. She's yet to speak. Without their mother's feistiness to reinforce them, the two older girls are adrift. Biddy's command of the world ends at the cabin door. She knows little outside the familiar comfort of her kitchen, which is now being reduced to ash.

"I wish Da was here," Annie says.

We are united in a solemn moment by this wish. Seamus's quiet assuredness is an anchor in rough seas. He'd know what needed doing.

Somewhere deep in the woods, a wolf howls and is answered by a second far-off wail. The sound strikes fear in my heart. In our first homestead winter, Seamus and I came across a deer carcass. A wide girth of bloodied snow had been tamped down around its remains—reduced to bones, fur and hide by a wolf pack. Since that day, none of us will venture outside past dark.

Biddy slowly turns her face toward me and the girls follow. They're asking me to lead—to act as the man of this family. How can I refuse?

My mind reels with the crush of responsibility. We can't risk staying here—not with Biddy injured as she is. The pain of her burn will only worsen once the shock wears off. Flaming shingles have begun lifting from the roof. A change in wind direction carries them toward the outbuildings. Within the hour, the sheds will be burned to the ground. Biddy and the children won't survive the night without shelter.

The closest neighbours are over a mile away, and the walk would be against the easterly wind. None will have food to spare given last summer's drought. Before leaving for camp, Seamus said I was to turn to the Newells in Bytown in case of trouble. And Fran Edwards may still have a stock of Biddy's arnica salve along with willow-bark tea to ease pain.

In Bytown, I'll be nearer to Thomas. Whether he likes it or not, this calamity will draw him back to me. In times of trouble, family bands together. Those for whom sacrifices have been made, so too must sacrifice.

Esmerelda has begun bawling in the cowshed, which sets the hogs to squealing.

"Elizabeth, come with me." With reluctance, she shuffles Katherine onto Annie's lap and follows as I set off toward the animals. "Free the chickens."

"But they'll freeze to death. Something might eat them," she says, breathing heavily as she struggles to keep up.

"Better set them free so they can return to us than leave them to meet a certain end."

I wade to the cowshed to retrieve a length of rope. We'll tie either end around the necks of the hogs so they can be guided to Bytown.

"The hog shed's on fire!" Elizabeth cries.

"Oh no!" Flames are leaping from the centre of its sloped roof. I open and shut the sty gate, then fling open the shed's low door, expecting the pair to bolt past me. Instead, neither one of them comes out. I drop to my haunches and squint. Inside the squat shed, the hogs grunt and squeal as embers drop through the roof and onto the straw spread across the ground. Both hogs are pressed against the far wall. I reach an arm toward them. "Come," I say, attempting to coax them to me. "You can do it. Stay close to the outside wall. Come on!" But they refuse to budge. Fire races across the straw and climbs the walls, the heat forcing me to draw back.

Then, a sudden swoosh of brilliant-yellow flame. I rise to my feet in disbelief as the hogs' squeals slice through me, their burning flesh turning the shed into a raging torch. Sobbing, I turn away.

Elizabeth runs back and forth outside the chicken coop. She flaps her arms and shouts at the hens and roosters as embers rain down. Some of them fly to the shelter of nearby cedars, but others rush back into the smouldering coop.

"Elizabeth! Come!" I call. I rush into the milking shed, where a sledge is propped across the end wall. Esmerelda quiets for a moment when she sees us, then bellows a high note. I lower the sledge onto its runners, and hand her its rope. "Go to the chair shed. Collect all of your da's tools from the workbench. Carry them to the windbreak, then come back here fast as you can." I take the wooden yoke from where it hangs next to a leather harness and a set of traces.

"We're leaving?" Elizabeth asks as I fit the yoke around Esmerelda's neck.

"Yes."

"In the dark?" Her voice shakes.

Another wolf howls in the distance. I busy myself hooking the traces to the yoke in order to avoid facing Elizabeth. Fear is contagious and she's already sick with it.

"We must be brave and do what is required," I say. When I look over my shoulder, she is gone. I hitch the traces to the sledge, then speak to the cow. "We must be brave, Esmerelda. The forest is full of terrors."

Two feet above my head, orange light flickers. The roof is already burning.

Hands shaking, I reach for the goad stick suspended from a hook on the wall. "All right, girl." I tap her hind quarter, but the sharp nail on the underside of the stick does not move her. There's no time for tenderness. I bring the goad stick down on her rump with all my might. "Move!"

The cow bolts forward through the door with her bell clanging. To my relief, she allows me to guide her toward the windbreak. Elizabeth, holding her scarf across her mouth, walks toward us. We've nearly reached her when, on our left, the cabin roof caves in. Flames shoot high and debris tosses up in the air. Without warning, the cow turns sharply and topples the sledge.

She's heading back to the shed.

"Elizabeth," I shout. "Run to the milk shed! Close the door!"

With one hand, I grab her harness and pull back with all my weight. It's no use. She drags me along with her. We can't afford to lose the cow, not after the pigs have died.

"Esmerelda, stop," I shout. Ahead of us, Elizabeth stumbles through the deep snow. She looks over her shoulder, sobbing as the cow bears down on her.

By some miracle, Elizabeth gets the shed door closed in time. The cow, seeing this, veers left toward the forest. I'm able to get ahead of her. A few thwacks with the goad stick, and I bring her to a halt a safe distance from the fire.

Puffs of steam billow from the cow's nostrils. I stroke her neck and wait for both our hearts to slow. Elizabeth, head down, plods toward the windbreak where her mother and sisters wait. "Well done," I holler, but she doesn't look up.

Nearly two hours into the woods, we're bone-weary and less than halfway to Bytown. My ankle throbs. Along the path stretching before us, snow gleams like a just-washed plate. Moonlight reflects from its crystalized surface and casts a dim light several yards into the woods on either side of us. Under different circumstances, I might have considered it beautiful. But below the icy veneer lies two feet of snow. Every crunching step forward is a struggle, as the burning muscles of my thighs will attest. The cow comes to a halt frequently. I allow her a moment's rest from pulling the sledge before urging her onward with a strong tug on the harness, checking over my shoulder each time to be sure my sister and the children are all right.

Biddy lies on the narrow sledge, a sack full of Seamus's tools and the loaded musket piled at her feet. She drifts in and out of sleep. A balled-up bedsheet cushions her head, and her bonnet is loosely knotted under her chin so the fabric doesn't stick to the oozing burns on her cheek and ear. Beneath the quilt I've tucked around her, she holds the sleeping Katherine in one arm and the cursed flour tin in the other. Her coughing jags have increased and she moans each time the sledge lurches.

Elizabeth and Annie follow along behind the sledge. Even with a trampled path to walk, the journey tests them. Where the snow is deepest, the girls sometimes trip on their skirt hems. To her credit, Elizabeth doesn't complain as she trudges along, staring into the snow. Meanwhile, Annie turns her head in every direction, scanning the forest for danger.

I understand her watchfulness. My own nerves are eased knowing that Seamus's rifle is loaded and within easy reach.

Suddenly Esmerelda jerks left, nearly knocking me off my feet. The front of the sledge lifts, then slams against the frozen ground, and Biddy cries out. Katherine begins to wail, and Elizabeth and Annie crowd onto the sledge.

As I step toward the cow, she lifts her muzzle high and rolls her eyes back until the whites show. "Shhh," I whisper and stroke her neck. I scan the forest on all sides of us for signs of movement and come up empty. But whatever trouble is out there can't be far away.

A trio of howls lifts from the forest and sends me running for the rifle at Biddy's feet. She and the children form a piteous scene, and the condition of my sister's face is another dagger to my heart. Katherine cries from inside the shroud of the quilt as Annie rests her head in Biddy's lap.

I sling Seamus's ammunition kit around my neck and choke down the lump of fear in my throat. "Up you get, girls."

Elizabeth begins to sob. "I can't go any farther."

"You can and you will," I tell her, reaching for the musket. "Think of your mother." There's no time for mollycoddling. What we do this night will either kill us or save us.

Biddy's eyes open. "The cabin is gone—all of it. How will Seamus find me?"

I tuck the rifle under one arm so I can reach out and touch the back of my hand to her forehead. She's red-hot with fever.

"I want Seamus," she whimpers.

What can I possibly say? That I want him too? I turn away from the desperation and agony written on Biddy's face. Tears scald my eyes as I urge the cow forward.

We're barely on our way when Annie hisses, "I see something! Over there!" She points into the woods on our right.

"I don't see anything," Elizabeth snaps.

A sliver of grey streaks through the forest. *Wolf!*

I ready the musket. "Girls, stay close to your mother."

Biddy struggles to prop herself up on one elbow, shushing Katherine. "What's happening?"

I wade to the opposite side of the cow, then cock the rifle and aim at the spot where I saw the wolf. Nothing. Slowly, I sweep the gun barrel left, then right, panning the shades of grey that conceal him among the trees. The weight of the rifle bears down on my already exhausted limbs. Muscles in my left arm are screaming. The scars around my right eye tingle with dread. My heart bangs inside my chest and I can barely breathe. The sharp-toothed beast is stalking us.

"I see it," Elizabeth yells. "By the stump!"

And there is my worst nightmare, standing in a gap between two birch trees twenty feet away. The full-grown wolf steps out of the shadows as if testing my resolve. His ears stand up straight and he studies me with such intensity that my knees nearly buckle. I fight to concentrate on lining up the wolf along the sight of the barrel. One shot—that's all I have. My aim must be true. If I miss, it will take several seconds to reload—even longer with my hands shaking in this finger-numbing cold.

A whimpered prayer spills from Biddy. "Jesus, Lord and Saviour, look down on us, your humble servants with mercy. Spare us, I—"

"Shhh . . ." I warn her, pulling the gun stock tight against my shoulder. My breathing slows. I squeeze the trigger. The end of the barrel jerks upward and the blast echoes in the night. Wood chips fly up from the stump next to the wolf's shoulder and a puff of snow kicks up from the ground. He yips and retreats to the shadows.

Biddy gapes at me with wide-eyed terror and my heart swoops low. The wolf will be back and he won't be alone. Where there is one, there are others. Elizabeth mirrors her mother's fear, but Annie appears relieved and Katherine, the same. Their faces are so innocent and trusting, huddled close to their mother.

"The wolf is gone. We're fine," I lie.

My hands are shaking as I grab a new cartridge from the leather kit. I half cock the musket and bite the paper from the top of the cartridge, taking with it the musket ball that, for the moment, I hold in my mouth. After shaking a bit of gunpowder into the pan, I close it and dump the rest into the barrel. As I spit the ball and a wad of paper into the muzzle, I steal a glance at the forest. The responsibility for four lives—five if I count the baby my sister carries—falls to me. My fingertips are so numb I can't feel the ramrod as I plunge it up and down inside the gun barrel, packing the ammunition in place. With the musket cocked and ready, I wonder where the damned wolves are hiding. After moments of scanning our surroundings, none of them reveal themselves, so I lower my weapon.

We've only begun walking again when, from the corner of one eye, I see wolves streaming through the forest. It's impossible to say how many. The cow falters in the deep snow, so I grab the traces and pull forward. My heart races as I keep watch over my shoulder for movement among the trees. We're doomed.

Suddenly, the cow stops and begins backing toward the sledge.

I look down the path. A wolf lurks there, head dipped and ears forward. He's a massive brute with a well-muscled chest. He's crouched ready to spring, his gaze locked on Esmerelda. When I raise the musket, his focus shifts to me.

If I manage to kill this beast, what next? Will the pack tear us to shreds before I can reload?

I lower the musket and slowly step closer to the cow, taking care not to remove my gaze from the wolf. With the gun trapped beneath one arm, I unhitch the yoke from Esmerelda's neck and let it drop into the snow along with the traces. Freed from sledge, she veers left from the path and thrashes into the forest. The brute speeds effortlessly across the snow to head her off. Two more bolt across the path and lunge at her heels. She bawls frantically. A ribbon of torn flesh soon dangles from one of her hind legs. I'm paralyzed with horror.

"Esmerelda," Annie cries out. She bounds a few yards from the sledge and stops when Elizabeth screams her name.

The lead wolf sweeps around and charges at the cow head-on. He lunges, then sinks his teeth into her throat. The two other wolves leap onto her back and clamp onto her haunches and spine, and she lets out a last strangled bawl. Her front legs buckle as she's wrestled into the snow.

The rest of the pack streak by me in a rush toward the kill. They pounce on Esmerelda and tear chunks of hide and meat from her carcass. Their barking and growling bring back the hot fetid breath of the Flynns' dog snarling next to my face. I feel sick.

"We have to get out of here fast," I tell Biddy and the girls as I step inside the traces to take up the yoke. "Elizabeth, help me."

"Seamus, where are you?" Biddy calls as if beckoning a stray child.

"Mam, you're scaring me," Elizabeth says. Together she and I push against the yoke, and the sledge moves ahead. For a moment, I am hopeful.

A high-pitched scream sounds behind us. It's Annie, motionless and staring at a wolf now emerging from behind a stand of pines. He's long and lean, a youngster trying to prove himself.

"Auntie?" Annie whimpers.

I raise the musket and aim at the spot behind the wolf's front shoulder. Everything slows. Minutes exist between my heartbeats. I pull the stock tight against my own shoulder and squeeze the trigger. *Blam.* A flash shoots from the barrel; acrid smoke fills my nostrils. The wolf yips and drops to the ground. Annie runs to Elizabeth and buries her face against her sister's coat.

At the sound of the shot, the other wolves leap away from the grisly remains of the cow and lift their bloodied jaws in our direction. We're done for, I fear, but they quickly return to feeding. One wolf raises his muzzle to the moon and howls a long and terrifying note. I should be dragging the sledge at top speed to put distance between us and the pack, but instead I hear their snapping teeth and my fear turns to rage.

I drop the rifle on the sledge and grab one of Seamus's tools—a narrow-bladed chisel.

My chest heaves as I stride through toward the body stretched out on the crimson bed of snow. The wolf is dead, his yellow eyes lifeless, but still I fall upon it and jam the chisel again and again into the wolf's rib cage. I howl with a wrath that scrapes my throat raw. When I'm spent, I look up to see another wolf standing in the shadows. I'm beyond fear. We hold each other's gaze for a moment, then he trots back to join his pack.

Pellets of frozen rain begin to skitter against the crust overlaying the snow. My fingertips burn from the cold. Strange how contrasting sensations are mistaken for each other. Resentment becomes compassion. Terror becomes boldness. The impossible becomes possible. The wolf no longer looks fierce. I bury my hands in his fur and thaw my fingers against his fading warmth.

When I sling the wolf's carcass over the front end of the sledge, Biddy and the girls regard me with a new sort of awe. And, perhaps, a little fear.

19

THOMAS

Since being tossed out of the smithy last night, I've been walking Lowertown streets and alleys. The freezing rain has set my teeth to chattering, and my hands are numb from the cold even though they're wrapped inside a bundle of my extra clothes. The swelling around my eye pains me when I yawn. Morning light reveals Michael's dried blood covering the front of my coat. Even my pant legs are stained. I can't get his look of stunned disbelief as his life drained away out of my head. He is—was—one of the few people whose motives I never questioned. It should have been Rory laid open instead; Rory, who expressed no remorse when I told him about Michael dying. I can't forget that either.

I'm circling through the whores' district for the hundredth time. Most people here have secrets and know how to turn a blind eye to unsavoury business. On these streets, a man covered in blood is a common sight. Such is not the case in Uppertown. Before I see Clara this night, I'll need to be cleaned up. I'll figure out how to manage that later. With all that's happened, it's hard to focus.

Mueller believes I'm the bad seed to blame for Michael dying and Rory's a good and respectful lad. It's pointless to tell him otherwise. He's been burning to get rid of me for a while. When people have their mind made up about things like that, talking rarely changes it.

Still, he refused to pay my wages before he sent me packing. In a few weeks, Gleeson and his men will return to Bytown and come looking for me. When they learn how I've been mistreated, Mueller will get his comeuppance. Let's see how bold he is when they burn his smithy to the ground.

Da once warned me that revenge is overrated. Whatever you do in anger will return to bite you on the arse. But he didn't witness the smirk on Rory's face last night when Mueller ordered him to drop my extra shirt and pants in a heap at my feet. I imagine telling Peter Aylen about the wrong done to me—the man who's helping him plot against James Johnston. The back of Rory's head will meet with a cudgel, and I'll be glad of it.

Life is stirring inside shanties along this street. I scoot into the shadows between two sheds and change into the spare shirt and pants I've been carrying. If volunteer riflemen spot me in this bloodied condition, they'll haul me off to Perth Gaol straight away. Near penniless, I can't do much about the state of my coat.

Woodsmoke wafts through the still air as I press onward. What I wouldn't give to sit in front of a roaring fire right now. Ahead is a low-roofed shanty and perched in its front window is a bottle, signalling an unlicensed whiskey joint. I'll go inside to warm myself and with a bit of luck there'll be a scrap to eat.

The door has frozen shut overnight and requires a couple of tugs to break it free from the ice. I duck to avoid striking my head against the lintel. At the far end of the room, a man—most likely the owner—looks over his shoulder and, after a quick inspection of me, returns to stoking the fire. An old-timer is passed out, face down and snoring, at a table a few feet away from me. His coat hangs unattended over the back of his chair. As I edge toward it, the first man stands, poker in hand. His opposite arm ends at the elbow, his sleeve knotted below the stump, but he's broad-chested and has the advantage of height. Even one-armed, he could do me harm. Without breaking eye contact, I begin removing my own garment. He looks at the old man's coat and back at me. An excruciating moment passes before he turns away and resumes shifting logs in the fire. I snatch up the new coat and throw mine on the table. Outside I break into a half run until I'm a good distance away, then wade into a snowdrift trapped between two shanties to catch my breath out of view of the street.

In one pocket of my new coat, I discover a one-pound note, enough for food and drink until Peter Aylen rewards me. There's also a jackknife, a clay pipe and a leather pouch half-full of tobacco in the other pocket. My luck is turning. I venture into the open and head toward Sleigh Bay on the river. There'll be cheap ale, warm bread and news enough to occupy me until I see Clara tonight.

Soon after setting off, I spot a half-dressed girl, just a bit older than me, shaking out a blanket in front of an open shanty door. Her bare legs jut out from unlaced boots big enough to fit a man. She catches sight of me as she turns to go back inside. Her dark brows pinch together as she squints.

"Hey, I know you," she says slowly. Her words rise on the white clouds of her breath.

I recognize her too—that black hair and sharp chin. She's one of the whores Gleeson goes around with, the one Rory likes. When I ignore her and continue walking, she hollers after me.

"You're a lot like your auntie!"

I spin toward her. Now it's my turn to squint. How does this girl know my aunt?

"Mariah doesn't like to talk either." The girl smiles and dips a shoulder so her shift falls below one breast. I can't help gawking. It's perfect. Her voice goes all lovey-dovey. "Bet I could make *you* talk. Come on and we'll find out. Virgins ride for free."

"I'm no virgin. And I'm not looking for charity either," I tell her.

Her smile annoys me. "Maybe I should marry you, then." Now she's making fun of me.

"How do you know my aunt?

"That's confidential information," she replies.

"What's that supposed to mean?"

She goes inside, leaving the door wide open. I stare after her until my good sense returns. How could I face Clara after romping with a whore? But more than that, I'm not mixing with anyone who's got ties to Gleeson, Rory and Aunt Mariah.

❧

At Sleigh Bay, the teamsters are out in full force. I'm invisible among the scores of labourers hoping for work hefting supplies from one sled to another. Pairs of draft horses clomp past en route to the bay. The horses fare better than me with their cork-bottomed shoes. My own boots slip out from under me easily on the slow decline of the icy road. Some sleds are loaded with barrels of whiskey and ale for delivery to taverns. Others carry sacks of flour, dried beans and hogsheads filled with salted pork destined for the timber camps. Maybe one will make it to Da's. I'm glad he's not here to give me an earful of I-told-you-so's.

A horse jingles past, drawing a sleigh. A smiling couple rides with a child wedged between them and furs pulled over their knees. They're probably on their way to a posh Uppertown hotel or maybe to visit family in an outlying town. I don't need to know them to hate them.

The Ottawa River is frozen solid. I pause on the bank to watch a convoy of teamsters ease onto the ice, joining the long line of horses and sleds that stretches along the centre of the river. Da once told me they travel two days from here before they branch off onto smaller rivers like the Bonnechere and the Madawaska to travel inland to various depots. For a fleeting second, I think about hopping on a sledge. I could go anywhere, be anyone I claim to be. I could distance myself from my family. I could bring Clara with me. Together, we could outrun bad Irish luck.

It's impossible. Clara's not the running-off type and the Shiner reach extends far in every direction. The quickest path to me owning a smithy is through gaining Aylen's favour.

Last night I'd been so excited to learn about the Nepean Township election. But really, what if my news is worthless?

Clara must know something more of value. The right kind of persuasion will coax details from her. I'm doing this for us. My future is her future. She'd understand that, I'm sure. *Don't let me down*, she'd said. The truth of my current situation would put an end to us. But if I line things up right, there won't be a problem. It's time I collect what's due me—a reward. Mueller and Rory can eat crow.

I wake in the pitch-black of Johnston's stable, exhaustion combined with the dinner I'd been able to buy taking me under as soon as I lay down beneath this horse blanket on a layer of fresh straw. I have no idea how much time has passed, and my heart races from nightmares about Michael. His whimpering haunts me, as does the weight of him slumped against my chest.

Think of other things. Picture Clara's smile and her silvery eyes. If I could put my hands around her waist, my fingertips would likely touch. She's slight but strong from hoisting kettles and toting provisions from the market. My pecker stirs at the thought of what lies beneath her skirts. Rory would tell me to bed her if I can. But Clara is special.

I fling the horse blanket off and brush the straw from my new coat. When I go to the window, light glows through the Johnstons' bedroom curtain. The rest of the house is dark except for the kitchen. My eyes strain, searching for signs of Clara beyond the snowflakes and coal blackness of the hour. So much rides on our few minutes together. What she does or doesn't tell me will alter the course of my life, for better or worse.

When she finally appears at the kitchen window, she presses one hand to the glass, a good-night wish meaning that she won't be coming out tonight.

"No." Disappointment squeezes from my mouth like air from a bellows. She disappears from view and my well-laid plan falls on its head.

A second later, I'm outside with the cold wind whipping my face. Patch stands and wags his tail as I approach. I hurry past the dog to the kitchen window, where I scrape my fingernails lightly across the glass. An eternity passes. I try again, and again, and she appears at last, carrying a lit candle.

I mouth, *Let me in*.

Clara points upward, indicating the Johnstons. But she doesn't leave the window, so there's hope of changing her mind. I rub my arms vigorously and pull a sad face. She smiles at my jesting and shakes her head again. When I press my hands together as if in prayer and pout another plea, her face turns serious. She's considering. In the snow accumulating at the bottom of the pane, I draw a heart. She gives a look of exasperation, then sets down the candle and moves to ease the kitchen door open. I'm quick to squeeze inside the house.

"Are you mad?" Clara whispers. Her copper hair flows loose and spills to her waist. She hugs a shawl around her chest when she sees my eyes on the front of her nightgown.

"You're so pretty." I'd no intention of saying such a thing, but don't regret it now that I have.

"You'll get us both fired," she says, smoothing her hair away from her face.

I reach out and return the strands to where they'd lain against her cheek. "You're perfect as you are." Her doe-eyed gaze puts a lump in my throat.

"You have to go," she whispers.

"One more minute."

She sighs. "A minute and that's all."

I salute her on our way to the hearth and she rewards me with a whole-hearted smile.

Although the fire is dying, the kitchen is warm. As I kneel to hold my hands near the dwindling flames, I steal a glance to where her bed juts from behind the corner. Her dress is neatly folded and lies at the foot of it. Had I arrived a moment sooner, I might have seen her naked.

"Are you warm enough yet?" She checks over her shoulder before I answer.

"Why so fidgety?" I say. "Aren't you Clara of Kinsale, County Cork, the girl who dodged the rent collector? Where's your nerve?"

She grins at me then and turns a kitchen chair toward the hearth. I do the same. As we settle onto our seats, my arm brushes hers. I'm burning to touch other parts of her. When my gaze drops to her breasts again, she snugs the shawl even more firmly around her shoulders.

I fold my hands over my lap to hide the bulge stirring inside my britches. On the table behind us, I notice a pair of lit candles and a puddle of dark fabric. "What've you been up to?" I ask.

"Sewing the pocket back onto Mr. Johnston's suit jacket. It was near torn off."

"Fit for a president," I say.

"I suppose," she replies. "He was wearing this very suit a year ago when he lost the agricultural something-or-other election to the Shiner King. A mob of Irish rioters beat him senseless after the meeting."

"You know about that?" I ask with surprise. I didn't.

"I make it my business to know," Clara says. "Mr. Johnston and the two Georges discussed it in the dining room today. It was the Shiners what torched his first house and his newspaper shop too."

"How terrible!"

"Well, they won't get away with it this time because—" Her mouth closes in a guilty line.

She's a loyal girl, a rare thing. I love her for it, and my heart twinges a wee bit for what I must do next.

"Clara," I whisper, staring deep into her eyes. "We're a team now. I need to know everything about Mr. Johnston's doings—for his own safety."

She looks away and toys with a loose bit of wool at the edge of her shawl. Then finally, she says, "The two Georges are helping him win."

And there it is. The gem I've been waiting for. It's a fight to keep my voice steady. "How?"

"In the Bathurst District, only property-owning men could vote for the president of the Agricultural Society. That Aylen fella found out, then started selling one-yard squares of his own land to landless men in his gang. They all showed up at the election meeting and outnumbered the men who'd promised to vote for Mr. Johnston. Well . . ."

"Go on . . ."

Her gaze turns toward the glowing embers on the hearth. "It doesn't feel right, telling their secrets."

"Clara . . ." My tone is the same one Da uses to underscore his disappointment in me. I'm about to say more, but her eyes cut to mine. They shine with doubt. If I let the silence stand, she'll fill it with words, all the right words. I'm a manipulative shit—which leaves me feeling a bit dirty but proud at the same time.

"The two Georges and Mr. Johnston are rallying more of their sort—rich Scottish and British men, merchants and half-pay soldiers—to vote him onto the Nepean Township council."

"So the rotters are scheming to bar Aylen from office." And there I have it, the thing that will leave Aylen indebted to me.

"It sounds like you want the Shiners to win? Have you no loyalty to the Johnstons?"

"Sure," I lie. "But we *are* Irish first."

"I never forget that, Thomas O'Dougherty. But I can't abide Shiner behaviour. They don't represent me with their drunkenness and going around with bad women. They beat good men senseless and burn people out. The Irish will never gain respect that way. We've got to show we're as good as the English and Scottish. Win fair and square."

She's wrong for a million reasons. But I won't tell her that *fair and square* doesn't exist. We Irish will get what we take. By claiming my due is how I'll gain respect among men, and with Clara on my arm, I'll be the envy of everyone. She won't stoop to serve another Orangeman or Brit for as long as I draw breath.

"Wise words," I say to appease her. "I thought about you today. A lot."

She regards me with skepticism. "What happened to your eye?"

"A horse that didn't much want to be shod." Another lie.

"Ah." She gently lays her hand on my cheek. "Does it hurt?"

"Not now." I take her hand in mine and kiss her palm and her wrist. My mouth lingers and I hope my love travels straight into her heart.

"Thomas . . ." Her voice is raspy. "We can't."

I slide forward on my chair and take Clara's face in my hands. Her lips part as if to speak again, but I kiss them before words can break the spell. My right hand has a mind of its own and wanders to her breasts. I can feel the alarm in her kiss before she pulls away. I've gone too far. It's cruel that God should make a girl so beautiful, then not let me lay hands on her.

"One day I'm going to marry you." There, I've said it. Nothing happens in the world without a flag being planted. Now I've planted mine.

"I suppose I'll have a say in the matter?" Clara says.

"Someday I'm going to build you a house as grand as this one."

Her expression lets me know that she thinks I'm dreaming.

"And I'll have my own business. People will respect me. I'll matter."

"Will I matter?"

The question feels like a trap. If the answer's not right, it will spring shut and crush my chances with her. All I can think to say is, "I love you."

Her eyes glow with affection, and she smiles at me with a contentment that warms me from the inside out.

"I don't give my heart easily, Thomas O'Dougherty. But if that was a proposal, I accept."

I draw her into my arms and my kisses wander from her mouth to her perfect earlobe. She loves me. I can scarce believe my luck. Our breathing grows ragged but when my lips skim her neck, she pushes me back. "Thomas—"

Our faces are inches apart. All I want to do is kiss her again. "Thomas, you really must go."

Upstairs, floorboards creak. Clara's eyes widen. I spring up and make a tiptoed rush to the door, where I give her a last hurried kiss before she eases me outside.

"I love you, Clara," I whisper.

"And I you." She blows me a kiss and closes the door.

Darts of happiness shoot through my heart. She loves me! *And* I got the goods on Johnston. I want to shout my victory at the stars. My moment is coming. I've only to endure one more miserable night with Johnston's horses. To be sure my tracks are hidden for Clara's sake, I decide to cross behind the outhouse on my return to the stable. There's a steady snow coming down in giant feathery flakes. My boot prints will be filled in by—

I'm yanked by my coat collar and a hand clamps over my mouth. Cedar branches slap at me as I'm pulled backward through the hedge. I try to break free, but a thumb presses hard on the outer corner of my wounded eye and subdues me. My feet scramble for traction, but I'm lifted from the ground and unable to stop whatever is about to happen.

Suddenly I'm flung downward. The back of my head thuds against the frozen ground and my eyes squeeze shut against the pain and the effort of remaining silent. I open them to a wave of nausea and discover, towering over me, Hairy Barney—a mountain huffing clouds of steam into the dark. He's flanked by three other hoodlums—all scrappers with bent noses and broad shoulders. If Hairy Barney is in town, Gleeson must be too and these men will bring me to see him. This is all wrong. I need to see Aylen first.

I brace myself for a boot to the ribs, although I've no idea why I deserve it. Is this a test? My eyes cut to the faces of each man. No one moves, but one word from their leader will unleash hell.

Hairy Barney bends forward and fastens his eyes on mine like he's getting a read on me. I'm scared enough to wet my drawers, but I try to keep my face blank. He snorts, then nods to his men.

This is it. I hold my head and pull in my elbows. Instead of being kicked, I'm pulled upright and dragged several feet until I manage to recover my footing. Saddled horses are waiting inside a copse of trees just ahead. Another armed Shiner waits among them. My gut ties itself in a knot. "Why do we need horses?" I ask, trying to sound brave. Gleeson usually summons his men to public houses in Bytown, a short walk from where we stand. No one answers. One of Hairy Barney's men unties a pair of reins from a low branch and hauls himself onto the saddle of a dark horse, then extends a hand to me. I freeze.

Hairy Barney glowers at me. "Get your ass on that horse—Tommy."

20

MARIAH

Elizabeth gave up pulling once we met Richmond Road. It's only me now who is straining to pull the sledge, the wooden yoke digging into my collarbone. With her hands tucked inside her coat sleeves, she walks next to me and no longer even looks over her shoulder when Biddy calls out for Seamus. Wide-eyed and watchful, Annie clutches a handful of Elizabeth's coat and treads along, pressed close to her side. Elizabeth's present meekness reminds me she's a child and not the adversary her sharp tongue often presents. She must be blaming herself for the fire as much as I'm blaming myself. Poor child.

Uppertown's grand stone houses are sheathed inside a skim of ice, glinting with a treacherous beauty. Much of the roadway leading to Sappers Bridge is slick, and it's near impossible for my leather soles to find purchase, though at least the sledge runners glide easily. Every time I want to cry or give up, I think of Thomas, sleeping soundly and untroubled with layers of blankets snugged beneath his chin. When we arrive, I'll wake him and he'll let us shelter inside the blacksmith shop.

Suddenly, one of my feet goes out from under me and my knee

smashes against the unyielding ground. Pain jolts through my bones, but I forbid myself to cry out in front of the girls. They need my strength and I will give it.

"Not much farther to Thomas now," I tell them as I struggle to my feet. Instead of responding, their gazes shift to the bridge, where a group of five men is crossing toward us. I'm too tired to be afraid. The men regard us with curiosity as they pass by, but don't offer to help. We're another woeful lot of filthy Irish. Nothing new in this town.

My son is the only unbroken thing in my life, a thought that keeps me moving forward. Thomas is a solid boy, dependable. We'll rise above this catastrophe together.

Finally, we arrive at Mueller's Blacksmith Shop. The windows are still dark, and a heavy chain is strung through the front door handles and padlocked. My sister and her children need warmth and shelter now and, if we're lucky, some tea to warm their insides. Without an ounce of strength to pull the sledge farther, I drop the yoke and trudge toward the narrow lane that leads to the back of the smithy. Elizabeth and Annie follow at my heels.

"Stay with your mother while I fetch Thomas," I tell them. But they tag after me anyways. "What if she or Katherine wakes and you're not there?" When I stop once more to turn them back, the girls look at me beseechingly. They resemble a pair of ghosts with the ice frosting their lashes and the hems of their skirts frozen stiff. I've not the heart to insist further.

At the rear of the smithy, a pair of dark windows look down on us from the second storey. I gather a handful of icy snow and lob the snowball at the first window and wait for Thomas's face to appear.

The girls and I stand shivering in the cold, but Thomas doesn't answer. Again, I gather snow, but this time I throw harder. The snowball makes a dull thunk on the glass and splatters across the pane. Almost immediately the window slides open.

"Feck off," a voice whispers loudly. "I just fell asleep!" Then Rory, Thomas's mouthy apprentice friend, leans out through the open window.

"Please get Thomas," I call up to him.

His voice softens with bewilderment. "Auntie?"

"We've been burned out. Just fetch my son."

The earth drops from beneath my feet. I've just referred to Thomas as *my son*. There's a troubling keenness about Rory as he pushes away from the sill.

My eyes, brimming with tears, cut to Elizabeth. "Don't know why I said that. I'm just so tired . . ." Elizabeth doesn't say a word, but her expression hardens like shale.

I steel myself for the reception I'll receive from Thomas if Rory has repeated my gaff. An approaching candle lights the ice-glazed ground-floor window in front of me. When the frame tilts outward, Rory's face appears. My heart sinks.

"Burned out, you say?"

His grin unbalances me. "We've lost everything."

"And you need your *son*?"

He's toying with me, the black-hearted scamp, but to what end I can't piece together. "Please let us in. We've been walking all night and the children are freezing. My sister is out front of the smithy. She's not well."

"Why not!" he says too exuberantly. "The quickest way in is through this window." When Rory catches sight of Elizabeth, he reminds me of Annie seeing hard candy at Edwards Mercantile for the first time. "Tommy never mentioned his sister was so beautiful."

Elizabeth is all smiles now.

I pin Rory with a warning look, which he ignores. "I'll be back in one minute—with her mother." As I set out to fetch Biddy, Elizabeth begins feeding Annie feet-first through the window and into Rory's arms.

Biddy mumbles when the sledge lurches ahead and Katherine begins to fuss. "Shhh," I whisper, desperate not to wake Mr. Mueller for fear he'll turn us away. Katherine bawls, "Mam!" and kicks the quilt away, but Biddy doesn't rouse enough to comfort her.

I lean against the yoke and concentrate on dragging the sledge. The sooner this child is inside with Elizabeth and out of Mueller's earshot, the better. As I round the corner of the blacksmith shop, Elizabeth— with skirts lifted above her knees—straddles the windowsill, then leans into Rory's outstretched arms. As he pulls her inside, I picture his eyes devouring her. Loathing ignites inside my chest.

"Where do you think you're going?" a deep voice shouts as light splays over me.

I turn to find Mr. Mueller standing on his porch with a lantern. He's pulled a coat over his nightshirt and stuffed his feet into unlaced boots. His face is contorted with a rage that lingers after recognition dawns in his eyes. "What's all this?"

He thinks I'll bow and scamper off as I usually do. But tonight I say, "Fire took our home. There's nothing left. Please unlock the smithy doors so I can bring my sister and her child inside."

"Go to your own people," he insists. "There's Irish everywhere."

"Thomas *is* our people. That's why we've come."

"Well, you're too late. He's not here."

That shocks me, and I falter. "Where is he?"

Katherine begins to wail.

He hesitates before answering. "I threw him out. Thomas is tangled up with the Shiners and he led the other two apprentices astray, drinking and cavorting. One boy's dead because of it. Young Rory's given me a full account of your nephew's misdeeds."

I can take no more. I cast the yoke to the ground and stomp toward him. "You take the word of that little ferret, Rory? Did you ask Thomas for his side of the story?"

Mueller's gaze lowers to the dead wolf on our sled, then slowly lifts. Where there was indignance, doubt has appeared. When I stop in front of him, in the full light of his lantern, he takes in my bloodied face and hands with astonishment.

"You've turned a *boy* into the streets among unscrupulous creatures— at night in this weather? He's all alone with no home to return to." I'm shaking. "How will he find us?"

"I trusted Thomas and he betrayed that trust," Mueller says.

"And we trusted his master. Had you sent word that he was heading for trouble, we would have come for him. None of this would have happened."

I stand, chin lifted and glaring, waiting to hear what he has to say for himself.

Mueller finally shrugs. "Give me a minute." He heads back into his house and my knees nearly buckle. I'd no idea I had it in me to be so forceful.

When Biddy coughs, I kneel and take one of her chapped hands in mine. She lets out a groan of discomfort as I rub warmth back into her fingers. "Look, Biddy, we're here."

"Mam, I hungry," Katherine says.

"There, there," Biddy says haltingly. "God will feed us."

A moment later, Mueller returns properly dressed. He drags the mutilated wolf carcass to a spot against the smithy foundation, then picks a key from the metal loop around his wrist. "Let's bring your sister inside."

He unlocks the padlock and removes the chain from the door. The hinges groan as he swings the plank door wide. I lean hard against the yoke, but it's not until Mueller comes around us and shoves the back of the sledge that the runners slide onto the hard-packed smithy floor. Biddy, still on the sledge with one arm still hugging the flour tin, gives me a faint smile. "Good job, a stór," she says in a raspy voice. She hasn't called me a treasure since we were wee girls. Her unexpected affection lifts me, but when she pats the tin, my guilt swells.

I'm grateful to be inside four walls and under a roof once more. Katherine, quiet now, climbs off the sledge and goes to Elizabeth, who stoops to pick her up.

Mr. Mueller asks Annie, "What's your name?" When she won't answer, he says, "I got a little girl right about the same age as you." Annie shyly buries her face in Elizabeth's coat.

He crosses his arms and eyes me thoughtfully. "You can sleep in the apprentices' beds, but only for a few days. I'm not running a hotel. There's a stove up there, so you'll all be warm."

"What about me?" Rory says.

The blacksmith ignores the question. "Can your sister stand?" he asks me.

"I think so."

Rory is indignant. "Where do you expect me to sleep? In the stable?"

Mr. Mueller hisses a response. "That's exactly where you'll sleep. Spare the poor woman. Her home's burned down and her trouble-maker nephew disgraces her." Rory quirks a brow at *nephew*, but my expression doesn't change.

Together, the two of them help Biddy upstairs—no small feat with the tin held fast in her arms. I light the way with Mr. Mueller's lantern and Katherine riding one hip. The two older girls stay close behind me. Once in the apprentices' room, I roll back the covers on the bed closest to the pot-belly stove and the men lay Biddy across the straw tick. Rory angrily grabs a wool cap hanging over the corner post of the upper bunk, then stomps down the stairs without as much as a word to anyone.

Before leaving us, Mr. Mueller stirs the embers inside the stove and adds a small log. Throughout our trek to Bytown, I longed for warmth. But now the flames call me back to the burning cabin and I'm momentarily paralyzed. The front hatch squawks as he shuts it. "Rest up," he says solemnly. "Morning will be here soon."

Tears sting my eyes. "Which bed is—was—Thomas's?" I ask.

As it is with Seamus, a woman's distress discomfits Mr. Mueller. He nods at the bed that Biddy is lying across and makes his exit.

It's a relief when he leaves. His turn of heart has surprised me, and my gratitude wrestles with my resentment over his treatment of Thomas. My son is somewhere out in the world alone in this ice-crusted hell, afraid to come home—to what home?—lest he disappoint his da and earn Biddy's rebuke. But there she lies, weak as a kitten, with her head on his pillow.

I tuck the three girls into the bottom bunk so they have a view of their mother. In the glow of the lantern and moonlight, their soot-smeared faces are a knife through my heart. The children have nothing but the clothes on their backs—and a worthless flour tin. I've no idea how to react when they discover the earbobs are missing.

Elizabeth's eyes pin me in place. No doubt piecing together the lie her mother, father and I have been living. I can't meet her gaze, so I turn away and make for the door. I'll sleep in the stable.

Her voice stops me. "It's not fair."

It's the truest hardship she's ever suffered. She's so young to shoulder the burden of the guilt she must be feeling. "I know, Elizabeth. But things will work out. We'll find Thomas."

"I don't care a fig about Thomas."

I can't have heard that right.

"Mam will take my earbobs and sell them to get money." Elizabeth pauses to sniffle. "They're mine alone! I am the eldest girl and she promised them to me."

Heat rises in my face. I leave the room without speaking another word.

21

THOMAS

My hat's long gone and the tops of my ears burn with cold. Snow continues falling in icy clumps as Hairy Barney's crew rides in silence across an expanse of empty field. The gathering drifts reflect just enough moonlight for navigating the horses. As we leave Richmond Road farther behind us, I do my best to note the surroundings—the tip of Victoria Island and the distant roar of Chaudière Falls—so I can make my way back to the road later and hitch a ride to Aylen's house, which I believe to be closer to Perth. The broad-shouldered rider in front me blocks my view forward, so I try to lean to the side of him to see ahead, no easy feat as we sway with the horse's uneven gait through the snow.

In the distance, spots of light burn like hot coals through the darkness. As we travel closer, I can see a scattering of outbuildings. At their centre stands a log cabin over double the size of Mam and Da's. The two chimneys, one at each end wall, explain the bright fire-lit windows that guided us here.

"Is this Gleeson's place?" I ask. No one answers. Their silence is a boot heel grinding my confidence into dust.

Maybe I have this all wrong. Maybe it's Gleeson I should be impressing, instead of Aylen.

But then again, why not gain favour from both? I can feed a morsel of information to Gleeson and reserve the choicest details for Aylen's ears.

As we come close, I notice a pair of men armed with rifles and posted on either side of the front door. Someone of means must own this place. The timbers are hewn square, not rounded like Mam and Da's log cabin. Are Gleeson and his men harassing a wealthy family and holing up in their house? Panic slaps me. I won't be an accomplice to terrifying women and children. But how will I refuse?

We slide from our mounts and one of the Shiners takes up all our reins and sets off around the corner of the house. I presume I'm meant to help him stable the horses, being the youngest and all. But when I move to do so, Hairy Barney jerks his head toward the house and says, "In here." One of the guards opens the door, then steps aside to let him pass. I hang back, expecting the other men to proceed ahead of me, but instead they're rooted in place and regarding me with sullen expressions. Then I understand. This is a house a man doesn't enter without invitation—or a summons. I could near piss myself. What am I walking into?

When I start through the door, one of the guards blocks my way with his rifle barrel. The other, an intimidating bruiser, spins me toward him and roughly searches my coat pockets. He smiles faintly when he discovers my new pipe and tobacco pouch. I say nothing as he holds them up to a wall-mounted lantern for examination—and nothing again when he shoves them into his own pocket. Straight-faced, he goes on to pat around my waist and the top of my boots. When he's done, he flicks a look at his partner, who lowers his rifle and shoves me over the threshold.

I brace for the sight of a terrified family cowering in a huddle. To my relief, this is not the case. In fact, nothing is at all as I expect.

Maybe a dozen men are inside, some warming themselves in front of a fireplace. Others are sitting on the lower steps of a proper staircase that must lead up to sleeping quarters above us, judging by the absence of beds in this room. A table fully lit by candles and strewn with plates, some streaked with gravy and balancing used cutlery, stretches at least ten feet along the centre of the room. It's flanked by benches, and a high-backed chair towers over one end.

On the far side, Hairy Barney already sits shovelling food into his mouth. At the left end of the room, more men, old enough to be my da, stand before the fire ladling stew onto their white china plates, so different from the wooden or metal sort in Mam's pantry.

Unease grips me. I've yet to see anyone fine enough to be the likely owner of this house. Or Gleeson.

On a wooden chair at the other end of the room, a man sits, backlit by the warm glow of the second fireplace. After a moment, it dawns on me that I'm looking at Gleeson. I didn't recognize him without a hat on his head. He's leaned forward, listening to whoever occupies the high-backed armchair across from him. Gleeson's posture tells me he's not in charge here.

When Gleeson notices me, he sits upright and turns toward me, his eyes narrowing like he's trying to decipher my expression. A peal of female laughter settles on us from upstairs, but he doesn't react.

I try my best to look calm, clasping my hands before me as if I'd just removed my missing hat. I swear he can see through me like I was morning ice on a water bucket—right down to my plans to bypass him and go straight to Aylen with my information.

He nods, and I take a couple of slow steps toward him. *You're a thinking man. Think your way through. You haven't frozen your arse off, lost your job and nearly been killed to come away from this empty-handed.*

Just then, the stairs creak in an offbeat rhythm. I look sharply over my shoulder to see Aylen's right-hand man, Andrew Leamy, coming down them with his shirt unbuttoned and his suspenders swinging loosely against his thighs. This must be his house. His clothes look expensive and men clear the lower steps so he can pass. The distraction buys me a few seconds to order my thoughts. I'll tell Gleeson about the election date—that's it. Tomorrow I'll find my way to Aylen and share the critical details of Johnston's conspiracy with the two Georges and Hobbs. Leamy spots me as his feet touch the floor. "Who the hell's this?"

Before I can answer, Gleeson pipes up in a voice not so deep and commanding as usual. "O'Dougherty."

Leamy strides along the table. "You've kept us waiting." A tousled-haired woman with a blanket wrapped loosely around her starts down the stairs. Her legs are bare below the knee. "Not now!" he says. She turns away in disappointment and hurries back up to the loft.

Suddenly, a knifepoint digs into my gut and I freeze. I look up into the deep-set eyes of Peter Aylen, who has leaned over the arm of his chair to encourage me with his bone-handled blade.

"This one's a right eejit," Leamy says to Gleeson. Then he turns to me. "You're standing before *the* Peter Aylen. He'll gut you easy as battin' an eye."

Aylen's an imposing man, but not because of his size. Many of his men tower above him, but his famed hair-trigger temper and the speed with which he dispenses violence make him a giant. I should be more scared, but instead I feel like laughing. Of all the dumb luck! Fate has delivered him to me—now I can tell him everything.

"It's an honour to meet you, sir," I tell him in as even a voice as I can muster. He greets this with a drawn-out silence that unnerves me.

Finally, Aylen withdraws his knife and says, "Yer standing in my blind spot."

"Sorry, sir." I turn sideways and shuffle closer to Gleeson. Aylen and I glance sideways at each other as I back away. His expression reminds me of a man at a card table itching to lay down his winning hand.

"Sit," Leamy says, his head jerking toward a chair beside Gleeson.

I drop onto the seat. Now I'm part of the inner circle. If Rory could see me now, he'd be green with envy.

"You've been watching Johnston's place," Aylen says.

"Yes sir. Every night for nearly a month," I tell him, then wait to see what comes next.

"I thought it best to keep tabs on Johnston," Gleeson interjects. But the big man pays no attention to him.

Without removing his gaze from my face, Aylen flips the knife deftly onto the side table.

One of the men who'd been serving himself dinner when I first arrived comes toward us with a glass of whiskey in either fist. He sets one on the table next to Aylen, and the other he delivers to Leamy.

"So, what's that shite-heels Orangeman been up to?" Leamy asks.

"Things are pretty quiet at his house, sir. No one's been there at night except a preacher," I say. Open with small details, save the exciting bits for last.

Leamy takes a swig, then hisses air through his teeth. With sudden violence, Aylen stabs the table, burying the knife in the wood. I can't help but lurch backward, and I catch Gleeson glaring at me. If looks could kill, I'd be facedown without a heartbeat.

While Aylen drains his glass, Leamy says, "Gleeson, you told this pup, still wet behind the ears, to watch Johnston's house at night? In the winter? The same house you recently shot up?"

I see the sense of what he's saying. No enemy of the Shiners would conspire with Johnston after dark for fear of meeting up with our men on the road. And especially not in the deep freeze of December.

For the first time I've ever witnessed, Gleeson is at a loss for words. My back straightens. This is my moment and I know just how to play it.

"I did scout around town, sir." It's cocky of me to pause, I know, but I'm savouring Aylen's attention. And Leamy's. Even Gleeson sits taller in his chair.

"Spill," Aylen says.

"There's to be an election for the Nepean Township council." There, I've said it. I relax against the back of my chair and wait for their awestruck gratitude.

"He already knows that," Leamy says. My heart sinks.

"What else you got?" Aylen says, his gaze still on my face. I'm back in the game.

Leamy takes a last gulp of whiskey. "The kid's smiling again. Feckin' eejit."

I've got him now. Everything is falling into place. "Johnston has been meeting in town with Patterson, Baker and a farmer named Hobbs."

Aylen's expression opens. "Go on."

Gleeson pipes up. "I'll find out what they're about and—"

"They're planning to rally more English and Scottish from throughout the township to boost the number of votes for Johnston." A dangerous game, stealing Gleeson's thunder. "They want to keep him in office and prevent a repeat of your glorious win at Bathurst."

Aylen leans forward and scowls. "And they just *told* you this?"

Hairy Barney speaks up. "He's knockin' boots with Johnston's servant girl."

The men all laugh, Gleeson the loudest. He took a gamble on me and I came through. I feel heroic when he punches my shoulder like we're old friends.

"We need resourceful men," Aylen says. "Men who follow orders but think for themselves."

The past twenty-four hours melt away. I'm on top again.

"You're losing your edge," Leamy tells Gleeson. "This pup outthought you."

I smile with pride—until I see the murderous look in Gleeson's eye. Humiliation builds grudges. I don't need enemies, especially not the type who retaliate. "Mr. Gleeson leads us well."

"I want particulars," Aylen says. At first, I think this is directed at Gleeson. Then I realize his words are meant for me.

"How many men support Johnston?" Leamy adds. "What are their names? Where are they from?"

I open my mouth to speak but no words come out. How the hell am I supposed to deliver on that? Even if I knew how to collect all the information, I could never hold it all in my head. Never learned my letters, so I can't put any of it on paper.

As if reading my mind, Hairy Barney shouts, "Work on the girl, Tommy." A couple of the men lean their shoulders close together and snigger. This is the second time he's called me Tommy. I don't like it any better than when Rory does.

Clara will thankfully never know how she's been spoken of. "We aren't that well acquainted."

"Bullshit," he yells around a new mouthful of food. "She's in the stable with you every night."

Leamy backhands my face. Tears sting my eyes, as much from disgrace as pain. Then he leans over me, his hands on either chair arm. "You lied, eejit. What else you lyin' about? Huh?"

I grit my teeth and press my knees together to stop them from shaking. If I'm cowed by him, they'll all treat me like a boy.

"Leamy, stand down," Aylen says in an icy tone. Leamy lingers for a moment longer, then pushes away.

"You go see that girl and find out what else Johnston's up to. All women are whores. Guaranteed she's holding something back for money. Give her coin. If she don't start dishing secrets, slap her around like Leamy done you. She'll talk."

My face gives me away. I can't use Clara that way.

"There's plenty here that'd like to give her a go if you're not man enough for the job," Aylen says.

"I'm man enough," I shoot back.

Aylen's expression deadens and the room falls silent while everyone awaits his reaction.

I've been too bold.

The corners of his eyes begin to crinkle, then his head tips back and laughter rolls from the cave of his mouth. *Thank God!* The men now assembled on either side of Hairy Barney chuckle too.

But Aylen isn't finished. "Get this man anything he wants to eat and drink and send him upstairs to the girls."

Leamy grabs the front of my coat and hauls me from the chair.

"Come on, little man," one of the Shiners hollers. Space is made for me along the bench and a full plate of stew is set before me. Bottles and glass clink together and the next thing I know, someone tousles my hair and a glass of whiskey lands next to my fork.

When Aylen claims the chair at the head of the table, everyone quiets and looks his way. The man who served him earlier sets a fresh glass and a bottle of whiskey in front of him.

"The boys will return you to Bytown in the morning. You got two days to find out what I need to know. I'll set you up with money. You've earned it. I take care of my own. But cross me, O'Dougherty, and . . ." Aylen grabs the whiskey bottle by the neck and smashes it on the edge of the table. I jump in my seat. He leans forward, with his elbow resting in a pool of whiskey and glass shards, and presses the jagged-edged bottle under my chin.

I'm not out of this thing yet.

The Shiners don't return me to town the next morning as Aylen promised. They have a score to settle with some French raftsmen staying across the river in Wrightsville, so they drop me on the banks of the Ottawa River east of Chaudière Falls. I don't mind walking the fifteen minutes to town. It gives me time to think. So much has changed over the past twenty-four hours. I've moved on from being Gleeson's lackey. Now I'm something bigger in this world.

When Leamy finished doling money into my hand this morning, Aylen gestured for him to give more. There's the equivalent of one month's smithy wages, and then some, filling my pocket. "Buy a hat and clean yourself up," Aylen told me.

He's right. If I'm going to be a respected man, I should look the part, so the first thing I do upon entering Uppertown is walk straight into the fanciest shop with hats in the window.

The shopkeeper waits behind his counter, all smiles until I wish him a good morning and he gets a good look at my black eye. "We don't serve Irish," he says.

"Yeah, well I want that one," I say, pointing to a black hat on a shelf behind him.

"There's a hat shop in the middle of Lowertown suited to your kind."

"How much do I owe you?" I grind the words out and slam a fistful of Aylen's money on the counter.

He goggles at the wad of paper money, then passes the hat to me. My face heats as he takes most of the money. My pride has cost me more than I'd expected. But that's okay. Once I'm strutting along Wellington, wearing my beaver felt hat tipped at an angle, I feel as if I were the Shiner King himself. I'm with Peter Aylen now. More money will come my way.

I puzzle over the problem of Clara. There must be something she longs for or needs badly enough that, if I dangle it before her, she'll set aside her loyalty to Johnston and help me. She said fancy things don't matter to her, but I don't believe it. I've seen how my sisters' eyes light up over Aunt Mariah's earbobs. Girls like shiny stuff, though I can't afford any of that.

I wander into a shop that sells sweets the likes of which I've never seen. The scent of peppermint, cinnamon and butterscotch makes my mouth water. A display of chocolates catches my attention. While I make my selections, the shopkeeper comments on my new hat. I choose a single square for myself and six for Clara. I don't want to look impressed as he wraps mine in paper. But I can't help myself when he ties red ribbon around the packet meant for my girl. She'll love it. Suddenly, I'm aware of my callused hands in comparison to his smooth ones, and after I slide payment across the service counter, I draw my hands inside my sleeves.

I enjoy his look of surprise when I pay with paper instead of coin. As I leave, he says, "Watch your footing, sir. The ice is treacherous under the snow."

Once outside and around the corner, I unwrap the single chocolate and pop it into my mouth. Flavour explodes across my tongue and I carefully move the melting square side to side to prolong the pleasure. This is what money and power taste like—bold and sweet. It's what I want for myself and Clara. I have to believe she'll come around. The prospect of explaining the threat of Aylen's men against her is unthinkable.

Tonight, I'll draw her to Johnston's stable. She'll be happy I've returned instead of being away for a few days as I'd predicted. I picture her cheeks flushed over the pleasure of the chocolates. Then maybe we will be together, there in the straw. We are getting married, after all. And if, afterwards, she feels doubly inclined to tell me more of what she's overheard about Johnston's scheme, all the better.

I walk past Johnston's house on the off chance that I might catch her eye. Some of the other house girls along the way are sweeping snow from their masters' front stoops and shaking out carpets. But not Clara. As I squint at the house hoping to see her pass inside a window, I relish how bold I am to openly walk in front of the house of a man who I'm so cleverly undoing.

The soft jingle of sleigh bells alerts me to an oncoming horse, its hoof-falls muted by the snow. Two well-to-do men—the sort that belong in this morning's hat shop—ride on the bench seat with buffalo furs pulled over their laps. One manages the reins and the other hugs a leather case, thin and held fast by a brass clasp, against his chest. As they draw closer, I realize the driver is George Baker. As the sled passes, I look down so the brim of my hat blocks his view of my face. He directs the horse into Johnston's lane.

A morning meeting! Plans for the election must be ramping up. What luck that I'll see Clara tonight to harvest details.

My hands are freezing as I continue on my way. I have a hankering for a hot cup of tea. Think I'll find a high-class establishment, belly up to a nice table, and set Clara's box of chocolates on their clean tablecloth next to my new hat. The waiters will call me *sir*. I'll stay as long as I'm allowed to, then figure out where to spend the rest of my day. It's a long time till dark when I'll see my Clara.

No sooner do I think of her than I spot her near Sappers Bridge. My excitement falters when I see she's stopped to chat with Rory, who stands easily with a bundle of wrought-iron pokers under one arm. Why the hell is she talking to him? They're so deep in conversation that neither of them seems to notice me approaching. Rory places a hand on her shoulder, then when her head bows—he better not be pestering her!—he slides his free arm around her.

Rory flicks a rehearsed grin in my direction. He *has* seen me.

"Hands off my girl," I say evenly.

"Thomas!" Clara, eyes glistening, looks up at me.

"Thank God you're back," Rory says with exaggerated relief. "Your aunt showed up at Mueller's last night. Or is she your mam now? It's a bit confusing. But no matter—she didn't know you'd been fired."

"Where did you sleep last night?" Clara asks, then hesitates. "Is that a new hat?"

I won't tell her I stayed at Aylen's. If she knows I'm mixing with the Shiners, it will be the end of us. And what's all this about Aunt Mariah?

Rory screws his face into a look of nearly convincing concern. "It appears you have two mams, Tommy. By the way, nice shiner."

My agitation flares. "Why did my aunt come to the smithy?"

"Oh, you don't know?" Clara says tearily. "Your family's homestead burned down last night. They've been left with nothing."

The news slams me in the gut.

"They came looking for you—the whole family except for your da. But you were nowhere to be found," Rory says.

"Well, you saw to that," I fire back.

"Oh, and some fellas from the Bytown Rifles want to question you about Michael's death. They dropped by the smithy this morning. I told them everything I know, but they seem quite eager to speak with you."

Clara's jaw drops. "Thomas doesn't have anything to do with that!"

"Murder, more like," Rory says. "That's what the law's calling it."

He wouldn't dare.

"Clara—don't look at me like that! Don't listen to him. It's him that's to blame. He—he started the fight and left me to finish it!"

"You promised me no trouble." Defiance glints in her eyes. If I don't fix this, I'll lose everything.

"By the way," Rory says brightly, "someone's fetching your da. He'll sort things out, being a hero and all."

"He can't come now or he won't get paid!" I reply. The timber boss will penalize Da if he leaves before the season is over. The family needs his wages now more than ever. But if he remains at camp, the family will expect me to give up my own dream and stand in for him. They'll trap me just like they did Aunt Mariah.

Clara speaks up. "Where *did* you stay last night, Thomas? Were you with another girl?"

I may as well give her a dressed-up version of the truth now. It won't be worse than what she's imagining. "I was a houseguest of Mr. Peter Aylen."

"Och," Rory says and crosses himself. "The Shiner King's den of carnal sin and earthly pleasures. Did you leave with your purity intact?"

Clara gasps and Rory's eyes sparkle.

"I had my chance, but I turned it down on account of I'm getting hitched."

Clara jerks her arm away when I reach for her. "I don't believe you," she says. "Were you even hired by Mrs. Johnston to protect the master?"

"Yes," I lie without hesitation. No one knows the whole truth except for me and Aylen's inner circle. And none of them are here to contradict me.

Clara's eyes begin to soften, but then Rory pipes up.

"Don't hurt her more with any more lies." He turns to Clara and speaks with a choirboy innocence. "Tommy's working for the Shiners. He hides out in Mr. Johnston's stable and spies on the house so he can gather information for their gang. They've got it out for the man, though only God knows why."

Wait! How does Rory know what I've been doing?

"Thomas!" Clara cries in disbelief. "I've been a fool—you were never going to marry me!"

"That's not true, Clara. I love you!" I thrust the paper-wrapped chocolates toward her.

As tears roll down her cheeks, she regards my new hat and the red-ribboned package. "I don't want any of this. You used me."

"I meant every word I said, Clara."

"I'm surprised Tommy had the nerve to go back to Johnston's after shooting his poor dog," Rory interjects.

"You did that?" Clara's eyes are wide. I can hear her next words before she says them. "I never want to see you again."

Even though my shooting the dog is true, I'm stung that she'd believe so easily that I could do such a thing.

"Clara, don't go!" I point to Rory. "It wasn't just me! Rory was there smashing Johnston's windows that night."

"I don't know what you're talking about, Tommy," Rory says.

Something clicks in my mind. Why did Hairy Barney call me Tommy? The only person who calls me that is Rory. How did Hairy Barney know that I'd been in the stable with Clara every night? Then it hits me. The figure I'd seen hiding in the shrubs alongside Johnston's house was Rory.

Bastard! I rush at him, knocking him to the ground. I kneel to pin his arms against his sides and put my face close to his. "You've been spying on me and telling Hairy Barney everything. Admit it."

"Stop," Clara shouts. "You're hurting him."

Instead of fighting back, Rory murmurs, "Your sister Elizabeth has been sleeping in my bed. Precious little thing. I don't even mind that she's so young." I ball up my fist and punch him square in the nose. The bone crunches like a dried twig and he screams. Blood gushes from his nostrils.

"Stop," Clara begs. As I stand up, chest heaving, she drops to cradle Rory's head on her lap. His eyes twinkle and he flashes a bloody smile. When I realize the trap he'd set for me, my heart sinks.

It's all over. I've lost my girl and my access to Johnston's plans.

Clara looks at me with such horror that I turn and run, slipping on the hidden ice at Sappers Bridge.

The merchant was right about treachery. It lurks everywhere, disguised as something else.

❧

The other side of the bridge is the familiar territory of downtrodden have-nots. I race along narrowing streets, dodging between sleds and horses. My mind reels. There's been a fire. I have no home. Mam and the girls are at the smithy with Aunt Mariah. And Da could be on his way back. He counted on me and I failed. My family must be hearing ugly stories about me from Rory and Mueller, who'll spare no detail. The Shiners will be hunting for me soon and the law already is. Rory has singlehandedly destroyed me, and on top of that, what he said about two mams scrapes at me. What does he think he knows?

Fear is a fine spur—so is rage.

With lungs searing, I arrive at the worst part of town still carrying the parcel of chocolates and with a pocketful of money. Instead of slowing, I run faster. I'm likely to fall on my arse at any moment, but I don't even care.

I know just how I'll get even with everyone who's hurt me.

There it is—the shanty I remember from yesterday. I pound my fist against the rickety door. The ice that had sealed it shut splinters away when it opens. The black-haired girl appears with an oak club and stares back at me. Her initial apprehension gives way to recognition and then to a look of concern. She lowers the club and for a few seconds we take measure of each other. In this morning light, her eyes shine green. She doesn't complain that she's freezing in her gauzy underthings or that the warmth from her hearth is escaping the shanty. I don't know what a man is supposed to say when he wants to plow a woman for money. Words are trapped inside the jumble of my mind. This girl is where the crossroads of my pain meet, connected as she is to Gleeson, Rory and Aunt Mariah, who stands in place of my family. But she is no Clara.

"I have money," I blurt.

"No charge for virgins."

"I don't take charity."

She opens the door wider. "In that case, you best come inside."

A short time later, I roll from atop her and lie on my back, grinning up at the smoky rafters. I'm so happy I could sing. This is the worst and best day of my life.

"You didn't kiss me," I finally say. Clara always let me kiss her and I didn't pay for it either.

"I don't kiss customers," the girl says.

Her answer relieves me of the worry that I'd done it all wrong. "The name's Peg, by the way."

"I'm . . .

". . . Thomas and you're a blacksmith," she says, sounding pleased with herself. This town is too small at times.

"How is it you know my aunt?"

"We're in business together."

I give Peg a stunned look.

"She's a deep well, that one. A bit odd, but she's got spunk. I like her."

"What kind of business?"

"Medicines for woman troubles. And saltpetre for man troubles. She sells to me and I sell to the other girls. We both take a cut."

Aunt Mariah is skimming Mam's herbs for her own gain. That tickles me. Mam would have a conniption if she knew Auntie and I were consorting with a whore. I laugh and wipe my eyes.

Peg rolls onto her side and props her head against one hand. "Why's that so funny?"

I shake my head at how alike my aunt and I are. Then Rory's words return to me and I'm not laughing anymore.

"I don't plan to be here forever, you know. I'm saving for the future. I'm going to be someone," Peg says.

"You and me both. What's your scheme?"

"You first."

"All right. I'm going to own my own blacksmith shop," I tell her. "I'll be the boss of me."

She sits up suddenly and scans our clothes strewn across the floor. From over the side of the creaking bed, she grabs my new hat and pulls it over her wavy hair. I only have eyes for her bare breasts.

"Guess my dream," she says.

I'm lost. "Point man on a riverboat?"

"Nooo. I'm going to own a milliner shop and make hats for rich women. Or maybe a seamstress shop. I'll go to a new town far from here. All the rich ladies will want my hats and dresses. Men say a woman can't be a businessman, but I'll prove them all wrong. I'll be somebody, I will."

"You already are a somebody," I say.

Peg tears up and I like that I can affect her that way. "We're both someone, then," she says, her voice wavering slightly.

My heart aches unexpectedly. "Two somebodies who are nobodies, for right now," I say.

"For right now," she repeats wistfully. "So, why aren't you working today?"

"Got fired. Long story."

"Life's shit sometimes. The girl I was sharing this place with took off last week and left me holding the bag."

"I know what that's like."

"Who let you down?"

I nearly tell her but decide against it. "Aren't you Gleeson's woman?"

Peg huffs. "Nah, he fancies my roommate. They deserve each other."

"And Rory. You know him?" When she shrugs and returns a blank look, I'm relieved. "He's Hairy Barney's skinny shadow."

"Ach!" She rolls her eyes. "He drools after me like a puppy. But I wouldn't take his money if he was the last lad on earth and I was down to my final shilling. Something's not right with that weasel."

"You've got that straight," I say.

She hugs my hat against her breasts. "When you landed at my door, you were fired up like something was chasing you."

I want to tell Peg everything. She's not at all what I thought she'd be. But still . . .

"There's a whole bunch of somebodies getting in the way of my dreams," I finally tell her. "And I gotta fix that—for me and for some other folks feeling let down by me."

Peg sets my hat aside and tenderly kisses my collarbone. And then my jaw. She pulls away and looks at me and I feel, all at once, like we've known each other a long time.

Lying on Peg's stained mattress with straw leaking through the sides, I tell her everything about my family, the Shiners and what Rory did to me. We stay wrapped together in her frayed blanket for hours. I describe Clara as a friend, that's all. Regardless of her line of work, after what I've just done with Peg, it wouldn't feel right to say more about another girl.

But Peg pinches my shoulder and laughs. "No man gets upset over a woman unless she's more than a friend." She can sniff out a lie from a mile away.

"So, you got to find out how many men Johnston is bringing to Bytown and what their names are?"

"That's the gist of it. Aylen will pay me when I deliver. I'll keep moving up in the world, and everybody who doubted me can eat crow."

"But?" she says, raising her brows. "There's always a *but*."

"But Johnston's maid won't speak to me anymore, so I don't know how I'm going to get the information." Or save her from being harassed or worse by Aylen's men. God only knows how far they'll take things. The thought sickens me.

"There's ways around that problem," Peg says.

"I can't be running around town asking questions right now. My family will be hunting me down." And the law too, but instinct tells me that's the one thing not to mention to Peg. "And Johnston will turn me in if he recognizes me from the night we busted up his place."

"Like I said, there's other ways. Each of those men coming to town will have a horse, right?" She waits for me to catch up to her logic.

Of course they will. They're travelling here from all across Nepean Township. Voters from outside Bytown will need overnight lodgings and secure stables for their horses and sleds. At last some hope. I'm grinning so hard my face hurts. She is too.

"Promise me fifty percent of Aylen's reward," Peg says. "I know people working at every hotel and livery in Bytown, and can tap them for the information. And you can hide out here until this whole thing is over."

"There's no way I'm giving up half of my reward. I put a lot of hours into planning this just right and I took a few good beatings for it too."

"All right, then," she says, "thirty percent."

"Twenty," I reply.

"Twenty percent and whatever's in that box tied with red ribbon."

"Deal." We shake on it.

Peg scampers out of bed wearing nothing but my hat and then pulls back the raggedy curtain separating us from the rest of the shanty to fetch the parcel. On her way back to me, she undoes the ribbon and folds back the paper to see what's inside. I've never seen a naked girl jump up and down before, but it's worth the price of those chocolates to see it now.

She settles back on the bed and offers me one. While I'm lost in the flavour, eyes closed, she says, "I would have agreed to fifteen percent."

I finish my chocolate and tell her, "That's grand. I was willing to give you twenty-five."

Peg swings a pillow at my head. Then offers me another chocolate.

22

SEAMUS

A crackle of splintering wood, followed by perfect stillness as I wait for the tree to give way. I never tire of the chain reaction I trigger by hacking into a white pine nearly twenty times my height and with a girth nearly three times my arm span. It's evidence that I can, on occasion, exert my will in this world.

The second axeman tips his head back and squints upward into the branches. Our patience is rewarded by the low groan of yielding wood. The tree shudders and together we shout, "Timber!" Then we scramble well back, knowing what will come next.

The tree leans away from us and sheers from the stump. Sharp pops precede the snapping of limbs on neighbouring pines as the mammoth trunk plummets to the ground. A thundering impact against the frozen earth sends a cloud of powdery snow into the air.

This is the sort of day a man lives for. From the treetops to the seat of God, blue sky stretches uninterrupted. We started work as the sun began to rise. The afternoon's just begun and our gang of five—the other axeman and me, plus the liner and hewer fellas squaring the logs and the skidder who hauls them away—has already brought down four pines and squared three. Every man sets about his work with focus.

There's a rhythm to the axe swings of felling gangs scattered through the woods. The strokes of blades, close by and distant, come together in a strange chorus of high or low notes, depending on the breadth of the trees they smite. I can tell which job a man's doing by the measured beat of two men felling pine, the woodpecker taps of blades skinning bark or scoring logs in preparation for the hewer's broad axe.

The blazed trunk of another white pine towers before me. There's no question about what needs doing. The other axeman sets off to top the newly fallen pine while I start chopping this new one. With every swing, the blade of my felling axe bites into the trunk as chunks of bark and pine spit back at me. I'll keep chipping at this beast until it weakens and topples too. Then I'll continue to the next one and do it all over again. Here everything is that simple: no need to walk on eggshells around two women always ready to pounce.

An entire day can pass without my speaking a word to anyone, and that suits me fine.

Thirty feet away from where I'm standing, two of our men stand atop a fallen white pine, skinning bark and scoring the log's roundness in preparation for its soon-to-be squared edges.

A funny thought occurs to me. Biddy would make a great hewer; she lives to measure and perfect things. The woman's been trying to square me since we first met, but I'm round and that's all there is to it. I used to speak my mind, but I've lost the willingness to do so, given my opinions never fall in a neutral middle ground between my wife and sister-in-law. Either Biddy accuses me of siding against her, or Mariah turns a cold shoulder to me for days. If Biddy tried to boss this camp with the same controlling stranglehold she exerts on our family, the men would revolt. She needs to learn that the only road to gaining compliance isn't through wearing down a man. At least Mariah understands that.

Dying light signals the day's end. The hewer is the most senior man among us. When he begins to gather his things, the rest of us follow suit. One of our men issues a sharp whistle that is answered by the rallying cries of other felling gangs spread throughout the woods. It's a two-and-a-half-mile walk back to the camboose shanty where a hot meal and a warm fire await us, and we're eager to get there.

I don't have much to carry, just the felling axe that rests across one shoulder. It weighs only six or seven pounds, but by the end of each day it bears down on me like a sledgehammer. My clothes are damp with sweat and, as we walk, I'm soon chilled to the bone, even wearing everything I own: long underwear under my trousers, three pairs of wool socks, three shirts—including the one Mariah sewed for me—and a coat.

Since leaving home, I've let myself think of her on occasion. She's a good woman and true to her word. There's lots of others who, in her situation, would have left us by now. She could have run off with Thomas, passed herself off as a widow and started a life with someone new. Biddy says no man would have her with that scarred face. I disagree. She's got a quality that makes a man see past that once he knows her.

Ahead of me, men make jokes about the bull boss and the way he lords over us day to day, keeping track of what gets done. I've lived with worse. If you pull your weight, he'll leave you be. That's worth something.

Our liner turns around and hollers, "Seamus, don't be an old woman." He waves an arm for me to catch up.

"In a minute," I tell him. I savour moments of solitude when I can find them.

Soon they're laughing about something new and, to my relief, they forget about me.

If not for having to get crops in the ground next spring, I'd do the river run to Montreal and only return to Bytown in May. What man wouldn't want to see more of the world, even if only from the corner of a raft? As long as I get home before the baby comes, Biddy might forgive my long absence in favour of the extra money I'd earn. I could buy a pair of sheep like she's always wanted, and assuming our cow survives the winter, I could afford stud fees for a neighbour's bull. There'd be a new calf next spring.

The more I think on it, the better the idea of a river run sounds. Mariah's always worked alongside me, good as any man. If I send word, Thomas could come home weekends and help with the plowing. The responsibility would make a man of our son, get him out of Bytown and away from the riffraff for short spells. Mariah could spend time alone with him, which might cure her of this fool notion about telling him the truth. Before summer, I'd be home to take over. The three of us could work the field. Together.

Biddy won't like it, not one bit. But with the burden of a new baby on the way, I can make my argument stick.

Her being pregnant feels like a trap, but maybe I've got it all wrong. Maybe the new baby will be the answer to some of my trouble—especially if it's a son. I'd finally feel like I'd squared things up with Biddy. Maybe she'd be gentler once she had a son of her own. Yes, a boy could set things right, and perhaps remove the target from Mariah's back. Biddy would need Mariah all the more while the child is young, so there'd be no more talk about getting rid of her.

Soft grey light pushes all blue from the sky as we trudge along the road, exhausted. More men emerge from between white pines to join the snow-crunching footfall of our procession. Halfway to camp, I turn toward a sharp whistle from behind me. I recognize Patrick Newell's horse before I even see him walking next to it with the reins hanging loosely from one hand. Behind them, dual sledges connected by heavy chains drag along the ice.

I wait for Patrick to catch up, then we walk together.

"Saw some deer tracks along the edge of a clearing just north of where we've been cutting," he tells me. "Me and some of the other fellas are going to head back there on Sunday. Some venison would be nice, eh?"

"No argument there," I reply.

"You in?"

"Yeah, sure. I'll come along."

"The tracks head east toward the river."

"We should go deeper in the woods at first light to where they're bedding. Mariah and I got a nice buck that way in the fall."

"Mariah and you?" Patrick says thoughtfully, then pauses. "Doesn't it upset Biddy? You and her sister alone in the woods?"

"Nah," I lie. "She don't mind at all."

"Hmm. Mariah *is* a fine woman." There's a question at the end of Patrick's statement, but he doesn't ask it.

I'm glad it's getting dark so Patrick can't see my face redden.

When he asks me a short time later if I've heard about the Shiners cutting trees from our camp owner's timber limits, I shake my head. He retells what he's heard, but I'm distracted by thoughts of Mariah.

For years, I've refused to think about the afternoon we made Thomas back home on the riverbank. We were just kids and I was half out of my mind with grief over Da. Even with her scars, it was to her I turned for solace, not Biddy. But I've made my bed with Biddy and I must lie in it, no matter how thorny. I swore an oath before God and man. *Till death do us part.*

Strains of someone tuning a fiddle cut through the night: we're close to camp. Although my stomach rumbles and the warmth of the camboose calls out to me, I follow Patrick to help unhitch and stable the horse inside the lantern-lit shed. A slight figure stands backlit in the doorway. As we get closer, Patrick hands me the reins and races toward him.

"Liam?" he calls out.

"Yes, Da."

Something terrible has happened for Liam to travel this far.

I bring the horse to a halt and wait.

Patrick holds the boy's shoulders. I can just glimpse Liam's face. His lips are moving. He stops speaking and Patrick's hands drop to his sides.

My first thought is that something's happened to Roweena or the children.

Liam's gaze travels to me, and then Patrick's stricken face turns slowly in my direction. I steel myself to withstand his grief.

"Seamus . . ." There's pity—not anguish—in his tone. Liam isn't here for Patrick. Roweena is fine.

The boy carries bad news for me.

23

THOMAS

I n the middle of the night, a loud bang wakes us. It's close enough that the windowpanes rattle and light flashes through spaces between the shutters. Peg and I run to the door and fling it wide.

Along the shanty row, neighbours lean outside to watch bright-orange flames shooting upward into the night sky to the east. Men race in the direction of the blast, some already dressed and others pulling coats on as they go.

The fire will spread as it must have at our homestead. There'll be injured people needing help. I think of Da saving Aunt Mariah from the Flynns and begin to fidget. I missed the chance to rescue Mam and the girls—and her too. My fists are clenching when I feel Peg grip my arm.

"You best leave the helping to others, Thomas."

Truth is a bitter pill, but she's right. All sorts will be nosing around the fire. I can neither risk being seen by Da, if he's got back to town, nor being captured by lawmen. Flames jutting above the rooftops cast an eerie glow. We close the door against the cold and stand at the front window. Peg shivers and rests her head on my shoulder. Together we watch the devilish dance of light against dark.

It's not easy being cooped up here while others take action. If I don't soon do something useful during daylight hours, I'll lose my damned mind.

Peg takes my hand and tugs me toward the bed. I remain rooted where I stand and, after a few steps, only our fingertips are touching. And then they're not. She turns and sends me a smile that beckons me to follow.

Soon after sunrise, news trickles to our street. The explosion happened behind the Victoria Hotel in Lowertown. I smell a revenge story. Since a run-in between the owner of the hotel and one of the Shiner gang, rumours have been spreading that the Shiners want to show the owner who's boss in this town. Then Peg returns from the market at midmorning with a story so shocking I can barely believe it.

Hairy Barney blew himself to smithereens last night. The Victoria was unharmed.

"One boot—with his foot still inside it—landed dead centre of that hellish mess," Peg says. She sits across the table sewing buttons onto a vest she's making for me. "If not for a shoemaker coming by and recognizing the boot as one he'd recently sold to Barney, no one would have realized it was him scattered around the place."

I picture bits of Hairy Barney being flung toward the stars. By the time we'd scrambled to the door last night, his pink mist was already speckling the snow. If circumstances had shifted slightly and I'd been sent to light the fuse, it would have been my leavings the crows picked over at first light. Pubs would have been filled with men shaking their heads over what a fool I'd been.

There are many ways for a man to blow up. I wonder if I'm being careful enough.

"Penny for your thoughts," Peg says and bites off a thread. She still won't kiss me on the lips, but I'm her only man. I asked her and she told me so. Since striking our bargain, she sews in every spare moment. Her rainy-day money and what her sewing fetches somehow keeps us fed and a roof over our heads, since I'm low on cash. But I find it hard watching her work for our keep while I do nothing.

"Just thinking of you," I tell her.

Her eyes flash mischief as she wets the thread with her tongue, and suddenly I'm thinking of her, wishing I was that thread.

"Now you're thinking of me, Thomas O'Dougherty, but you weren't earlier. You might have fooled the Virgin Clara, but I know better." She threads the needle and continues her work.

I wish Peg would stop poking fun at Clara, but how can I complain when she's sewing handsome clothes for me? Eventually I'll be free during the day to venture outside the shanty, and she says that I need to clean up for people to take me seriously. But I think she wants to show off her skills too. *Friends*, as she calls her customers, have left pieces of clothing behind. She tears out seams and cuts the fabric to make new things—a coat becomes two vests, a tie becomes lining for a pocket, and a torn bedsheet a shirt. Whatever else is needed, she liberates from drunken patrons of Uppertown taverns.

"Since I'm on your mind," Peg says, "it'd be nice if you figured out how to make me howl next time we knock boots. Women need that too, you know."

That's a kick in the teeth. What's all her moaning been about?

"The good book says it's better to give than to receive. And Thomas, I'm ready to receive."

I've been giving it all I got and working up a good sweat doing it. "Sorry, Peg. I thought . . ."

"It's a beginner mistake. Easily fixed if your heart's in it."

Embarrassment heats my face. I don't want to be a beginner at anything, least of all screwing. Maybe I can ask one of Aylen's Montreal whores what she's talking about.

She looks up and doesn't speak again until my eyes focus on her. "I overheard some fellas say they saw Barney roll a barrel of gunpowder behind the Victoria Hotel. Dumb ox sat on it to enjoy a good pipe. He lit a match and blew himself to kingdom come."

I wonder where this leaves Rory. With Hairy Barney out of the picture, he'll be conniving to fasten himself to a new higher-up. He needs to be dealt with, but I have no idea how.

Peg smooths my vest on the table and gestures to where the shirt she finished yesterday hangs from a wall hook. "Here you go, fancy man. Put those on."

I undress and pull the new shirt over my head. It's the nicest I've ever worn, and the vest with all its tiny buttons makes me feel like a rich man. Peg turns me around and examines her handiwork. She grabs my new hat and plunks it on my head.

"Pleased to meet you, Mr. O'Dougherty," she says with a curtsy. "'Tis a fine blacksmith shop you run here. Four apprentices, I see. Business must be good."

I lift her from the floor and spin her around until she begs me to put her down. After I kiss her forehead, her cheeks turn pink and she playfully shoves me away.

"Forgetting a debt, sir, doesn't pay it. Come round my shop later and square up your account." On her way to the hearth, she grins over one shoulder and waggles her brows. Then she tips her head back and laughs the most boisterous laugh in the world.

I'd smile longer at her jest if I weren't running out of money. While I'm caged here during the day, Peg winds through inns and taverns collecting gossip and questioning the working class. Chambermaids and livery workers tell her which Orangemen supporters have made advance arrangements for overnight stays and stabling horses on the night of the township council vote. It takes coin to loosen lips, so most of the money Aylen gives me in exchange for names is spent paying off our network of spies.

GWEN TUINMAN

Many nights under cover of darkness, I've met him at another of his houses closer to town to pass on the names of would-be voters. I've seen impatience building in him and Leamy. They want more names and faster, but I can only tell them what I'm capable of memorizing at one go. If Peg or I could read and write, I'd supply him with a complete list.

As she ladles water into a pot simmering on the fire, I change back into my old shirt. "Peg, I've been thinking about Aylen. Once he gains his seat on the township council, he'll reward me—*us*, I mean."

"And?" She wraps one hand in a rag and returns the hot lid to the pot.

"There's only two weeks left until the election. I've got to bring him information so impressive that if he uses it to his advantage, he's guaranteed to fill every council seat with a Shiner. If he gains control of the entire township, he'll fill our pockets with money. Maybe he'll even award us some land."

Peg's face lights up. "Go on."

"I'm going back to Johnston's house."

"To see Clara?" she says. Her jealous tone warms me.

I shake my head and her expression softens. "Before I came here that first day, I saw two men in a sleigh turning onto Johnston's lane. The first was George Baker, who I've told you about. Baker's passenger was holding a leather case with a brass clasp. He must have been delivering important papers. If I search Johnston's house and find them for Aylen . . ."

"One problem with that plan, mister. How will you know if you've found something good? You can't read."

"Neither can you!"

Peg thrusts her chin out. "Well, that's where you're wrong."

"You can read?"

"A little. And I know my numbers. Some." Hands on hips, she says, "I'm coming with you."

"Absolutely not. I'll go on my own and see what I can find. It's Sunday and everyone will be at church. Even Clara attends mass at

Notre Dame in Lowertown. The Johnstons take a cold meal on the sabbath, so she's free to go out."

"You need me," Peg insists.

"I'm better on my own."

"My future depends on the outcome of this plan as much as yours does," she says. "I won't be left behind."

Her heels are dug in. "Well, you'll have to listen and do as I say."

"Right. Sit down," she says, pointing at the stump seat she'd previously occupied.

"What for?"

"If you're going to pass as a gentleman, you need a haircut."

"I thought you were angry with me?"

"I am," she says, picking up her sewing shears.

The church bells have stopped ringing, which means the sermons are starting. Peg and I travel as many backstreets as possible to get to Johnston's house. Once we reach Wellington, I tuck her hand in the crook of my elbow. One of the other working girls lent her a wool cloak and a bonnet; I'm wearing my new clothes. Together we look like a respectable couple.

By now, the Johnstons are sitting smug in their church pew and dropping extra coins in the collection plate to help poor sods like me and Peg.

Clara is probably at her church lighting a candle for her gran. Maybe she'll pray for my soul, or more likely for Rory's. The thought of his hands on her sickens me, despite all I do with Peg.

Peg's hand tightens on my arm. Her eyes say, *I know you're thinking about Clara.* The woman is like a hound who's picked up a scent. How she does it is beyond me.

In no time at all, we're hurrying along the cedar hedge beside Johnston's house. Fresh tracks lead from the back door to the stable. Patch recognizes me from a distance and wags his tail hard enough to snap it off in this cold weather. I fish part of a biscuit from my pocket and give it to Peg so she can feed him while I pick the lock on the back door. The tumblers click softly, then we go inside and close the door behind us.

Peg looks around the kitchen and sucks in her breath. "Sweet mother of—"

I raise a finger to silence her. We listen closely, but the only sound is the *thunk-thunk* of a clock somewhere in the house. Once I'm sure no one's home, I set off for the front of the house in search of Johnston's study. Clara told me about it. All the rich buggers have one.

I peer into the dining room. Empty. To my left is the door to the pantry where Clara hid me the first night we met. I glimpse her small bed in the corner. No more sleeping on a pallet for her. Above Clara's pillow the wire daisy I made hangs from the wall by the hair ribbon I gave her. What does that mean?

"This little beauty is going home with me," Peg says. I turn to see her tucking a china teacup inside her cloak.

"Put it back!" I won't see Clara lose her job over a missing cup.

Peg's brows lift and she points to oranges lined up on the window-sill. She pulls one of Annie's pouty faces and says, "Just one? There's cloves stuck in them!" When I don't give in, she abandons the oranges and returns the cup to its shelf, then follows me along the hall that leads to the front half of the ground floor. We find Johnston's study across from the parlour.

I don't belong here. Floor-to-ceiling shelves around the room are packed with books that Clara probably dusts every week. There are stacks of newspapers too. A painting of a man who looks much like Johnston, but older, hangs on the wall. His father? I imagine Johnston sitting behind his desk and looking up at it while smoking his pipe. I picture him puffing smoke while he dreams up new ways to undermine Peter Aylen's efforts to free our Irish brethren from the tyranny of the gentry. I want to pull every book from the shelves and fling them across the room.

"This could be our life soon," Peg says brightly.

I turn to find her leaning back in Johnston's chair with the heels of her scuffed boots resting on his desk, her ankles crossed. Across her chest, she holds the leather case and points to its brass clasp.

I laugh in utter disbelief.

"Found it right here in the bottom drawer. Men have no imagination." She opens the flap and removes some papers.

"What do they say?" I look over her shoulder and marvel at the columns of gibberish. She puffs out her cheeks and says, "Letter vee, oh . . ."

"Hurry!"

"Don't rush me." She pauses for a second. "V-v-v. O-o-o. T-t . . ."

"Vote?"

"Voters," Peg says triumphantly. "L-l. Is-is . . ."

"Voters list. You found the voters list?" I'm gobsmacked. "You know what this means, Peg? We're set, you and I. These papers change everything."

"We'll have our new lives." A mischievous look smoulders in Peg's eyes and she lowers her bonnet.

"More than that," I say. Thoughts of revenge taken on Johnston set my below-the-belt parts to stirring. I take the case from Peg's hands and toss it onto the desk. "We're going to cut the legs from under this Orangeman."

Peg stands and takes my face in her hands, then presses her mouth, soft and wanting, against mine. She tastes peppery and sweet all at once. We exchange knowing smiles. A kiss on the mouth confirms she's mine and no one else's. Hungrily, I kiss her back. My pulse bangs inside my ears.

"And," I add, "from under the rich bastards that look down their noses at us."

I groan when she roughly unfastens my britches. She works her skirt above her waist and rests her bare bottom on Johnston's desk, then wraps her stockinged legs around my waist.

"And I'll charge a handsome price to dress their rich wives in silk and taffeta." She squeezes me tight and I'm inside her. I lose track of time, and our plans for the future, as our bodies buck against each other on that desk. I'm nearing a perfect explosion when Peg's eyes open wide and she sucks in her breath.

"Stop, stop, stop," she says. Now I'm wide-eyed too.

"D'you hear that?" she whispers.

I shake my head. But then I hear the rattle of the back door.

Peg and I scramble apart. While I struggle to button my britches, she's already opening the window behind Johnston's chair. She lands in the snow outside and by the time I'm dressed, she's disappeared. Peg has left me to be caught red-handed. *Eejit!* I should have known better than to trust her.

"Hello? Is someone here?"

It's Clara!

Oh no. I'd rather it was Johnston and I was about to be shot. Floorboards creak along the hallway.

"Mr. Johnston?" Clara's voice is hesitant. I want to take the voters list and run, but if I make a sound, she'll hasten into the room thinking her master has returned early, and then I'm done for. I cannot abide disappointing her again.

Bang, bang, bang! Silence, then more pounding at the back door.

"Coming," Clara sings out. What a relief when her voice travels away from the study. I ease the voters list from the case, roll it up and tuck it inside my coat.

The back door rattles open. "Good day to you," Clara says.

"A good day for some, miss." Peg's voice is unmistakable. What a woman! She's buying me time. "I pray you can open your Christian heart," she says, breaking into sobs convincingly. "My husband's run off and left me with a pair of youngsters. I haven't anything to feed them."

"Poor dear, come and sit by the fire," Clara tells her. "I'm sure we can spare something for your little ones."

I return the empty leather case to the drawer Peg took it from. If I leave everything as I found it, Johnston will think he misplaced the voters list and Aylen will have the advantage of surprise. From my pants pocket, I remove a piece of red ribbon saved from the package of chocolates I bought days earlier for Clara. For a moment, I think about leaving it in on a bookshelf, somewhere Clara might discover it. Instead, I push the ribbon back into my pocket.

Once through the window, I slowly lower the sash. No one's around, so I walk to the road and wait behind some cedars.

It's not long before Peg comes strolling toward me, munching an apple and swinging a plump sack with her free hand. She's ditched her bonnet and messed up her hair to look down and out. I'm such a shit for doubting her loyalty earlier. When she's close enough, I whistle like a snow bunting, as Aunt Mariah taught me. Peg wades through the snow to join me.

"Well done, little bird. Apple?" She offers me a bite of the half-eaten fruit.

"You were brilliant!" I say.

"I was. Got the list?"

"You bet," I tell her, then reach for the sack. Inside there's a half loaf of bread, four hard-boiled eggs, a slab of fruit cake, some carrots and potatoes. I hang the sack from a bough and break off a piece of cake. Of all Clara's cakes, this one's like nothing I've ever tasted—all sugary with bursts of dried fruit.

GWEN TUINMAN

"So, you're sure about Aylen paying up?"

My mouth is so full with cake all I can do is nod.

"Men in power are selfish, you know. They'll use you up until you're of no further use, then toss you out."

"That's not the case here. Aylen is for the people. He takes from the rich to benefit his countrymen—not himself."

"I hope you're right." She takes one last bite of the apple and pitches the core into the bushes.

"We best get out of here. I'll carry on to Aylen's right now," I say. "He's back at the farm, rather than in town, so I can't dally."

Peg tucks the sack under one arm. "Your Clara is a fine one. We had a good chat. She even sat with her arm around my shoulder. My make-believe *husband* ran out on me and it seems her betrothed ran out on her. We both chose liars."

I wince at Peg finding out I'd asked Clara to marry me.

Peg laughs at my discomfort. "But I don't think her man is a liar. I think he's a good storyteller and that sometimes stories need telling if we're to get what we want in this world."

"But once you and I have what we want—my smithy, your sewing shop—there'll be no need for stories and lies. We can live like good honest folks."

"Right, but for now . . ." Peg winks and pulls two clove-studded oranges from under her cloak, then holds them on either side of her broad smile. "One for you. One for me."

I can't help grinning. We're peas in a pod, the two of us.

She tucks the oranges away and steps in to kiss me goodbye. When she holds me in a tight hug, I catch a whiff of Clara's clean soap smell.

"I'll see you later," Peg says and pulls away. "Sewing awaits and there'll be soup over the fire when you get back."

"Very good," I tell her. She seems pleased as she sets off. I stand up my coat collar, raise my wool scarf to cover my mouth, and pull my hat as low as possible. There aren't many travellers on the road today, but I can't risk being recognized. Several minutes into my walk, I can still smell Clara's soap.

I try to chase Clara away with thoughts of the Shiners and the reward I'll reap when I put the voters list in Aylen's hands. But she won't leave. She hung the wire daisy from my ribbon. Is it possible Clara still loves me? Well, I don't love her. I can't. I'm with Peg now. She understands me. I don't need a religious woman who makes me feel guilty for chasing my dream, a woman who clobbers me with the Bible and all the *thou shalts* and *shalt nots*.

I turn off Richmond Road and cross Aylen's land and its familiar ridges of frozen earth tufted with dead grass. The homestead should be visible soon. I'm proud to be associated with the likes of Aylen. He is a visionary. He and his army of Shiners will undermine every rich Brit's and Scot's attempt to re-create the hold they've had for generations over the Irish. Aylen even helps push French Canadian timbermen aside to make way for Irish workers. He truly is a selfless man of the people, a leader who offers feast and women to his lonely and hungry men.

From a distance, I see two figures shovelling snow from Aylen's rooftop. A cold wind picks up from the north and gusts drive swirling snow across the field. In still moments, fiddle music rolls through the air to meet me. Once I leave the uneven ground behind, guards move to either side of Aylen's cabin door and wait there. No matter how many times I report in, I'm sickened by nerves.

"Yer back," says the guard who now smokes my pipe.

"Aylen's expecting me," I say, trying to sound confident. Inside people clap and stomp in time to music. A woman shrieks happily and glass breaks.

The guard eyes me for a moment, then opens the door. There's barely room for me to squeeze inside among the celebrating men and the whores Aylen has brought in from Montreal. One much older than Peg winds her way toward me, pointing at me and then at herself. In slurred English, she says, "You, me—make some fun, yeah?"

"I need to see Peter Aylen," I yell over the music. "It's important."

She turns to a man next to me. "Some fun?" she asks.

As I look around the room, trying to spot Aylen, a sharp whistle sounds. All eyes turn to Leamy, standing halfway up the stairs and flanked by two bare-shouldered women. "We're here to bid farewell to our friend, Hairy Barney. Where's Peter at?"

Across the room, men lift Aylen onto their shoulders. He dips a hand into the crowd and brings it back up, holding a glass of whiskey.

"To Barney," Aylen says. "He died as he lived. Loud as hell! Men who love danger will perish. But what a way to go!"

Cheers rise around the room. "To Hairy Barney," repeated over and over. Then the crowd erupts in laughter and applause. I'm pushing my way across the room.

"Where you goin', kid?" someone asks.

"To see Aylen. It's urgent."

Music kicks up and I'm lifted from my feet and passed hand over hand above the heads of the crowd. I manage to take the folded-up papers from inside my coat and stretch them forward to Aylen's outstretched hand.

"What is it?" he says and takes a drink. There's irritation in his voice.

"The voting list, sir. For the township council election."

Aylen skims the first page, then looks sharply upward.

Leamy has muscled his way over to us and demands, "How'd you get that?"

The pairs of hands holding me up begin to shift. "I took it from Johnston's study. Sirs."

For a long moment neither man speaks, and then Aylen's face splits into laughter. He waves my papers overhead and toasts the rafters.

"This election is in the bag, boys!" Whistles and cheers are deafening. "A bottle for O'Dougherty!"

But it's not a bottle I want. It's money, for me and Peg.

Someone else shouts, "Now we know which heads to knock together." Another voice adds, "There'll be a few less Orangemen voting this year! Hoo hoo!"

"Mr. Aylen!" I'm lowered to the floor and jostled by men who've begun dancing with each other. I'm quickly swallowed up by the surge, my voice lost.

In the small hours of the morning I awake on the cabin floor with my head thudding, nearly buried among the bodies of people sleeping where they dropped the night before. My mouth is parched and I desperately need to piss. I lift someone's arm from my shoulder and draw my left leg from beneath a woman who's lying across it. My foot is all pins and needles when I stand up, which causes me to nearly stumble over a tangle of snoring Shiners on my way to the door. Outside, a different man stands guard. He barely pays me any notice. Around the corner of the cabin, I let loose my stream. The air is still and the scent of pipe smoke reaches me. Funny how smells and sounds travel so clearly late at night. I recognize Aylen and Leamy's hushed voices coming from the back of the cabin.

"So, we have potential buyers for the two hundred and fifty acres in Nepean?" Aylen says.

"Yes, they're interested. It's a good time to sell," Leamy answers.

"Hmm." Aylen pauses. "See how high they're willing to go." Silence again.

"Things are lining up in Aylmer," Leamy says. "Still good acreage to be had. Some on the waterfront."

"Lower Canada and a clean slate will be good for both of us. We've made decent money here. We should be ready to pick up stakes and clear out if things get messy."

Things go quiet. I smell more pipe smoke, and skulk back to the cabin when they go on to talk of other things.

Inside I search for an empty space and lie down, but sleep won't come.

For the rest of the night, I study the rafters. Aylen—who I've pinned every hope on—is leaving. He's not the hero I believed him to be. Or am I leaping to conclusions like a gossipy fishmonger?

He could be planning to take the Shiners along with him to share in these new opportunities. Aylen must have his people's best interest at heart, or why would he be so set on himself and Shiners winning town council seats?

Yes, that must be the case. If not, I've blown myself up as surely as Hairy Barney has.

24

MARIAH

A week and one day after the fire, I'm still sheltering at the black-smith shop. Mueller doesn't much like it, but he allows me to muck out his stable and care for the horses in exchange for food and a place to lay my head. But next week, when his new apprentices arrive, I must leave. God only knows what I'll do then. Biddy and the children are safe at Roweena Newell's cabin in Corktown, but I've no wish to be among them.

I share the loft with Rory. My first day on my own here, I awoke with a start. An ear he must have sliced from the wolf I killed lay on the pillow, inches from my nose. Rory's ability to catch me unawares fails to raise my opinion of him. He's claimed Thomas's bed next to the warmth of the stove while I sleep on the bottom bunk that belonged to the murdered apprentice. To block my view of Rory, I curtain myself behind horse blankets tucked under the edges of the straw tick over-head. The weasel's steady breathing in the dark is unjust. Tears wet my thin pillow nightly while I pray for Thomas's safety and that I'll see him soon. Hopefully God still recognizes my voice.

Desperation returns all of us to the Father, sooner or later.

Mostly, I lie awake thumbing the soft wolf ear like a Catholic's rosary and reliving all the moments in which I've failed my son and Seamus. I picture Biddy, where I last saw her six days ago, laid out on the floor in front of Roweena Newell's fireplace—and with the flour tin peeking out from the blankets. The vision of my sister's face the night of the fire is seared in my mind.

She won't let anyone pull back the cloth I'd earlier laid over her wound so it can be treated. Guilt holds me back from visiting her again as a good sister would. The longer I stay away, the more impossible it becomes to see her again.

When I think of my earbobs in the pocket of that burly Frenchman, I feel sick. Benoît. I hate him and his brother. They're miles away from me now at the Sinclair camp on Round Lake. Little good it does me to know this. They may as well be on the other side of the world.

This morning, I rise while it's still dark, tuck the wolf ear inside my boot for good luck and head downstairs through the smithy to the stable door behind the forge. All three stalls are occupied. The demand to board horses increases with all the Christmas travellers passing through Bytown, and there's to be some election brouhaha in the first few days of the new year. Out-of-towners have already written Mueller about keeping their horses here.

I unlatch the plank door and it swings open easily. There's something familiar and comforting about a stable in the half light that returns me to childhood mornings when I helped Da at the Harrises' stable. Maybe Mueller will let me continue to work for food and a place to sleep in the straw. I'd be off the street at least; vagrant women are arrested or worse.

Of the horses staying here this week, my favourite is a dappled grey stallion in the centre stall. He reminds me of Lord Harris's horse, which Da used to shoe back home. I nickname him Rainy because his coat resembles water droplets splashed against a glass pane. His liquid eyes are trained on me as if he's been awaiting my arrival. I stroke his nose and press my forehead against his, and his warmth and steady breathing lull me. I don't think of fires. I think of the endless green of County Cork, the song of water splashing along our river and the kindness in my da's eyes.

I wish there was no poverty. I wish cruel tongues could be stilled. I wish Da could have been his own man. Then I might have become a different woman.

Dawn breaks and Mrs. Mueller arrives with breakfast—potato soup, which Rory and I hastily devour. The forge is soon lit and work begins. I put a halter on the bay mare in the first stall and tether her to a wrought-iron ring on the far wall. While I'm spreading fresh straw in her stall, I hear the smithy's front door open, then bang shut. My attention is captured not by the sound that follows, but by its absence. Usually Mr. Mueller shouts a welcome over the puffing bellows and clanging hammers. This time, the hammers have stilled and there is only the hushed murmur of secretive talk. I strain my ears to hear it.

Most of the words come from a commanding Irish voice deeper than Mr. Mueller's.

The horse closest to me nickers but quiets when I scratch his forehead. "Check the loft," that voice now says clearly.

My alarm is instant. This has something to do with Thomas. I know it. More than one set of boots thump up the stairs.

I creep to the door that opens into the smithy to listen. From here I can see only a sliver of the stairs. Floorboards creak above me in the loft, then dust sifts from between the planks and onto the straw pile.

Rainy pricks up his ears and watches me from over his stall gate. I understand why Da spent his life with horses. Their dark eyes are like wells you can keep looking into and never see the bottom. In that split second of calm, I decide that doing nothing isn't an option. I must get a measure of this situation, and it begins with seeing who the deep voice belongs to.

I scoop oats from the bin behind me and fill my pockets. Then I take a deep breath and walk past the open door to where the mare waits, shifting her weight from hoof to hoof. She eagerly munches oats from my hand while I steal glances into the blacksmith shop. Mr. Mueller and Rory stand facing the street. Before them is a gaunt man with a pointy chin and a nose like a harrow blade. They call him captain. The shoulders of his coat are sharply squared and a fur collar bunches at his throat. His brimmed hat conceals his hair colour, but he's clean-shaven with a pale brow so I wager he was red-haired in his youth. Stern-faced, he scans the inside of the shop.

The mare nudges my arm. I reach into my pockets for more oats. Boots tromp down the stairs, and within seconds two men step off the landing.

"He's telling the truth, Captain Baker. The boy's not here," one says. There's a pistol in his belt and a rifle is pinned under the second man's arm.

Their leader scowls at them. As he turns away, his attention lands on me. Panic jolts through me. When he nods my way, his henchmen appear startled to see me there.

"Well, well," the pistol man says.

I want to bolt, but for Thomas's sake I cannot. Even so, when the two men stride toward me, my gaze darts to the stable's side door. Through the window next to it, I see another man stationed outside. He lifts his brows and waggles the butt of his rifle at me to make his point. I'm not going anywhere.

They're only men. Only men.

"Thomas O'Dougherty. You know him?" the pistol man asks. My breakfast rolls up the back of my throat.

"What do you want with him?" I ask.

"Answer the question," the second man says gruffly.

"I'm his aunt."

"Where's the boy at?" he says, planting himself a few inches in front of me.

I shrug and stare straight back at him.

The pistol man looks me up and down. "Nasty scars you got there."

"Thomas is a good boy," I say.

"He's a Shiner," Captain Baker snaps back at me. "Your *good boy* cut the throat of Mr. Mueller's youngest apprentice. Yesterday, he laid a beating on this lad," he says, indicating Rory. "We have men willing to testify that O'Dougherty urged members of the Shiner gang to bust up Blackmore Tavern in Uppertown."

No, not my Thomas!

"He's also been identified as one of the hoodlums who shot up the home of a respected businessman, and he may pose a danger to the family's young woman-servant to boot."

My mind reels under the weight of these accusations. They can't be true.

"Thomas O'Dougherty will be found and made to answer for his crimes. You have my word on that." His gaze remains locked on mine as he addresses the others. "The rest of O'Dougherty's family is in town. They're next." He searches my face for a reaction as he slowly pulls his gloves on.

My son would never turn to the Newells for help, knowing their close relationship with Biddy and Seamus. The law won't find him there.

Captain Baker tells the rifleman: "I don't want her warning the family. Keep her here for half an hour, then meet us at Blackmore's."

I glance up and catch Rory suppressing a smile. He's the root of all this, I know.

Thirty minutes drags on like thirty years. Grooming the horses helps distract me from Captain Baker's man watching my every move. I suddenly realize I've been brushing the same section of Rainy's mane for the past several minutes. When I stop, his head swings toward me and I pet his velvety muzzle. Since the fire, I feel as if I'm in a mile of water and drowning in doubt. My hope fled with the earbobs and Thomas.

He is somewhere alone and frightened out of his wits. I could tear those Shiners from stem to stern with my bare hands for the trouble they've caused my son.

"Eh," says Captain Baker's man at last. "I'm off now. If you see O'Dougherty, woman, leave word for us at Blackmore's." Then he turns up his coat collar and heads into the smithy.

Once the front door bangs shut, I make a straight line for Rory, who's sharpening the tip of a metal hook he has clamped in a vise.

When I grab his shoulders to spin him around, he lifts the rasp over his head to threaten me. His cheeks are grazed with scabbed-over cuts and green-yellow bruises from the beating Thomas delivered. In his eyes there's a fury that equals mine.

"Where is he?" I ask. We both know I mean Thomas.

"I. Don't. Know."

"You're lying." I grab the front of his coat and shout into his face. "Where's Thomas?"

Rory's eyes narrow. "Get your hands off me. Now."

"Mistress Lindsay," Mueller shouts. "Let the boy go, and be on your way! You're no longer welcome here. And if I see your no-account nephew, I will turn him in to the authorities. You should do the same."

"My boy is innocent." My slip of the tongue causes Rory to beam with devilment, which only makes me angrier. "Thomas is better off without the lot of you."

I barrel toward the front door. "A curse on this place and everyone in it!" I shout at them and fling the door wide.

As I steam along the snowy streets toward Corktown, I feel my anger shift to fear.

How can I navigate this world of men without Seamus's help? I have no choice—I must go to the Newells' cabin and pray for Seamus's return, even if it means seeing Biddy.

The charred skeleton of our former life will bring Seamus to his knees. My rescue of his chair-making tools won't make up for my fault in the fire. How will I face him?

The snow around the Newells' front door is well tramped down, a sign that Captain Baker and his men made good on their threat to visit. The latch yields when I lift it, so I quietly let myself inside.

Biddy, eyes half-closed, still rests on her pallet in front of the hearth. She's been persuaded to remove the dressing I laid over her burns, and the right side of her face resembles a melted candle, her hair scorched off from temple to ear. She still has the flour tin nestled under one arm.

Elizabeth regards me warily from the end of a bench at her mother's feet. Annie and Katherine sit cross-legged on the floor next to Biddy's shoulder with a cornhusk doll on the floor between them. The five Newell children are bunched around a small table, chattering as they eat gruel from wooden bowls.

Roweena, kneeling at Biddy's side, flicks a glance at me and nods. I understand. The baby is not lost. It's a relief to know and one less cross to bear. Then she continues trying to spoon broth into my sister's mouth.

"You must eat something, Biddy, if you are to recover," Roweena says. But Biddy, who hasn't noticed me yet, refuses.

Then the back door of the cabin swings open and in comes Seamus, his arms piled high with firewood. He's wearing the shirt I mended for him before he left for the timber camp. I stifle a sob, and the urge to run to him and bury my face in his neck. He closes the door with one elbow, then kneels to stack the wood next to the fireplace. After he tosses a log on the fire, he stands back to watch the flames rise. Then he turns toward us, and finally he sees me.

When our eyes meet, he looks at me like a sailor seeing land after too long at sea.

Roweena eyes the two of us with disapproval. "The law was here looking for Thomas," she says to me.

"I saw them too." Tears blur my vision.

Annie gets up and runs over to Roweena.

"Hello, Annie," I say, but she doesn't respond.

Roweena slides an arm around the girl's shoulders. "She hasn't spoken since she arrived." Poor, sweet Annie.

Elizabeth speaks up, accusation in her voice. "We know."

She means the earbobs, of course.

Seamus looks at me, seeming as lost as he was the day his da passed on. I want to hold him and say everything will work out as it's meant to. But first we must save Thomas.

"Did you steal them?" Elizabeth again.

"No." A lump catches in my throat.

"Then where are my earbobs?"

Biddy's head slumps against the wall, as if she's swooned.

"You're upsetting your poor mother," Roweena says to Elizabeth.

"They're gone," I choke out.

Seamus drops to his knees beside Biddy. He lays one ear against her chest, and his eyes lock on my face. I think he loves me. I'm a cow for thinking that now, but I think he does. Am I smiling? I hope not. God forgive me.

"Is she all right, Da?" Elizabeth is now close to tears.

"I hear a heartbeat," he answers, voice quavering.

Elizabeth and Annie hug each other.

Now Seamus rests his forehead between my sister's flattened breasts.

"Oh, Biddy, my darling, don't leave me," he says, voice breaking.

The floor dissolves beneath me and the ground swallows me up.

25

MARIAH

When Biddy and I were girls, we often encountered an old woman, bent and slightly mad, who wandered the village market begging for scraps of food. Her hair hung in greasy ropes and she reeked of sweat and urine. Other impoverished women, younger and maybe more stunned by their circumstances than she was, sat on the cold ground with their threadbare children hugged against their sides. Their silent glances implored passersby to offer coins or a bit of food.

Biddy once told me, "It's a sin against God to allow oneself to fall so low."

Then a sinner I am, for I am brought low. I spend the day hoping for Biddy's survival as I roam the side streets of Bytown. All the while, my stomach growls and I have no idea where I can take shelter before the night. I think of Peg, but I can't turn to her, and interrupt her livelihood, such as it is. Where does a woman go when there's nowhere left? The fire transformed my only shelter into a nightmare. Each time I close my eyes, I'm haunted by roaring flames, hogs screaming, yellow wolf eyes gleaming in the dark.

At dusk, the sound of a choir rehearsing Christmas hymns reaches out from a white clapboard church like an angel's arms. I slip into a back pew, then bend my head as if in prayer and weep in relief at the enveloping warmth. When the practice ends and the choirmaster begins snuffing oil lamps, I push out of the church doors into the failing light.

Funny how things go, that after turning a cold shoulder to God for so long, my rescue should come from one of his servants. One of the choristers, wearing a lace collar and a look of concern, calls me back with a wave of her smooth hand.

"You might try the Home for Friendless Women, just one street over." I'm so grateful for the suggestion, I feel no shame.

A stocky woman, accommodating enough if stiff, receives me there. She leads the way to a room where a row of four beds stands along opposite walls, then walks me into the kitchen. A scrawny teenage girl ladles broth into my cup and passes me a bread crust.

Light slants through the shuttered windows of the strange room where I awake for the second day in a row. I'm no closer to knowing what I'll do next than when I got here. Across the aisle from my bed, a girl younger than Thomas sits at the foot of a cot and rubs her swollen belly. She needn't tell me her story. I am her story. I know the girl will promise her baby that she'll always look after him. But without means, she's bound to disappoint—and where she doesn't fail through her own flawed nature, others will create circumstances that steer her off course.

"Morning," whispers the woman lying on the bed next to mine. On her forehead is an angry cut surrounded by a purple welt. She's drawn her blanket up to her chin, probably to hide more bruises. When I make no reply, she closes her eyes and her tears wet the grey pillow. I'd like to be more caring, even ask her what happened. *Did your husband beat you? Will you be all right?* But I've got enough problems of my own.

I consider returning to the homestead to scrounge for belongings that survived the blaze.

But as I know too well, wolves roam the forest. Then there's the two-legged sort, desperate folk who prey on others' misfortune. Likely scavengers have already sifted through the ashes and charred timbers and run off with whatever they can make use of—iron cauldrons, pokers, any implement rendered on a blacksmith's forge.

Making chairs will be Seamus's salvation. I'd imagined how his face would be lit with gratitude for my rescuing his draw knife, spoke knife and chisels. That moment will never happen.

Biddy, my darling, don't leave me. No, my sister is too cantankerous to die. If only I was given to drink, anything to rid myself of the image of his cheek pressed against my sister's breast as he uttered that plea.

Thomas is all I have left. I'll search night and day to find him.

I sit up fully dressed and reach for my bonnet. At the scent of rose-water, I look up. A well-to-do woman sweeps into the room, skirts swooshing against frilly leghorns that jut from beneath her hem. I tie the strings under my chin, refusing to meet her eye. She was here last night too, in a getup like a fluffed-out chicken. She tried to coax Seamus's coat away from me and Mam's shawl too. I wouldn't let them go, but I did trade her my dress for a new one. The hem of mine was shredded and the skirt riddled with burn holes from the fire.

"I'm back," the rosewater woman announces in fluting tones.

Yes, back from her stone house filled with children, no doubt, and with a fully stocked cupboard and a servant girl tending to her every whim. I imagine she's my age, but easy living makes her look younger. Not a callus on those hands, but gold rings instead. In her story, there's a husband who dotes on her, buying her fancy dresses. And she has plenty of places to wear them. I'll never be her. She'll never be me.

The woman stops at the foot of my cot. "I brought you a visitor!" she says.

Thomas?

I look up in foolish hope.

At her elbow is a girl about Elizabeth's age, who sucks in her breath and steps back when she sees me. The woman squeezes her eyes shut briefly and sets her large basket on my blanket. She slips an arm around the girl's shoulders and hugs her close.

"Her face," the girl whispers too loudly. What's left of my dignity flees.

"I'm sorry, my darling. Mamma should have warned you." The rose-water woman then looks at me. "Poor thing," she says.

At first I think, *She does have a heart.* Demeaning, yes, but it's at least a bit of empathy, which is more than I've received for some time. But when she kisses the girl's hair again, I realize she is speaking of her daughter. Shame paints my face red.

"Well," she says next, letting go of the girl and plying me with a saccharine smile. "Yesterday you wouldn't part with that coat, although only God knows why, my dear. It smells of smoke and horse barn." From her basket, she lifts a brown wool coat, far nicer than my own. "My husband has tired of this. I'd like to have offered you something of mine, but . . ." Her eyes measure my large frame and she finishes her thought. "Well, you know."

Yes, I do. She's letting me know she's finer and daintier than me. Just like Biddy is finer and daintier than me. I've been reminded of it my entire life.

She extends the coat toward me, eyes aglow with expectation—that I gush with thanks, no doubt.

"Not interested." I lift my chin to signal that I'm the victor in this exchange just as I hear a "Hey!" from the doorway.

It's the home's cook, addressing me in a tone so like Biddy's that I wince. Her face is slick with sweat and her sleeves are rolled above her elbows. "Finish your tea party and march yourself into the kitchen. Work's waiting. No free rides here."

I rise from the bed and draw myself to full height, allowing my gaze to fall on the line of white scalp between the rosewater woman's plaits. She cranes up at me warily.

"Mamma, let's go," says the girl, tugging her mother's hand.

"Have a blessed day and a merry Christmas," the woman says. Her mouth smiles but her eyes don't. She begins to tuck her charity coat back into the basket.

I find myself bending forward to scowl at her, meeting eyes filled with confusion bordering on fear.

My trapped-animal rage cuts through her, as do my scars, as does the ache of guilt and shame and every tragedy heaped upon me. My glare is as bitter as valerian root, and twice as hateful.

The woman's eyes moisten as she takes her daughter by the hand and the two back away from me.

Shoulders squared, I stride toward the door. I don't know where I'm going, but not to the kitchen to do the cook's chores. I do know one thing. Never again will I let my old existence slip back over my head like a noose.

Outside, white light jabs my eyes. Somehow I must find Thomas and warn him about Baker's search.

I keep to the trampled snow along the roadside to avoid being run over by the carters hauling supplies to Sleigh Bay. The earthy smell of the passing horses and the puffs of steam from their nostrils calm me. Through the tunnel of my bonnet, I watch a dog sitting between a pair of barrels in the back of a passing sled. His mottled fur droops over his muzzle like a rich man's moustache, and the long bits falling over his eyes resemble Da's shaggy brows. The mutt responds to my attention by cocking his head with such humanlike mutual curiosity, I can't help but smile.

Me smiling over a dog. The world is changing. Or perhaps I am.

I search for Thomas along Wellington Street and as far west as Richmond Landing, where I watch the comings and goings of customers from the drinking houses along the Ottawa River. No sign of him. I then walk the side streets, past every public house. At one, I scrape up the courage to peer through a window. But a meaty fist bangs against the glass from the inside and I scramble away. No better luck awaits along Sussex Street. Nearer to Sleigh Bay, I encounter bleary-eyed men stumbling along inside the sled tracks. Their blasts of laughter startle me.

A safe distance from where the sleds gather at the mouth of the bay, I watch the few late-departing carters trail onto the frozen Ottawa River. Oh, what I wouldn't give for a glimpse of my Thomas. I remember every patch I've sewn onto his winter coat, but I see no sign of it here. Wind gusting off the river ice cuts through the thin cloth of my skirt, and the tops of my thighs sting from the cold as if prickled by nettles.

Maybe Thomas already knows he is a wanted man and has fled south across the American border or into Lower Canada to avoid arrest. That's what the Shiners do, the ones who escape Perth Gaol. Four horse-drawn sleds, lined up like stitches on a shirt, travel along the frozen Ottawa River. If Thomas has ridden off on a sled already, I'm searching in vain. He could be anywhere in the valley—or beyond—waiting for this storm to pass.

If only I could hop a ride on one of those sleds and leave for parts unknown. I could do it right now. I've nothing to retrieve—no money, no belongings, no lover to hold me here. Who would miss me, really? I could disappear so easily.

But I am a mother and so I must wait and trust that Thomas will surface. At this moment, though, my feet are freezing and I must move. I won't go back to the humiliations of the women's shelter, so

I worry about where I will sleep as I retrace my steps along Sussex Street, averting my eyes from the shabby string of public houses.

The loud crack of splintering wood startles me. I look up in time to see an airborne man busting through the closed door of a low-slung shanty. He lands squarely on his back atop the newly broken planks and laughs even as he swipes a hand across his mouth to check for blood. A second man—the groggery proprietor, I'd guess, judging by his filthy apron—steps outside. He's portly and his cheeks are as red as if he's been working behind a plow all day.

"That's the second time I'll be fixin' that door 'cause of you. Don't show your face here again!" He dusts his hands off, then ducks his head under the top of the door frame and disappears inside.

Two gaunt-faced men, oily and unshaven, saunter outside to join the first. One helps the drunkard to his feet. The other lights a pipe. They're standing no more than ten feet away from me.

Look away. Keep walking.

I give them a wide berth and pick up my pace, continuing to walk quickly even after I'm well past them.

When finally I slow, footsteps crunch the dry snow behind me.

"Hey darlin'," a deep voice slurs from over my shoulder. "Who you been running from?"

My heart beats faster, fuelled by a hodgepodge of fear and anger. They're following me.

Another voice joins his, calling "How'd you like to earn a few shillings?" Although my bonnet blinkers my view of him, I can tell he's caught up and is walking next to me.

Then on my opposite side, a younger voice chimes in: "Got a friend? Bring her along."

Suddenly, one of the men cuts in front of me. He walks backward, hoping, I'm sure, for a glimpse of my face. Instead of lifting my head, I keep my eyes on his scuffed boots.

They're spotted with blood—he's the drunk man who got tossed from the groggery. His laces trail in the snow. The smells of whiskey, tobacco and piss lift from him.

"Come on now. Don't be shy." The drunkard reaches out and yanks at the brim of my bonnet. I bat his arms away.

"Feisty 'n' tall. I like that," he says.

Laughter slashes at me from all sides.

I am a flesh-and-blood human being—a woman, not a possession or an object. I'm tired of being belittled.

Suddenly, the strings of my bonnet feel like they're cinched too tightly under my chin. I just want my son. I want to be what I say I am. I want to be his mother. My hands are shaking too hard to untie the knot. The men chuckle as they each jockey for a glimpse of my face.

"Whores can't be choosers," the drunkard says. When his blood-smeared hand grips my elbow, I aim a strong kick at his shins. It connects and he lets go, cursing. His friends laugh harder.

Something breaks loose deep inside me. *Not a servant. Not someone's workhorse. Certainly not a whore.*

My efforts have only tightened the strings, so I work them over my chin and cast the bonnet onto the snow, straightening to face my tormentors.

The men's laughter cuts short. My face is not a sight for the faint of heart.

"Holy Mother of God, she's stitched together by the devil himself!" the drunkard yells.

Oh, the irony! His own nose is as crooked as a Virginia fence. His lower lip is split, and through the gap where his front teeth should be, I see blood pooling in the cracks between his bottom teeth.

For the second time today, my loathing for my fellow human beings is so thick I taste metal. The men's faces melt into those of Flynn and his no-good sons. I'd like to shoot every damned one of these bastards and drive chisels through their scrawny rib cages to skewer their still-beating hearts.

I brace my feet and raise my fists. I will claw, bite, kick them bloody and strike my way out of this. What can they take from me that hasn't already been taken?

My gaze darts from face to face. No one makes a move.

One of the gaunt-faced men takes a step backward and touches the rim of his hat. "Ma'am," he says. The second follows suit, and soon the two of them are gone.

The deep-voiced drunk gapes after his friends, then calls out, "Come on, lads. We're just havin' a bit of fun." When they ignore him, he steps in so close we're nearly toe to toe. "Ugly as a dog," he hisses.

I withhold the reaction he seeks, a flinch or teary eye. He thrusts his face sharply toward me. "Woof!"

I lunge toward him. My forehead smashes his nose as I shout the primal battle cry of Celtic warriors told to me in fireside stories of my youth.

"Aboo!" *Victory!*

He stumbles backward, blood pouring from both nostrils. "You bitch," he groans, fishing out a grimy handkerchief he brings to his nose. Casting a nervous look my way, he turns away at last and tromps after his friends.

Nothing falls from the sky to strike me dead. No one challenges me or tells me I must leave. For the first time in my life, I feel powerful.

I want more of this. I want what is mine. I want to reclaim all that's been taken from me. This face that's held me back, convinced me I'm indebted to those who would limit me, will now be the very thing to carry me forward.

At full tilt, I press east toward the roughest part of Lowertown. I mustn't overthink, like I usually do, and reason myself out of taking action. The first step is to go see the one person I can trust.

If there's one thing I associate with Peg, it's her green dress with its low neckline that affords even the most unwilling set of eyes a full picture of what lies beneath. So when she opens the door to me, I'm puzzled by the high collar and the buttoned-up blouse front she's stitched inside the dress's deep scoop.

Then, instead of inviting me inside, she closes the door so that there's only room for her face to peek out at me.

"Red!" she whispers. "How are you?"

"I must speak with you, Peg."

She blinks. "I have a gentleman caller."

"It's urgent," I say.

She closes the door completely. I don't know what to make of this. Her words have always flown freely. It's important that we talk, so I wait.

Half a minute later, Peg swings the door wide and invites me inside. The fire is burning strong and a day's worth of split wood is stacked next to the hearth. The air tantalizes with the smell of meat broth simmering in an iron pot; my stomach growls loudly on cue. Peg has moved up in the world.

Instead of offering me a bowl, like she would have in the past, she bites her lip and positions herself between me and the curtain drawn across the foot of her bed.

"If not for your mam's shawl around your shoulder, I'd not have recognized you," she says.

"What?"

"I've never seen you without your bonnet." Then I realize I left it in the snow at Sleigh Bay. We smile warily at each other.

"You've been sewing," I say, gesturing at the work spread across her table.

"My luck is changing. I told you I'd be a seamstress one day."

"That you did." I notice a vest and fine white shirt hanging from a hook on the wall, along with a man's hat, the sort found in an Uppertown shop.

Peg follows my gaze and her face lights with pride. "He's a well-to-do gentleman." Her mouth opens as if she'd like to say more, but she catches herself. *Most strange.*

"I need to speak plainly. Is he asleep or . . .?"

"Oh yes! Sleeping, very soundly." She nods vigorously. "He's travelled a great distance and arrived in the small hours. Won't wake until the evening, I'd wager."

I choose a stump seat at her table and sit. The impatience—or is that disapproval in her eyes?—makes me question why I've come here. Finally, she relents and sits across the table. I decide I must risk it. Who else do I have to confide in?

"Peg, what I'm about to tell you can go no further than this room," I say in a hushed tone. "Do you swear?"

She nods, leaning closer, her elbows on the table.

"I'm leaving town for a while."

"Where to?"

I swallow hard. Until I say the words out loud, I won't believe it either. "Round Lake, then farther along the Bonnechere River to a timber camp."

"When? How?" Peg asks.

"I don't have the particulars figured out yet, but I'm going."

She slumps back on the bench. "Why on earth would you do that?"

I unpack the story, carefully setting each detail before her. I tell her about hiding Mam's earbobs and about the Frenchmen, Maurice and Benoît, who stole them. My voice breaks when I describe escaping the fire, sacrificing Esmerelda to the wolves, and then shooting one myself. Her face turns unexpectedly ashen when I tell her that Thomas has gone missing, and about Baker, the lawman, who is determined to try him for a long list of crimes.

Peg glances toward the curtain, like she's afraid her caller is waking, even though we haven't heard him stirring. "Why are you telling me all this?" she asks.

"Because you're the only person who knows me. And I think you'd recognize Thomas. If you see him or hear where he is while I'm away, you must tell him to wait for me." I swipe tears from my eyes with a corner of Mam's shawl.

Peg studies my face, squinting, with her head cocked to one side. Now she more closely resembles the Peg I know.

"So, you're frightened of men. Yet you're willing to risk your life to go up to the middle of nowhere among the worst of the worst and do what, I've no idea! Do you think this Maurice and Benoît will say, 'Oh gosh, missus! So sorry we stole *your* earbobs. Had we only known . . .'" Peg pantomimes the remorseful return of my earbobs, then rolls her eyes. She's not finished yet. "Even if you manage to take back the earbobs and sell them, you can't spend the money if you're murdered. Some of those scrappy timbermen at the camp will take one look at a warm body in a dress, then devour you like Sunday dinner."

"I'll dress as a man," I shoot back.

Peg folds her arms across her chest and sizes me up. Finally, she says, "You'd have to cut that hair, then maybe you could pass. But if you're found out—what then?"

"I can't think about that now. My mind is made up. I *must* go to the camp and take back Mam's earbobs."

"And why is that worth risking your life for?"

Bile rises in my throat. "I need the money for my son's future."

Peg is momentarily speechless. Her glance flicks toward the curtain, but then she smiles and seems genuinely pleased for me.

"A son! You never mentioned being married."

My face heats.

"Oh," Peg says. "I see." We hear a sudden snoring from her gentleman caller behind the curtain and neither of us speaks for a moment. But then her brows press together. "If the earbob money is to help your own son, there's no reason for Thomas to wait for you."

I let the statement hang and will her to do the work of making a connection. I suppose it's my way of keeping the upper hand in this conversation.

Realization sweeps Peg's green eyes. "Thomas isn't your nephew!"

The truth spoken out loud fills me with joy and fear. "The earbobs are pearl and gold, a gift from the wife of an English lord," I say. "They should fetch enough money to buy a place for me and Thomas— someplace with a forge."

"A smithy," she says breathlessly.

"For a blacksmith and a farrier," I reply.

"And a farrier?" Again, after a moment, understanding dawns on her face. "You? Shoeing horses?" She leans back and her hands drop into her lap. "Well, I'll be damned. 'Tis absolutely grand."

A pleasant sensation fills my chest. I think it must be pride.

I leave Peg's shanty with a flannel shirt, a pair of wool socks and a scarf tucked under one arm. I'd rather not imagine how she came by these items, but I appreciate the gifts. The next leg of the plan is to visit Edwards Mercantile. Fuelled by determination, I tromp through snow- drifts along the streets and think of what I'll need to survive the cold journey to Round Lake plus a few days in the bush—long underwear, pants, a warm hat and gloves. Hopefully I can barter with Fran—these items in exchange for the promise of my labour upon returning.

The sun is low in the sky when I reach the shop.

Fran stands behind the counter making small talk with two women while she binds their purchase with twine. She doesn't acknowledge me when I come inside, but I catch her glancing in my direction as I'm considering a folded pile of men's long underwear. I can't make out the price of them. It's a hardship and an embarrassment not being able to decipher the writing on the paper squares pinned to their fronts.

The women leave and Fran tucks a pencil behind one ear, then turns away to organize jars on a shelf behind her. When she finishes, I'm examining some leather gloves, warm but far above my means.

"What brings you by?" Fran finally asks. I turn to see her with her elbows resting on the counter and her hands clasped in front of her.

"You asked me once what I wanted out of life."

"I remember."

"I want what's mine."

Quick as a sneeze, Fran darts out from behind her counter and lowers the blinds on the mercantile's front windows and draws the wooden bar across the door. She places a bench before the fire, then sits and pats the seat next to hers.

"Tell me everything," she says. "Start at the beginning and leave nothing out."

The shop darkens as I purge myself for the second time this day, but to her I disclose every detail from my life in Ireland and Bytown—Da shoeing horses, the Flynns' dog attacking me, falling in love with Seamus. She passes no judgment on my being Thomas's mother, but shuts her eyes and clucks her tongue at tales of Biddy's treatment of me. When I tell her about the Frenchmen stealing the earbobs and describe the fire that drove us to town, Fran reaches for my hand. She squeezes when I tell her of Seamus's renewed declaration to my sister. After I confess to Thomas's troubles and say that my plan is to retrieve the earbobs to fund our future together, she releases my hand.

"Tomorrow morning, I'll go to Sleigh Bay and make inquiries about sleds travelling along the Bonnechere. I can hitch a ride with a carter." Then, hoping it's true, I add, "Dressing as a man will keep me safe, and I'll pose as a latecomer searching for work. I'll be at the camp only a few days. It can't take that long to steal back a pair of earbobs." Whether I'm trying to convince her or myself, I'm not sure.

A cold stone settles in the pit of my stomach when Fran's only response is silence. *Here it comes.* I brace myself for naysaying, a warning that the idea is pure folly. When at last she turns to face me, her eyes are glistening with tears.

"It's a commendable plan. How can I help?"

I laugh from sheer relief. "Long johns."

"You'll need more than long johns to be credible as someone search-ing for work. The men who come here to be outfitted stock up warm clothing, axe handles, axe heads."

Really? My confidence flags. "I have no money."

"None required, my dear." Fran stands and smooths her apron. "My late husband was nearly your height. Let me go through his things. His boots may be a good fit." As she hikes up the stairs to her living quarters with the agility of a woman half her age, she calls over one shoulder, "Of course, you'll sleep here tonight. I have lots of leftover stew and cornbread."

I'd respond but I'm choked with emotion.

After a night of patchy sleep, I greet the morning shot full of nerves and self-doubt. At first light, I toss Seamus's coat aside and stand in front of a looking glass in Fran's storage room, her shears in my hand.

I didn't think it would be this difficult to cut my hair.

It's not just vanity that holds me back. The cloud of frizz and stray curls around my face shields my scars from gawkers' scrutiny.

Tears roll down my cheeks. I lose heart and set the shears on top of a sealed barrel.

What am I doing? But even as I question my wisdom, I undo the buttons at the back of my dress, which then slides from my shoulders and falls to the ground, leaving me standing there in only my shift, covered in goosebumps. As a girl, I used to marvel at my body, passing both hands along my flat belly to the soft swell of my breasts. Now my breasts are irrelevant, so long out of use by a babe or a lover.

And soon I won't look like myself. I'll resemble the enemy.

Mr. Edwards's long underwear is flopped over a flour sack. I pull off my shift and teeter as I stick one foot, then the other, through the legs. The fabric is soft and forgiving as it stretches over my broad hips. I slip my arms through the sleeves and button the front, then blow my cheeks out and examine myself. The backside hangs loosely and so does the belly, but the fabric is stretched taut across my chest. I frown and squash my breasts flat, but they fight back, spilling out from beneath my palms. I fumble hurriedly to undo the long john buttons to my waist and wriggle out of the sleeves. I tear strips of fabric from my shift and knot them snuggly around my chest. That does the trick.

With the flannel shirt buttoned to the top, any remaining swell is hidden. Mr. Edwards's pants are too big around the waist and I must cinch them in with a belt. Fran has also found a roomy pullover she'd knitted for him that falls a good ten inches below my hip bones and obscures any hint of a womanly figure.

Next, I assess which of my undisguised attributes might point to my being of the weaker sex—the thin neck, the delicate narrowness of my foot, or the lack of a beard.

My voice.

I dip my chin and speak in the lowest possible register. "Good to meet you, sir." *Shite!* I sound like a woman trying to sound like a man. I stare into the mirror and breathe deep. *Try again.* This time, I speak the same words in a monotone. The effect is only slightly better. The contents of my stomach roil.

Last night, Fran asked about my monthly courses. I'd lost track of them. To delay and lighten my monthlies, for the entire timber season if necessary, she prepared a packet of ground black pepper, dried yarrow and raspberry leaves left over from her stock of Biddy's medicinal herbs. I pray it works. To be on the safe side, I tear the rest of my shift into wide strips and shove them into the burlap sack Fran gave me to carry extra clothing.

GWEN TUINMAN

Sleigh bells jingle along the street outside the mercantile as I shove the wolf ear into my pants pocket. Carters are already at work. I must hurry if I'm to catch a ride today.

I take up the shears in my shaky right hand. In my left, I grab a hank of red hair, the same locks Mam used to stroke and Thomas used to tangle his spit-covered fists in as a babe. I feel a tug on my scalp as the blades slice through, and the hair comes away in my hand. There's no going back now. I cut the other side, then a couple of handfuls at the back.

The storeroom door flings open.

Fran bursts into the room and closes the door behind her. "Someone on high is looking after you, my dear!" She takes the shears from my hand and gestures for me to sit on a low keg. "Brother James Stewart is here." She snips at my hair as she fills me in. "He's leaving on the hour by sled to visit a Quaker meeting house, established by his wife's cousin northwest of Round Lake. On his way there, he's delivering salt pork to the Sinclair camp, west of the lake on Bonnechere River. Is that not the very camp where your earbobs are?"

"Yes." I breathe out the word in disbelief at this possible stroke of luck.

Fran steps back to examine her handiwork. "I'm sure he'll take you there, but he wants to meet you first." She brushes hair from my shirt as I stand. "Quick! He won't wait all day. Come out before I finish up his order."

Fran's about to leave when she stops where she is and pulls a packet of brown paper tied with string from her apron pocket. I reach to take it from her, but she doesn't let go. She regards me with deep serious-ness, and then says, "You might need this."

"What is it?"

"Just a little powdered bloodroot. Use in self-defence and *only* as a last resort." She releases the package to my care. "A tiny bit will kill a man. You'll know when the time comes if you need to use it."

260

"All right," I say uncertainly.

"I'll feel better if you take this too." Fran reaches into her apron again and passes me a bone-handled knife with a six-inch blade, then dashes from the room.

My mind whirls as I wrestle Mr. Edwards's tall boots over my wool socks and put on his coat. I'm tying the wool scarf under my chin when I absently turn toward the looking glass. I freeze. The reflection is shocking.

A curly-headed youth, maybe eighteen, peers back at me in disbelief. My slow smile spreads across his face—our face.

"William," Fran shouts from the mercantile. It's not until I hear her a second time that I understand she's calling me. I put on her husband's hat and snatch up my burlap sack, then crack the door slightly open, hoping for a view of this stranger who's offered his help.

Brother Stewart, examining a bolt of grey fabric, stands in the middle of the mercantile.

He's a tall, apple-cheeked man, clean-shaven with dark eyebrows, and dressed head to toe in black. At his feet sit two crates filled with provisions—tinware, butter, bags of sugar, salt and cornmeal—and next to those a sack of flour.

"My wife will use this fine cloth to good effect," he says to Fran. You can tell a lot about a man by his tone, and his is laced with warmth. I'll be safe travelling with a godly man concerned for his wife's happiness.

"Three yards there. Plenty for a dress," Fran tells him.

"Then purchase them, I must. Content wife, joyful life," says Brother Stewart with a laugh that lights his face. The silver streaking his sideburns hints that he's much older than me. His hat is black and flat-rimmed. It'll be airborne in a strong wind gust, although it strikes me that this Quaker would chase after it in good humour.

After one final look back at the storeroom to check if I've forgotten anything, I'm on my way. I've left my dress puddled on the floor next to Mam's shawl, folded in a neat square, and Seamus's coat resting on top of my old boots.

I close the door gently behind me and step into my future.

"So, this is the boy!" Brother Stewart's eyes crinkle at the corners when he smiles at me.

"Yes, this is my nephew, William," says Fran.

Brother Stewart nods at me, waiting for me to speak.

I gawk dumbly. How to best disguise my voice in a manner that I can sustain?

Say something. Anything!

In the awkward silence, I sense Brother Stewart taking measure of my face and trying to guess my story.

"Fear not, William. You can speak plainly," he says.

How can I go through with my plan? I can't even speak to a kindly man of God. My eyes cut to Fran, desperate.

"Brother Stewart, forgive me. I omitted to tell you that William doesn't speak," she says.

"Shyness can be overcome, praise God."

"No, what I mean is that William cannot speak, sir. Hasn't done since he was a boy. His father was cut down by intruders and his mother—my dear sister, God rest her soul—was found nearby in an awful state and poor William cowering in the bushes with his face torn thusly. A wolf encounter, I'm afraid."

Brother Stewart reaches out to firmly grip my shoulder. "You have been spared for a purpose known only to our Lord."

If only that were true.

Then, as if the moment has become too serious, he says, "What need have you of words when a man's actions speak clearly?" He squeezes my shoulder, then lets his hand drop away.

Bending forward to hoist a crate, he says, "Bid your aunt farewell and secure your possessions in the sled. We've a great deal of hard

travel ahead of us and should set off while the sky is clear, praise be."
He heads outside with the boxes.

I hug Fran around the shoulders.

"You're a good lad, William," she says into my chest. "Be safe and remember the end always justifies the means."

I kiss her cheek just as Brother Stewart returns, then I pick up my belongings to follow him outside.

"Are you not forgetting something, William?" he asks.

Nothing springs to mind but panic. I look to Fran, who appears equally baffled.

"Chopping trees will go easier if you bring your axe." He erupts in hearty laughter.

26

THOMAS

Peg left the shanty over an hour ago to scare up something for us to eat. My stomach's so empty its walls are touching, and Peg is the same. Whatever extra people have, they save for themselves. Hardly anyone is selling food at the market this winter, and with the crop failures of summer, there's less coin for people to spend anyways. The rich have cleaned everything out to make their fancy Christmas dinners and now all their servant girls scour the market in preparation for New Year's Eve—so Peg tells me. Odds are she'll return empty-handed.

During famine times back in Ireland, Mam and Auntie Mariah said they sucked stones to trick themselves out of feeling starved. Right eejits. How is that supposed to help?

I swear this room shrinks every day. My new clothes wait on their hook as they've done since the day Peg and I broke into Johnston's house. Though I left Hairy Barney's wake with nothing to show for our efforts, Aylen's men have been roughing up some Orangemen on the voters list—mostly English and Scottish farmers living outside

Bytown. He and the Shiners are in a high mood, as if the election is already won. Maybe he'll stay here.

Aylen better feckin' remember who set him up for the win.

Jaysus, but I'm hungry. I swallow the last bit of water from a tin cup on the table. It's been a week since I drank anything but. Everyone's out at the pubs at night. Not me, though. I'm stuck here, keeping my head down, pacing eight steps in one direction and ten in the other. A man can't live on water. I hurl the cup against the chimney and it clatters to the floor just as the shanty door flings open. Peg is home.

"What's this about?" she says.

"I dropped a cup," I answer grimly.

"Against the wall?" She grins at me.

Peg is always happy now. And why not? When pressed about a reward amount, I told her three hundred quid, a complete falsehood. Honesty would kill the good thing we have going. She trusts the tall tales I've been shovelling about promises Aylen hasn't made. It's Clara all over again. Why do women make me do this?

"You've been gone a long time," I tell her.

"And here's the reason why!" From a basket hidden inside the folds of her cape, she produces a loaf of bread and a cloth bundle the size of two fists.

"What's that?"

"You're a sour thing." She lays everything on the table. As she hooks her cape on a wall peg, I unfold a corner of the cloth.

"How'd you come by a ham hock?"

"A friend. Here's the best part." She produces a half-full bottle of whiskey from her basket and plunks it on the table. "You could use some cheering up."

I should be happier about that, but I'm not. When I tip the basket to see inside, a few potatoes and some wrinkly carrots roll onto the table. "Did this friend require coin—or was it a favour he was after?"

Peg narrows her eyes at me and wipes her nose roughly on the sleeve of her dress. I catch a disgusting glimpse inside one nostril. You'd never see that from Clara.

"What's eating at you?" Peg says.

"Nothing," I tell her. A log settles in the fire and sparks leap upward.

"If you must know, on the way to market, I chanced to meet a kitchen girl from the Union Hotel. We struck up a bargain, although she got the better of the deal. I gave her the blue flowered dress in trade for the meat and the rest of it."

"Oh," I say, my face turning red. "I thought—"

"I know what you thought," Peg says. "Whoring was a means to an end. But my old ways are behind me now that there's money in our future." She puts her arms around me, and lays her cool cheek against my hot face. "I'll soon be sitting pretty in Peg's Dress Shop. No, *Margaret's Dress Shop for Fine Ladies*." She hugs me tighter.

My chest aches.

"About before—it's just, we're short on coin and all . . ." I tell her, then hastily add, "Until Aylen comes through with the reward, of course."

"I know," Peg says, nuzzling my neck.

I'm such an arse. She bartered the flowered dress she worked on for days to feed us. I've bet everything on Aylen, and it's yet to pay off. Peg and I may never see a penny from him. What then?

Peg begins kissing my ear, but I shrug her off. She gives up on getting a rise out of me and drops onto the bench across the table. "You're so tense. If you're fretting about money, you needn't."

"How's that?"

"Mariah is ponying up money for you—for us by default, according to our deal."

"Auntie Mariah? Where did you see her?"

"She came here one day when you were napping."

"You should have told me!"

"Relax, I didn't let on I knew anything about you." Peg's gaze is steady. I think she's speaking the truth.

"You couldn't have heard right. Auntie Mariah hasn't a penny to her name."

"Not now, but she will once she gets the earbobs back."

Of course, Gran's earbobs. "What d'ya mean—gets them *back*?"

Peg talks a mile a minute as she recounts how Auntie plans to recover them, pausing only to laugh in disbelief over our turn of fortune. "Mariah has earmarked the money for buying a place with a forge. She's got it all worked out—you blacksmithing and her shoeing horses."

I leap to my feet. "She's off her head going off alone like that. It makes no sense."

"But your own smithy, Thomas. Think of it!"

"The woman's afraid of her own shadow. Picture her in a camboose jam-packed with bruisers. The men sleep two to a bunk, you know. She'll piss her knickers. Auntie has never slept next to a man in her entire life."

Peg opens her mouth, then clamps it shut.

"What?"

She looks me hard in the eye for a moment, then grudgingly says, "Maybe she has. Once at least."

"If you got something to say, Peg, spit it out."

Peg reaches for the tin cup lying on the floor. She sets it in the middle of the table, pours an inch of whiskey. "You might want a drink before I tell you what I'm gonna tell you."

My gaze locks on hers. I'm stockstill now.

She tips the cup herself and drains it in two swallows. "Mariah is not your auntie. She's your mam." Peg looks up to gauge my reaction.

My mouth falls open. I must have misheard her.

"Your mam is your auntie," she repeats.

I hear laughter. It's mine. But Peg's expression sobers me.

"That can't be true," I say. "I'm the spitting image of my da. Since the day I was born, people have said so."

Peg quirks a brow at me. She's figured something out and I need to catch up, but I can't stay here. I pull my hat on and grab my coat from its hook.

Peg stands so quickly she knocks the table. "Thomas, don't go!"

"I've got to stop Auntie Mariah before she gets herself killed."

"You won't find her. She left town three days ago."

"All this time you've known and said nothing!" I slam my fist against the table. Peg holds her ground without flinching.

"I did it to protect us. I knew you'd chase after her if you found out. But your place is here. We've worked hard to win Aylen over. The vote is in four days, Thomas. You need to see it through and collect our reward money."

"But you should have told me!"

"Your mam will be fine," Peg insists. "She's tougher than she looks."

"For God's sake. She's my *auntie*. For her to be my mam, she and my da would have had to—"

My world screeches to a halt. Suddenly, everything makes sense: the tension between Mam and Auntie Mariah, Da's long silences, his unwillingness to tangle with Mam over anything. Mariah and Da, so comfortable together in the field, in the woods. I sensed something was wrong the way you can feel a presence in the dark. All along, it was me—my very existence—that was wrong. *My life is a lie.*

"Does my mam know?"

Peg gives me a compassionate half smile. "I'm so sorry, love."

My throat aches and tears burn my eyes, but I won't break in front of Peg. "Don't matter," I mutter. But it does. Everything matters. They've all misled me—Da, Mam, Auntie Mariah. And Peg. Who do I trust now?

I snatch the whiskey bottle and escape outdoors into the biting cold.

"Thomas, you'll be seen," Peg shouts after me. "Bytown Riflemen are looking for you."

I don't care. The worst has already happened.

After nightfall, I linger in the darkened corner of a low-slung drinking house more fit for hogs than men. An open fire burns in the centre of the dirt floor. Most of the smoke draws out through an opening in a roof that is only half a foot taller than most men. No whiskey here, only poteen, which suits me fine. Homemade brew is all I can afford and, not having eaten all day, the effects go straight to my head—which is the point.

I've just enough sense left in me to realize it's time I go home to Peg. I stumble outside and, once I have my bearings, head toward her shanty. It burns my arse that she's spot-on about my needing to stay put. I'd like to be the one who is right for a change. But that's Peg. She sinks her teeth into a plan and there's no shaking her loose.

Clara would have let me be the boss.

"Who's Clara?" a woman calls from an open window.

I'm puzzled. "You're reading my mind now?"

"You're shoutin' her name, you drunken fool!"

She laughs when I clap a hand over my mouth. A scowling man pulls her inside and lowers the sash.

I walk forever. Funny, only one of my hands is cold. Seems I lost a glove. When I was a boy and Elizabeth was still too small for winter play, Auntie Mariah used to bring me outdoors. She taught me to roll snowballs and dig tunnels in the drifts. If my hands got cold, she'd hold them in hers, blow her warm breath over my fingers, and then tuck my hands inside her giant mittens. She gave me hugs that squeezed the air from my lungs.

An image slides into my mind—Mam watching us, stern-faced, through the cabin window.

"Oh, Thomas, sweet lad," Auntie says as she holds me close. From over her shoulder, I see Mam's disapproval. My stomach is upset and I push her away. She holds me at arm's length. The way she looks after this rejection, I think her stomach hurts too. But then her face lights up and she says, "Snow angels, Thomas!" And so we lie in the snow and sweep our arms and legs open and closed, again and again. She sings an Irish tune. I don't know the words, but I try to keep up. It's a nice daydream and I don't want to leave.

The back of my neck has grown numb with cold and I can't feel my hands. Fat snowflakes settle on my face and collect on my eyelashes. I'm laughing. Da will need to shovel the roof tonight if this keeps up. There'll be more piles to tunnel in tomorrow and—

"Thomas O'Dougherty, you'll catch your death of cold out here!" A candle hovers above me. It's Clara who holds it. I reach for the red braid lying over her shoulder. She's wearing a thin shift and I can see her bubbies, which makes me laugh out loud.

"What are you doing?" Her free hand pulls at my sleeve and I try to stand.

"I'm making snow angels, with Auntie." Then, raising a finger to my lips, I whisper. "She's really my mam, but don't tell. It's a secret." I try to kiss Clara's cheek. "You're pretty."

"And you're drunk. Come inside before you wake everyone on the street."

Clara sits me on a bench in front of the fire. She takes my hands in hers and rubs, then blows her breath across my fingers until the feeling returns. When she lifts her head, I see her green eyes and sharp chin. I blink and look again. Her hair is now the colour of a raven's wing.

"Peg?"

"Who'd you think it was, you daft bugger?" She kneels in front of me while I look around the room, then wrestles the boots from my feet. "Thank goodness I heard you singing. Otherwise you'd have frozen to death two feet from our front door."

As she banks the fire, a rush of affection and grief brings tears to my eyes and burns my chest. Peg guides me to the bed and unbuttons my coat. We lie down together, her body snug against my back. She reaches an arm over my shoulder and strokes my hair. I'm a small boy again with my head resting on someone's lap. Auntie Mariah's lap. I can't remember my mam doing that. Mam's just my auntie now? It's too much change for one day. A new wave of tears come on and I sniffle.

"There there, love," Peg says.

"You're too good to me," I tell her.

"I know it," she says and dances her fingers across my eyelids.

On the morning of the town council election, I rise long before Peg and stoke the fire. My shoulders are stiff and my back aches. It's time to flip the straw tick on our bed. The ropes dug into my back all night. I barely slept a wink.

My mind swings from worries about Aylen not paying up to Mariah in certain danger.

I've begun to think of her as only *Mariah*. She's not my aunt, yet I can't bring myself to call her Mam, not until I've heard the story from her mouth.

If I ever see Da again, I won't waste the breath it takes to say hello. I'll come at him with a nice right hook, drop him like a sack of rocks. No need for words between us. I know what he did, leading Mariah on, having his way with her, and then marrying Mam. I mean Biddy. Da's a down-and-dirty dog for tangling with the two sisters. Was probably him that came up with the idea to pass me off as hers.

I gotta push all that from my mind and concentrate on more immediate problems. I've been counting on a reward, but what if Aylen doesn't win the council seats as he wants? Will I pay the price for his disappointment? If he gets it in his mind to lash out at me, for damned sure neither Leamy nor Gleeson will hold him back.

The sun is well up by the time Peg wakes. When I hear the bedstead groan, I take a seat on the bench facing the fire and wait, my right knee bouncing rapidly.

She steps from behind the curtain with a blanket around her shoulders. "Morning," she says, yawning as she passes me on her way to the hearth.

"I'm not staying cooped up today," I tell her. "And that's the final word."

Peg lifts the lid from the pot hanging over the fire. "There's enough soup for breakfast."

She lifts a ladle from its hook and stirs. All along, she's warned me away from nosing around town during the day. Where's the scolding now? I give it a minute before testing her further.

"It's best if I keep watch on the comings and goings from Stanley's Tavern today, see if I get a measure of how many out-of-town Orangemen's horses are being stabled."

Peg leaves the ladle in the pot and rests the lid askew. As if I haven't spoken at all, she reaches for a pair of wooden bowls atop the mantel.

I can take the silence no more. "For God's sake, woman. Have you heard nothing I've said?"

Peg wheels on me with a frown. "Oh, I've heard you. I heard you say you're going to skip around Bytown in plain sight of the law and risk getting yourself arrested or worse. Then Aylen for sure won't pay you when he wins—and he will win—and then ole Peg gets nothing out of this whole deal but a cold bed and an empty purse. That's what I heard."

"I know what I'm doing."

Peg comes to me and cups my face in her hands. "We're so close, Thomas. Now's not the time for mistakes."

"No one will recognize me."

She slips onto my lap and rests her cheek against my head. "Midmorning and this afternoon, I'll check around town and bring you news like I've been doing." Her hand slips inside my shirt and her fingers trace my collarbone.

Of course she's right. But I don't like it.

Peg kisses my hair. "I won't steer you wrong. You know I won't." She gives my shoulders a squeeze, then scoots to the door and steps into my boots. Cold air gusts into the shanty when she dashes outside to the privy.

I pace the floor like a wild thing in search of physical release, something to punish with the full brunt of my frustration before she returns. I'm supposed to be the strong one, the leader. Instead I feel like a child sat in the corner.

Tonight, everything could come crashing down. When Peg sees I've been exaggerating the possibility of a reward, I'll lose her just like I lost Clara. My life is crumbling. *Shit!*

I grab the straw tick and heave it as far as I can. The bedframe and the ropes are exposed—and so is Peg's blue flowered dress, the one she claims to have bartered for food a few days ago. It's neatly folded and laid across the ropes. I think I know what this means but I don't want to believe it. Is she whoring again? *I'm supposed to be her one and only now.*

Peg's voice rings out in conversation with someone in front of the shanty. I don't understand the urgency I feel to pull the straw tick back onto the bed. But I do it anyways. By the time she kicks the side of shanty, knocking the snow from my boots, I've finished. She comes inside looking so beautiful in the morning light, I can't speak.

"My stomach is talkin' to me," she says and makes for the pot. I'm always one step ahead of the axe and waiting for it to fall.

❧

That night is dark as coal dust, with only a thin slice of moon. I huddle with Peg between two buildings across the street from Stanley's Tavern. No one will see us here. I stamp my feet for warmth, but Peg scarcely moves. Her rigid posture reminds me of a cat set to launch on a mouse.

"Where the hell is Aylen?" she says at last.

"Patience," I answer, as if wise to his plans.

Stanley's Tavern, built of stone, looms two storeys tall. Twenty-five well-dressed men, several grey-haired with heavy jowls, have arrived over the past half-hour. Judging by the commotion we see through the side windows, there's a big crowd inside. Most voters arrive on foot and a few by sleigh. Drivers deliver them and wisely return home. I wouldn't leave my team here either, knowing the likelihood of Shiners turning up.

Come on, Aylen.

Three men in suit jackets exit the tavern and stand beneath the light of the oil lanterns hanging on either side of the entrance. Straight away, I recognize Johnston and the two Georges—Baker and Patterson.

Peg and I flatten against the board-and-batten wall. She squeezes my elbow.

While Baker does the talking, the other two smoke their pipes and survey the street, maybe for late arrivals. Johnston checks his watch, then tucks it inside his vest pocket. He adjusts his collar and taps Patterson's shoulder before they both return inside. Baker unbuttons his jacket and continues smoking his pipe as if he had not a care in the world.

Someone's approaching, whistling a jaunty tune.

I inch forward and steal a look north. From the darkness emerges a man, robust but not particularly tall.

Aylen!

With a determined stride, he roosters toward the tavern. Gone are his scuffed boots and raftsman flannel shirt; tonight, he's dressed like money.

Aylen's left shoulder knocks Baker's as he passes him headed for the door. The lawman holds his ground without retaliation. After Aylen is inside, Baker returns the pipe to his mouth and directs his attention toward the opening of our alley. My mouth goes dry and my knees buckle. No way he can see us—but still, it's a relief when he turns away to join the meeting.

"I gotta get closer," I tell Peg.

She grabs my sleeve. "Be careful, Thomas. If Baker is here, so are his volunteers." She kisses my mouth, then pushes me forward.

I dash across the empty street. The north side of the building is darkest, so I duck beneath a window there. My heart bangs inside my chest like hooves on hard ground and I'm sure someone will hear. I take a deep breath, then pull my hat low and hide my mouth and nose behind my scarf before daring to rise slowly and peek inside.

My view is blocked by voters, so I shift around until I can see across the room to a long table where three strange men and Johnston sit side by side facing the crowd. Johnston laces his fingers across his doughy middle and studies the gathering with a satisfied smile. A bailiff, stern with a thick moustache, stands guard and scrutinizes the crowd from his end of the table. His broad-knuckled hands are clasped in front of him. I scan the room for a glimpse of Aylen but cannot spot him. He must have claimed a back corner. There are no other Shiner faces in the crowd. His being here alone among the enemy doesn't seem so smart to me. Maybe I've given him too much credit.

Soon the Orangemen at the front table introduce themselves, and the crowd applauds and settles. George Baker stands at attention in the left corner. From the seat next to Johnston's a man with a nose like an axe blade reads from a large-paged book, the sort Mr. Mueller kept accounts in. Heads begin turning toward the middle of the room. I can't make out the words through the window glass, but I recognize the boom of a familiar voice. Here's Aylen, claiming centre stage.

One of the voters closest to my window removes his suit jacket. I drop out of sight when his friend turns to raise the sash to let in some air, then rise quickly to see what's happening.

"Magistrate O'Connor," Aylen shouts at the axe-nosed man, "you're a disgrace to your people." The audience heckles him and the bailiff takes a step forward. He's at least a head taller than Aylen. If it comes to blows, my money's on him.

Johnston leans in and whispers something to O'Connor, then sits back wearing a smirk. He's drawn the magistrate to support Orange interests at this meeting. No wonder Aylen hates him.

O'Connor announces the first item of business. He talks loud enough for me to hear, but his rich man's words splash out too fast for me to keep up. Every so often, Aylen hollers a new complaint, refusing orders to cease his disruptions. The bailiff flexes his fists, sizing him up.

O'Connor continues. "We'll be voting in three councilmen this evening—one from the Ottawa front, one from the Rideau front, and one from Bytown."

"No damned way! They should all be from Bytown," Aylen shouts.

"What?" Johnston shouts back. "And set you up to feather your own nest? I think not."

"Back to Corktown with you and all your Irish Catholic riffraff," someone calls out. The comment is met by thunderous applause.

A stocky man leaps to his feet. It's Hobbs, the farmer Clara told me about, the one who met with Johnston and his men at Blackmore Tavern. "Reaching above your station doesn't change who and what you are, Aylen!"

"Be careful, Hobbs." Aylen's index finger taps his temple. "I have a long reach and a longer memory."

O'Connor's gaze darts around the room. Eight newcomers, raftsmen in tall scuffed boots and worn coats, have just come in. He turns to the bailiff and two other men and swears them in as special constables.

"You can swear in everyone in this feckin' room, for all the good it'll do you. I'll say what I like."

Now, the moustached bailiff squares off in front of him. "If you don't comply, *sir*, I'll escort you from the room using whatever force necessary."

"Lay a finger on me, I'll drag you into the street and beat you senseless."

"Shut it, *Shiner King*."

Aylen lets out a roar and rushes the bailiff. The newly sworn-in constables grab him by both arms and drag him to the corner he'd stepped from earlier, out of sight. Several voters thump whiskey glasses against tabletops. "Hear, hear," they chant.

"That's your last warning," says O'Connor.

Once the voting starts, fellas stand up, then sit again. Hands are raised and lowered. I can't see the front table anymore, nor can I hear O'Connor's words above the din. An occasional cheer rises, but for what I've no idea. In the midst of the chaos, Johnston yells above the fray, "Only landholding inhabitants can vote." A remark greeted by booing and whistling.

The crowd begins to settle. But Aylen is riled up again. "I want a recount."

"But you won your Bytown seat."

Yes! Thank you, Jesus.

"I demand a recount by my people. Patterson and that other gobshite have no right to represent Nepean."

No, no, no. If you push too hard, we'll lose everything.

A whistle cuts through the night. Across the road, Peg is waving her arms. What now?

When I wave back, she points south toward Wellington and I'm suddenly aware of voices rising above the racket from inside the tavern. The jingle of horse harnesses gets louder along with men's voices singing a boisterous rendition of "Forget Not the Field."

Could the chain for an instant be riven
Which Tyranny flung round us then,
No! 'tis not in Man, nor in Heaven,
To let Tyranny bind it again!

A team of bays trots into view, pulling a sled loaded with Shiners. Some men sit with their legs dangling over the sides and a few stand behind the bench seat. I see one of them glugging whiskey from a jug and passing it along. Gleeson is at the reins. Next to him on the front bench, a man holds a large painting of St. Patrick himself. I recognize it from Aylen's house. Other men march alongside—sixty or eighty Shiners at least.

Gleeson must be acting on Aylen's orders, but his timing is all wrong. If the brawling starts now, Aylen will get booted out of the meeting. Johnston and his lot will block him from the council and I'll get no reward. If I run inside to Aylen, tell him about what's ready to bust loose out here, he could put a halt to it. But Baker will nab me. I won't survive being locked up.

Across the alley, Peg bunches her shoulders and turns her palms skyward. She sees trouble and I know she wants me to do something to get in the way of it.

Before the team draws to a stop, Shiners leap from the sleigh and into the snow. Cudgels are clasped in fists. I spot the butt of a holstered pistol. They shout threats as they swarm the street in front of Stanley's Tavern. Someone fires a gun skyward and the men start whooping.

Above me, the window sash rattles as it's raised higher. An Orangeman leans out to take measure of the Shiner rabble. With a start, he notices me crouched below the window. "Was that gunfire? What's happening, boy?"

I'll take any help I can get.

"I need Mr. Aylen straight away," I call up to him. In the street, men hurl empty bottles against the tavern.

His eyes narrow. "You part of this mob?"

"Peter Aylen can head this off, but I need to speak with him first."

He turns back to the room, "Aylen," he shouts, "messenger for you." O'Connor and Johnston flash a look at each other.

"Bailiff, bar the front door," O'Connor calls out.

Aylen makes his way to my window, patting shoulders as he goes. He grabs someone's half-full glass of whiskey as he sweeps past the last table. "Geez, O'Dougherty. What a night!"

"Yes sir, but it looks like trouble's brewing."

He chuckles and drains the glass. "I won the council seat for Bytown. But I need those two other seats filled by Bytown men." He shouts back into the room, "The first vote's a sham. But my lads are here now and we'll win on the next one." He tosses his glass past my head and turns back to the mayhem.

I remain dumbfounded at the window. *What just happened? Is this really Aylen's plan?*

Outside, men hoot and holler, drawing O'Connor's attention to the street. "For the love of God, do something," he says to the men he's just sworn in. None of them budge.

There's wild banging at the front door. "Let me in!" someone shouts.

The constables unbar the door briefly, then a red-haired Scot bounds inside gasping for breath. Men ease him onto a chair.

"The Irish scourge set upon me," he says.

With an awful crashing of the front door, two muscle-bound Shiners careen inside. At the same time, the far windows shatter and glass shards fly through the air. The tavern owner protests, but it's too late.

Andrew Leamy's head pops over the sill and he climbs inside, followed by a second Shiner. Before the Scot can escape a second time, their blows rain down on him. Throngs of new men pile inside. The tavern is jam-packed and I lose sight of Aylen. Shouts ring back and forth as the pandemonium kicks up.

Most of the original voters grab their coats and dodge the fisticuffs on their flight to the door. Others escape through unguarded windows. Outside, more Shiners lurk, eager to agitate the fleeing Orangemen. Violence escalates quickly.

If I'm to have a chance at that reward, I must stay close to Aylen and be seen helping him. I crawl through the open window and push my way to the centre of the room, where Aylen is shoving Johnston against the wall.

Patterson swings a chair for the back of Aylen's head. Here's my chance.

I rush Patterson and tackle him so the chair barely grazes Aylen's arm before it clatters to the floor. Aylen releases Johnston and whirls around to launch a blow at Patterson's jaw that drives him to the ground. Patterson lies there with his eyes rolled toward me, pleading for mercy. I need to show I'm with Aylen, but aside from punching Rory, who deserved it, I've never caused injury to another person. Still, I grit my teeth and boot Patterson, full force. When he cries out, three other Irishmen join in kicking his gut.

Aylen doesn't give me a second look. His eyes are locked on Johnston, who's scrambling for the door.

"Run, you feckin' coward!" Aylen jeers, then chases Johnston into the night. I've little choice but to follow after them.

Outside, men fuelled by drink battle each other in the bloodied snow. I don't know where to leap in. Aylen chases Johnston toward Wellington until the darkness swallows them. Perfect. I draw a deep breath and charge after them, casting a look in Peg's direction. I stop cold.

Bastard!

Rory has Peg backed against the wall. She pushes him away, but he presses in on her again. I look back to where I last saw Aylen. Gone!

If I give chase now, it might be possible to catch up. In the alley, Rory buries his face in the crook of Peg's neck.

As I pelt toward him, Rory grabs a handful of Peg's skirts and lifts them. Peg knees him in the balls. He doubles over for a second, then recovers himself and swings a fist at her jaw. She cries out as her head snaps backward.

I charge at Rory. His face turns toward me last minute. "Hey, Tommy!" he slurs drunkenly.

Down he goes like a sack of flour dropping off the back of a wagon. He lands with a sickening crunch and a howl. In a heartbeat, I'm on top of him. I'll teach him not to manhandle women!

"You all right, Peg?" I ask.

"Yeah," she answers shakily. "Right as rain."

Time to even another score too. The son of a bitch has once again cost me the opportunity to deepen Aylen's indebtedness to me. I'm coiled tighter than a spring, but Rory just lies in the snow, eyes closed. He'll try bucking me off any second now. I know it.

Peg sniffles. "Is he dead?"

"Nah. He's faking it." I push his shoulder roughly. No response. My eyes cut to Peg's. She drops to the ground next to us and slides a hand inside his coat. "He's breathing." *Thank God.*

Gunfire blasts above shouting from the street.

I stand and pull Peg to her feet. "We gotta get of here."

Peg looks back at Rory. "The little shite will freeze to death if we leave him there."

She's right. As much as I hate Rory, I've no wish to bear the guilt of his dying. As if by some miracle, a riderless horse saunters across the mouth of the alley, its reins dragging through the snow. I know this dappled grey stallion from Mueller's livery. Its owner is likely getting his head bashed in right now. He won't miss his horse.

"Grab the reins," I tell Peg. "I'll fetch Rory."

"What are you up to, Thomas O'Dougherty?"

I smile for the first time today. "Just hold the horse steady."

Fifteen minutes later, I guide the horse onto Mueller's front porch and tether it to a railing. Rory is slumped forward in the saddle with his cheek resting against the horse's mane. On the walk here, Peg pulled a rich man's hat from a snowbank. Initials were sewn into the lining. We push the hat onto Rory's head. He reeks like a distillery. Mueller will detect the scent of whiskey straight away once he recovers from a horse blocking his front door. If there's one thing he can abide less than the evils of drink, it's thievery—especially of horses.

"My mam was right. Whatsoever a man soweth, that shall he also reap." I grin at Peg.

"I could have dealt with him in that alley, you know. You should have gone after Aylen."

My shrug brings a warm smile to her face. "Are you ready?"

"Ready." She winks.

At the same moment as I bang on Mueller's front door, Peg launches an ice boulder through his front window, shattering three panes of glass. Shards fly into the house. We're shocked into silence for a second. Then Peg starts to laugh and excitement courses through my heart.

As Mueller's roar resounds from inside the house, Peg gathers her skirts above her knees and we take flight. Hand in hand, my girl and I run west toward Sussex Street, where our boot prints blend with hundreds of others left by Lowertown's forgotten poor.

27

MARIAH

This morning I wake in the upstairs bedroom of a Quaker house a few miles west of the Bonnechere River and about eighteen miles from the Sinclair timber camp. It will be my third and final day of travelling with Brother Stewart. He figures we'll arrive at the camp close to noon. He makes this journey to see his wife's cousin every winter and overnights with a different family of Friends on each leg of the journey. From what I've witnessed, they share a kinship that makes me wish I'd been born Quaker.

Last night the two of us bedded down on the floor in the boys' room, on either side of their bed. I slept deeply, waking only once, when one of the wee lads piddled into the chamber pot in the middle of the night. Brother Stewart stayed put all night. He's a man of God who glows when he speaks of his son and loves his wife deeply, the way I wish—wished—Seamus loved me.

I get to my feet in the semi-darkness, already dressed head to toe, and fold the blanket. The three little boys lie snuggled together beneath layers of quilts on the bed. One stirs slightly and lays an arm over his brother. An unexpected homesick feeling drops like a lead sinker inside my stomach. There's no time to waste on melancholy, so I carry my boots to the washstand next to the door. I break a hole through the ice on top of the water in the basin and wash sleep from my eyes.

On my way downstairs, I hear Brother Stewart's distinctive voice. Even in prayer, his tone carries the lilt of a smile that brings Da to mind.

When the stairs creak under my weight, the missus raises her head and, with a soft smile, waves me to the chair next to hers. She's already ladled soup into a bowl and buttered a slab of bread for me. 'Tis a grand and simple gesture, so rare that the pleasure of it travels straight to my eyes. The warmth of the missus's smile only deepens when she notices.

Brother Stewart reaches for the water pitcher and refills his cup. "The fellowship of Friends is water to a thirsty man," he says. "If I'd spent the night at an inn, it's doubtful I'd arrive at my destination with the same count of pork barrels in my sled as when I left home. Unscrupulous thieves roam the roads."

"'Tis true," our host says solemnly, then adds, "and desperate ones too, the poor, the Irish . . ."

Everyone nods. Everyone but me.

The men dive into serious conversation about rising tensions between Loyalists and rebels and rumours of an imminent uprising at York. A few times I glance sideways to find the Quaker woman studying me.

The youngest of the couple's sons, about four years old, comes shyly down the stairs and climbs onto his mother's lap. Together, they form such a lovely picture. I tamp more tears and gather my bowl and spoon. The kitchen worktable with a wash basin for dirty dishes is next to the door.

As I start to push away from the table, the missus whispers, "Brother William." I pause, expecting her to say more, but she only looks at the dishes in my hands then returns my gaze with brows raised.

She knows.

A man would not clear the table. I've given myself away. My eyes cut to Brother Stewart and our host. They're thankfully consumed with talk of politics and have noticed nothing. I rise from the table, leave the dishes behind, and hurry outside through the biting cold to the solitude of the outhouse.

It's more complicated than I expected to play at being a man. In the gloom of the outhouse, I fumble with the buckle of my new belt, my fingers already numb and uncooperative in the freezing temperatures. At this rate, I'll wet my drawers before I can undo these cursed fly buttons. Finally, I drop onto the wooden seat and release an urgent stream. Wind whistles through a gap in the plank wall. I think of my Thomas, all alone, then of Seamus and Biddy, and the likelihood I'll be found out at the camp, the unlikelihood of recovering Mam's earbobs.

I let my tears empty out too, in a scalding torrent. This is the last cry I'll allow myself until I can weep with joy at being reunited with Thomas.

☙

For much of our travel, the only sound has been the harness bells and the sled runners gliding through the snow. A buffalo hide drawn over our laps this morning helps us stay warm, but the ever-shifting wind numbs my cheeks. As we travel, Brother Stewart's storytelling and jovial nature have occasionally pulled me away from my troubles. He is a well-read man, stocked to the hilt with anecdotes and commentary about everything, but he never makes me feel his lesser, even though I, as William, can't speak.

Three hours into the last leg of our journey, he looks around him, then says, "This country is amazing to behold, William. Beauty for as far as the eye can see—yonder trees set against silver skies, this pristine blanket of snow upon which we advance."

He looks at me. I nod and smile, which sufficiently pleases him.

In the distance, strands of smoke wind upward in the pale sky. Dread washes over me.

"Ah, we're nearly there. And a fire awaits," Brother Stewart says. With a flick of the reins, his team quickens their step. "The horses will be glad to be rid of our load, I'm sure."

He continues talking, but his voice becomes a hum in my ear. My mind turns to the image of the two burly Frenchmen who have Mam's earbobs. Today I'll come face to face with them. My knees shake when I recall the towering bulk of the loudmouthed Benoît.

The consistent strike of a distant blacksmith's hammer sings into the still air. 'Tis a good reminder of why I'm risking all—the hope that Thomas at my side in our own smithy will be the happy ending of this foolish mission.

Brother Stewart gently pulls back on one rein, and the team curves right toward a wide clearing hacked into the dense expanse of pines. Ahead of us, a column of sky cuts through the woods, an indicator that buried beneath last night's snow is the camp road. The blacksmith's hammer stops. As we enter this stretch of looming trees, my hands tremble.

I can do this for Thomas, live among the men, take back the earbobs. I need to believe I can to make it so.

"William. You all right, son?"

My curt nod furrows Brother Stewart's brow.

"I'll do your talking to get you hired on. My wife sent along slates and chalk for my nieces. I could spare you a set so you can communicate."

My gaze drops away from his face. I can neither read nor write.

He takes my meaning. "Oh! Well, I'm sure you'll be fine," he says uncertainly. "Sinclair's a good sort."

Just before we're spit into the open, I brace myself for the sight of men everywhere, in crowds thicker than in Bytown.

A cluster of squat log buildings hunkers amid mounds of snow. In the centre of the yard, a lone brown stallion, harnessed to a twelve-foot sled and waiting for its driver, raises its head and nickers at the approach of Brother Stewart's bay mares. On the ground surrounding the horse, hoof marks and sled tracks criss-cross the snow—signs of a large timber crew, yet to my relief, not a man in sight. I'm spared for now.

"Whoa," Brother Stewart says, pulling back on the reins. We stop next to a hitching post and our sleigh bells fall silent. He pushes the buffalo hide from his knees and jumps into the snow with vigour. But I am frozen to the bench seat. The moment my feet touch the ground, there'll be no turning back. Brother Stewart tethers his horses and sighs with satisfaction as he surveys the camp. "Come, William. Let us get to the business at hand—my wares and your job. We shall find our man yonder," he says, and sets off toward a small shanty partly concealed behind a cord of firewood stacked chest high along the full length of its foundation.

I'm no longer Mariah, a woman who would steady herself with a hand on the edge of the sleigh. I am William, fearless in the sureness of youth.

I rise to my feet. And leap.

I wade after him through calf-deep powder, toward the trampled roadway slicing through the camp. As we near the stallion, a pair of men wearing white canvas aprons shuffle out of the larger building, gripping opposite ends of a wooden pole threaded through the handle of a wrought-iron cauldron. Each man's jaw clenches with determination as they heft the wide-mouthed pot onto the waiting sled.

The taller of the two men rests the pole across one shoulder and regards Brother Stewart with mistrust before addressing us in French.

I've no idea what he said. In my early days of living in Lowertown among the French, I learned a few simple words and phrases. How will I function here knowing so little of the language?

"Good day, friends," Brother Stewart answers without breaking his stride.

Emboldened by his example, I look back at the Frenchman to offer a smile, but he's already turned back to his companion.

"Anglais," he grouses loudly, wiping a hand on the bib of his apron. The two men walk toward the shanty, duck their heads and disappear inside. I'd like to avoid that building. And them.

I adjust my gait to match Brother Stewart's, draw my shoulders back and lift my chin. If I'm able to be a boy's version of a man, I'll blend in. I'll take whatever job is available and keep to myself during this brief stay. A week at the most—just until I can reclaim what's mine. Then I'll be on my way home. Somehow.

Muted laughter sounds from inside the shanty. Brother Stewart removes his gloves and knocks on the door.

"Oui, entrez," a male voice calls out.

French again. My mouth goes dry.

The door squawks on its wood hinges as Brother Stewart swings it open. Past his shoulder, I see a bedstead positioned along the left wall beneath a narrow shelf of personal effects—a razor, a cup and the handle of a hog's-hair brush. A coat and hat lie across the blankets.

"Qui êtes-vous?" comes the gruff reply from the opposite side of the room. Two men are sitting next to the only window at a simple table stacked with books and scrolls of paper.

"In English, if you might," Brother Stewart requests.

"Huh, anglais," says the second man, thin-faced and wearing a stained apron. Chair legs scrape across the plank floor. "Au revoir, Renard." He squeezes past us and continues in the direction of the large shanty where we'd seen the other two aproned men.

"What the hell do you want?" Renard asks, leaning back in his chair. I would give anything to warm my hands by the fire crackling behind him.

"I am looking for Mr. Sinclair," Brother Stewart says, removing his hat. He steps deeper into the room and I push in next to him to escape the cold.

"I'm the man in charge. You deal with me." Renard looks me up and down, grimacing openly at my scars. "Close that door, boy. You're letting the heat out."

I gladly do as he asks.

"Mr. Sinclair and I have an arrangement. I was to deliver four barrels of salt pork this day and five sacks of dried beans with the promise of payment."

Renard crosses his arms and stares at him.

"It's a standing agreement," Brother Stewart adds. "We shook on it six winters past."

Renard rocks his chair back on its hind legs and rubs his jaw, then drops back on all its legs and says, "Pull the sled close to the camboose. The cooks will help unload the barrels."

"And you'll honour the agreement struck with Mr. Sinclair?" Brother Stewart says.

Renard snorts and flips through papers on his desk. "Unload, then come see me," he says without looking up.

Brother Stewart is quiet for a long while, then slowly settles his hat back onto his head. "There's one more thing. This lad is looking for work."

"Not here," Renard snaps. "I don't hire any man—or boy—who can't ask for himself."

"William has been speechless since childhood, so I speak on his behalf."

I remove my hat and crush it against my chest to still my trembling hands.

"Is he Irish?" Renard says. "We don't hire those damned bog-jumpers. They ruin everything they get their grubbing hands on."

"He's English. A nephew of a merchant in Bytown."

"No hair on his chin," Renard says. "He belongs at home sucking his mother's teat."

Resentment rises bitter in my throat. I'm as able-bodied as those cooks. If not for the prison of my disguise, I would have told him so. No, I wouldn't have. As Biddy has so often reminded me, I'm often a mouse of a woman.

Brother Stewart's voice continues calm and steady. "His aunt tells me he has experience working in a smithy and skill handling horses."

"Don't matter," Renard answers with a sneer. "There are no jobs and even if there were, I wouldn't give him one. His plums haven't dropped yet."

"The boy's family needs the money."

"I run a timber camp, not a charity."

Brother Stewart clears his throat. "But surely, you could find something for him to do." There's shouting outside. At least two or three men. A horse whinnies.

"No," Renard says, and points toward the door. Irritation sparks in his eyes. "We finish our business and you go."

Brother Stewart's mouth works as if he might press the issue further. But then he casts eyes, full of apology, at me.

My plans are dashed. Or can I impose on Brother Stewart to take me to another camp? For all his shrewdness, Renard has taken me for a teenage boy. Others will too. I can work the winter and return with a full season of pay. But then what?

"Keep 'im calm, for God's sake. And cut his coat open," a voice booms from outside.

The door flings wide, narrowly missing me, and a distinguished man bolts through it.

Renard leaps to his feet. His arrogance crumbles to ash. "Mr. Sinclair! I wasn't expecting you back so early!"

Mr. Sinclair pitches his coat and hat at Renard, then yanks the blanket off the bedstead followed by the sheets. Blood covers his pale hands. He shouts over his shoulder as he rushes outside with the bedding. "Round up some men! François's been crushed."

"Yes sir." Renard follows him out the door wearing a black look. His shoulder slams mine, shoving me sideways.

A horse-drawn sled carrying the injured man stops outside the door. A second figure in a red flannel shirt bends over him, blocking the view of all but the injured man's legs trembling against the sled. I recognize the signs of shock. Mam once brought me along to help a neighbour man whose bull had crushed him against a tree. The aftershock had set his teeth to chattering with such ferocity we thought they'd shatter. His arms and legs shook so, they nearly danced the bed across the room.

Renard calls, "You want him brought inside?"

Mr. Sinclair spins to face him. "Christ, no, he's a busted-up mess."

Renard sets off toward the cooks' building, shouting for hot water.

"Come on," Mr. Sinclair barks, and when I start forward, he thrusts the bedding toward me.

I take the blanket and sheets from him, but my feet won't move. This is all happening too fast. Renard has already doubled back to the sled with one of the cooks in tow.

"Let's go, son," Brother Stewart says, passing me on his way to the sled. "Prove yourself useful and your fate may change, God's will be done."

I do, and as I approach the sled, I can see that the man called François has his shirt and long underwear torn open to the waist and his eyes are bulging and glassy. Mr. Sinclair tugs the man's boots off and Renard sets to work cutting through the blood-soaked pant legs and long underwear. The horse nickers and shifts back and forth, made uneasy by the smell of blood and excrement.

"It was an accident, boss, I swear it was," the red-shirted man says. "I told him the tree was coming down. Preach, Benoît, Maurice—they all heard me!"

I could laugh and cry at once. Both the thieves are actually here.

The cooks and Renard look away. Guilt is catching, even if you haven't done the wrong yourself.

Brother Stewart closes his eyes in prayer as François cries out in his mother tongue. His eyes search the sky as he shivers. My heart breaks for him.

Mr. Sinclair pats the injured man's shoulder, then looks up at me and barks out an order. His French is too fast for me to understand what he wants from me.

"Cover him up, simpleton," Renard says. He wipes the knife clean on François's jacket and continues cutting the buttons away from his bloody pants.

I step forward, and my boots slip and I'm flat on my back, staring up at the blank sky. My eyes water in pent-up frustration. Even if I did understand French, William couldn't have answered. I scramble to my feet and lay the blanket across François's torso, then tuck it carefully around him. Renard glances up from his task and squints at me with the look of a man who'd just seen something that didn't add up. I've been too tender with the blanket. Too motherly.

Renard finishes cutting. Just as he peels back the waistband of François's pants, the youngest cook edges toward the sled for a closer look, then turns away and vomits onto the snow. Behind me, the horse whinnies and steps sideways. The sled jerks and François screams.

His groin is a bloody pulp. Shards of bone spike through skin like snapped-off trees. Blood swamps the bowl of his pelvis, and his pale member slumps as if resigned to what we all know is surely to come. Red soaks the bottom edge of the blanket, drizzles over the edge of the sled, and bleeds into the snow.

It won't be long now, but the horse can take no more. He rears, front hooves thrashing the air, and we all jump out of the way. Mr. Sinclair and Brother Stewart leap in front of the horse to prevent it from bolting as one of the cooks makes a futile grab for the reins.

This is my moment.

I drop my gloves in the snow and press my bare palms against the horse's flank. I run hands along his ribs as he blows hard, then finally along his neck. I watched Da calm spooked horses so many times, I know just what to do. The horse's head swings around for a better view of me. When François moans again, the men rush in to hold the sled steady. Soothing words rise to the surface, but I push them back in. Instead, I stroke the horse's jaw and whistle one of the French melodies that spills from taverns in Lowertown.

With nostrils still flared, his liquid-brown eyes focus on me. I place a hand over the white diamond on his forehead and the other on his muzzle. The sled is still.

The cook who'd been with Renard in the cabin approaches, carrying white rags and a small cauldron of steaming water. He stops to stare sombrely into the sled, then sets the cauldron in the snow and crosses himself.

In the distance, the steady beat of the blacksmith's hammer is Da's voice calling to me from the grave. *Pay attention*, it tells me.

The other men step closer to the sled. Maybe they picture themselves in François's place, laid out and shivering near death. When their shoulders slump, I know it's over.

François is dead.

The red-shirt man blurts, "My hand to God, it was an accident!"

With his gaze riveted on the dead man, Mr. Sinclair replies, "You cost me a skidder."

"It won't happen again!"

Sinclair's eyes narrow. "That's the first right thing you've said. Pack up your gear."

"You can't fire me! I need to finish the season to get paid!"

Sinclair tips his head toward Renard, who smiles, then launches himself at the red-shirt man. Red-shirt man's arms fold over his face to fend off the rain of blows, but the wiry Frenchman's fists pound him until blood sprays into the snow and he collapses.

Maybe it is good that I'm leaving this place. I'd never make it among these vile men. I catch Mr. Sinclair sizing me up. He's onto me for sure. Pray he lets me leave without repercussion. There'll be no mercy here for a lone woman—an Irish woman at that—with men like Renard and Benoît in the mix.

Renard straightens his clothing and wipes a bloodied hand across his forehead. He points at the fallen man. "What do you want done with this one?"

"Leave him," Mr. Sinclair says. Then his eyes cut to mine. His finely trimmed moustache barely moves as he speaks. "You're hired," he says and stalks past us toward the cabin.

"He don't talk," Renard says in protest.

"All the better. What language does he understand?"

"English," Brother Stewart pipes up. "And he's very good with horses. The lad has some blacksmithing skills also."

"Renard, put him with Preach's crew. He'll take over skidding from François. You train him," Sinclair says, and carries on walking.

"He can't manage the horses to skid timbers out of the woods if he can't speak the commands," Renard protests.

Mr. Sinclair wheels around, his face fiery red. "Make it work!"

We all stand in silence until Mr. Sinclair returns to his shanty. Once he slams the door shut, Renard runs me through with a look of pure loathing.

28

MARIAH

Towering pines flank the frozen roadway and block all but a narrow strip of sky as we travel to the cut. I bump along on the bench seat of the cooks' sled, wedged between the man simply known as Cook and his helper, Étienne, a tall and gangly boy around Thomas's age. Uneven ground jostles us and I rock against Cook's arm. He elbows me sharply and topples me onto Étienne, with whom I share a look of mutual suffering.

Ahead of us, Renard bounces Sinclair's sleigh over a chunk of ice and shouts curse words at the horse. Although I can't yet see the men at work, their axe strikes echo through the forest. In a matter of minutes, I'll come face to face with the two Frenchmen who took Mam's earbobs. Mr. Sinclair mentioned another fellow on the crew— Preach. A godly man to offset the devil is a bit of luck, something to hang on to.

Cook brings the sled to a halt. Before us is a steep incline. A team of horses edges down the hill toward us, hauling a double bobsled stacked six timbers deep. Could it be that a log like that is what

GWEN TUINMAN

crushed François? I shudder to think of that full load shooting freely toward us.

Étienne reads my mind. "Sandpipers. No worry." He points to a road-side sand pile with a fire burning at its centre. Boys even younger than Étienne move back and forth sprinkling shovelfuls into the ruts carved by sled runners, then they get out of the way and watch the team until it and the load safely reach the bottom, leaning on their shovels.

Ahead of us, Renard urges Sinclair's mare up the hill. She stumbles, turns her head sideways, and nickers. He cracks the reins like a whip and shouts at the sandpipers, who dash forward to spread hot sand into the ruts under the runners. The mare tucks her muzzle close to her chest and strains the rest of the way. After Renard disappears over the crest of the hill, Cook gives a light flick of his reins and the stallion steps forward. As the ascent begins, we are tipped hard against the backrest.

"Is okay. The horses wear cork shoes," Étienne says with an air of importance that reminds me of Thomas. I reward him with an impressed look.

Cook grouses at the boy in French. "D'accord," Étienne replies and checks the cauldron behind us as we crest the hill. "No spilling," he confirms to Cook and then leans toward me. "He worries too much. Each trip, no spilling."

"Except that one time, eh?" Cook says. "Beans everywhere."

The boy rolls his eyes, then balloons his cheeks and makes explosion sounds. Then he grins. "Only one time, I don't tie things down so good, and he never lets me forget it. He is my uncle, so I put up with him."

"Ha," Cook says.

"So, you don't talk, eh?" Étienne says. I shake my head.

"Quaker fella said some wolves got at you," Cook says, craning his neck for a better view of my face. I look straight ahead.

"They did one hell of a job." There's no judgment in his voice.

"How'd you get away from dem sons of bitches? I know you don't talk, but you could show us, at least!"

I pull an imaginary knife and plunge it into my lower belly as I had done to the wolf on the night of the fire. Then I pull my fist in a line upward to my chest and drag an index finger sideways across my throat.

"Sacrebleu!" The boy exhales.

I glance up at Cook. His eyes narrow and he nods slowly at me. "You take," he says, passing me the reins. I hold them loosely in my hands as Da taught me and, as I've seen teamsters do on countless occasions, rest my forearms across my knees.

"Those deerskin?" Cook asks, scrutinizing my gloves. I nod.

"You need moosehide gloves for skidding timber out of the woods. Better for feeling the reins," he says.

Étienne chimes in. "An old Algonquin woman sold us three pairs last week. You can buy them out of the van back at the camboose where we sleep." He pauses a moment. "I'll show you around tonight. Your Quaker friend put your packsack in the camboose. You get François's bunk."

I force a smile, although my stomach swims at the notion of sleeping close to all those men.

"You'll have cold nights for a while. We sleep two men to a bunk, but no one'll want to share a dead man's bed. No offense."

Thank God for small mercies.

Another twenty minutes along the skid road, the chorus of axes has grown loud and incessant, and it chips away at my delusions of courage. I'll soon be within reach of my earbobs, but the risk I must take to steal them back terrifies me. I'd rather face another wolf than the gathering of strange men that awaits me there.

Cook lifts a steel triangle from under the bench seat and clangs it loudly for several seconds. One by one, men drift from the forest to follow after us, their axes over their shoulders. Each acknowledges

Cook and Étienne, but stares at me with a gloomy curiosity bordering on mistrust. They wouldn't have yet heard the news of François's death, but they must have known when the sled hauled him away that their friend was done for.

Mr. Sinclair's sleigh sits among some fresh stumps in a clearing straight ahead. Cook tells me to stop next to a circle of logs with a fire burning at its centre. The lightest tug on the reins brings the stallion to a halt. Étienne jumps down from the sled, wraps rags around the handle of an oversized tea kettle, and lugs it toward the fire. I'm uncertain of how to conduct myself, so I stay put. Men lay their axes against the logs and draw tin plates from the sacks they carry. A lineup forms at the sled, and Cook doles out baked beans, salt pork and fresh bread. The loggers take their seats in front of the fire and bring their plates close to their chins, eating in silence. My mouth waters at the smell of molasses and pork rising off the bean pot, but I have neither a plate nor the courage to ask for one.

I catch a glimpse of Renard's red wool coat moving among the trees beyond the clearing. I gather my courage and hop down from the sleigh and wade through the snow to where he stands at the end of a felled trunk whose diameter reaches his elbow. Planted stoically atop the trunk's hewn surface, a giant of a man watches me approach, a broad hewing axe leaning against his thigh. Renard raises his voice and his hands flap like crow's wings as he shouts at the man, "Preach, you hear what I say?"

Preach ignores Renard, directing all his attention at me. In spite of the cold, he wears neither hat nor gloves, and his coat is open at the throat. The wind lifts his silver hair to reveal its tarnished roots. He resembles the Old Testament Moses from the Bible stories Da told Biddy and me as children. Clenched in the corner of his mouth is a white clay pipe, its bowl sculpted into the face of a beautiful woman. Preach withdraws the pipe to puff smoke into the frigid air, studying me so curiously I'm compelled to turn away. I focus on loosening my joints and swinging my arms as men do when they walk.

Nearby, a pair of men are skinning bark from another log. I recognize them instantly. *Oh my Lord!*

Renard notices my reaction. "You know the Chartier brothers?" he asks suspiciously.

My eyes dart to his and I shake my head vehemently.

"Benoît! Maurice!" Renard calls.

Both men quit their work and join us. They're taller than I remembered. Renard shouts more instructions, but in French. Surely they hear my heart banging.

Benoît shrugs and glares up at Preach. "Off the log, old man. I could have hewed that log stick twice as flat in half the time you needed to finish the job. Everyone here knows it."

Preach slowly taps the ashes from his pipe and returns it to the inside of his jacket, as Benoît and the other men take up hardwood poles double their own height and spread out along the length of the log. I understand immediately that they will use the poles as levers to roll the log, like Seamus and I have done before.

Only after Benoît and Maurice wedge the ends of their poles beneath the log does Preach jump down, landing near me. "Your Christian name?" he asks.

"William," Renard answers. "He don't talk." He spits and mutters something to the Frenchmen. Benoît's teeth flash and laughter thunders from his mouth. Maurice looks away, grimacing.

My face goes warm. I don't need to understand the language to know I'm being mocked.

"'Tis by deed alone a man best be judged," says Preach. "So many speak falsely." He too takes up a pole and wedges it in place at the centre of the trunk. "Come, William. This beast of a log needs to be rolled forward a quarter turn."

I lean forward and brace a shoulder against the underside of his pole. From the corner of my eye, I see tendons flex in Preach's wrists.

His fingers are thick as kindling, but his right index finger, from the second knuckle up, is missing.

Benoît shouts, "Un."

In a duel of sorts, Preach calls over him. "One!"

We push together and the log rocks forward, then back.

Benoît and Preach shout two simultaneously in their different tongues. I push with all my might. The log teeters ahead then rolls back to us.

On three, we groan with effort and the log rolls away from us a quarter turn, halting abruptly when the flat hewn side thumps against the frozen earth, ready to be squared after these men have eaten.

"Well done, son." Preach extends a hand and I remove my mitt to accept it. Instead of a quick shake, his fingers close around mine with a powerful grip. His skin is unexpectedly warm and the stub of his finger presses into my palm. "The Lord has shone upon you, William." He continues to crush my hand. "I see by these marks you've been spared from death. Our Heavenly Father has plans for you." His dark eyes are serious and I do not flinch, for to do so would betray me as weak and this is not a world that tolerates weakness.

"Let's eat," Renard calls over his shoulder.

Preach's mouth twists with the hint of a smile, then he winks and lets go, punching my arm. Once his back is turned, I slip my hand back into my mitt and stretch my fingers, then follow him to the clearing.

At the campfire, everyone is finishing up their beans and wiping their plates with bread. There must be forty men, plus a few at the sled getting seconds from Cook. Étienne is making the rounds with the kettle, pouring tea into their extended cups. A ruddy-cheeked man takes a sip, and says, "This batch is thick enough to hold my fork upright." The men on either side of him chuckle.

Étienne spots me, and says, "Where's your plate?"

A lone sack sits beneath a spindly Jack pine a few yards from the fire. We both know who it belonged to.

"François can't use it no more," he says. Men within earshot exchange long-faced glances, then look away.

I retrieve the bag and fish out François's plate. Cook loads it up and I find an empty spot next to Benoît and Maurice. Maybe I can learn something about where the earbobs are hidden. As I raise François's spoon to my mouth, I hear Renard telling a story in French that raises laughter among the Canadiens.

"Again, in English," someone shouts in a Scottish brogue.

Renard nods in my direction. "This boy showed up today, now he's skidding for a crew. But he don't talk. So, if you see him coming with a horse, jump out the way quick and yell 'Whoa' en français. Else the damned horse won't know when to stop!" He slaps his knee and guffaws kick up again.

My face goes hot, but I'm saved from having to respond when Cook hollers from the sled, "Renard, don't judge him too quick!" He switches to lightning-quick French, then claws the air, howling like a wolf, and draws his fingernails down his cheek. Men lean forward on their log seats. He repeats my earlier gestures—knife to the gizzard drawn upward to this chest, an index finger across his throat. His dark shaggy brows rise as he eyes the reaction of his audience.

When they look to me for confirmation, I make a slicing motion across my throat. "That's a fine scar," the Scot says above murmurs of approval.

And that's when I understand that a scarred man is a heroic creature. He'll unbutton his shirt or roll up his sleeve and tell anyone willing to listen how he came to earn them: shot by musket in service to his king, slashed while barring marauders from his home, beaten while defending the virtuous name of his sainted mother. Whereas a woman seeks to hide the signs of an ordeal she struggled to survive, a man bears his scars with pride.

I suppress a smile and keep my head down, waiting for the attention to pass. My purpose is better served by fading into the background as best I can.

Soon Cook and Étienne leave with the sled. As they disappear along the ice road, the lumbermen finish their tea and scrub their plates clean with snow. Some change into dry socks before they repack their sacks and trickle back into the woods.

Before I finish eating, Maurice and Benoît abandon their sacks on their log seats and return to the cut. The earbobs might be in one of their bags. Could it really be that simple? While none of the stragglers are paying attention, I discreetly swap my bag for Benoît's and prepare to ease it open.

"Remember me?"

How do I know that loathsome voice?

When I look up, my breath catches in my throat. It's the fur trader from Fran Edwards's mercantile. His wild stench and red woollen hat are forever stamped in my mind.

"I know'd it was you by those scars." I can't think.

"Never thought you'd see ole Gustave again, did ya?" His eyes gleam with pleasure. "What would Sinclair say if he know'd you was a woman. And Irish, ta boot! He don't cotton to your kind since the Shiners stole from his timber limits."

I have no choice but to stand and face him. Before I'm fully on my feet, he pushes me hard in the chest and sends me reeling backward over the log. I land so hard on my bottom my teeth rattle.

"Eh, stupide!" Renard calls from a distance. "Let's go."

I flick a sideways glance to where he waves me toward François's horse.

"This ain't over," Gustave says through his browned front teeth.

"We got a score to settle. You best let me under your skirts all winter, otherwise, I'll be obliged to tell everybody the truth 'bout you." He backs away slowly, then turns, whistling a tune on his way to the ice road. My gut squeezes with fear. As I get to my feet, I notice Preach's stormy eyes follow Gustave from atop the log as he walks away. Preach and I lock gazes for a moment. Then he bends slowly forward, chokes up on the handle of his broad axe, and begins chipping away at the bark skin. My knees wobble, but I set off after Renard.

Well behind the log, where the Chartier brothers hack bark at one end and Preach does the same at the other, Renard waits next to a chestnut mare that regards me with the calmness of one recognizing an old friend.

The horse is easily a head taller than Renard's. Twists of long hair cascade over the top of her hooves, which are wider than pie plates. Her winter coat is shaggy and a wayward forelock sweeps like a wild thing across her forehead. God never made a creature more commanding and beautiful. This horse deserves the name Queenie.

Renard points to the squared logs around us, their ends hewn to form pyramids. "You and this horse skid all these sticks to the heap. I'll show you a shortcut through these woods."

He flicks the long leads. "Hup, hup!" Queenie drags a skid chain and a pair of opposing hooks through the snow. She stops at one end of a log that lies skinned and hewn flat on all four sides. Its surface gleams like bone pulled from a soup pot.

Renard lifts a short-handled sledgehammer and drives the sharp tooth of each iron hook deep into either side of the timber. "Log-dogs, these are," he says and yanks the skid chain hard to be sure they're set. Upon hearing the clank of metal, Queenie strains against her traces and the timber eases forward like a ship pulling away from the dock. Intent on observing Renard's every move, I follow him on the right side of the log, a quarter the way along its sixteen-foot length.

Maurice, who's been scoring the new log ahead of Benoît, shouts to me as we advance. "You too close!"

Just then Renard steers Queenie left, and the back end of the timber swoops toward me. I lunge behind a thigh-high stump just as the end of the squared timber sweeps the very spot I'd have stepped in if not for Maurice's warning.

Behind me, Benoît laughs at the near miss. It will be especially satisfying to take the earbobs from that man. I look back over my shoulder in time to see Maurice scour his brother with a disapproving look.

"Angels watch over you," Preach says quietly as I pass by.

My da used to say that very thing right up to the time the Flynns' dog got after me.

Queenie plods surefooted around trees and stumps to a well-used skid path. There's no evidence of sled runners here, only a single groove worn into the frozen snow by previously dragged logs.

Away from the others, Renard addresses me and Queenie in torrents of scorching French. Some words I pick up on—*shit, stupid,* insults to my mother—but the rest is a blur.

Walking behind him, I commit his every move to memory. I can mimic the subtle flick of the reins, but I need to figure out how the silent William will issue Renard's spoken commands.

Pine boughs above us yield to open sky and we emerge into a new clearing where two rugged characters await us next at a pile of nearly twenty squared timbers. My heart pounds with worry. What will I be expected to do here? Queenie knows, and she walks across the end of two short logs leaning like ramps against the bottom layer of timbers in the stack.

"Whoa," Renard says, pulling back on the reins.

"G'day," one of the men offers. His pleasant tone doesn't match his gruff exterior.

Renard doesn't bother with introductions. "Come here," he snaps at me. "See this?" He backs Queenie up so that the skid chain goes slack, then he hammers at the log-dogs until they sprawl open and release the timber.

"One more stick before dark, eh?" The man earns a grin from Renard, who tosses the leads onto the snow and pulls a flask from his coat pocket.

"Nip of whiskey?" Renard asks him.

"Sinclair doesn't abide drinking in camp," the man replies, all the while measuring me for loyalty to the timber boss.

"Don't worry, this one's lips are sealed." Renard laughs at his own joke. "Go on," he tells me. "I catch up."

I scoop the leads and flick them lightly. Queenie doesn't budge. Behind me, I hear Renard sniggering, which burrows under my skin like an old insult. I click my tongue and flick the reins harder. Off she goes with a sudden lurch that pulls the reins through my gloves. When I tighten my grip, Queenie nearly tugs me off my feet, which sends Renard into a fit of laughter. But I don't fall and that is a victory.

Along the skid path, Queenie moves steadily, towing the bobsled without any urging from me. The way is obvious and she's walked it more times than I'll ever know. Twenty minutes in, another skidder follows a draught horse toward us dragging a stick. To allow them a wide berth, I direct Queenie off the path and into snow deep as her knees. She halts after a few steps, so I wade next to her shoulder and hold her bridle to lead her forward. After a few heaves, we're on our way. The man nods in passing.

"Good job," he says, without reaction to my scars.

I'm several yards past him before I realize my heartbeat has at last slowed to its normal rate. My mood further lifts as I reflect on his compliment. I'd be hard-pressed to remember the last time I received one for a job well done.

Renard is slower than promised to return to the cut, so I hitch Queenie to a second log and set off to the heap. We encounter him on a flat section of the skid path flanked by dense woodlands. When our eyes meet, he turns his head away and spits. After we pass each other, I can't help my smile. Renard hopes I'll fail without him at my side. He's going to be disappointed. If he and Biddy were ever locked in argument, I wonder who'd prevail.

On the return trip to the cut, the shadows have grown longer. Mr. Sinclair's sled is gone, and with it, Renard. Both Frenchmen and Preach are deeper in the woods with two other men I've yet to meet, choppers I presume, heads bowed and hats pressed to their chests. Prayers for François, no doubt.

Benoît's pack still slouches in the snow next to the one I've inherited. I'm eyeing the bag when Queenie nickers and turns her head toward me. With my back to the crew, I trudge toward her, then remove a glove and pet her muzzle, quite possibly the softest thing I've ever touched. My heart is captured. She's unflinching, as if I'm a returning friend and not a stranger.

Snow squeaks behind me. The two men I hadn't met trudge past with felling axes resting across their shoulders. "How's it going," they say.

The French brothers trail behind them. With each new step, Maurice lifts his feet above the deepest drifts. Benoît plows forward, kicking up sprays of snow. The way men move tells much about their character. These two are night and day, like my sister and me. I need to watch each of the Frenchmen and learn their ways. Then, and only then, will I act on reclaiming the earbobs. My stay at camp may be longer than I first planned.

Queenie raises her muzzle and looks back the way the men have come. Just as I turn to follow her gaze, a strong hand clamps my shoulder. It's Preach. In his other hand is François's pack. "I'll carry it for you," he says and searches my eyes, for what I know not. But I am discomfited by it.

The flow of departing men cues Queenie to tug against the reins, and I let her lead me toward the ice road that will return us to the timber camp. Preach drifts along at my side. Halfway through the long trek back to camp, Preach says, "That trapper gives you trouble."

I direct my eyes to the ground and keep walking.

"Gustave is a heathen of the worst order. He boasts openly about forcing himself on Indian women. The man's lower than a snake."

It's a struggle to appear calm, knowing that I could be next.

"We are Christian men, and we shall smite down sinners in the Lord's name, William," Preach says. He casts me a sideways glance and pats my shoulder.

When his hand lingers there, I swallow the lump in my throat and look at him.

"I intend to pen a letter to my Florence and tell her about the speechless young man who so strongly resembles what our own son might have looked like had the Lord not called him home."

This revelation explains why he's been paying such attention to me. Poor man.

"Florence is much younger than I and struggles to accept His will. I tell her there will be others—sons, that is. She's so delicate in body and mind. These months without me are difficult for her, and my letters are her only solace until we are reunited once more in spring."

My interested expression satisfies Preach and he carries the conversation for both of us. "Do you have a girl, William?"

I shake my head.

"When you do, treat her well. Buy her a good wedding ring. Then while you're away, it serves as a constant reminder to her that she is yours. I bought my Florence a gold band etched with vines."

A ring should be given in love, not to mark a woman as a man's property. I'll never wear a gold band, not that I'll ever be asked to. Florence is both cursed and blessed, where I am only cursed. What I wouldn't give to be taken under a protective wing.

The sky is wrought-iron black when we finally reach camp, but at the entrance of each building a lantern lights our way. I smell food cooking when we pass the blacksmith's shed. If only I were so lucky to be that blacksmith so I could also eat away from the others. Most of the men stream quietly to the camboose door and duck inside. Gustave is about to enter when he looks back and catches sight of me. He takes a stride in my direction, but the glee fades from his face when Preach steps in front of me to block his path. I move away, following the other teamsters and their horses to the six low stables several yards opposite the camboose. Between the first two log stables waits a short, portly man with a fully whiskered face. His wire-rimmed glasses reflect the light cast from the lantern he holds.

"You're William?" he asks. I raise a thumb.

"I'm Henderson, the barn boss," he says. I follow him to the last stable on the right, and he directs me to Queenie's lamplit stall and gives me instructions for morning feeding.

"Everything comes off—the bit, harness, log-dog, whiffletree," he says. "Hang them from pegs at the back of the stall or on either side of the stall gates."

All this unbuckling and hefting paired with animal smells reminds me of our lost Esmerelda. For a second, I'm transported to the dark forest after the cabin fire, snapping teeth, the cow's frantic bawling cut short, and the wolves' crushing jaws.

In front of a grey mare in a neighbouring stall, Henderson and a taller man, curly-haired with a dark beard, discuss reshoeing the horse tomorrow. Must be the camp blacksmith. The smith pets the horse's muzzle and promises the full job will be done by midmorning. While the men chat about other jobs that need doing, I brush Queenie's coat like Da used to do for the Harris horses. There's a patch of hair rubbed away where the harness makes contact above her right shoulder. I squat to run my right hand the length of her leg to check for swelling or soreness. Then I lift each of her shoes to check for wear.

"You know your way around a horse," the blacksmith says. I turn to find him and Henderson now standing outside Queenie's stall. He's likely a year to two older than me and he's taken the encouraging tone a man uses to put a shy boy at ease. "My father wants to apprentice a farrier at his smithy. Think about it."

My cheeks blaze with pride. I want to shout *yes* but instead I nod and point to the balding spot above Queenie's shoulder.

"Ah, yes," Henderson says. "I'll fetch a tin of ointment for you to rub in tomorrow morning. She'll thank you for it. This one's a company horse and will give you no trouble, not like those farm horses some of the fellas bring. They work best for the man who brought them."

He sets off with the blacksmith toward the stable door but then pauses and turns back to me. "William, a word to the wise. I saw you walking with Preach. Take care what company you keep. Many of the men here are hiding from the law. Not saying he's one of them, but no one knows his story and it pays to keep your eyes open. Right?"

I give him a thumbs-up and he leaves, explaining to his friend that the new boy can't speak.

"Talking is overrated," the blacksmith replies and casts a smile my way.

After I snuff the lantern, I stay with Queenie, who lets me scratch her forehead while I consider Henderson's warning. Preach is the least of my worries. I'd rather sleep in the straw at this horse's feet than spend a night trapped in the camboose with all those strange men. If not for Mam's earbobs, I'd do just that.

I sigh and head for the camboose. No one is around, so before going inside, I venture beyond the lamplight behind the stable and relieve myself quick as I can. I mustn't be caught squatting. At the very moment I'm about to reassemble myself, the camboose door flings open. My eyes widen. I don't move.

Gustave steps into the night. He checks left, then right, and skulks toward the first stable.

He takes a brief look inside, and then I watch him as he continues to the other stables. I hear him curse when he doesn't find me in Queenie's stall.

He reappears and, with his back toward me, calls out slyly, "Oh, William! I know you're out here."

My stomach knots as he scans the stable yard. If he turns around, lets his eyes adjust to the darkness beyond the light, I'm sunk.

"I just want to talk," he says. When I don't answer, his voice turns harsh. "Stop wasting my time. You know I'm gonna find you."

I hold my breath for fear of making a sound.

"Bitch," he mutters after a long, tense silence and then he stalks off toward the blacksmith's shed, a few yards beyond the rightmost column of stables. I close my eyes and thank God.

When I open them again, Preach is standing in front of the camboose. I'm afraid to move. How much has he seen? He strides purposefully in the same direction taken by Gustave. I count to ten and hoist my trousers and fasten my belt, then run toward the dreaded camboose. Off in the darkness, I hear the two men arguing. Their voices carry and, despite my fear, I stop for a moment to listen, hugging François's bag to my chest.

Preach growls, "You will not corrupt that boy."

"I never did nothin'," Gustave hollers back.

I shove the heavy door open and lurch inside.

A wall of stench slams me—unwashed bodies, damp wool, smoke. Along the back and side walls of the camboose are double-tiered sleeping platforms. Oh no. One long endless bed for all of us to pile into. Silent shantymen balancing tin dinner plates on their knees sit on benches at the feet of the lower platforms. Above them, others sit dangling their legs from the upper level. From every available hook, corner post and rafter hang ropes over which socks and long underwear are draped. At the centre of the floor is a firepit framed in squared timbers. Cook has hung pots and kettles of all sizes above the flames.

Although most of the smoke rises through a large square opening in the roof, a haze blankets the room. Memories of the cabin fire rise momentarily. My heart pounds as flames climb my imagination.

"Eh, William!" Étienne smiles brightly next to Cook's fire. "Wash up. I show you around."

I turn to see a stand next to the door on which sits a basin of dark water and a towel black as coal with the dirt of every man who arrived before me. I rinse my hands in the cold water and dry them against my pant legs.

"You sleep there," Étienne tells me, pointing to a narrow vacant space on the lower-level platform against the rightmost wall.

Panic floods me. I'm meant to sleep snugged between strange men. No matter which way I roll in the night, I'll be facing the one thing in life that frightens me more than a dog. Still, half of the space is laid out with pine boughs and a folded blanket. My rucksack rests against the exterior wall. I'm surprised to see a black slate and four lengths of chalk peeking out from under one edge—a gift from Brother Stewart. *Good men do exist*, I remind myself.

"That's yours too." Étienne points to a peg wedged between two logs and then across the room to the van, a tall, padlocked chest that contains necessities—gloves, socks, wool underwear, axe heads, knives. "Whatever you take, Cook writes in his book. Sinclair pays you at end of season, minus what you owe," the boy says. "Now, come and eat."

I dig my plate and spoon out of François's sack, which I hang on the peg. Étienne ladles me out potatoes, boiled pork and broth until juices nearly overflow the edges. Although my stomach has hounded me since late afternoon, my appetite disappears as I think about how scarce food is for Biddy and the children in Bytown. Maybe even less for my Thomas, wherever he is.

Anger rises in my chest when I think of all the winters I felt sorry that Seamus had to be off at the camp. And here he was, eating his fill while I so often went hungry so his children and Biddy could eat. If ever I see him again, it will be through new eyes.

I find a sawed-off stump seat at the front of the camboose and eat alone, relieved that aside from Étienne, no one here has as much as acknowledged my presence.

I finish eating and rinse my plate and spoon in a water bucket as the others are doing, then tuck them away. Yawning, I crawl over the foot of my platform and settle in, discreetly sliding Fran's knife from inside my boot and tucking it under the blanket. Whatever comes my way, I'll be ready. Then I wrestle my boots off, hang my damp socks from my peg, and put on a dry pair from home.

With dinner over, tobacco pipes are lit. Their smoke is sweet and reminds me of Da's after-dinner puff. Directly across the room, the blacksmith hauls out his fiddle and tunes its strings.

Neither Preach nor Gustave have returned to the camboose, and I'm grateful for it. All around me, men play raucous games like grown schoolboys and share stories. There's an ease among them that helps me forget, for a moment, the gravity of my situation. It occurs to me that Thomas hadn't been running away from home, from me, from our disaster of a family. Perhaps he was running toward this.

"Ezra," someone calls out to the blacksmith. "Play dat jig we all like!"

Ezra cradles his fiddle beneath his dense beard, a soft smile tugging at the corners of his mouth. His fingertips dance along the violin's neck as he plucks the notes right-handed without dropping the bow. I've heard nothing like this tune before. He strikes up a faster beat, and four men leap from their benches to dance. Another four rise to partner with them, knotting their handkerchiefs beneath their chins in pantomime of women. They ham it up, preening and batting their lashes coquettishly, which raises cheers from onlookers.

On a bench across the fire, one of the fellers from our crew leans in to look at something in the palm of Benoît's hand. I strain to see past the dancers, twirling through the room with elbows hooked. But when they move on, I'm rewarded with a glimpse of gold and pearl between his beefy fingers.

Benoît truly does have Mam's earbobs. *And he's flaunting them like an eejit!*

As Ezra's fiddle playing reaches new heights amid peals of laughter, Preach eases through the camboose door and unfolds himself to full height. His expression shows no trace of the anger I heard earlier. Like a vapour, he trails to the back of the room and plants his foot between two men. When they jump to clear the way, he boosts himself onto a top bunk.

I look back at Benoît in time to see him tucking the earbobs into the breast pocket of his shirt. Of course, he carries them with him. How naive of me to think they'd be stashed in his pack.

How will I retrieve them when he carries them everywhere? I bite the inside of my lip, then give myself a shake. Although I cannot imagine it now, I must believe the opportunity to take back the earbobs will reveal itself to me. I will be ready.

As Étienne snuffs candles, Ezra plays a tune that raises a burning lump in my throat. The grief that warbles inside each note quiets us all. The blacksmith must also come from people who understand suffering.

"Bonne nuit, les hommes," Cook says when Ezra lowers his bow.

Wood slats creak as men climb into their bunks. Using my folded coat for a pillow, I lie straight like a board with my head inches from the wall and the scratchy blanket gathered beneath my chin. The camboose grows still except for the breathing of my bunkmates and the sound of Cook and Étienne burying bread tins under the hot coals of the smouldering flames.

I lift my head and dare one glance at the door. Gustave will surely return soon. The hilt of my knife is warm and solid inside my grip. He won't catch me off guard again. I will not back down.

29

BIDDY

Darkness snuffed out the sun an hour ago. Roweena's five children and my three are hungry and irritable while we wait for Seamus's return from his new job clearing trees to make way for Bytown roads. This has been the evening pattern at the Newells' cabin since we took refuge here after the fire. Each night my husband comes home a bit later. His neglect is a sour enough pill without Roweena bearing constant witness to it. That she overhears our bickering is total humiliation.

All I want is for Seamus to stay with me and protect our land from squatters. And to love me. But he wants to travel back up the Gatineau River to finish out the timber season. He says it's because we need the money, but I see that our life, which once made him happy, now fuels his restlessness. His body is here but his mind is far away.

I deserve better than I've gotten. God will forgive me for thinking so, because He knows it to be true. Every day for the past month, from sunup to nightfall, I sit inside the front window of the Newells' cabin waiting for my old life to return. Maybe *hoping* better describes what I do. No, I think *wishing* is more to the point.

I wish the flames that leap in my mind each time I close my eyes would disappear. I wish the burns along my cheek and jawline would heal and that I would be beautiful again. I especially wish I could go back in time and leave Mariah behind in Ireland.

The devil is at work in my sister as he was in my da, who squandered our money and stumbled around in drunkenness. Her sin is covetousness. She's always wanted what was mine—my looks, Seamus, the earbobs. My sister has robbed me of everything. When I told Seamus that she's probably in Lower Canada or America squandering our money, he left the room.

"Help Annie set the table," Roweena tells her eldest daughter. "Seamus will be back soon and expecting to be fed." Annie leaves Elizabeth's side and begins laying out spoons. Roweena notices me watching and the soft smile drops from her face.

From the moment we first landed in these Corktown swamps, Roweena Newell has been a friend, but now she wears on me and so do her children. She has kind looks and thank yous for Seamus but not for me.

"Need help?" I say. Her back is turned as she stirs the largest pot hanging from a crane in the hearth. Her tone is all business when she turns her head to answer. She frowns at my belly. "Dinner's well in hand," she says. "Rest up." I can tell from the squint of her eyes and sudden pallor that she's brewing a headache, and she can't help but snip at any of her children who get in her way.

"Elizabeth, tend the little ones so they aren't underfoot." I try to sound in charge, like my old self.

Roweena withholds her thanks. It's remarkable what you learn about people when forced to live with them in cramped spaces.

Her melancholy brood show no enthusiasm for Elizabeth's attempts to organize them in games of Jack Straws or tell them stories about the grand house she'll one day live in. They look as if she's tied them to a pole and is torturing them.

Liam rolls his eyes. "Do you know any stories from timber camps or back home?"

"Tell us one about a horse," says his youngest sister.

And Elizabeth soon gives up. When Katherine fusses, Roweena is openly annoyed. The racket will only double when this baby is born. Children cry. It's a fact.

At least Roweena can't find fault with Annie, who hasn't spoken since the night we arrived in Bytown. Her silence will pass, I'm sure, but for the time being, one less nattering voice to grate on my frayed nerves is a blessing.

Elizabeth rolls out her bottom lip and huffs, "Da's late again and I'm starving. Can't we eat?"

"We'll wait a bit longer. He's working very hard cutting trees," Roweena replies. "You should be grateful that he finds work," she says, walking over to pick up the whining Katherine and settle her on one hip. My daughter sucks her thumb and rests a cheek against my friend's shoulder. Watching her do everything I should be doing in my own home is its own kind of slow-burning hell.

"I'm not a baby. Da comes home smelling of whiskey," Elizabeth says.

"Then you're old enough to know a man needs an occasional drink to forget his troubles," Roweena tells her.

Elizabeth turns to me as if *I'm* the source of our woes. "You let him waste our money."

Her dismal expression is more than I can bear, so I turn away and stare once more out the window. It's history repeating itself. She sounds so much like me at her age, complaining about my da.

It's going to take money for us to start over. When Seamus went to take the measure of the damage at our homestead, he found that our *trusted* neighbours have scavenged my best cauldrons for their own use. May they choke on all the food they cook in those pots.

I know Seamus regrets leaving camp and forfeiting whatever wages he'd earned to that point. He resents me for it too, but he should be angry with Mariah. If I still had the earbobs, I could have sold them and fixed all our problems.

In turn, I resent him for missing Mariah. He never says it, but I know he wishes she was at the homestead, working alongside him as I've never done. How was I to know that the way to a man's heart was through firing a musket with precision, hefting fence posts, or planning the next year's crop rotation.

I am—I was—the pretty one. I am the one who shares Seamus's bed. I gave him the most children, daughters who neither rebel against him nor look down on his achievements. *So why can't he love me?*

Roweena touches my arm and I jump. "What?"

"I called you three times," she says and holds out a cup of broth. "You must try to pull yourself together. A home can be rebuilt and possessions regained, but a family . . ."

I see that our children are at the table and the eldest have already finished eating.

"Seamus isn't home yet," I protest, pushing the cup away. "You should have waited for him."

"It's nearly bedtime and none of us can sleep with our stomachs empty," Roweena replies in exasperation that quickly melts into pity as she looks at me. "Let's at least take your bonnet off and give it a good washing tomorrow. We'll wash your hair too."

I shake my head.

"It's growing back so nicely," she coaxes. "I'll heat enough water so you can bathe."

"Not yet," I say forcefully.

The back door opens and a gust of wind sends snow across the floor.

Seamus comes inside with a snow-white hare dangling from one fist. Annie launches from the bench, hurls herself at him, and wraps her arms around his waist. But I am aghast.

"Get it out of here!" My hand trembles as I point at the hare. "You've cursed our unborn child!" I cross my arms over my belly. "He'll be born with a harelip for certain. Never bring a hare near a pregnant woman unless its tail's been cut off." I try to tear the hem of my dress to offset the curse. But as hard as I wrench, the fabric will not give. My chest ratchets with panic.

"What's Mam doing?" Elizabeth asks shakily.

"Biddy, calm yourself," Seamus says. "That's nothing but an old wives' tale. And let go of your dress. You're scaring the children."

Doesn't my husband understand by now that telling me to settle down only winds me up tighter? Sometimes I think he doesn't know me at all.

Roweena hurries to him and he hands her the hare. "Thank you, Seamus. You do well for us. Have a sit down. Soup's still on the fire." There's warmth in her voice.

"I already ate," he says, and turns away to hang his coat on a peg. He glances in my direction for a fleeting second and takes a seat in front of the fire. My husband can no longer abide my face.

"Annie," he says. "Fetch the awl handle I've been working on."

On one of his sabbath outings to the homestead, he uncovered the metal remains of his larger tools. Most evenings he whittles new handles. With the carpentry tools Mariah rescued, he's begun to make chairs again, fashioning a shaving horse and trading labour for a few planks of dried wood. He often works late into the night. By the time we lie next to each other, he's too exhausted to speak.

The youngest children have begun yawning, and Roweena trundles them off to bed. Soon all of her children have climbed to their beds in the loft and she follows. Our girls spread bedrolls on the floor behind Seamus and snuggle beneath their coats.

Seamus's back is a formidable wall between us, and his silence is intolerable. I want to say something, but where do I begin?

Elizabeth pipes up. "Da, where have you been? We were waiting for you."

"Go to sleep" is all he says.

This answer doesn't satisfy Elizabeth, who flops over onto her back and pouts at the ceiling.

Seamus is still for a long time, leaning his elbows on his knees. And so am I. I can see that our child's question affected him. A woman learns to read her husband. He's about to disclose something and he's choosing words carefully. I can barely breathe for fear of devastating news.

"We'll start again," he finally says. "The land is mine and I'll not walk away from it."

I'm relieved by his decision, yet feel bruised. If only he thought of it as *our* land and said he was determined *we'll* not walk away from it.

"After the spring thaw, I'll build a lean-to and put up a tent for shelter. We'll all live there," he says. "When the ground dries, I'll begin work on a new shanty. It'll be slow going without an extra set of hands, but I'll manage."

"What about the baby? He's due around that time. Who'll be there for my labour, and after, who will cook for us?"

"Elizabeth can help," Seamus says.

Elizabeth begins to cry.

Tears burn my eyes too. He overestimates my strength and her ability. What does she know of delivering a child into the world? And I've tried my best to spare her from the day-to-day toil expected of women. I won't work her like a dog to make up for Mariah's absence. My own mam did that to me and I hate her for it.

"When is Mariah coming back?" Elizabeth asks.

"I'm sure it will be soon," Seamus replies.

He's deluded, but I bite my tongue. Mariah's taken our single most precious possession and made off.

There is one silver lining to my sister's betrayal. She's no longer here to poison my marriage. With her and Thomas gone to parts unknown, the deceit that casts its shadow on my family is no longer necessary. Seamus and I can scrub her from our history and be as newlyweds building a new life together—with our own son, I pray.

Now he turns to me and says, "I've already felled and topped two pines. Come spring, I'll arrange for a horse and plow to ready our fields for planting. Our seed burned up, so we'll need to buy new."

"Will you have enough money?" I ask, knowing the answer. We're next to penniless. But there are admissions I hope to drag from my husband's mouth. *Mariah robbed us, burned our home, and left us destitute. You're right, Biddy. This is all her fault.*

His eyes on mine are sharp and angry. "If I must clear trees from a hundred roads by day and make a hundred chairs by night, I'll do it! Thank God for Mariah saving my draw knives," he says, then slowly turns back toward the fire.

I want to shout back, *Thank Annie for waking us up before the fire took us all. Thank Elizabeth for saving our children from the inferno. Thank me for surviving with your son still in my belly.* But I can say nothing. My authority left with my beauty, my home, my earbobs.

I take a deep breath, calming my heart. "Seamus," I say softly. "I miss you. Why were you late coming home?"

"I was looking for Thomas."

I did not expect that answer. "Where?" I ask, hands shaking.

"Drinking houses at Richmond Landing and along Sussex." His tone softens. "No one's seen him, but he's somewhere in Bytown. I feel it."

"Thomas is gone, husband. Gone with his mother and my earbobs."

Seamus's expression hardens. "Mariah's earbobs, you mean."

"You forget who you're married to."

Seamus leaps to his feet. If not for our daughters lying on the floor between us, he might have come at me. "You know full well your mam gave her the earbobs. You drove Mariah away."

I'm stunned. "She burned our home down, nearly killed me and the children. And left me with this!" I tear the bonnet from my head and point to the right side of my face.

"She did not," he says. "Elizabeth should know how to bank a fire safely. You could have overseen her."

I struggle to my feet. "So now it's my fault?"

"Your words, not mine," he says.

"Don't you dare speak to me this way. I'm bearing our first son."

"I have a son!" he shouts.

"With my sister," I fire back. "Maybe you should have married her!"

"There's something we can agree on." Seamus reaches for his coat.

Roweena starts down the ladder. "For the love of heaven, you two. There are children in this house!"

"Where are you going?" I call after Seamus—but it's too late. He's stormed outside.

"Aunt Mariah and Da?" Elizabeth shouts. "Mam, have you gone mad?"

"Da, come back!" Annie runs to the door. For the first time since the fire, my sweet girl has spoken! Hallelujah, even though her words aren't for me.

She stands there, framed in darkness, and cries out, "Take me with you." She stamps her feet and sobs, "Da!"

I feel as though a claw is gouging out my innards. If Mariah were here, I'd scratch her eyes out. I hope she dies. I never want to see her again.

30

THOMAS

O n this raw February night, Peg and I sit across the table
from each other separated by candlelight. And again, she's
sewing. Cutting and stitching consume her every waking
moment. We haven't rocked the bed in four whole days. It ain't natural. I reach my socked foot under the table and rub the inside of her
calf. She ignores me, but I don't let up. She knows what I want. Even
in semi-darkness, the hitch of one corner of her mouth is unmistakable. When I slide my foot higher up toward her inner thigh, she
knees me away.

"Not now, Thomas," she says. "I'm busy."

"You're just sewing. What I've got in mind is a lot more fun."

"Yeah? Well, I get paid for sewing," she says. "I haven't forgotten
my dream."

I rest my crossed arms on the table. "I remember mine too."

Peg tucks her hair behind one ear and resumes sewing. Her mouth
is set tighter than a rich man's purse.

"Come out with it, Peg. You've been holding it in for days. Just say it."

"Very well." She plunks her sewing on the table. "You could do better by us."

"That's it?" Peg keeps looking at me. I shrug. "I earn enough doing Shiner mischief for us to get by."

"Exactly. Getting by was never the deal. What happened to owning a blacksmith shop? Have you given up on claiming the reward you deserve from Aylen? You don't talk about it anymore. He used your information to win. Where's the damned money?"

I've never told her about overhearing Aylen's plans to sell off land-holdings in Nepean and move to Lower Canada if things went bad. And Peg will sour on me altogether if she finds out I've lied about the reward. My gut tells me if I push Aylen for my money, I'll lose out. Especially now that he's facing charges for inciting a riot on election night. I'll show loyalty by accepting the trickle of work he offers through Gleeson. That'll get me something.

"You haven't answered me," she says. "The day you landed on my doorstep, we agreed you'd stay here for free, collect the reward money, and we'd split it. I've come through on my half of the bargain . . ."

"A good businessman has his eye on the future," I tell her. "I'll rise through the Shiner ranks, you'll see. It's already happening. I'm becoming a big man in town."

Peg's drawn-out sigh makes me feel small. "You're nothing but a lackey," she says.

"That's not true. What I do makes a difference."

"They puff up your ego, throw a bit of money your way, and you eat it up, as if scraps meant for dogs taste like top-notch roast."

"I earn the same as I did from Mueller and for working fewer hours. And I get paid by the job, so the money comes in faster."

"Aylen pays you just enough so you're not bitter, but not so much that you can strike off on your own."

"You got it all wrong. Look at what I've done since the election! When that pub owner insulted Shiners at Richmond Landing, it's me Aylen called in to set fire to the bastard's place." I fish matchsticks from my pants pocket and wave them in front of her disapproving face as proof that I'm always ready for the call. "Aylen and Leamy respect my talent for sneaking into places in broad daylight to liberate items of importance—the account book of a crooked Orangeman, a pistol from behind a merchant's counter, a priest's gown from the French Catholic church."

"You're doing their dirty work. When you get caught—and you will, because everyone does—you'll rot in a cell alone."

There's a knock at the door. Peg and I look across the table at each other, still worried about George Baker siccing the law on me.

"I'll get it," Peg whispers. She jerks her head toward the rear of the shanty and I grab my boots and scurry behind the curtain drawn across our bed. There I wait, eyeing the back door and bracing myself to run to an abandoned shed by the river. If anything goes wrong, Peg will bring me food and money so I can flee to the United States and wait for things to cool down. It's what Aylen's men do.

Once more a fist bangs against Peg's door.

I hear the wood brace lift, the hinges squawk, and cold wind sweeps across the floor. A man's deep voice mumbles, the door closes. It's quiet again.

"You can come out," Peg says.

I step into the open. "Well?"

"Gleeson wants a word," she says grimly. "He's waiting at Christie's Tavern."

I clap my hands together. "There must be a new job and that means coin in *our* pockets," I say as I tie my bootlaces.

"Thomas, it's time to leave this place," Peg says.

"I need to get out of this shanty too," I tell her. It's been a month since Michael's death brought the law on me and I've mostly kept hidden away, but it's hard to stay careful.

"Get out of Bytown's what I mean," Peg says. "I'm making a wee bit of money taking in mending work. But there's more out there for me. I feel it."

"More whoring?" I think of the lie she told me about her flowered dress.

Peg actually looks hurt, which makes my innards knot up with regret. "Oh, feck off," she says. "I told you whoring's over with, eejit."

"Just joshing you." I try to sound playful, but she's having none of it. Truth is I can't bear the idea of other men touching the woman I love.

Love? Well, I'll be damned.

"We need to leave Bytown, go to a new town where no one knows us. Maybe a city, like York. There's lots of rich women there needing dresses. And I can make anything."

"There's unrest brewing in York. Word is rebellion is coming," I answer, eager to demonstrate I'm a man of the world.

"There's unrest right here," she says. "In case you hadn't noticed."

"But here, I *add* to the unrest and it makes us money."

"I got a bad feeling is all," Peg says. "Move on with me, Thomas. I want my dream now."

"I can't leave, Clara! Not when I'm this close to getting what I've worked so hard for."

Peg's mouth falls open and she glowers at me. I'm in trouble, but for the love of God, I've no idea why.

"What?" I shrug.

When she doesn't answer, I push away from the table, nearly overturning my seat. I make a beeline for my coat and hat. My hand is on the door latch when Peg's boot sails past my left ear and ricochets off the wall. I spin around, ready to dodge the second boot she's gripping.

"You called me *Clara*! You son of a bitch!" she roars, and hurls her ammunition full force. I duck in the nick of time.

"I did? Peg, it didn't mean anything." A pair of scissors flies past my shoulder as I turn to run outside. I close the door and lay my ear against it. She can't leave me. "It's you I need, Peg, honest to God, I—"

Something heavy thuds against the opposite side, hard enough to make my eyes water. I step back to find two men smoking their pipes on the front stoop of a neighbouring shanty, enjoying the show.

"Go for a pint. She'll settle down," one says with a chuckle.

I sure as hell hope so. My certainty about my future splits wide open. Without Peg to mend the tear, all the little pieces of me will fall out.

I'm miserable and burning for a drink by the time Christie's Tavern comes into view. The two Shiners guarding the entrance greet me by name. Though the place is jam-packed, I spot Peter Aylen and Andrew Leamy eating dinner at a table in the middle of the room. I wave, but they're too deep in conversation to notice.

It takes a moment to spot Gleeson sitting ramrod straight, alone at his own table. As I make my way toward him, his eyes narrow and he lowers his glass. The thing with Gleeson is you never know what mood he's going to be in.

I drop onto the rough stool next to his. "Your glass is empty," I say, raising two fingers to the barkeep, who nods. He brings us two clean glasses and a bottle.

Gleeson pours himself a glass and I do the same. He raises his, saying, "Death stares old men in the face and lurks behind the backs of the young." We drain the whiskey and pour another. I'm trying to figure out what he's getting at.

"We're going to Goulbourn tomorrow morning," he finally says.

"Who's there?" I ask. That's Orangemen country, loaded with British half-pay soldiers turned farmers and some Scots.

"Hobbs. He needs to be knocked down a peg or two. No one calls Aylen *lowbrow* and gets away with it."

"What's the plan?"

"You and me, we go to his farm and stir things up."

Stir things up was code for fire. "What about the wife and his brats?" I ask, trying to sound tough. I'm all for Orangemen getting their comeuppance, but I draw the line at terrorizing women and children.

"Don't know. Don't care," he says, then finishes his whiskey. "You?"

"Nah, me neither." I tip my glass back to avoid looking at him. It's all talk, I tell myself. Push comes to shove, Gleeson would never bring harm to the innocent.

A cold wind gusts inside when the door opens anew. My mouth drops open. For Chrissake, it's Rory! Next to my kin, he's the last person on earth I want to see.

I stand so quickly my stool topples backward.

"You're leaving early," Gleeson remarks, eyeing me.

"Got things to do." I toss a few coins on the table. "Are we riding to Goulbourn tomorrow?"

He shakes his head and fills his glass. "Walking," he says. "We'd draw attention to ourselves on horseback and we can't risk hitching rides with teamsters who'd remember us."

I understand the reasoning, but I don't have to like it. Goulbourn is at least a three-hour walk in the cold. Giving him a nod, I slide out the door, avoiding Rory.

I step into the road and immediately feel snow filling one of my boot tops. Damn it, the laces are untied. I drop to one knee to fix things.

"Thomas?"

Oh shit. I know that voice.

I stand slowly and look Da in the eyes. Since hearing the awful news from Peg, I've haven't been able to shut off the part of my mind teeming with questions about Da and my mam. How could he betray Biddy and deceive me? I could kill him.

"Thank God you're all right," he says. "I don't believe you hurt that boy. You should know that up front." When I don't speak, he keeps blathering even though his voice breaks. "I've been searching for you everywhere. Your mam and I—we've been worried sick about you."

"Which *mam* would that be?"

His expression of relief gives way to dread.

"That's right, Seamus," I say, hands shaking. "I know about you and Mariah. Now, get out of my way."

I try to push past, but he blocks me. "Let me explain."

"Save your explanation for Aunt Biddy, you randy dog!"

Da rushes forward and grabs me by both lapels. I push against him, but he pulls my face closer to his. How I loathe him. His breath smells of whiskey as he shouts in my face. "Listen to me. You have no idea how—"

Behind me, pistols are being cocked. *Click, click.*

Da's grip on me loosens.

"You know this eejit, O'Dougherty?" one of the guards asks.

Da lets go and steps back, regarding me with open desperation. "These are bad men. Come with me. I can help you."

The door of the tavern squawks open. "What's going on?" Gleeson calls out. "Come back inside, and we'll finish off the bottle."

Da's gaze darts from me to Gleeson and back again.

"Everything's fine," I answer. "Just a pathetic drunk who thinks he knows me."

Light drains from Da's eyes and I feel victorious. The guard waves the barrel of his pistol down the road and Da lifts his brows in a final silent plea. I shake my head, and he turns and slowly walks away from me. *Who's the man now?*

The next morning, I wake in the tavern. My mouth tastes like something died in it. Pale light streams through a hole in the roof and makes my head pound when I lift it. The barkeep's wife is collecting dirty mugs and her daughter follows her with a wet rag. Gleeson sits next to me, wide awake and eating breakfast. His beard catches a glob of barley that falls from his spoon. He gestures toward a ripped-open loaf of bread next to his bowl. "Eat," he says.

Three other bearded men from Gleeson's crew sit at a table near the door, still drinking. One of them raises a bottle and takes a swig. The other two wait hollow-eyed for their turns. I'll never allow myself to be so hopeless as they look. When my chance to be someone shows up, I'll grasp it with both hands and let it carry me upward. Peg's wrong. I've forgotten nothing.

While Gleeson finishes eating, I tear into the bread and think further of Peg. She'll cool down today. I'll be home tonight with a gift in hand, maybe a lace collar or china buttons from one of those fancy shops she likes. That'll fix things.

Gleeson drags a sleeve across his face and belches loudly. It's so unexpected from him, a laugh escapes me. His eyes cut to mine like a dare, and I try to turn it into a coughing fit. From inside his coat, he pulls a flask and passes it to me. "Top this up with whiskey and let's go." I do as I'm told. He wobbles when he rises from the stool, and I realize he's still drunk from the night before.

The men stand and together we follow Gleeson into the raw cold of the February day. To avoid being recognized, I pull my hat low and draw my chin inside my collar.

As we pass through Uppertown, I can't resist long sideways glances at Johnston's house in hopes of glimpsing Clara. It's ridiculous. At best, I'll see her shake out a rug on the front step. She doesn't want to see me or speak to me. What do I hope for? That she'll throw herself into my arms and declare her love? At best, she'd let me pass without reporting me to the law.

By the time we reach Richmond Road my feet burn with cold, and I wish we could hitch a ride.

A sharp whistle slices the air and we spot a dark-clad figure waving an arm and running toward us from the direction of Richmond Landing. It's a Frenchman, judging by the red scarf tied around his waist. We brace for action.

The man slips and falls on all fours, then sends an arc of snow into the air as he struggles to his feet. His distinctive laughter carries through the still air and my shoulders drop.

Rory. He's like a bad smell I can't get rid of.

When he reaches us, he's still hooting, oblivious to the alarm he's caused. He doesn't acknowledge me, which, although I hate to admit it, riles me. Also, I don't want this mission I'm embarking on with Gleeson tainted by Rory. Everything he touches turns to shite.

He hustles ahead to walk with Gleeson. But I've been working to regain the boss's favour for weeks. I push my way between the two.

"You're wearing an enemy scarf," I say, hoping Gleeson will lash out.

"Won it in a card game," Rory says. His goofy expression tells me that he's half-drunk.

"Get rid of that damned scarf before one of ours mistakes you for a Frenchman," Gleeson says. "You'll get us all shot."

"Where ya off to?" Rory says, unknotting the scarf and dropping it in the snow.

"No place you're welcome," I say.

"Ain't asking you, *Tommy-boy*," he replies. That greasy smile floats across his face, but hatred burns white hot in his tone.

"I'm telling all the same!" I give Rory a strong shove that sends him reeling sideways into the snow. He recovers quickly and tackles me around the waist, but the men pull us apart.

Gleeson smirks.

"Well, all right!" Rory crows, jerking his arms free of the men. He laughs as if nothing has happened. I'm left to fume.

Gleeson takes a swig from his flask, then offers it to me. I know the order of things. Sharing his flask with me means he ranks me highly. Still, as a show of respect, I take only a sip and return it to Gleeson. He then passes it to Rory, who tips the flask and swigs as if he's deserving and he belongs.

"Ahhh," Rory exhales. Gleeson reaches an arm across my chest and hooks Rory's neck, and pulls him ahead of me. They walk along like bosom buddies trading the flask back and forth.

What the hell! Rory can't just waltz into this mission and unseat me. Yet he has. If I didn't need the money, I'd go home to Peg right now. My pace slows and soon I'm trailing behind the three other Shiners. One of them drains the remainder of a whiskey bottle, then lobs it against a tree trunk. It smashes and glass shards scatter on the snow. A few steps later, they're passing a new bottle between them, but no one offers me a drink. Peg is right. I'm just another flunky.

Harness bells approach from behind us. I turn to see a woman in a fur-trimmed hood and cape at the reins of a blinkered team. The seat next to her is piled high with a mound of purchases, neatly wrapped in brown paper and tied with red ribbons. As the sleigh jingles past, three girls, similar in ages to my sisters, peer over its side. One lifts her doll's arm and waves it at me, her face lit with recognition. It's Hobbs's daughter, the one I met at Mueller's Blacksmith Shop.

Should I go home before this day gets worse? But she's seen me now, and after Hobbs's house or barn burns down, she will name me and I'll stand trial whether I set the fire or not. *Calm down.* May as well stay the course, collect my pay, then get out of town until things cool down.

Gleeson and Rory have heard the sleigh. They turn and stand shoulder to shoulder, blocking its path, weaving slightly. The snow on either side of the road is too deep for Mrs. Hobbs to steer her horses around them. In a last-minute panic, she whips the team to speed them onward, but Gleeson and Rory shout and wave their arms in the air until the horses jerk their heads back and falter.

One of the Shiners pulls himself into the sleigh, setting off a round of screams among the little girls. He shoos them aside, then reaches over Mrs. Hobbs's shoulder and wrestles the reins away from her. The two other men drag the furs from the children's laps and cast them onto the snow as the sisters cower against one another and cry out for their mother.

"Everything will be all right, my darlings," Mrs. Hobbs says shakily.

Rory grabs the bridle of the rightmost horse.

"Jumpin' Jehoshaphat," he exclaims. "This is Hobbs's sleigh. I recognize the horses."

Gleeson's head snaps toward Mrs. Hobbs. "Is that true?"

The woman's chin lifts. "We've come from shopping in Bytown. You are welcome to all that we've bought. Take it and we'll be on our way."

The Shiner behind Mrs. Hobbs flings her brown-paper-wrapped packages and a hat box to his friends, then wrenches the doll from the youngest child and smashes its painted face against the edge of the sleigh. The girl howls. When her older sister protests, he draws the cudgel from inside his coat and waves it menacingly.

"Leave her be!" Mrs. Hobbs tries to reach over the back of her seat to console the three girls, but they only cry louder.

"Shut those kids up!" Gleeson says. "Or I will."

"Yeah, a good whuppin' is what they need." Rory bounds through the deep snow toward a roadside tree and starts yanking on a branch.

The Shiner crew still on the ground tear the paper from Mrs. Hobbs's parcels. Together they unroll a bolt of shiny dress fabric, and wind it around themselves, swishing their hips like women. Soon they grow bored with that game and the tallest Shiner rips open a second package. He pulls out a lacy corset and twirls it overhead by its strings, crowing with laughter at Mrs. Hobbs's embarrassment. The other Shiner tramples her expensive cloth into the snow and churned-up dirt as he models her frilly new hat. Green silk ties dangle on either side of his wolfish face. He lurches toward the sleigh and makes a taunting grab for the girls, who shriek and shrink away.

"Stop it! They're only children," Mrs. Hobbs cries. "When my husband hears of this—"

"He will hear of this. I'm banking on it," Gleeson says, running a hand along one horse's side as he approaches the front corner of the sleigh. "That's a fine animal."

"You can't have him," the eldest daughter pipes up with a sudden brashness that reminds me of Elizabeth. The Shiner raps her shins with his cudgel, and she falls back against the seat, wide-eyed and sobbing.

Rory is back now with a branch four feet long and as broad as a thumb. "Cry some more," he tells her. "I dare ya."

I didn't sign up for hurting women and children.

I step between Gleeson and the sleigh. "Let's leave them here with nothing," I say in a low voice. "We can drive the sleigh to the farm and do what we set out to do, then run off."

Rory overhears me. "We can't just leave 'em. They've seen our faces." He tosses his stick to one of the Shiners and hauls himself astride one of Hobbs's horses. He pulls a knife from his boot, slashes off a handful of mane, and holds it above his head like a trophy, screeching.

Gleeson takes a drink from his flask and shoves me aside. He's drunk and I don't have the measure of what he might do.

I try a new tactic. "She knows better than to squeal on a Shiner, don't you, Mrs. Hobbs?" The woman nods fervently.

I lean in and whisper to Gleeson, "And it's her husband that needs learning a lesson, not the missus and his children."

"The best way to hurt a man is to hurt what he loves," Gleeson says and nods at his crew. The man in the sleigh picks up each girl in turn and lowers her into the arms of a Shiner waiting on the ground. The girls kick, scream, reach for their mother, but it's no use. Seconds later they're huddled together in the snow with no boots on their feet.

"Don't hurt my babies," Mrs. Hobbs cries out, standing up in the sled as if preparing to leap. Her cloak parts. Her belly, several months pregnant, swells like an accusation. I feel sick. She braces a hand on the sleigh.

Gleeson cocks his pistol and attempts to level it at her, but he's too drunk and can't hold his aim steady. "Sit down. You're coming with us."

"I will not," she says resolutely. Her attempts to lower herself over the side of the sleigh unaided are hampered by the length of her cape as much as her pregnancy.

"For God's sake, leave her alone," I say.

He shifts his aim to the left of her head and fires. Mrs. Hobbs screams as the team whinnies and bolts, knocking her sideways out of the sleigh. As she falls, I flash back to Mam tilting off the bench.

Mrs. Hobbs's skirt catches on the runner as she slams to the ground, and soon she's bouncing over the snow like a rag doll, with Rory whooping from atop the galloping horse. At first she shrieks, grasps at her skirt, clutches at the ground. Then she goes limp, her daughters watching in shocked silence. The three Shiners chase the sleigh, leaving me behind with Gleeson.

I think we've killed Hobbs's wife. Like I'm not in enough trouble already. This can't be happening.

Heartbroken sobbing from the little girls seems to sober Gleeson up. He spits on the snow and begins walking back toward Bytown.

The girls shiver violently and look up at me. "I'm going for help," I lie. "So just stay here and wait, right?"

"Thomas, I want my papa," the littlest girl cries. I want to cry too.

I turn and run to catch up with Gleeson. "We should go to Aylen's. He'll take care of things."

"Shiners don't carry trouble there," he replies, trudging steadily along. "Not unless they want to wind up dead or worse."

I don't ask what's worse than death.

"Find a place to hide," Gleeson says. "If you're caught, don't turn me in or I'll feckin' kill you."

Now I see how it is. I don't matter at all.

31

MARIAH

In the early hours of morning, while the other timbermen still sleep, I lie awake listening to the fire crackle as Étienne shifts the logs under the cauldrons. Soon, Cook will begin lighting lamps to wake us all for breakfast.

Da used to tell me a person can pretty much adjust to anything. A short time ago, I could barely tolerate passing strange men on the road, yet here I am waking among men for the forty-ninth day in a row. My excuses for not yet stealing the earbobs from Benoît's pocket have been many—his ready violence makes it impossible to risk stealing the earbobs while he's awake, too many men are still awake when he falls asleep, or a storm approaches making escape impossible once the deed is done. Perhaps I should work to the end of the season and collect my full pay from Sinclair in late March, then steal the earbobs just before the men head out for the spring river drive or continue back to their farms. In the mayhem of departures, I'll be harder to track if Benoît realizes I'm the culprit.

When I wake at night despairing over the earbobs or where my son might be, this small army of timbermen breathing in unison lulls me to sleep. After the first three sleepless nights, cocooned in my blanket between a newlywed farm boy from south of Cobden and a veteran chopper with an impossible Scottish accent, I finally gave myself over to sleep. At least they shield me from Gustave, whose spot is kitty-corner from me on the opposite wall. I've avoided his attentions so far, but I often feel his eyes on me across Cook's firepit. And now I'm accustomed to men's snoring and the sound of them taking a midnight piss against the bottom of the door because it's too cold to go outside. In truth, I worry less about Thomas now I have experienced camaraderie inside this world of men. There's good among them, which makes me believe that there must likewise be at least one Samaritan among the Shiners, someone to take Thomas under their wing so we can reunite.

Here, I've become a mascot of sorts—the silent boy who knows horses and kills wolves armed with nothing but a knife. The men appreciate my efforts and even joke with me.

William's muteness isn't a problem because the work doesn't have much call for words. Days run according to a pattern and everyone knows their role. I do have Brother Stewart's chalkboard upon which I draw pictures when my pointing and hand gestures don't communicate what I want. Figuring out what I mean by my drawings and gestures has become another game for men in need of distraction.

Finally, it's the moment I wait for every day. Henderson stands and ties a woollen scarf around his neck. He's the last man to leave the stable each night and the first to arrive there each morning. I roll my blanket back and crab-walk to the foot of my bunk.

While Henderson chips away frozen urine to unseal the door, I pull on my boots and hide the knife inside. Soon men will begin squeezing past each other in the cramped quarters to get breakfast, find a friend or head to the outhouse, which I need to get to first. Another reason why I'm happy to follow Henderson out of the morning bedlam and into the predawn dark.

I choose one of the bank of six outhouses that sit side by side, jutting out of snowdrifts. I reach for the wooden block nailed to the inside of the door and turn it sideways to lock out any early-rising ne'er-do-wells. The wooden seat is icy and a swoosh of cold air from underneath sets my teeth to chattering.

Men enjoy freedoms, like standing up to piss. Though some men are less free than others. One day I came upon a pair in tender embrace deep in the forest. It looked to me like sweetness, not sin. Such risk they take to be together. Their love for each other is stronger than any Seamus has shown for me.

No one questions that I, William, am male. I've been mixing Fran's herb blend in my tea each morning and night since leaving Bytown, and have only a couple days of dull ache in my lower belly, accompanied by a light monthly easily managed, thank God for that.

Soon I'm kicking an overnight snowdrift away from the bottom of Queenie's stable door.

True, five other horses share the stables, but I still think of it as hers. Henderson has already lit the kerosene lamp hanging from a bracket next to the door, so I take it inside with me and hook it on an overhead beam. She nickers and extends her neck over the gate to rub her muzzle against my shoulder. I scratch under her chin as she nuzzles my ear.

Henderson enters the stable, blowing warm air into his cupped hands. "That horse is in good hands." He watches me for a moment, then adds, "The men say you're doing well at the cut."

On the inside, I'm ten years old again and receiving Da's praise. I serve Henderson with a smile so big and prolonged my cheeks hurt as I watch him inspect the other horses' hooves. Morning silence is pierced by the coarse whine of an axe being sharpened on a grindstone, a sure sign that the camp is springing to life.

After Henderson leaves for the next stable, I open Queenie's gate and go inside. Her water bucket is frozen over, so I stomp it full force with the heel of my boot as she nudges my arm with her nose, ready for a drink. The ice is so thick I can't break it with my heel.

Suddenly, I detect a waft of burning tobacco.

I turn around sharply to find Preach standing in front of the stall, smoking his sculpted clay pipe. As usual, he's dressed in shirt sleeves, yet not shivering. His tolerance to cold is mystifying.

"Try this," he says, passing his axe into my hands.

To spare the sharpness of the blade, I hammer at the ice with the blunt side. Soon hairline cracks form and I break through. Queenie lowers her head to drink the water, avoiding the ice chunks. I return the axe to Preach along with a nod—insufficient thanks for the kindness he's shown me each day since my arrival.

Preach draws on his pipe. I can tell he's rolling something over in his mind. His brow furrows like Da's used to before he dispensed wisdom or warning.

"William, about Gustave. I've seen how he watches you, son."

His forthrightness reddens my face, and I shrug, palms up. I want the conversation to end here.

"He's an immoral man," Preach says. "If he attempts to bother you in any . . . unnatural manner, you must tell me. I'm a man of God called upon to do what is required by the Heavenly Father. Do you understand?"

Yes, I understand. Preach will take Gustave aside again and berate him with scripture, fire and brimstone. Gustave will feel no shame. He keeps my secret and bides his time with me, as I do with Benoît.

I watch Preach through the open door as he heads back to the camboose. A couple of men returning from the outhouses slow their pace to let him pass. All the men here walk a wide circle around Preach. Their reluctance to engage him is a mystery. He's brooding and stone-faced, yes, but I've never seen him commit violence.

While I apply balm to the wear spots on Queenie's neck, I think of my da. What I most remember is how he made me feel that what I wanted out of life mattered. By the time Biddy and I woke up after sunrise, Da would've already left for the estate where he shod horses. Biddy wanted him to come home for his midday meal, but he liked me to carry it to him. He would wink and tell her that her cooking was grand but it tasted better when I delivered it. He understood how much I loved the horses, and that our wee cottage was like a cage for me. Each time I'd run up the road to meet him at the stable, he greeted me as if I were a long-lost friend. He'd update me on how each horse was faring until I knew as much about them as Lord Harris himself. After lunch I'd sit on a bench for a time and watch Da shoe horses. And he didn't laugh when I shared my dream of becoming a farrier one day. Instead, he smiled with pride.

The afternoon is perfect—clear skies, no wind. The thwacks of axes striking white pines echo throughout the forest, and the snow is so crisp it crunches underfoot. My belly is full of pork and baked beans, and as I walk Queenie to the cut after having skidded a stick to the dump, I realize that except for Thomas, I don't miss my old life—Biddy's criticisms, Elizabeth's snobbery, Seamus's taking me for granted while reaping the benefits of my labour.

I decide I really will stay on to the end of camp and claim my full wages. I'll steal back the earbobs from Benoît once I've been paid and hide them in the woods so they won't turn up if I'm searched. He's more brawn than brain, but still, it won't be easy under Maurice's eye. I could find a way to dose Benoît with Fran's powdered bloodroot, just enough to knock him out for hours. But I must be careful not to deliver a fatal dose. I'm no murderer, after all.

Sometimes I see only the impossibility of it all. But today, my reasoning feels solid. I'm on top of the world. Everything will—

"Don't say a word or I'll spill your guts in the snow."

There's no mistaking Gustave's voice nor the sharp point jabbing into my lower back.

"Drop the reins and start walking into those trees." He shoves me into knee-deep snow. "You been making yourself scarce. No more holding out on ole Gustave. We're gonna get to know each other real well."

Ahead is a thicket of snow-covered pines. I want to vomit. My mind reels for a way out. It's useless to run in such deep snow. I'd only fall and he'd be upon me even faster. I search the forest, hoping to spot another teamster.

"Ain't no one here but us two," he says, as if reading my mind. "You're gonna be good to ole Gustave. If you keep making it worth my while to stay quiet, I'll take your secret to the grave. But you better make it worth my while."

I fight the urge to scream. One shout and I'd reveal my true identity. But to comply means killing a part of myself I've fought to reclaim. Which do I sacrifice—earnings and earbobs, or dignity and my body? He pushes me through the wall of snow-laden pine boughs and spins me around to face him, pinning me roughly against a tree trunk and shoving the knife blade against my throat. His face closes in. And then his mouth snaps on mine like a trap. I taste stale tobacco, rotten teeth and pork gone bad. I feel his hand clutching between my legs and it's like being attacked by the Flynns' dog all over again. But this time my scars will be on the inside. I may die right here.

"Turn around," he orders. "Hug the tree."

I tremble with dread and loathing. Fran's knife is in my boot, too far away to reach. There must be another way.

He takes a half-step back and jams the knifepoint into the hollow of my throat. "Now," he says. "I'm done waiting."

Slowly, I turn. He pushes the knifepoint behind my ear, shoving my face into the tree trunk. His breath is ragged. His belt jangles. I'll wait for his pants to drop around his ankles and then I'll fight back, hoping to tangle him in the trousers. Gustave hoists the bottom of my coat.

When his icy fingers tear at the waistband of my pants, rage sets in. A growl rolls from my throat. I'm striking backward with hands, elbows, feet.

"Hold still, you Irish slut," he hisses, "or I'm gonna—"

There's a sharp intake of breath next to my ear. The knife falls away and Gustave's weight is yanked from me.

I whip around to discover that Gustave's neck is trapped inside the crook of Preach's right arm and Preach is ratcheting it tighter. My hands shake, but I pull the knife from my boot and point it at Gustave's chest.

Gustave's bare legs flip and flop like beached trout as he struggles to regain his footing, hampered by his buckskins. Gustave claws at Preach's arms, his eye bulging, then confusion rises in his face like a strange dawn and his movements slow. Finally he slumps, his arms dangling limp from his shoulders.

Preach lets the unconscious body slide to the ground, Gustave's back ending up resting against his shins. He tips the Frenchman's head so his neck is exposed. "Deliver him to hell," Preach says, sounding only slightly winded.

As much as I hate Gustave, I cannot bring myself to do murder. Preach closes his eyes and brings his hands together, as if to pray, but instead traps Gustave's head between them. A hard crank to the left and the Frenchman's neck breaks with a gut-turning crack.

Preach's eyes smoulder, dark and ferocious. I'm free of Gustave but trapped in a new way. He's killed on my behalf.

We stand, catching our breath, staring down at Gustave's body. Preach's grimace relaxes until he resembles his old self. Although he asks nothing, I sense he has questions about what he witnessed between Gustave and me.

Shame burns within me. Must I always be saddled with the consequence of men's aggression?

Preach nods at me. It's a signal for me to do something, but what? I look down on Gustave's purpling face, and I spit on him. Preach studies me without satisfaction, so I kick Gustave's ribs for all I'm worth. And then I continue kicking until my legs scream so loudly with exhaustion that I must quit. I regard Preach with raw fury. Already I'm wondering about the cost of his willingness to do violence for me.

My defiance softens Preach's eyes. "Be on your way, son," he says.

I glance at Gustave then at Preach and shrug with my palms upturned. *What about the body?*

"Go," he says. And so I do.

When I rejoin Queenie on the path, I hug her neck and she rests her jaw on my shoulder. Emotion rises in me, but I swore that William wouldn't cry so I hold it in. We'll be a man of action, not of self-pity. I gather the reins and take one last look back.

Preach has hauled the body away from the tress and laid it flat on the snow. He's squatting, holding one of Gustave's limp arms by the wrist. At first, I can't make out what Preach is doing. But then I see the glint of metal and the sawing action of his right arm. My stomach pitches. Before he lets Gustave's hand fall to the ground, I spy the bloody gap where Gustave's index finger had been.

I urge Queenie forward at double speed.

At the cut, Benoît is doing Preach's job, hewing the top of a felled pine tree. He spits French curses in angry bursts. Maurice works quietly on the ground, scoring the bark farther along the trunk.

Benoît raises his head as Queenie and I approach. His face splits into a broad smile. "Eh, what d'ya think?" he shouts. "I look good up here, no?" He kneels and strokes the gleaming pine. "She's straight like my woman's back."

I raise my brows and muster the exaggerated nod his ego demands. I try to act like everything is normal. But nothing is. My body moves through the clearing, but my mind is still trapped in the woods with a blade jabbing my throat.

Benoît immediately reverts to his former state of rage, spitting French as he seizes Preach's axe and hurls it end over end into a swath of toppled trees. "Sinclair should give me your job. You hear me, old man?" he shouts into the forest. "I'm better than you!"

Maurice, who usually pays his brother's rantings scant attention, pauses mid-chop to direct a warning glance his way.

That night in the camboose, I sit at the foot of my bunk pretending to enjoy Ezra's fiddle music as my mind jackrabbits in every direction. Preach is something darker than a defender of the innocent. The harder I try to act like nothing's happened, the tougher it is to act like a boy. I'm Mariah pretending to be William pretending to be more like William. It's a matter of time before someone notices Gustave is missing. And not much longer after that before men begin asking questions.

Renard will be keen to hunt him down: men who desert camp are tracked and hauled back into service. No matter how well Preach hid the body, it'll be found eventually. Gustave will have left tracks through the woods, from the site his crew is clearing through to where he found me on the skid road that runs from our cut to the heap. The men don't typically walk the stretches of woods between crews, and only me and two other teamsters use that section of road. Accusations will fly and nervous behaviour will point to guilt.

I could take a lesson in calm from Preach. He studies the Bible in his upper bunk and smokes his pipe steady-handed. It's as if this afternoon never happened, as if he hasn't murdered a man. Is he mad or does he feel justified? The Methodist preacher of my youth did tell us stories about killings in the Old Testament. Men are always killing in the name of God.

Maybe I worry too much. Gustave was a blight on the world, the sort no one would grieve to see gone. Maybe everyone will assume he slunk away to get drunk and froze somewhere. I'm safe now. Maybe Preach did me a favour and my days of worrying are over. Maybe.

Preach lays his pipe on top of his closed Bible. Tin cup in hand, he slides over the end of his bunk and makes for a tea kettle hanging above the fire. Around the corner of the raised firepit, Benoît is playing a card game with two other men known for betting against their wages. Gambling is forbidden in camp, but then again, so is drinking. While the players study their dealt hands, one sips from a corked liquor bottle he's stashed inside his shirt, then passes it discreetly to a friend.

Benoît fans his cards out on the bench they're using as a table, and his laughter booms above the din.

"I win again. No one can beat Benoît," he says, pounding his chest with a clenched fist. He notices Preach filling his tin cup and rises from the bench. "I am the best hewer," he announces.

Several men look at Preach. He turns slowly toward his bunk, sipping his tea.

Benoît ignores Maurice's warning glance and his voice becomes more insistent. "I am the best hewer in camp. Better than Preach."

Preach stops dead.

The Frenchman's card mates clear the bench on either side of him. The fiddler stops playing.

"I'll play you at cards, old man," Benoît says. "If I win, tell Sinclair you do my job now. And I'm the hewer for our crew because I am the best." Preach turns toward him.

"Ah, you don't want to play because you know I am the best. Not even your God will help you defeat Benoît."

"Proverbs 16:33," says Preach, dumping his tea into the firepit. "'The lot is cast into the lap, but its every decision is from the Lord.'"

A number of men cross themselves.

"I'll play you," he says, "on one condition."

"Anything you want, old man. You're not going to win anyway," Benoît says. He's a showman, all smiles for his audience.

"I'll take those earbobs you brag about—for my wife."

Benoît frowns, caught in his own trap. All eyes are on him now. He must accept Preach's terms or lose face in front of all the men.

"Let's do it," he says.

Cheers ring around the room as he and Preach square off on the bench. Benoît shuffles the deck, then deals the cards as Preach sits across from him, his hands folded in his lap. The men squeeze in for a closer look and my only view is of a wall of backs and shoulders.

Cook calls, "Thirty minutes to lights out, game finished or no." Someone shushes him. Seconds later, the crowd groans. The tension is killing me.

If Benoît maintains ownership of the earbobs, I have some hope of retrieving them. He thinks all battles are won through physical strength and isn't on the outlook for trouble from a timid boy like William. Preach, on the other hand, is watchful and canny, and is able to murder without remorse. If he wins the earbobs, everything changes.

A final cheer goes up. Men fall away one by one and Preach, appearing no more jubilant than when he first came down for tea, returns to his bunk and I am relieved.

But then I see Benoît's crestfallen expression and my hope plummets. Preach has won and Mam's earbobs may forever be lost. I search the fire for my future until Cook and Étienne snuff the last light.

What now?

32

THOMAS

I t's dark and cold in the wooded lot next to Johnston's house where I've been hiding. I can't shake the picture of poor Mrs. Hobbs bumping over the snow, nor the sound of those little girls wailing. If she dies and they're left motherless, I won't be able to live with myself. I came here hoping to sleep in the stable, but the door handles are now strung through with heavy chain and double padlocked. The Johnstons have just completed their nightly trek to the outhouse, and their lantern light bobs horizontally toward the house as they scud hellishly slow across the snow, their combined silhouette a nightmarish creature with two heads. I jounce, rub my arms, blow into my hands. Nothing warms me. What I wouldn't give to be hidden in their kitchen pantry again, knowing Clara rests by the fireplace on the other side of the door.

Once they're finally inside and their upstairs light is snuffed, I bound through the powdery snow and the long shadows cast by the stable, around the back of the building, past the hen coop, and toward the outhouse. Patch is hunkered inside a new doghouse and pays little attention to me.

I've never spent the night in an outhouse, but there's a first time for everything.

Fortunately, Johnston's is spacious, so I can sit sideways with my legs across the seat and my back against the wall. Moonlight reflects off the snow and enters through gaps around the door. So here I am hiding in the reek of my enemy's shitter. I'm half-frozen and shivering, with my collar turned up and a scarf covering my nose and mouth. My teeth chatter loud enough to shake snow off the roof.

There'll be one more visitor to the outhouse tonight, and I'm at the mercy of her Christian conscience. And how much she drank today. Clara's need to take a piss might be the difference between life or death for me.

I could've stolen a horse and been halfway to America by now. The punishment for horse thieving can't be worse than the penalty for beating an Englishman's pregnant wife. While I had no part of that, I'm probably the only man the little Hobbs girl can identify by name. Their father will be out for blood and Baker, who already has it in for me, won't care which Shiner he captures so long as the public can see an Irishman swinging from a rope. My name begins with an *O*, which will suit all the papers. *O'Dougherty*, sired by parents from Cork, they'll say. In my new life, I'll pick an inconspicuous last name like Smith or Brown.

I'm figuring the last place Baker will look for a Shiner outlaw is on the property of Peter Aylen's most outspoken adversary. Gleeson kept heading along Wellington toward Lowertown, but Gleeson is a fool. Can't believe I ever looked up to him. Lawmen will scour Lowertown, hunt through sheds belonging to the Irish underclass in search of him and the rest of us. They'll start at Mueller's, in case I was stupid enough to go there, and spread their search north to the Ottawa River and east to the Rideau River. I'll be long gone before they think of looking here.

I can't chance returning to Peg's to borrow money, no matter how desperate my situation.

She'd never say the words *I told you so*, but I'd read them in her eyes. And our neighbours would give me up to the law in a heartbeat if there was any form of reward or benefit to be gained. If we'd stolen Mrs. Hobbs's shopping—her hat or that dress fabric—and given it to some poor half-starved widow, we'd have been hailed as heroes. But the Shiner bastards taunted children, beat them and their pregnant mother with sticks. For that, we won't be forgiven by either side—and rightly so.

Suddenly, yellow candlelight shines around the edges of the door. Please, God, let it be Clara. With nowhere to hide, I cram myself tightly into one corner and prepare to spring in case it's not her. Hinges creak open. I see Clara's lantern-lit face just as her eyes flash wide. She scrambles backward with her mouth wide open as if to scream.

"Clara, it's me!" I tear the scarf away from my face. When she spins toward the house and starts running, I race ahead of her through the light of her jerking lantern. "Wait," I say, blocking her path. "I just need to talk with you."

"Go away. You won't be squeezing secrets from me again."

"You want me to beg?" I say, dropping to my knees in the snow. "I'm desperate, Clara, please. A little food and a few coins, then you'll never see me again."

She gives me the same look Mam—Biddy, that is—gives when she thinks I'm trying to lie my way out of a tight spot. But she blows out the candle in her lantern and hauls me into the shadows of the cedar hedge. "Are you trying to get me sacked?"

I take courage when she allows me to touch her sleeve. "You're going to hear bad things about me," I tell her. "But I promise I haven't done what they're going to accuse me of."

She yanks her arm back. "You're part of the gang that attacked poor Mrs. Hobbs and her girls?"

"I was there, but—"

"Get away from me before I scream."

Patch is on his feet now, ears perked.

"Clara, I tried to stop things. I swear. But the men were hell-bent on violence. You know I couldn't hurt them. I got sisters the same age as Hobbs's girls and my own mam is pregnant." That last bit felt strange to say. "I need to get away from here quick. Please help me. I'm begging you."

"Mr. Hobbs found his horses wandering the countryside. Their ears were cut off and their tails too. One had flesh cut from its back haunch."

Feckin' Rory, trying to be like the Whiteboys back in Tipperary.

When the dog starts to whine, Clara shushes him, then turns back to me.

"I've risked enough already and you lie too much." Clara's eyes narrow. "A woman was here, just before Christmas. Dark hair. Green cape. Important papers of Mr. Johnston's went missing that same day. I think you had something to do with that. You know her, don't you?"

"Yes."

"I told the Johnstons no one had been in the house," she says angrily. "I had to lie because of you two."

"I had no choice. You don't understand."

"Right! I'm just a woman. And Irish to boot. What would I under-stand about not having choices?"

"Of course you understand, Clara. Please forgive me. I should have never come asking for help, not after what I put you through. And you're right about me lying. I've been a fool who thought there was a shortcut to getting ahead. Now I'm paying the price. You don't deserve to be caught up in any of it. I don't know how I'm gonna make it up to you, Clara, but I swear to God I will."

Clara's eyes search mine, but she says nothing.

I break the silence. "Thanks for hearing me out. Pray for me, please." I feel myself beginning to choke up and begin walking toward the road.

"Thomas," she says. When I turn, she meets me with an uneasy look. "I'll put some food in a sack for you. And I can spare four pence, that's all. Promise me you'll get out of here if I do."

"I promise." Words stick in my throat, but I manage to say, "Mrs. Hobbs, did she . . ."

"There's been no news."

I hold Clara's gaze a little too long. When she looks away, her eyes track a lit candle passing across an upstairs window. "Someone's up. Better hide in the outhouse again. I'll sort them out and meet you there."

It feels like just minutes have passed before I awake in the outhouse with a start. Something's not right. I shove open the door to find the sky beginning to lighten. Damn, I've lost a full night of travel. There's neither a sign from Clara nor a sack of food in sight. My skin is crawling. What now? The roads are too risky for me in daylight.

The Johnstons' house rests in darkness, so I return to their wooded lot. A hundred feet from the stable doors, there's a dead pine whose trunk is hollowed out by rot. I'm able to squat inside it to escape the wind while keeping sight on the house. An hour later, a faint glow appears in the kitchen window. Clara must be awake. I pray she'll come looking for me soon, with provisions in hand. My stomach twists with hunger.

When the kitchen door swings wide midmorning, I'm still hopeful. But instead of Clara, it's Johnston who exits. He heads for the stable with a sense of urgency that sends me scrambling for more cover. Through a screen of bramble, I watch him open both padlocks and go inside. Soon after, he drives out in a sled pulled by both his horses, with the Brown Bess across his knees. *Oh no.* He could have taken the cutter with two seats. That he's taken a heavier sled with room for several passengers suggests he intends to transport other riders— probably a search party.

Or I'm a right eejit, thinking the worst. Maybe he has business in another town a distance away. Or he needs the sled for carrying goods home over rough roads.

I know I should wait and only take to the road tonight, under cover of darkness. But what if I'm wrong? Maybe it's best that I flee now. I know just how I'll go. I'll follow the Rideau River to Kemptville, bear south, walk across the frozen St. Lawrence and into New York State. There are timber jobs; I'll get one of those. Or I could work for a smithy. I'll earn enough to help Peg get her business, like I promised her. Dear God, I'll make everything right. Just give me the chance to get away.

Then the kitchen door opens and Clara appears. As she heads for the outhouse, I creep through the woods and call her softly from its edge.

She spots me and I wave her over, not wanting to risk crossing the yard in daylight.

"Clara, I didn't think you were coming."

"Neither did I. Mrs. Johnston came downstairs yammering for a cup of warm milk just as I slipped in, and even so she was restless all night. I couldn't get away until just now. And then there was another matter." Clara pulls a bundle from beneath her cape and pushes it into my arms. "There's enough bread, cheese and meat to last a few days. The money's in there too." She pauses a moment and frowns. I can tell she's deciding whether or not to tell me more. Finally, she says, "Johnston just left with his gun."

"I saw."

"A rider carrying news knocked on our front door this morning. Mr. Hobbs has rallied an army of neighbours to search Bytown and flush out the culprits."

My lungs empty like bellows over a forge. "I'm a dead man if I stay here."

"Thomas," she says softly.

I look at her, tight as a knot and sweating all over. When someone speaks your name before delivering news, you can be sure it's bad.

"Mr. Hobbs's little girl remembers you from Mr. Mueller's smithy. George Baker and his men are already searching Lowertown for you. Mr. Johnston has gone to see him with news of Mr. Hobbs's plan. Too many men know who you are. If you leave now, someone is bound to recognize you, whether on road or a trail. Promise you'll hide here and leave after dark."

"Jaysus, Clara." I back away, ready to run. "If I'm found here, they'll figure you're helping me. And then what?"

She meets my eyes. "I'm still angry with you, but I don't think you'd go along with hurting Mrs. Hobbs and her children—or your friend Michael, for that matter. I don't know what demons follow you, but the past is never the past. You have to turn around and face it square on, or you're going to die young. A man can't outrun himself."

Clara comes near and takes my face in her hands. She kisses my forehead. I can't tell what she's thinking when she looks into my eyes and I don't want to cry, but emotions are surging into my throat. I suddenly wish with all my heart that she was Peg. I'm shaking as Clara's mouth gently presses against mine. When she draws back, I look away and wipe a sleeve under my nose. Her kisses used to light me up, but this one leaves me heartsick over how I misused her.

She turns and walks away, and I'm so alone it hurts.

Just then I see that in his haste Johnston has left the stable doors open. All right, then, I'll do what I must to avoid trouble. Sleep by day. Travel by night.

I slip into the stables and climb the ladder to the hayloft above the horse stalls with the food bundle. My stomach is yelling at me, so I sit and eat one of Clara's rolls. Then I try to sleep, but my mind reels with thoughts of all that could go wrong. At the top of my list is other Shiners hoping to divert blame from themselves by helping the law to find me. I expect Rory's far from Bytown and having a good laugh at the bedlam he left in his wake.

A few hours later the whinnying of a horse rouses me—I must have dozed off. I sit up and look over the edge of the loft and out the window I once used to spy on him. Above the snow piled on the outer sill, I see the muzzle of a rifle aimed straight at me.

I throw myself back on the hay, but it's too late. "He's in the loft," the gunman shouts.

"O'Dougherty, this is George Baker of the Bytown Rifles. Come out with your hands up!"

Shit, shit, shit! I'm unarmed and there's not so much as a window to climb out of.

I peer over the edge of the loft. In a shaft of daylight spilling across the stable floor, Baker stands with his rifle pointed at my head. I scramble backward against a wall.

"Climb down the ladder, nice and steady," he shouts.

"I didn't lay a hand on anyone!" I yell. I hear scrabbling sounds on the exterior of the stable wall at my back and my panic spikes.

"Throw your weapons on the ground!" Baker shouts.

"I got nothing!"

"Then do as I say and come down that ladder. Don't be making any kind of trouble. I got deputies here dying to take a shot at you."

Footsteps cross the rooftop above me. I hear Baker cock his gun.

Oh God, this is it. I'm caught and there's no way out.

"I'm comin' down. Don't shoot." I'm on the last rung when I'm grabbed by the back of my coat. Men shout all around me and someone lands a punch to the gut that winds me. I'm sucking air as two men take either arm and drag me into the blinding daylight. Next thing I know, I'm mashed face first in the biting snow and someone's boot heel is crushing the back of my neck.

"Tie his hands good," a new voice says. "And I'm warning you men, this son of a bitch better make it to Perth to stand trial." Whoever's binding my hands together pulls so tight on the rope it burns my skin. I want to go home. I want for none of this to have happened.

"He'll face justice, Hobbs. You have my word," Baker replies.

I'm hoisted to my feet. I see Johnston first, standing proudly with a handful of men, farmers judging by their axes and pitchforks.

Then Hobbs slides from his horse and storms toward me. "Who else was with you?"

"I don't know, sir."

Quick as a blink, he pounds me in the face. My head snaps back and my nose explodes in a burst of white-light pain. Blood fills my mouth.

"That's for my wife. And this"—he lands a punch to my gut that doubles me over—"is for my girls."

I vomit in the snow and blood drips from my nose. His wife must be alive, thank heaven, or he'd have done more than punch me. I send up a thank you for this.

"We know there were other Shiners involved," says Baker. "Where are they?"

If I tell, worse will be done to me than any judgment handed down at Perth. I keep silent.

Baker huffs. "You should be more like your friend Rory. He told us you'd be here. I only had to ask him once." When I glare at him, Baker says, "He'll be joining you at Perth. Don't you worry about that."

"George," Johnston now interjects, "your deputies are welcome to use my horses and sled in the transport of this vile specimen to the gaol."

Baker nods, and a pair of his men drag me onto the sled. Two others climb onto the bench seat and urge the horses forward. When the sled lurches into motion, another armed deputy hops onto the back.

As we pass by Johnston's house, I glance shame-faced at the dining room window, where Clara watches with a hand over her mouth. A lump in my throat practically chokes me. She must hate me for bringing trouble to her doorstep. If Johnston ever realizes the connection between Clara and me, she'll be out on the street and no family in Bytown will hire her. I turn around to keep looking at her, hoping she'll see how sorry I am.

The butt of a rifle nudges my shoulder. "Eyes straight ahead," the deputy warns me. As the sled turns onto the snow-covered road, I see another of Baker's men at the end of the lane with a pistol aimed at Rory's head where he kneels, hands bound behind him, in the snow. Right now, I hate Rory more than any Orangeman or rich bugger I've ever met. The horses slow to a stop and Baker's deputy shoves him onto the back of the sled. He falls face first onto the wood floor, then rolls sideways to right himself opposite me. His left cheek is scraped up and his right eye is nearly swollen shut. But when he sees me, a grin spreads across his face that quickly ends in a groan. There's a dark gap where one of his front teeth ought to be.

"Together again, eh, Tommy?" he teases, then breaks into a cough and winces.

If my hands were free and these men weren't watching, I'd knock out more of his teeth.

"Don't worry. Things are going to work out for us. You'll see." Rory brazenly winks his good eye at the lawman riding just on the back of the sled. Instead of reacting, the man continues scanning either side of the road for trouble. "Yep, you better watch out," Rory says. "It's a long ride to Perth." The man's eyes skewer him, but Rory only smirks, then settles in and closes his eyes.

What does Rory know that I don't?

Every bump in the road jars my spine and my teeth chatter from the cold. Baker's men take turns eating and guarding. No one cares if I'm hungry. Even if they did, it's doubtful I could keep food down right now. Fear has my stomach twisting. I keep imagining what's going to happen once I'm turned over to the Perth gaoler.

Rory is wide awake now but shows no sign of nerves. He catches me staring, then smiles knowingly.

"I knew right where to send Baker. You know what your problem is, Tommy? You're predictable and lacking in imagination."

My eyes dart to the man guarding the back of the sled.

He grins at my reaction. "I'm not saying anything I haven't already told them about you." Then he adds mockingly, "I told Baker a few places to search for Gleeson too."

"You son of a—"

"C'mon now, Tommy, a smart man's gotta look out for himself," Rory says. "Because I've been a helpful and repentant citizen, one night the door to my cell is going to be left unlocked. And I'll wander out of there free as a bird. Maybe I'll find my fortune in the United States. Haven't quite decided who I'll take with me. Peg is a saucy one, and from the long line of men she's bedded, I understand she gives a good ride."

Before Rory can turn away from me, I swing my head downward like a club and bash his face. Momentum carries me forward, so I fall on him. I'm scrambling back onto my knees for another go when a guard hauls me off him and tosses me in the opposite corner of the sled.

Blood is running from a cut above Rory's left brow. "You're finished, Tommy."

The deputy riding in the passenger seat turns sideways and hits Rory with the butt of his rifle. "Shut up, you."

"Hey, you can't touch me," Rory shouts at him. "Baker's protecting me now."

The driver twists toward Rory and spits, "Pipe down. We're all sick of your talk."

Rory's eyes go dark. "You can all kiss my—"

Thunderous musket fire splits the air. The horses rear up as I flatten myself against the sled bed. Baker's men scramble behind the sled for cover and cock their rifles.

"Do you see where the shooter is?" the driver calls out. One of the guards replies, "I can't spot the bastard."

Aylen has sent Shiners to rescue us from the gaol transport. I just need to stay down until the firing ends.

For a long time, no one moves.

"Where the hell is he?" It's the deputy at the back of the sled.

All remains quiet. I wait, with breath held, for new gunfire, for hands pulling me to safety.

"I think it's over," the driver says.

Where are the Shiners? I look over at Rory. His head is slumped forward. Blood drips onto his lap.

"For Christ's sake," the deputy hisses. He climbs onto the sled, then grabs Rory by the hair and tilts his head back.

Dead centre of his forehead is a hole steadily dripping blood. So that's his reward for giving us up.

I can hear him in my head, saying *Left you holding the bag again, Tommy-boy.* The outcry to avenge Mrs. Hobbs's beating will drive the law to make an example of one of us. With Rory alive, I could've possibly convinced someone that he was the chief culprit. Now that Aylen's men have gotten him, I don't stand a chance.

"Seems your friends don't like a snitch any more than you do," the driver says.

They sent a man to kill Rory but not to save me.

"They're no friends of mine."

33

MARIAH

A Methodist circuit rider, Reverend Eli Bagwell, has arrived in camp hours after Gustave's body was found. After we ate supper, he performed a brief eulogy for Gustave and offered a prayer. When asked if anyone would like to say a few words, Renard said Gustave was the best damned card player around and whoever murdered him should swing at the end of a rope. I thought I'd pass out on the spot when those beady eyes swept over me.

Even Preach measures me. Since that day he found me pinned against the tree, I swear I can see him wondering how I could be so unmanly as to allow Gustave to come up on me that way.

Now when the men call out "Preacher," both Bagwell and Preach respond. The two men couldn't be more different. Preach is solid and imposing, while Bagwell is gaunt-cheeked and peaked-looking beneath the wide rim of his black hat. Cook tells me he refuses to eat meat on account of him following the ways of church founder John Wesley, who himself never touches to his lips a morsel that doesn't come from a plant. The reverend's manner is stern but softens greatly when teaching some of us how to read English after dinner. He peers at us from over the top of his spectacles like a doting father.

I sit with the others to try to learn a few words, but Bagwell can't figure how to teach me. As William, I can't sound out the words, so he can't tell if he's making inroads.

Along the benches on either side of Bagwell, eight men hold reading primers toward the candlelit lanterns. Benoît doesn't tease Maurice for taking part as I'd expect of him, but the burly Frenchman has been quieter since losing my earbobs to Preach. The young man who bunks to my left is an eager student. He already knows the sounds of the alphabet and enough words, he tells me, to spare him from being taken advantage of by dishonest men. He sits beside me in deep concentration, moving his lips and sliding one finger beneath the print.

Bagwell is helping a Scotsman to read an advertisement from a newspaper when an older student throws his primer on the floor. "I give up. I cannot make out a single word."

"You need help is all," Bagwell says. He looks around and spots Preach reading his Bible in the upper bunk. "Master Preach, would you please join us and lend your guidance."

Preach's gaze lifts sharply, then darts around the camboose. I've never seen him flustered before. When he notices me watching, he resumes reading his Bible.

"Master Preach," Bagwell calls again.

"Heard you the first time."

"Will you help?"

"I'll help *him*," says Preach, pointing at me with his old certainty.

I walk to the foot of his bunk, primer in hand, and he lowers his tin mug over the end. "Tea starts with *T*. I could sure use some." Bagwell frowns when the others chuckle. I fill his mug with Cook's strong brew and return it to him. Preach smirks in Bagwell's direction before enjoying his first sip.

The camboose door creaks open and, to everyone's surprise, Renard steps inside. He looks to the front of the room, where Gustave's belongings are piled. Next to it, François's bundle still sits, topped with his capote, red tasselled hat and a long scarf.

Since the discovery of Gustave's murder, Renard worries there may be Shiners afoot. Stories circulate camp about them setting fire to competitors' timber piles. At the stable, I've overheard talk that he's questioning all the men about the day of Gustave's murder. He'll be getting around to me soon enough.

I've been staring too long, but I can't look away. Renard settles on a bench close to Benoît. The two French brothers must be next.

My bunkmate starts reading out loud. "Listen to this from the paper: 'Irish members of the Shiners gang have been charged with beating the pregnant wife of Mr. Hobbs of Goulbourn and their three daughters. Hobbs's horses sustained grievous mutilation at the hands of the Irish bandits.'"

The men jeer and shout obscenities at the mention of the Shiners. "Ship the lot of them back to bog they crawled out of," one shouts.

"They caught two of them so far," the newlywed says. Everyone quiets and waits for names.

Oh please, God. Don't let Thomas be one of them.

Encouraged by the crowd, the young man continues reading. "One of them won't be going to Perth Gaol. 'Rory Whelan was shot and killed by an unknown gunman during transport to Perth Gaol.'"

Rory is Thomas's workmate.

"There's a second man awaiting trial." The newlywed squints and tips the paper toward Bagwell. I'm holding my breath. My boy, my baby, my flesh and blood. Thomas could never beat a girl, much less a pregnant woman.

Bagwell studies the print and says loudly, "The other Shiner arrested is—Thomas O'Dougherty."

I fight to hold back from wailing. They'll hang my son.

There's no time to waste. I must steal the earbobs back and get to Perth, where I can trade them to a barrister in exchange for Thomas's defence.

As though Preach can read my thoughts, he leans back in the shadows and discreetly removes my treasure from his shirt pocket. Where he puts them, I can't see. He shuts his Bible and slips it into his pack, which he then stows beneath the rolled-up coat that serves as his pillow.

"Lights out," Cook shouts, and I've never been more grateful to see the end of a day.

After Étienne snuffs the candles, I remove Fran's satchel of powdered bloodroot from my pack and tuck it inside my shirt cuff. She told me to use it as a last resort, and this is it. I've no idea of the proper dosage, only that too much will kill a man and that's not my intent. I only want to incapacitate Preach long enough to safely search his pack and his person.

If, God forbid, I do end his life, won't I be doing some manner of justice? He's killed a man. According to his own ministry, a life for a life is fair. Still, how would I live with having silenced a heart that beats so strongly for his wife? Can a man be all bad who loves his wife so truly? If the dose kills him, Florence will be left a widow in a world unkind to women. I'll have reduced her to my situation. How is that just?

Once everyone is asleep, I sit up and gather items into my pack— my socks and sweater, a few hunks of bread I saved from dinner. With the pack tucked beneath my head, I try to rest. For the first time in a long while, I fish the wolf ear from my pocket. And I remember that night in the woods, when courage took me over and I murdered a beast that would do us harm.

Dear God, watch over Thomas and protect him, I pray silently. *I call on you now to help me be brave. Please forgive me for what I must do tomorrow, but I act as a mother who loves her son. Amen.*

I rise early the next morning, but I don't go to the stables as usual. Instead, I visit the outhouse and linger there to pour a half tablespoon of the powdered bloodroot into the palm of my left hand. I'm about to return to the camboose when I reconsider the amount I'm holding and pour out the rest of the bag.

Someone bangs on the door. "Hurry it up in there!"

Startled, I jerk and spill a portion of the bloodroot on the ground.

No, no, no! I hope there's enough left to do the job.

Inside the camboose, men eat breakfast and prepare for the day. Preach is reading his Bible as usual. I take a deep breath, then cross to his bunk and tap the sole of his boot. When he looks up, I mimic taking a drink. His brows lift and he passes me his tin mug. I smile; he winks, like we're a team. My hands shake so badly I'm sure everyone will see.

I set his cup on the timber-framed edge of Cook's firepit, allowing my palm to rest across the mouth of the cup as if to steady it while I hoist the kettle from over the fire. Clumps of powdered bloodroot drop into Preach's cup as I slowly pour the tea. All but a few specks dissolve. I don't think he'll see that. I tap his boot again and he leans forward to take the steaming cup from me. Anyone watching might think it odd that I've poured tea for Preach and not one for myself, so I wipe both hands against my pant legs, retrieve my cup and fill it too. Then walk back to him. I hope he won't notice that I'm sweaty all over and have to work to hold my cup steady.

He takes a first sip. "Thank you, William," he says in a fatherly tone that sparks a twinge of guilt.

What's done is done.

On my way out the door, it takes all my willpower not to look over my shoulder. I slop tea all along my path to the stable.

Seeing Queenie quells my panic. I lay my forehead against her neck and pray for the strength to do what I must for Thomas. She turns her head and nickers as if she understands how I'm feeling.

"You're here later than usual," Henderson says as he passes Queenie's stall. "I was wondering what became of you."

He's noticed. Will someone else?

Teamsters begin trickling in as Queenie chomps on her morning oats. Outside, the stable boys are hitching Reverend Bagwell's horse to his sleigh while they wait for the stables to clear out for mucking.

Timbermen now head for the trail that leads to the cut. In the midst of the exodus, Étienne steps outside alongside Bagwell, toting the crated primers. They stand aside to let a pair of teamsters pass with their horses and sleds. Suddenly Preach runs outside in his shirt sleeves and vomits in the snow at the corner of the camboose. Newly exiting men give him a wide berth, then join Bagwell at his sled. While they form a circle to pray, Preach catches his breath. But a moment later he's retching again.

Now is the time to act.

I grab a horse blanket and head back to the camboose, casting a quick look at Preach as I pass by. He's hunched over and weaving a bit. When I sneak a look back, he leans to scoop fresh snow into his hands to wash his face.

Only Cook remains inside the darkened camboose, but he's distracted taking inventory at the van.

In a flash, I scramble onto Preach's bunk. His mug, still holding an inch of tea, sits on a shelf above his pack. A quick search turns up his Bible. I flip open the cover and bile rises in the back of my throat. I blink to be sure that what I'm seeing is real.

A large rectangle has been cut out of its heart, so the Bible is transformed into a treasure box. Inside is a jumble of wizened fingers and a freshly bloodied one that must be Gustave's. Could seven fingers mean seven murders? I dump the contents of the Bible onto the bunk. My earbobs aren't there. They must be in his pocket. And oh, dear God! One of the dried fingers, long and slender, is circled by a gold band engraved with a twisting vine. It's Florence's ring, the one he described to me. That son of a—

"Hey!" Cook stands below, studying me warily. "What you doing up there?"

With my heart in my throat, I grab Preach's mug and hold it up for Cook to see. He nods, satisfied that I'm retrieving it for Preach, and goes about his business as I scramble to the ground.

I go to my bunk and wrap the horse blanket around my pack, then I sweep up François's capote, hat and scarf over one arm to disguise myself later and carry Preach's remaining tea outside.

Preach is now slouched on a bench at the front of the camboose, his head in his hands. When he looks up, I can see his pupils are unnaturally large. It won't be long now.

"I'm coming down with something awful," he says, taking the cup from me. "I don't feel so good."

Impatience replaces my panic. He deserves to die.

Across the yard, Bagwell finishes his prayer and shakes the hand of each man before they head off to the cut. Étienne loads the reverend's leather trunk onto the sled, then continues to the stable with the other boys. Bagwell pays us no mind. Men are sometimes ill, and he likely presumes I am helping. He climbs up onto the bench, flicks the reins, and his horse eases the sled toward the lane through which I entered the camp all those weeks ago. I must hurry things along before he leaves without me.

I make a drinking gesture to Preach.

He winces, then tosses the cup back and finishes the last dregs. "Ahhh," he says, grimacing. "That's some bitter-tasting shit, worse than usual." Suddenly, his gaze locks on me and his mouth gapes.

Preach knows!

He pitches forward to throw up again, then falls into the snow with his hands grabbing at his chest. His eyes bug with fright. I kneel and shove my hand into his shirt pocket, searching for the packet containing my earbobs. It's all I can do not to recoil from the fiery heat his body gives off. He grabs feebly at my wrists, but it's too late. The earbobs are mine.

His mouth contorts grotesquely but the words won't come.

There's time to catch up to Bagwell's sleigh yet, so I lean in close to Preach. I will say what I wish and enjoy it.

"You're no man of God, and I know you can't read or write letters. Now you know I can talk and that I'm Irish. Here's the kicker. I'm also a woman." I hold up the earbobs. "And these are mine."

Tears leak from the corners of his eyes and spit dribbles from his mouth.

"You're dying. But where you're going, you won't be seeing your dearly departed Florence. I know what you've done to her."

A faint protest escapes his throat as I cover him with the horse blanket.

"Burn in hell, you son of a bitch," I tell him.

I wheel around to chase after the sleigh, then suck in my breath. Ezra stands two feet from me. He must have overheard everything.

Ezra studies me calmly.

He's a decent man with liquid eyes and a still mouth. A man unafraid. The sort of man shaped by kindness and love given freely during boyhood. A man led not by vengeance and an urgency to break things, but by reason.

"I can explain."

"Another time." He glances around. "You need to get out of here, my friend."

I shove the earbobs into the breast pocket of my shirt. "I won't forget this," I say, hastily gathering my belongings in my arms.

He speaks again, but I'm already running and all I hear is *find me* and *Matawatchan*. Bagwell and his sleigh are nearly out of sight, so I place two fingers in my mouth and whistle. He stops the sleigh and turns around in his seat. I wave my free hand above my head.

And he waves back.

Worry scrambles my brain through my first hours of travel with Bagwell. Have I killed Preach? If I haven't killed him, what then? I do know we journeyed east along Bonnechere River for the first half of the day, then swung south until Round Lake came into view. It feels like we've been travelling along the curve of the lake forever. The reverend is expected at an old fur trader's shanty three hours still from where we are now. We'll overnight there, then Bagwell will continue west and I'll hike southeast in the direction of Golden Lake. Henderson once told me about a camp he'd worked at in the area. With a prayer and some luck, I'll catch a ride with a supply sled returning to Perth. It's not much to go on, but it's all I've got.

Brother Stewart's banter was much friendlier when we were on the road together. Reverend Bagwell asks questions that feel like traps about to spring. No one leaves a timber camp on good terms at this point in the season. He wants to know why I'm wearing a Frenchman's coat and red wool hat, if I had a falling out with Sinclair and do I need to ask the Lord's forgiveness for anything? Maybe he's hoping to expose a sin on my part so he can fill the silence with a sermon. At the moment, I can't imagine which parts of me are worth rescuing. I watch the shimmy of the horse's tail as it trots and fight to steer my thoughts back to saving Thomas.

That's where my mind should be.

After an hour more of silence, the reverend tries a different tack. "Has a family emergency prompted you to leave camp?" he asks. When I don't respond, he speaks louder and slower, repeating what he's already mentioned at least three times. "You are forfeiting your wages. Do you understand?" He's one of those people who thinks that my not speaking implies a lack of intellect. And that suits me fine. Less pressure to react. I actually can't bear to look at him, knowing I've killed Preach. My eyes will give me away and he'll never quit fishing.

It's like he's overheard my thought. "Do you worry about Preach?"

My head torques toward him before I can stop myself.

"Ah, there we have it," he says, looking into the distance with a satisfied expression. "You burden yourself overly much. The man is tough as nails. He'll be up and about in no time."

Reverend Bagwell is wrong about that.

We ride a little farther and he adds solemnly, "Be careful of the company you keep, lad. All men are God's children, but some carry the devil inside them." He pauses to sneeze, then pulls a handkerchief from his coat sleeve to wipe his nose. "There is a darkness in Preach. The other men at Sinclair's camp realize it too and keep their distance from him."

As he studies my dismay, his grey and stony eyes begin to brighten. "For a good tree does not bear bad fruit," he says. "Nor does a bad tree bear good fruit."

Which tree am I?

❧

After spending the night at the first trader's shanty with the reverend, at daybreak I set out on my own, glad to be away from him. I'm running on nerves and barely any sleep. So many things have to go right in order for me to save Thomas. Our host has confirmed that if I continue in a southeasterly direction, I stand a chance of intercepting a supply sled and hitching a ride to where I'm going, so that's what I'm doing.

All morning, I walk just off the path, inside the treeline, to avoid being spotted by anyone, especially Renard, who tracks men who run out on their contracts before the end of the timber season, doles out a good thrashing and hauls them back to the cut. If he connects me to Gustave's and Preach's murders, he'll chase me to the ends of the earth and I'll be useless to Thomas.

In the clearings the snow is beginning to melt, but it's rough going in the woods where there are still high drifts. I'm constantly scanning for movement among the trees and watching for tracks in the snow, any sign of paw prints. It's hard to shake the sense of being stalked, by wolves or men. My heart beats faster to think of it.

Shortly after noon, I break out of the woods, winded and thighs burning. Before me is a finger lake. I can see easily to the opposite side, but the shore where I stand stretches far away, to the left and the right. It's impossible to know how many hours it would take to walk around the lake in either direction. The shortest distance is straight across. Even though it's too early for a total thaw, I see dark-grey patches where water seeps into the snow cover. To attempt a crossing is too great a risk. If I fall through and the current sweeps me beneath the ice, who will help Thomas in my stead?

But all day I've also sensed a lurking danger. I turn to check behind me. Though I see nothing amiss, the feeling grows more intense. I find myself stepping with caution onto the edge of the lake. Ice crackles under my heel and water pools around my boot. Farther out, the ice should be thicker. *Should be.*

As I'm weighing my options, a crow caws. Three more fly over me toward the opposite shore. Something has spooked them.

Then I hear a horse whinny from deep in the woods. Panic tears through me. Is Renard closing in? I rush onto the lake and run for all I'm worth. My best bet is to cross the ice and hope he won't risk following. On the far shore I spot a lone figure paused against the treeline. *Pray he'll be a friend.*

About a quarter of the way across the lake, an eerie groan travels through the ice and I slow to a near halt. I cast a look over my shoulder to solid ground. Should I turn back and follow the shore-line or keep going?

Suddenly a horse bursts through the treeline. It's Queenie. At first the rider is slung forward and resting against her neck. But then he pulls himself upright and his face is revealed.

Preach!

Holy shit! He's not dead?

I suck in my breath and start to run. I slip and smash my right knee on the ice and almost pass out from the agony, but there's no time to stop. I scramble up and keep running. Over my shoulder, I see Preach slide from the horse and lurch after me onto the frozen lake.

"Traitorous whore! I'll kill you!" He slips on the ice too, and I gain a few more yards.

Pain sears my lungs and my knee throbs, but I forge ahead. I search the far shore desperately, but I can't find any sign of the figure I saw earlier.

At the centre of the lake, my boot prints fill with water. Preach is howling again behind me, an incomprehensible jumble about forked tongues, lying and forsaking. "God is on my side," he shouts. "I fol-lowed Bagwell's circuit and then your tracks led me here. It's a sign. I shall slay thee!"

He's mad!

I angle right to avoid a sodden grey patch and pray I avoid weak spots. Again, the ice moans and I stop, uncertain where to step next.

Preach is charging toward me when the lake gives up an ominous sound, like low thunder. I turn around.

Preach is locked in a motionless half crouch only fifteen or twenty feet behind me, staring at a hairline crack that runs through the ice from between his boots to where I stand. All else is quiet. Slowly, he raises his head, his hair wild around his pale face. He claws at the air and shouts, "I will smite thee down and reclaim those earbobs for my Florence!"

Oh hell, no! I start moving again, stepping as lightly as possible through the questionable area. At last I reach a safe span, evenly dusted by snow, and I run full out toward the shore.

Behind me Preach lets out a startled yell. By the time I turn around, he's disappeared. All that remains is slush bobbing inside a gaping hole in the ice. The only sound is wind and my own ragged breathing.

It takes a minute for my mind to catch up to what's happened. Preach is gone, this time for good. It's really over.

I start laughing and crying from sheer relief.

Again, the lake rumbles. My heart catapults into my throat as lines in the ice spiderweb toward me. Then everything goes still again. I lean forward, hands braced on my knees, and send up a thank you to God. The shore is only about forty feet away and—

Crack! The ice gives way and the lake swallows me up. Cold water stabs me from chin to toe. I paddle my arms, drawing quick half breaths into my burning lungs. Muscle spasms jerk through me. I try shouting for help between my chattering teeth, but who will hear me? As I grab for the edge of the hole, I suck in a mouthful of icy water amid my coughing and sputtering. I stretch my arms across the ice and try to hoist myself out, but my legs are numb and I keep sliding back into the water. My strength is waning. Everything is slowing down. Am I kicking my feet? Don't know.

Shivering stops. Sky fades and black moves in.

34

BIDDY

S pring thaw has barely begun, yet here we are—Seamus, the children and me—too early back at the homestead. We are ghouls drifting through the burned-out skeleton of our former life. Our tent, staked inside the remains of my kitchen, shudders against the buffeting wind. Damp seeps through the seams and I am left chilled to the bone.

I've asked Seamus to keep the tent flap tied back during daylight hours, so I can take in a sliver of life beyond these dirty canvas walls without leaving the discomfort of this pallet or the reassurance of Seamus's musket tucked next to my leg. When I do venture outside, I keep it brief on account of worrisome twinges inside my womb and I avoid looking at the scorched fireplace and chimney, both reminders of that horrid night. If only I could unhear the roaring flames, maybe I'd sleep. Blackened timbers fence us inside a bogus fort even a child could overtake.

Around us, the forest teems with men of evil intent. They're out there watching, I know it. Safety is a fairy tale for children. Something will always get us, from within or without.

My wee Katherine toddles into the tent. I reach out to pull her toward me, but she struggles free and begins to wail. "Don't cry, my girl," I tell her. But I hardly set a good example, given I'm squeaking out the words between sobs. In a huff, Elizabeth ducks in through the tent opening and takes stock of the situation.

Katherine reaches for her sister, calling her "Mamma." *Oh, my heart.*

Elizabeth picks her up and takes the time to sneer at me before whisking her outside, leaving me to call after her to be sure to stir the pot of broth hanging over the fire. Seamus will soon be here for his lunch.

It's the Lord's day, his reprieve from clearing roads for the township. Annie's with him, out in our woods, where he's working this morning. My dear silent girlie follows him like a dog and will not leave his side. I can hear the blade of his axe striking wood. He tops each tree he fells, chops their limbs away, then leaves them lying in the snow and goes on to the next. Soon he'll cut pines he felled in earlier weeks into the lengths required for a new home. We'll be starting over again—like just-off-the-ship Irish—crammed into a ten-by-eight-foot shanty with a sloped roof and a back wall only four feet high. This is what Seamus tells me. I am informed these days, not consulted.

My leverage is gone—no herbs, no kitchen, no say. And this ruined face. What is left of my worth to exchange for a husband's loyalty?

There'll be no loft in the new house, no means of escaping each other. But the constant presence of children will hopefully distract from the unease between us. A shudder reminds me of the building urge to relieve myself. The baby presses on all the wrong places. I try to think of other things to delay leaving this cursed tent to seek out the outhouse.

"I've made a decision." Elizabeth blusters into the tent midsentence. "I'm old enough to find a position in Bytown—cleaning houses, helping in a kitchen."

"I need you here," I insist in a shrill voice. "Where is Katherine?"

"But you're fine now! Look at you, sitting up." Elizabeth's smile is so sugary it makes my teeth ache. "And Katherine's right outside the tent. She's no trouble at all. Annie could help you while I'm gone."

"Elizabeth . . ."

Her cheeriness falters. "I'd come home on Sundays. All the girls do. Mrs. Newell told me so."

"There are men in Bytown," I say, leaning toward her. "Bad men. I cannot lose another one of you."

"I can take care of myself. I'm twice as smart as Thomas."

Oh, the cheek of her! "Elizabeth O'Dougherty, your duty is to kin. I forbid you to leave!"

"That's not fair! I didn't make these babies! Why should I stay here and be poor like you and Da?"

Furious, I point at her. "You're a wicked, ungrateful girl!"

She fixes me with a hateful expression that slices me stem to stern. After she storms off, something inside me breaks and I'm crying again. She's as good as gone.

The Newells cited a lack of room as the reason for our sudden ejection from their home. I'd have respected Roweena more if she'd told the truth—that she feared that the disease of our discord might spread through her house. Her Patrick is still away at the timber camp, but maybe she worries that his feelings could cool if he comes back to such a strain. If my marriage can deteriorate, so can hers.

Seamus thinks we're lucky that Roweena consented to lend us this tent after we overstrained her hospitality. I suppose she thinks this gesture makes us even for all the times she didn't pay for the medicine I sent her.

A woman is meant to be a giver, after all. A giver of life, affection, kindness, forgiveness, forgetfulness to ease the way, acceptance, compliance, sacrifice. Where am I in all of this?

I'm an empty vessel. Even the child in my belly does not fill me up.

My attempts to win back Seamus's love only drive him further yet. And so I'm waiting—for this baby to arrive, for my husband to return to me. I'm waiting for healing plants to resurrect in the spring so at last I'll have dominion over something.

Still, if anything happens to this baby, I'll be nothing. In fact, I'll fall lower than Mariah—than Mariah *was*. I expect by now she's sold my earbobs and is living handsomely somewhere on the proceeds. Have I done something to deserve this reversal of fortunes? I'm beginning to wonder.

When was my fate set? Maybe when I was a twinkle in Da's eye. More likely it happened when I resigned myself to Mam's insistence that I shepherd Mariah across the ocean to hide her loss of virtue. Yes, that was it. Now that Mariah and I are far apart, we are more sisters than ever. Same scars, although the ones on the inside are different. Hah!

Elizabeth is now tending our small cauldron over the hearth. I hear her scolding Katherine. Her patience is short because she's angry with me. Instead she should thank me for that broth she's stirring. Last fall, I instructed Mariah to lay away our meagre supply of potatoes, carrots, turnips, onions and a few ratty cabbages in a cold-storage pit topped with straw and levelled over with dirt. I didn't share any of these vegetables with Roweena because I knew we'd be back and charity does begin at home, after all.

Near to bursting, I can no longer put off leaving the tent, but I won't do so without Seamus's musket. Anything or anyone could be out there.

I carry it outside with the barrel aimed at the ground, as Seamus taught me. My gaze combs the treeline for intruders as I head to the outhouse at the backside of the chimney. All I see is a pair of red squirrels leaping from bough to bough in a tall pine.

The outhouse is the only building untouched by the fire. Is there a message in that? Maybe that God has a strange sense of humour.

I step inside, stand the musket in the corner and hike up my skirt. While piddling, I ask for God's protection of my family. Is it a sin to speak with Him while using an outhouse? I've not seen rats since leaving Ireland, but my pulse quickens nonetheless when I imagine them scouring through the filth beneath me.

I'm rushing to complete my business when I hear the warning call of the red squirrels. Danger is coming! Quick as a flea I bolt from the seat and grab the musket. I'm outside standing in the snow, barrel raised, before my skirt settles around my ankles.

I swing the gun left, then right and back again, squinting to see between the tangle of bramble, tree trunks, scrub and low-hanging pine boughs. I hear a twig snap. I knew I did. There's a movement in the branches straight ahead, twenty or thirty feet inside the treeline.

"Elizabeth," I shriek. "Take Katherine into the tent."

She's crying already. "Mam, what's—"

"Do it!"

Now Katherine is crying too. When the whimpers become muffled, I know they've gone inside.

The musket weighs heavy. The muscles in my left arm burn and my hands shake.

My eyes are playing tricks on me. I stretch them wide, then squint again.

"I know you're there. You better move on or I'll fire." I'm answered by silence. A bush rustles. My finger is firmly on the trigger and I'm ready to shoot. Ten feet to the right of the spot I'm watching, another movement catches my eye. Oh dear God! There must be two men—maybe more. I aim the musket left, then right, then left again. *Where are they?*

"Show yourself," I call shakily.

Then, from the right, a shout. "Stop! It's—"

I swing the musket toward the voice, close my eyes and squeeze. First comes an ear-splitting boom, then the smell of sulphur. The musket muzzle bucks and the stock slams my shoulder, causing me to stumble backward.

"Annie, Annie!" It's Seamus's voice I hear. He's running from the place I just shot at to where the first intruder is hiding.

Elizabeth is behind me now. "Mam, you nearly shot Da!"

"No, no. I fired at the stranger! He was right there." I'm so confused.

Seamus storms into the clearing with Annie in his arms. She's howling and her face is buried against his neck. I think I may be sick. What have I done? My husband's eyes brim with loathing. The anger in his face frightens me like nothing I've ever seen.

It feels like forever until he reaches me. Tears now stream down his face. "What in the hell were you thinking?" he shouts at me. How can I respond when I have no idea?

"Annie ran ahead of me," he says.

"I called out. She could have answered me." As soon as the words are out, I realize my error. "You should have announced yourself."

Seamus's mouth trembles with anger. "For God's sake, woman. I was trying to when you shot at me."

His mouth continues moving, but his voice fades until I can't hear it anymore. I'm vaguely aware of the musket barrel dangling loosely from one hand. I should be crying too, but I'm not. Earlier, I'd tried to decide the moment that sealed my fate. It's come back to me now. Such strange timing.

Mam was sick for a long period after Mariah was born. At five years old, I was already charged with my sister's care. How I resented her, all new and pink, draining Mam's life away.

Mariah was only a few months old when I lugged her down to the river. I arranged a raft of branches on the mossy shore. Like Moses in the Bible story, I would send Mariah floating down the river. A new family, far away from here, would fish her out and raise her with their own brood. I settled her onto the raft and dragged it out until I was knee-deep in the water.

Before I pushed her away, I pinched Mariah's arm hard so she'd cry. She'd need to be making noise if her new mam was to find her. I remember my sister's toothless quavering mouth as she wailed. She thrashed her arms and the stick raft bobbed a foot or two away on the current. Then her wee body submerged and sank to the silty bottom.

I watched her face distort just a few inches under the surface. Before long, her eyes closed.

Bubbles rose up. I remember being so angry. The little cuss wouldn't float.

Then the moment that changed my life: I pulled her out.

35

MARIAH

Gentle humming slowly pries my mind open and pulls me close to waking. I don't recognize the tune, but the voice is as calming as my own mam's. My eyes refuse to open, so I linger in a fiery heat at the upper edge of sleep. Something niggles at me. It's important that I wake, although I don't know why.

When finally I come around, nothing appears as I expect. Six feet above me, saplings arch like pale ribs. They're lashed together and covered in sheets of bark except for a large hole in the centre through which smokes escapes into the sky. Bundled herbs hang overhead and woven containers sit along the curved wall.

What is this place?

Then something traces the line of my scar and I'm jolted fully awake.

From the corner of one eye, I see a small hand hastily pulling away from my face. I follow it to see four black-haired children scrambling backward, giggling. Their skin is the colour of copper.

In the span of a breath, everything floods back to me, like a gush of ice water—Preach, dropping through the ice, the figure racing toward me across the shore. Now I understand. I'm lying here between two thick furs in the home of my rescuer.

An old Native woman sits cross-legged on her own fur not eight feet away. She's too old to be the children's mother. When she glances up from her needlework, I find it difficult to gauge if she's displeased that I'm here; her face gives nothing away. Suddenly it hits me—I have to go. Thomas needs me.

I grab for the earbobs in my shirt pocket. *Oh no!* Instead of cloth, I feel only the warm skin of my breasts. I run my hands farther south. To my horror, I'm completely naked. What now? My eyes cut to the old woman, who wears the whisper of an amused smile as she feeds more beads onto her needle. From a horizontal sapling beside the animal-hide doorflap hang my coat, pants and shirt.

One of the children, a girl, edges closer and settles cross-legged, about a foot from my right hip. She watches me closely. I'm not sure what she expects. Two others, little boys, soon wriggle forward to join her. Their dark eyes sparkle and the eldest boy smiles at me. One of his front teeth is missing. *My son is missing.*

The fire is dying down, but I'm so hot.

"My clothes," I whisper to the little girl. Even this takes such effort, but I need to know the earbobs are in my pocket. She smiles and reaches to pat my hair. She says something to the other children and they giggle again. I try to smile as if I'm in on the joke. "Please," I mouth and slowly raise one arm to point in the direction of my clothing. Now the missing-tooth boy touches my hair and grins.

The doorflap peels wide and a younger woman ducks inside carrying an armload of firewood. When she sees us, her weary expression switches from one of distraction to concern. She lightly scolds the children with words I can't understand, then gives me an apologetic look. My eyes flutter closed for a second. When I look again, the children are taking sticks of wood from her. The smallest boy wraps his arms around her knees and looks up at her until she leans forward to kiss the top of his head. While she dusts her hands off, his sisters pile kindling on a patch of exposed dirt next to the firepit at the centre of the room. The eldest girl, no more than eight, adds a new stick to the fire.

The two women speak gently to each other, and I am but an intruder on their quiet moment. Their intimacy moves me and my heart aches with wanting this closeness of kin for myself. The elder continues to bow her head over the beadwork while the daughter—daughter-in-law?—studies me. Where are my earbobs? My eyes grow heavy, but I'm powerless against closing them.

I hear the mewling of an infant. *Thomas, don't cry.* I want to call out to him, but as I struggle to sit, all I can manage to say is, "Baby."

The young woman approaches carrying a wooden bowl with a rag draped over its edge.

She sets them on the floor, then calmly pushes my shoulders back down. I know she won't understand me, but I speak with slow urgency. "My ba-a-aby needs he-e-elp." My tears are hot.

"Shhh," she says, wetting the rag. The old woman begins humming again and the baby sounds fade.

As I lie there—weak and sweaty—the young woman wipes my burning forehead with the ice-cold rag. I'm travelling backward through a dark tunnel to Ireland and the days following the dog attack. The woman's face shifts and becomes Mam's. I tell her, "I love you."

"Sleep now," she says. "You are safe."

Abiding love in Mam's blue eyes is the last thing I see before exhaustion pulls me deeper into the dark.

I'm woken in the morning by a fit of coughing that scrapes my throat raw. Although my head still hurts, I'm not as hot as before. My clothes are folded and stacked next to my head. I feel the shirt pocket. The earbobs are still there. Now I must figure out how to reach Perth.

The old woman is in her place, drinking from a small wooden bowl while her granddaughters brush her thinning grey hair. Inside a shaft of light from the smoke vent, the young woman sits facing me. The shoulder of her buckskin dress droops low while she nurses an infant swaddled in rabbit furs. Skin tightly drawn around her collarbone hints at the family's lack of food. All the more reason for me to leave quickly. I don't wish to be a drain on their stores.

"Your fever has broken," she says. The baby releases her breast, and she lays him against her shoulder, rubbing circles on his back with the flat of her palm.

"Thank you." I wince from the pain in my throat, then turn away briefly to cough again.

She speaks English, which is both good and bad. I'm braced for her questions. *Why am I dressed as a man? What trouble am I bringing to her home?*

Instead, she switches the baby to her other breast. The simple beauty of this moment drives home my separation from Thomas. She smiles tenderly as if recognizing my sadness, which presses harder on the bruise.

"Am I near Perth?" I ask.

"You fell through the ice on Golden Lake. My husband found you and brought you here, to our hunting camp."

"How far to Perth?"

"You are too weak for such a journey."

"But I have to go!"

Her baby fusses, so she begins rocking back and forth. "You have been asleep for two days. You are too sick."

Two days? Thomas could be facing trial by now.

Beneath the fur, I wriggle into my pants, then sit to wrestle on my shirt. The other women pretend not to notice, but I see them stealing curious glances. The cloth strips I used to bind my chest are rolled up next to my socks. I'll take them with me. It will be necessary to hide my sex when I'm dealing with the authorities in Perth. Otherwise, I'll be dismissed as a hysterical mother and perceived as an easy mark by any jeweller I approach to purchase the earbobs. I finish the last button and pull on my socks easily enough. But when I stand, the world tilts sideways and I sink onto the furs again. I rest my face in my hands and wait for the dizziness to pass. When the sensation leaves, so must I.

A light tap on my shoulder rouses me. The eldest girl extends a roll of tree bark that serves as a plate. On it are dried blueberries and another food I don't recognize. Perhaps eating will help me feel better. After I take it from her, with thanks, and start to eat, she watches me until the old woman calls her back. Meanwhile, the young woman seems pleased by my appetite.

"I am called Madeleine," she says. "The old one is mother of my husband. She is known as Mary."

I expected Native names, something long and difficult to pronounce. Madeleine regards me placidly and waits. It's clear she wants to know my name, but I hesitate to give it. As I'm choosing my words, the doorflap lifts and her sons dash inside followed by their father. My heart zings when I spot a horse's forelegs outside before the flap closes. It must be Queenie. She'll carry me to Perth at top speed and I can make up for the two days I've spent resting.

"Kòkomis," the missing-tooth boy cries out to his grandmother. A miniature bow is hooked over his shoulder. Wide-eyed, he holds up a limp rabbit by its hind legs to show it off, speaking in excited bursts.

His older brother's chin lifts with pride as he adds to the story, paying no attention to his sisters' giggles.

"We will eat well tonight," Madeleine says warmly. When the old woman raises her hands, the boys take the rabbit to her for inspection.

While the father settles in front of the fire, Madeleine laces their baby into an animal-skin bag attached to the front of a cradle board.

One of the girls carries a large square of bark, topped with the same kind of food I'd just finished, and sets it in front of her father without speaking. While Madeleine leans the cradle board against a pole of the exterior wall, he takes off his shirt.

Madeleine goes to him to remove and twist water from his knee-high moccasins, then unties his leggings and sets them aside. All that covers his groin and backside are two large squares of animal hide. I'm embarrassed to no end by his near nakedness. Unfazed, his eldest daughter gathers his wet clothing to hang from a horizontal pole in the frame of the wigwam.

He sits now and Madeleine lifts a thick fur to cover his shoulders. When she adjusts it, his hand reaches up to cover hers. For a moment, they gaze at each other with such tenderness I'm undone. Love reveals itself most truly inside small gestures, not in grand demonstrations.

Finally, Madeleine's husband raises the bark plate nearer to his chin and eats steadily. When he finishes, the youngest girl hugs his neck, then takes his plate away. She scampers back to hand him a white clay pipe—with the face of a woman sculpted on the bowl. The sight of Preach's pipe sends a shiver along my spine. But then I remind myself that it's just a pipe.

I clear my throat and announce to the family, "I have questions."

"Yes, we will talk," the man replies. I'm relieved that he speaks English too. But first he addresses his mother and wife in their Native language. His children giggle as he holds his palms two feet apart, communicating the size of something as he speaks. All this happiness suddenly annoys me. It's a relief when Madeleine, knife in hand, goes outside and the two boys follow at her heels with the rabbit.

The man adjusts the fur around his shoulders and turns to me, waiting for me to speak.

"I am Margaret." Giving my middle name feels right. "You saved me and I thank you."

His eyes close briefly and nods. "I am Joseph."

He must have seen Preach chasing me, and he'll want to know why. After a lengthy pause, he says, "Madeleine tells me you wish to leave."

"Yes. I'm headed to Perth with my horse," I say. "Thank you for finding her."

His lips form in a straight line. "Not your horse. I saw the man riding it."

I'm sweating with fever again. "But he's gone now, so . . ."

"Yes, he's under the ice. I found the horse and brought it here." Joseph reminds me of this as if it settles things.

My head pounds in time with my heart. I can't have come this far and risked so much to fail. Da used to say a good negotiation is when each man gives up a little something.

"Keep the horse, Joseph. She's yours. But take me to Perth." My request is bold but raises no reaction from him. "I have a son in Perth. I love him as you love yours. There are men who will hurt my son if I don't reach him."

Joseph draws on the pipe and watches the fire thoughtfully. I'm on tenterhooks waiting for him to voice his decision.

My tears start to flow. "Please, Joseph, I have only one son."

Finally, he says, "Children are a gift from the Creator."

"You will help me, then?"

"I will."

"Thank you!" I stand a little too quickly and stagger sideways.

"Tomorrow," he says.

"No, we must go now," I tell him.

"Perth is a two-day ride. At first light, we go."

When I study Joseph across the fire, all I can see is Thomas slipping away. Suddenly I'm blubbering so hard my sides heave. Joseph's brows gather and his daughters edge closer for a better look, so I hide my face behind my hands.

A morning departure is wisest. I understand this, but still my heart is torn in two.

Madeleine returns and, in their language, questions Joseph. All goes quiet and I imagine how I must appear to them—so beleaguered and mangy.

Cool hands pull my fingers away from my face. It's the eldest daughter, lowering my hands onto my lap. Her eyes reflect my sorrow, but the burden is mine to carry. I've no business spreading worry to children, so I draw a sleeve across my face and take in deep breaths to compose myself. After Madeleine finishes threading the rabbit onto a spit above the fire, she removes her drowsing baby from the cradle board and circles around the pit to sit next to me.

Madeleine leans against my shoulder and shifts the baby toward me. His dark lashes flutter as he sleeps; his tiny, bowed lips purse, then relax. He's a heartbreaking miracle. She smiles at me until I accept him into my arms. My eyes well up again at the comfort of holding this wee life. Calmness inches through my veins like warm syrup.

Mary speaks out in a halting voice that we fall silent to hear.

"My mother asks that you tell us a story," Joseph says. "She wishes to know about your son."

I start at the beginning and tell about everything, from the rolling green hills of Ireland to Thomas's birth at sea and our closeness throughout his childhood. I leave out the bit about him thinking Biddy is his mother. Joseph interprets for Mary. Her head cranes forward when I describe the cabin fire and my bout with wolves. I feel guilty that my story is more like a list of hardships, knowing that their family's challenges cut far deeper than my own. But their interest is genuine and their eyes are free of judgment, even when I tell them about Thomas's alliance with the Shiners and that he's landed in gaol. By the end, my voice is flagging.

"You are brave," Joseph says.

His words surprise me. I am anything but brave. I act out of necessity, to spare myself loss and shame. And even then, I sometimes act too late.

"You must be very strong to survive whatever did this." He draws a line from his eye and downward along his cheek.

"Dog attack," I say. "My son's father saved me."

"You and this man are still together?" Madeleine asks.

"No."

"He fears the strength of your will," she says knowingly.

Her conclusion stumps me. Seamus has always been the rock.

"He is a good father?" Joseph says. "Where is he now?"

I hesitate. Although I don't love Seamus as I once did, it hurts to speak of him. "My son's father is a good provider." Then, embarrassed, I continue, "He is married to my sister now."

Joseph tells this to his mother. Mary thinks a minute, then replies quietly.

"Hmm." Joseph nods slowly. "She says love is earned, not owed. And that you should make good your heart. Life is a circle. Your son will walk a path back to you. Heal yourself and prepare. He will need you as much as you will need him."

He speaks of Thomas's return with such certainty.

Mary beckons her eldest granddaughter. The child listens to her carefully, then sifts through birchbark containers along the wall. From one she pulls a small rectangular bag attached to a thin leather drawstring. She stands behind me and places it around my neck.

Madeleine says, "Mary honours you with a medicine bag made by her own hands."

I smile my thanks to Mary and pass a thumb over the soft hide. Fringes along the bottom edge trickle over my fingers. Since leaving Ireland, I've not received such a thoughtful gift.

"Fill it with plant medicines and things of the earth that speak to you. Carry them against your heart, hold them when you pray," Madeleine says, pressing a fist to the centre of her chest.

The baby stirs in my arms and I hold him closer. A new sense of possibility blooms inside me.

36

THOMAS

I don't want to die. All I think about is how much is left undone in my life. I want to go back to the first time I thought of crawling out through the smithy window to visit a tavern and talk myself out of it. If only I'd abided by Mueller's rules, I'd be waking up in his loft and warming my hands next to a pot-belly stove. Instead, I'm lying under a thin, scratchy blanket on a rough wooden bunk, trapped in a six-by-eight-foot cell in Perth Gaol.

My cell is one of six and the closest to the entrance connecting the gaol to the courthouse next door. Opposite my bunk is a plank door with a peephole eight inches square. There's a piss bucket in one corner. A small window high on the wall lets in a bit of light through its iron bars. If I stand on my bunk, I can see outside, though there's nothing much to see on the street except for the odd sleigh gliding past or sometimes a woman on her way to the village shops.

For eight days I've been cooped up in this log gaol. That's some kind of irony, considering how hard I've fought to keep away from my family's log cabin. I've had lots of hours to think about the last time I went home.

If I'd listened to Da's advice, I could be chopping trees with him right now, with sun shining on my face. It would have been good, honest labour and I'd have come home in the spring with my pockets full of money. But I wanted to prove to him that I was a man and no longer a boy. And now I'll never lay eyes on the new baby or my sisters again. Or Mam . . . Biddy . . . I still can't decide what to call her.

Da tried to steer me right, but now he's given up. He hasn't bothered to come to see me, not that I can blame him.

I lashed out too hard at Da outside the tavern in Bytown. He let himself get caught between two women, left each of them hoping for a piece of him. I'm seeing things from a new angle now, though. He didn't *let* anything happen. It crept up on him. He fell in love with both a gentle woman and a fiery one.

Who am I to judge? I spent weeks pining for two women, and in the end I hurt them both and ruined their prospects. Now I'm powerless to make amends. It's me that's made a mess of things. I was a fool for believing I could be tangled up with Shiners and still woo Clara, and worse yet, that a reward never promised to me could move Peg and me up in the world.

A man can't just think up what he wants, then sit on his arse spying through a stable window and expect his dreams to come true. Staying in that pretend wishing world is the opposite of freedom. It's a trap.

Been thinking about my real mam, too—that's still so hard to grasp. I wish to hell I'd been nicer to her the last time I saw her too. I should never have told her not to come back to the smithy again. It must have been tough for her to sit on the truth for all these years, hearing me call her sister *Mam*. And Biddy's hard on her. We all saw that, and none of us did a damn thing about it.

All I can do now is pray to God the law will listen to my side of things, but without a barrister, I don't stand a chance once Mrs. Hobbs starts talking. No one's going to listen to an Irish fella my age who's a known Shiner. The judge is gonna see in me all the other Shiners who've escaped justice and come down on me hard.

No one is coming to save me. I'm alone.

I've heard tell of Shiners, Peter Aylen himself included, who've busted out of this gaol. Last summer, two prisoners escaped by tunnelling through the dirt floor and out under the bottom log. True enough, they were recaptured soon after, but at least they tried. In case I get ideas, the gaoler claims there's a guard posted outside, but I've never seen evidence of one. He's a lax sort, prone to stretching the truth—and other things.

Sometimes through the small window in my cell door, I watch him stroll past, jingling the keys on his chain, accompanied by another man. The gaoler makes money on the side by renting bunks out overnight to travellers passing through town. Their snoring ruins whatever chance I have of sleeping. When I ask them for news of the outside world, they try to strike bargains I won't make. They offer news in exchange for information only a Shiner could know. *Does Aylen really have that magistrate O'Connor in his pocket? And some of the deputies too? Is it true about all those French whores at the Shiner parties? Heard there's two for every man.* My mouth's gotten me in enough trouble. I'm done telling stories.

Feck! The walls are closing in and my heart is jumping like a jackrabbit. I spring from the bed and pace the cell with my head clamped between my hands. The gaoler is late picking up the night waste bucket and the place reeks of piss and mildew. I miss home. Peg's shanty, I mean. Tears and snot drip from my nose. I have no home and no one to blame but myself. I miss the freedom to go where I want without worrying about who's coming after me. I miss curling up behind Peg and burying my nose in the sweaty woodsmoke smell of her long, dark hair while we talk about our future.

"Step away from the door."

The gaoler waits until I back up against the bunk, then his keys rattle in the lock and the door creaks open. When he squats to retrieve the breakfast tray from the ground, opportunity presents itself. I bound over him. I'm in mid-air when his elbow juts out and catches my left foot. Thrown off balance, I lurch forward and smash my forehead against the cell door opposite mine. Hands clamp tight around my ankles and drag me, kicking and screaming, back into my cell. I manage to hook my fingers on the door frame and hold on for dear life.

"I didn't do anything to that woman. I swear it!"

The boarder who'd been so eager for gossip the night before leans into the hallway.

"Help me," I cry out.

Instead, he steps forward and boots my knuckles until I let go. Just like that, I'm in the cell again.

The gaoler is panting from his efforts, but his expression is nonchalant.

"You best learn to accept your fate. The future is out of your control now." He backs out of the room and locks the door behind him.

I kick the bucket and my piss flies everywhere.

Shortly past noon, a team of horses pulls close to the building. I stand on the bunk and look out through the window. From this angle, I see the corner of a sled, and the gaoler traipsing outside to welcome new arrivals. At least two other men are speaking, but the wind carries their voices away and I can't make out the words.

I stand in front of the cell door, straining to hear. There's a further hum of voices. A lock clicks at the end of the hallway and hinges squeal.

"This way," the gaoler says as he trots by.

I recognize the man he's leading past my cell. He's one of the Shiners who beat Mrs. Hobbs. Who else has been caught? I cram my face into the window opening to see farther into the hallway.

My stomach drops. Gleeson is the next prisoner. He turns toward me as he passes by. Our gazes lock for seconds that feel like minutes. One of his eyes is ringed with purple and the other is swollen shut. Grazes rake both cheeks. His beard's been hacked away and strips of cloth are wound under his chin and over the top of his head. The strips covering both sides of his head are saturated with blood, some of it already dried and brown.

"I never said a word!" I shout after him. He's followed by the same two deputies who brought me here. The first one's rifle is aimed at Gleeson's back. The second deputy beams victorious.

Air squeezes from my lungs as I drop onto my bunk. The law has been holding out until they caught the big fish. Now that Gleeson is here, the trial will race ahead. Nothing to do but hope for mercy.

That evening, I leave my dinner on the floor to go cold. I can't eat because I can't stop thinking about all the wrong I've done and the people hurting because of it. During the trial, news is going to come out about me—deeds and associations that will shame my family. Maybe I *should* pray for a death sentence to spare me having to face them. Peg knew everything and stuck with me. Of all the people in my life, she's the one I could truly be myself around. She knew the real me and still loved me for reasons I can't figure out. I should have asked her what they were, and then worked to become the man she thought she saw in me.

How will Peg ever get her shop now? She's far too clever and good-hearted and talented with a needle to waste herself on whoring. Yet I may have left her with no other choice. If I just had the chance to do things over—

"Psst."

I look up to see the nosey bastard who'd kicked my knuckles. His face is pressed close to the window in my door; his eyes are lively.

"Bugger off, arsehole," I tell him.

He smiles harder. "Did you hear about what happened to the bearded Irishman they brought in today, the one with his head all wrapped up?"

He has my attention now.

"The farmer, Hobbs, cornered him in a stable and cut off both his ears, just like your fellas done to his horses." When my mouth drops open in shock, he says, "Thought you should know." He flashes a satisfied smile, then disappears.

Oh my God, this situation keeps getting worse. Shiners have pushed the Orangemen and Uppertown gentry too far. Every retaliation is fair game now. And here I am, alone with no one to save me.

I let myself slide off the front edge of the bed. My knees touch the ground and I lower my forehead to the cold dirt with ribs heaving. Tears rain down as I smother my sobs.

In the dead of night, the creaking of unoiled hinges wakes me where I lie shivering on the floor. Eyes straining, I try to make sense of what's happening. A hand reaches out from the pitch-black and grabs my arm, but I tear away and retreat into a corner.

"Come with me," the gaoler whispers.

I stand, and gather my wits, then follow him warily. At this point, I have nothing more to lose.

He leads me to the entrance to the courthouse. The gaoler opens the door, then locks it quietly behind us after we've passed through. He collects a lantern waiting on the floor and continues along the row of shuttered windows toward a fancy table behind which hangs a British flag and a painting of King William. I'm shaking with terror. Are they skipping the trial and going straight to the hanging?

"Where are you taking me?" I whisper.

The gaoler raises a finger to his lips and beckons me to a door on the left wall.

"Put those on." He gestures to a chair next to the door where a woman's long cloak is draped over a chair, along with a dress and a bonnet. I look at him in confusion.

"You can't waltz out of here looking like a man," he says.

"Out of here?" I repeat, even as I pull the dress over my head.

"I've been known to sneak whores into the courtroom at night for the pleasure of a barrister or two, even a judge. Nobody will look twice if they see a woman leaving the courthouse after dark."

I slip the cloak around my shoulders and study him as I fasten it at my throat. "To be absolutely clear, you're setting me free?" I can't believe it.

"Head north through the burial ground, cross the stone bridge over the Tay River, and wait on the other side by the road." He extinguishes the lantern before opening the outside door.

I quickly tie the bonnet under my chin. "Wait for who?" I ask with one foot over the threshold. "Is this a trap? Tell me."

The gaoler smirks. "Get going before I change my mind."

I do, and hurry toward where the burial ground should be. Between headstones jutting from the snow, I try to step inside the boot prints already criss-crossing the ground. Up ahead, there's a bridge, right where the gaoler said it would be. I crouch and run across. Just as I'm about to reach the road on the other side, I hear a horse snorting. Distracted, I get my ankles tangled in my skirt and go sprawling onto the frozen ground. The impact knocks the wind from me and I curl up on my side, wheezing for breath.

What am I to do now, caught out on the bridge? I hear hooves clomping toward me. The rider is closing in. The gaoler told me to wait here, but how do I know if this rider is the one sent to help me? I'm in the open with nowhere to hide. Then I realize, I *am* hiding—in these clothes.

I rise slowly and dust my skirts down, as women do when they want to look presentable. Then I turn around and begin walking back to where I came from. *Steady, not too fast.* I can wait there in the shadows until the horse and rider have passed.

From behind me comes a bird call—a snow bunting. I hear it again. I turn around to find a man standing with his horse at the opposite end of the bridge. He must be sent by the Shiners, but I don't recognize him from here. He waves me over. As I walk toward him, I feel oddly let down in spite of my relief at being helped. There's always a hook when Shiners are nice to me. I won't go back to that life. Ever.

Once the stranger sees that I'm coming, he busies himself checking the two pairs of large cloth sacks tied together and laid over his horse. He's finishing as I come up behind him. I stop about four paces away. When I clear my throat, he turns to greet me.

I'm struck dumb. Men's clothing cannot disguise that sharp chin and those green eyes.

Happiness radiates through my entire body.

"Oh, Thomas," Peg says. She's laughing with both arms outstretched. Tears stream down her face.

I run to her and sweep her up in a tight hug. After all the ways I've let her down, she still sees something in me worth saving. *God, I love her.* We kiss each other so wildly that the peak of my bonnet knocks her hat to the ground. Her hair tumbles over her shoulders. She's the most beautiful thing I've ever seen. "I can't believe you're here," I tell her.

"Where else would I be. I love you, eejit."

"I love you too," I say and kiss her again. "You've stolen a horse?"

"Gleeson no longer has need of his mare, so I liberated her from his *estate*," she says with a lopsided smile. "The Shiners owe you a horse at the very least."

As I pick up her hat, I can't help laughing. This woman can do anything. "Let's get out of here," I say, and move to help her onto the saddle.

"It's all right. I can manage," she says, and hoists herself atop the horse. "Hop on. Our new life awaits."

A new life with no more lies.

"Peg, I have something to tell you."

"Let's talk on the way. We must hurry." She reaches a hand down to me.

"You should hear this now. And if you want to leave me here and ride back to Bytown, I'll understand." I take a deep breath. Her look of concern makes it difficult to begin. "Aylen never offered me a reward. I'm sorry. I wanted so badly for it to be true I started to believe my own story. The more often I told it, the more impossible it became to admit it wasn't so. I hope you can forgive me for being such a fool. I love you, Peg. I wanted the windfall for both of us."

Peg shrugs. "I knew you were lying from the start."

"What?"

"Thomas, get on the horse! We can talk on the way."

I swing into the saddle behind her and she spurs the horse into a full gallop along the moonlit road. Several times I check behind us to be sure no one is following. A few miles outside of town, she slows the horse to a walk to let him catch his breath.

I have my own urgent need. "Peg, why did you stay with me if you knew?"

"You're savvy and ambitious. That's why I bet on you. Seemed like good odds that you'd come around. But you had to admit the truth yourself first. Once your plans began falling apart, you tried to protect me from the truth. It's the kindest thing anyone has ever done for me. But more than that, you didn't want me to leave you. I've never had anyone fight so hard to keep me. How could I abandon that?"

"I don't deserve you."

"Well, maybe you do. There's something I've been keeping from you too." I brace myself.

"I told you a while back that I traded the blue flowered dress I'd made—to a kitchen girl at a hotel—in exchange for food."

This confession will crush me, I'm sure. I remember too well finding that dress hidden under the mattress. I figured that Peg went back to trading herself for money to buy the food.

"I lied too," she says. "The truth is that I got that food from a man who worked at the same hotel. He paid me to . . ."

Here it comes.

". . . write letters to his sweetheart. And I spent the money at the market. I thought I'd just do it once, so I concocted that story about the dress to spare your pride, because I knew you were embarrassed that you couldn't read. I thought telling you the truth would bring you lower still. We needed the coin, and I thought, no harm done. But then he wanted more letters written and his friends did too. I'm not the fastest, but I get the job done. And everyone was paying me. The longer it went on, the harder it was for me to tell you, especially with the disappointment you were already facing because of Aylen."

I'm too humbled to speak. Even when she lied, it was to help me.

"But I did sell the dress, recently in fact. That plus a wee bit of my savings was what I used to pay off the gaoler tonight."

My eyes water up. "Peg, it's grand—what you've done. I'm going to work to pay you back."

Her face splits into a smile. "You've got the rest of our lives to make good, but we must be off again."

As the horse shifts into a canter, I hug her waist and nestle my face into her neck. "Oh, you feel good, woman."

"I do." Peg aims the horse northwest.

"Peg, turn the horse east. In a few days, we'll cut due south toward America."

"No, Thomas. We're going to Lower Canada."

"But, Peg . . ."

"We're following my plan this time around," she says firmly.

"Right. Well . . . I'm good with that."

I think back on what I decided in gaol, to ask Peg why she loved me, and whatever her answer, to make sure I do that over and over again for the rest of my life to make her happy.

"Peg, why did you come get me?"

"I told you. I love you."

"But why . . . after everything I've done?"

"At the start, we needed each other to get ahead. But that's business, not love. Then I realized that you take me for who I am, not for what I was. You don't scoff at my dream; you want to help me make it come true. That's love. In your head, there's a vision of the life you want and the man you must become to get it. True enough, your map to getting there has been ill-drawn, but you're trying for something better. There's never a dull minute with you. I couldn't take dull minutes. Neither one of us have been perfect people, but we're growing up together."

I thought I'd been in love before, but I was wrong. This was love.

"I want to build you a home—on the up-and-up—where you can operate a seamstress shop. I'd do anything for you, Peg."

"I know it. That's why I'm here. But what about your smithy?"

"It can wait."

We ride on in silence. Nothing else needs saying. Seems to me we have this love thing figured out pretty well.

37

MARIAH

I leave the hunting camp with Joseph at first light. Madeleine wakes to see us off, but the old woman and children do not stir. Both Joseph and I wish to reach Perth as soon as possible, even if it means riding well into the night. I am eager to see Thomas before the trial and secure a barrister willing to trade services for the earbobs; Joseph wishes to return home from this journey before the sun sets on the second day of his return trip.

Cold morning air starts me coughing. Each swallow is a dagger inside my throat. Never having ridden on horseback before, it takes me a few miles to adjust to its sway. I sit behind Joseph with both hands clamped on the back edge of the saddle, hoping not to slide off Queenie. By noon, my backside and legs ache more with every step the horse takes.

All day, we ride cross-country along Algonquin trails. After a short sleep, we do the same the next day. Changes in direction are marked by trees resembling twisted old men. Their trunks grow vertical but bend sharply at waist height and jut horizontal for several more feet. Joseph tells me his ancestors trained them to grow in this manner as signposts to guide travellers. I ask him to walk Queenie close to one such tree so I can snap off the end of a twig and tuck it inside my medicine bag, where I've already stuffed the wolf ear. I will need it to pray for guidance in the days ahead.

My son is my North Star. Fate passed the earbobs through many hands, from a wealthy estate owner's wife to a Bible-toting murderer. And now I hope they will buy his freedom.

On the last leg of our journey, we stop to let Queenie rest. After so many painful hours in the saddle, I welcome the chance to stand and stretch my back. The sun is warm when the breeze stills. With a front hoof, Queenie paws at the snow and nibbles at the tufts of grass she uncovers.

Joseph offers me a strip of dried venison, but I'm too nervous to eat, so I put it in my pocket.

"You will soon be with your son," Joseph says.

I am glad of it, yet worry writhes inside me.

I am brave. I am strong. Madeleine, Joseph and Mary told me so, and it would serve me well to believe it. I'm beginning to see the light, but a nagging voice in my head drags me back into the dark. It's so much easier to see these qualities in others.

A while after we resume riding, the snowy path widens into a road and we begin to encounter people driving sleds. Safe to presume Perth must lie ahead. Travellers glance sidelong at Joseph and me—a Native and a scarred-up youth dressed in Frenchman's garb. I'm accustomed to being gawked at, but not for the reasons that these people do.

Joseph pulls back on Queenie's reins and she stops. "This is as far as I go," he says.

His chin lifts proudly, but his eyes follow a sleigh bearing a pair of well-to-do men, one with a gun resting across his knees. After I slide from Queenie's back and bid her farewell, Joseph produces a knife from his waist, then cuts off an inch of her mane and hands it to me.

A lump rises in my throat as I add it to my medicine bag. "I will remember everything you have done for me." My voice comes out half-strangled and I must turn away to cough.

"All things are as they must be," he says.

I do not understand his meaning. Not one bit.

The road leads me straight into Perth. Sights and sounds of village life grate on me after the seclusion of Sinclair's camp and the peacefulness of the wigwam. Above the front door of one stone building on the main thoroughfare hangs a black sign bearing gold print. A barrister, perhaps, judging by the letters I can identify. I've yet to see any indication of the gaol, but it must be close by. Up ahead, a one-legged man balances on crutches as he smokes and watches the sleds dash by.

"Sir, where might I find the gaol? Or the courthouse?"

He looks me over, head to toe, and begrudgingly aims the stem of his pipe across the road and to the right. I thank him and continue hastily on my way, looking for an official-looking establishment. Thomas is within reach and I cannot wait to lay eyes on him. There it is: a pale stone building with tall windows and proper panes of glass. Although my legs shake with fatigue, I hurry forward, eager for a look inside. Shutters block my view until I come across a window with sprawled slats that permits me to see a few rows of chairs. Surely someone here can direct me to Thomas. I pound the door at the centre of the building. No one answers.

"Come on!" The condition of my throat constrains my voice, so I bang with both fists.

Shutters soon open wide inside the nearest window and a man appears. His hang-dog eyes regard me with relaxed curiosity and I spy a ring of keys resting against one hip. I've located the gaoler. When I smile and nod at him, he casually jerks his thumb toward the log building I now see extending from the end of the courthouse. "Go to the other door," he shouts through the glass and closes the shutters.

I rush along the courthouse wall to the only visible door on the log building. I test the knob, but it doesn't turn. High up on the wall to my left is a row of small windows, one of which must be Thomas's. I know it.

My short hair and manner of dress will shock him. Perhaps he'll realize I'm different, not at all like the old me. New Mariah would never have tolerated the lie we lived or my servitude under Biddy. I pull back my shoulders and lift my chin. To bolster his own morale, Thomas needs to see confidence in his mother and the possibility of a better life.

I hear wood sliding across the inside of the door and then the gaoler's face appears through a cut-out window.

"I'm here to see Thomas O'Dougherty."

"You're too late."

I'm too late. Thomas has been hanged!

I open my mouth to howl, but no sound comes out. Weak-kneed and blinded by tears, I stagger back. My boy . . . I didn't get to see him. He'll never know that I was his mother or how much I loved him. Now he's in the cold ground.

"Hey!" the gaoler calls out. "O'Dougherty's not dead. He busted out last night."

At first I'm not sure I heard right, but then the words sink in.

"Hey, only a woman could cry like that," the gaoler says. He reads my surprise and winks.

"Ahhh, you *are* a woman. O'Dougherty's mother, I'll bet. Your secret is safe with me—and you don't have to worry about that boy of yours either. He's likely halfway to the US border by now and hiding out with a pretty girl."

"Right," I whisper hoarsely. Everything has changed. If Thomas is on the run, my plans are useless. My mind whirs with new worries. Will he ever come back?

The door opens and the gaoler steps outside with eyes twinkling.

"If you need a place overnight, ten pence pays for a bunk here. But if you have no coin, I'm sure we could come to some arrangement."

Rolling my eyes, I turn away from him and head for the main street.

"I wager you're a good-looking woman underneath all that getup," he calls after me. I answer with both my middle fingers. That shuts him up. Amazing what rubs off on a woman after living in the bush with a bunch of timbermen.

It's an easy matter to wave down and hitch a ride with a teamster who's returning to Bytown. Soon I'm shivering in the back of a distillery sled loaded with kegs of scotch. If not for François's red tasselled hat, his capote and scarf, I'd be frozen. My body aches all over, wooden staves press into my back, and my legs dangle over the end of the sled. But my pockets are empty and the ride is free.

Thomas is gone and no one loves me. Still, my boy lives, I tell myself, and that is the most important thing.

Do I just try to go on as if he never existed? Not knowing where he is will kill me. How can I sit idly by hoping he'll one day find *me*? I'm not sure that life truly is a circle, as Mary said. The way things stand, I'm nothing to Thomas but a spineless auntie.

Seamus springs to mind for the first time in weeks. He's probably rebuilding the homestead now, a home for Biddy I'll never live in. I wasted my life waiting for him to come around, settling for any scrap of affection left over after my sister had taken her fill. I hate myself all the more when I realize how much I want to see him.

Seamus is the only person in this world who will understand my grief and feel it with me. Also, I cannot in good conscience shirk my duty to tell him what's become of our son. Keeping our secret put Thomas on the road to self-destruction. Surely together we can imagine a way to find him.

It's been nearly three months since I set foot on O'Dougherty land. It's a relief to walk among trees this morning, after days on a horse and then a sled. And yet, the closer I come to the clearing where the cabin once stood, the heavier my old guilt weighs on me. I look above the treetops and imagine the sky glowing orange as it did on the night of the blaze. For a minute, I consider turning back to Bytown. But then I receive a sign—the distant sound of an axe. Seamus is here. I carry on, hoping he is alone, for I cannot tolerate Biddy or Elizabeth needling me today.

I spot him and stop a few feet inside the treeline at the north edge of the clearing. I watch him as he notches the end of a log. There must be a hundred yards separating us, but when he pauses to wipe a sleeve across his forehead, my heart pangs unexpectedly. Something in the way the wind lifts his hair takes me back to the simpler days of our youth.

Seamus has so far built the shanty walls four logs high, but it's much smaller than the original. He must be living in the white canvas tent set up next to it. Will he be more angry that I disappeared so many weeks ago without a word to anyone, or that I've returned?

Either way, it's unlikely I'll visit the homestead again. From the nearest tree, I remove a tuft of moss. Before I place it in the medicine bag, I hold it and pray Seamus will talk with me.

Disappointment strikes when I open my eyes. I see Biddy stretching her back outside the tent, her rounded belly jutting through the opening of her cloak. A ragged bonnet conceals her face, and although I fight the feeling, my heart breaks for her. Annie suddenly skips from around the corner of the new shanty with Katherine scooting after her. Elizabeth must be nearby as well.

I slowly inhale the earthy scent of the forest to quell my unease, setting off a volley of deep rumbling coughs.

"A man!" Biddy shrieks. "There!" She's pointing in my direction.

Seamus looks up first. Then faster than I can make sense of what's happening, he lunges for the musket leaning against the log wall and raises it.

My throat seals shut.

"State your business or move on!" he shouts.

I raise my hands and step forward.

"Shoot!" Biddy screams.

I strain to call out, but it's no use. In the shape I'm in, my voice cannot travel the span between us. Seamus takes aim.

"Come no farther," he yells.

I slowly raise an index finger, a signal for him to wait, then reach upward with my right hand. If I remove the hat, they will see that it's me. No sooner do I lift the toque from my head than Biddy charges at Seamus, grabbing for the musket.

A thunderous boom splits the air and I feel a searing pain in the flesh of my upper left arm. I clutch at the wound in stunned disbelief as blood streams from between my fingers. When I look up again, I see Seamus jerk the musket from Biddy's hands and begin to reload. I drop to my knees on the snow and wait for him.

He approaches with the barrel raised. As he draws nearer, an expression of horror crosses his face and he lowers the gun. "Mariah?"

Tears trickle down my cheeks. My arm hurts and it's been such a long time since I've heard my name.

"Oh my God," he says upon seeing my bloodied sleeve. He squats in front of me while his eyes travel frantically over my body. "Why didn't you say something?"

"I tried."

Understanding crosses his face, followed by woe. "Biddy grabbed the musket. I . . ."

"What's happening?" Biddy shouts, and she begins to inch toward us with her arms wrapped around her belly.

"Stay back!" Seamus tells her, then faces me again. "Please tell me you've come back to stay." His bottom lip trembles. "I love you. I can't live without you."

I've waited sixteen years to hear those words. I don't want to feel longing for Seamus, but I do. "I've come about Thomas—"

"He's locked up, I know." Seamus fumbles with the buttons on my coat. "I should have gone to see him already."

I can't have heard right. "You knew he was in gaol and you didn't go to him?"

Seamus eases my arm from the coat and tears open my shirt sleeve. "It's a flesh wound, but it needs tending."

"Answer me."

His eyes turn overly bright as he clutches my hand. "You and I, Mariah, we can go to the gaol together."

"Mariah?" Biddy has come close enough to recognize me. Her hair hangs in greasy strands from beneath the bonnet and there's a new wildness to her. "Judas!" she screams, and she charges at me. She stops short, though, and lowers her bonnet to reveal her scarred check. "You burned our home to the ground and look at what else you've done! Marked me the way the dog marked you."

"No one's to blame," Seamus says. "That fire was an act of God, Biddy. We've gone over it a hundred times. Go back to the tent and rest. Tell Elizabeth to bring what's left of my whiskey."

Biddy's chin quivers. "You're not my sister anymore. You dare to dress like a man and wear that heathen thing strung around your neck. What debauchery have you been up to?"

"Mind your tongue, woman. She's back. That's all that matters," Seamus says.

Defeat twists Biddy's mouth, and her eyes cut to mine with a look of utter despondency that drives the air from my lungs. She is my sister, blood of my blood.

"I do love you, Biddy," I say.

Her face goes hard. "I should have let you drown."

"What do you mean?" I ask, but she turns away and trudges back to her children, all standing in front of the half-built shanty. I'm still trying to understand what she meant when Seamus grabs my shoulders and tips my chin up. This is all wrong, and yet he gazes at me with such earnesty that hope warms my hollow chest. I've waited a lifetime for what he's about to say.

"Mariah, my darling, don't leave me."

My heart cools like a stone. He spoke these exact words to Biddy in December as she lay ill by the Newells' fireplace. It's as if I'm outside my body, watching strangers from a distance.

"Thomas escaped from gaol," I say.

"Let's find our boy together. We'll bring him home, get him in line. We can be family like we used to be, but better. I'll set Biddy aside and build separate quarters just for you. For us. Say you'll stay."

I shake my head. It's not that simple and it was never going to be. I can't be a party to returning my son to the same prison I refuse to be trapped in. I once dreamed of a moment like this, but I won't do to my sister the very thing that pained me for so long.

Seamus's brows gather as he realizes that I'm refusing him. "But I can't manage without you. If Biddy dies, how will I raise four children alone?"

I look at him and feel nothing. I won't explain all the reasons why I'm leaving. If I do, he'll find a crack to wedge himself into and pry me wide open. Those days of letting him manipulate me are over.

Just as I'm putting on my coat, Elizabeth arrives, all smiles, with the whiskey in hand. "You're back, thank heaven. Mam's gone off a bit."

Seamus takes the bottle from her. "Mariah, I need to cleanse the wound."

"I'll do it myself," I say, taking the bottle from him and tucking it in my coat pocket as I stand.

Elizabeth narrows her eyes at me in disbelief. "You're leaving?"

"Mariah, you can't go," her father says urgently. "How will you survive with no home, no skills?"

This is the argument of a weak man trying to pin me down with fear. All along I thought he carried me when the opposite was true. I carried him. Without me to bear the brunt of Biddy's frustrations, they would have landed squarely on him. He doesn't truly love me and never has. He needs me like he needs a horse to pull a plow, and that's no love at all.

"Goodbye, Seamus." I turn away and head back into the woods.

"I want my earbobs back, you old cow!" Elizabeth hollers.

It pinches me to ignore her, but I do.

Once I'm some distance away, I hear Seamus call. "Thomas knows you're his mother! If he comes looking for you and you're not here, what then?"

I smile and continue onward. He hopes to sting me, but instead my heart swells with happiness. Life is a circle. My son will find me when it's time. And I will be ready.

I've sacrificed my happiness for others long enough. Mary said, *Heal yourself. Be ready.* And that's why I'm headed now to Bytown to sell the earbobs, the first step toward my new future.

There's a jeweller in Uppertown who I'll trust to be fair, because if he was unscrupulous, he'd have been out of business long ago. I'll repay Fran for the axe she gave me and use the remainder to buy property with a shed suitable for a smithy and a farrier.

I'll travel as the boy, William, and take odd jobs as required until I get settled. All things are possible if someone perseveres and keeps faith. There'll be no holding me back.

※

At midday, I walk through Uppertown with my shoulders squared and chin lifted. I feel different. Everything feels different. The sky is a brighter blue and winter's harshness is breaking. No one gives me a second look. There's a sense of lightness in people moving along the street; perhaps it's the anticipation of spring that cheers them. Men lingering outside taverns no longer give me pause. They put their pants on one leg at a time, just as I do. Not even dogs trotting unaccompanied along the roadside send me into a panic.

The jeweller's shop is up ahead. I hold the medicine bag inside my fist and think of Mam sending me off with the earbobs the day I left Cork. She could never have pictured me selling them to follow in Da's footsteps as a farrier.

A woman is leaving the shop with a fair-haired boy as I arrive. When I hold the door open, she nods politely. The child tips his head way back and gapes upward with awe before he follows after her. To him, I must look like a rugged giant. I catch myself chuckling and go inside.

Behind a counter to my left waits a heavily browed man wearing a proper suit and tie—his shirt collar cuts into the excess of his neck. The jeweller, I presume. "Can I help you?" he asks.

When I begin reaching inside my coat, his mouth tightens.

"Just fetching earbobs from my shirt pocket," I tell him.

"Ahhh!" He relaxes and smooths a red velvet cloth on the glass counter. "You wish to sell them, no doubt."

"Yes sir." I lay the first one on the cloth and glimpse the upward flinch of his brows as he sniffs.

"These once belonged to a fine lady," I assure him. "Pearl and gold. They've been in my family for three generations." But I drop the second and it skitters across the room. Red-faced, I search the polished wood floor and stoop to retrieve it from in front of a glass cabinet. The shelves display a few pocket watches with gold chains, some sparkling lockets strung on plush ribbons, and row upon row of earbobs—many gleaming with pearls. My jaw drops as I spy every conceivable size and shape, singularly mounted or clustered like kernels of corn.

I lay my second earbob on the red velvet cloth and wait for the jeweller's assessment. He peers at them through a tiny magnifying glass with a brass stem. After a few seconds, he tucks the brass apparatus into his vest pocket.

"At best, I can offer you a few coins."

"But they're gold and pearls," I tell him. How will I build a future with that piddly amount?

"Have you had them appraised before?"

"Well, no. I just thought . . ."

The jeweller shrugs, as if I should have known better. "These pearls are not real. The setting and screw back are made of gold-plated brass."

"You're certain?"

"Beyond a shadow of doubt," he says. "Do you still wish to sell?"

A lump rises in my throat. "I need a minute."

I pick up an earbob and turn away from the counter, wandering over to stand at the shop window overlooking the street. Sunlight warms my face through the glass. Although its brightness forces me to squint, I don't try to escape it.

I will not cry. Life is never as it seems, that's for damned sure. The only thing a body truly owns is what's inside.

Across the street a riderless cart waits for someone. The horse hitched to it is grey-whiskered and tired looking. Black leather blinkers prevent it from seeing sudden movements that might spook it into bolting. For the benefit of the rider, the animal is deprived of a full view of the world. As I watch, the owner returns, but the horse neither raises its head nor nickers. Only when the whip is applied does it plod forward.

Another man leads a horse at the end of a rope down the centre of the street. This animal is magnificent, with a sleek brown coat and silken black mane. The handler pulls the rope taut to encourage the horse to go faster. Instead of complying, the horse rears, front hooves pawing the air. What a marvellous and powerful creature. It tosses its head and yanks the rope from the man's hand. People scoot out of the way, expecting the stallion to buck and cause mayhem. But it does not. The horse stands majestic, enjoying its new freedom.

Weight drops from my shoulders. I'm buoyant. I stride back to the counter and lay the earbob on the red velvet cloth next to its mate.

EPILOGUE

June 1843

It's been a good summer so far. Our garden flourishes and neither deer nor rabbits have overly ravaged it. We hope for a harvest equally bountiful as last year's, but both having experienced famine, we don't take abundance for granted. The doors sprawl wide open at the front of my shed to give me a full view of hollyhocks now blooming along the garden fence.

I'm doing brisk trade today. This Percheron whose hoof I'm filing is the fourth horse I'll have shod before my husband's afternoon prayer. As I work, the draft horse stands inside the snug shoeing stall Ezra built in the centre of the shed. I dislike restricting horses, but Ezra reminds me that one kick would finish me and he couldn't live with that.

Our smithy, once his father's, is situated at a crossroads west of Matawatchan and draws plenty of business. At first local men hesitated to do business with a woman farrier, but they soon discovered my work is top-notch and my prices fair. Word spread about the red-haired woman who dresses like a man, wears Native trappings around her neck, and can calm a horse no matter how cantankerous its temperament. I know folks around here speculate about how my face came to be so scarred, but I let them wonder. They seem to enjoy trying to figure it out, and whatever they imagine will be more exciting than the truth.

They know better than to question Ezra about the scars. Their curiosity annoys him and he lets them know it. He doesn't see my scars, only the courage it took me to get this far. I am a blessed woman.

My husband would do anything for me, as I would for him. He's a burly, big-fisted man with the heart of a lamb who sometimes leaves a wildflower on the horseshoes he makes for me. He doesn't always tell me he loves me or that he's proud of me, but I know it by the way his eyes drink me in and how he speaks of me to others. At night he undoes my silver-streaked braid and we hold each other close. His love for me is boundless.

I'd rather shoe horses any day than talk to most people other than Ezra. Animals are more honest. And forgiving. It's not right for a serviceable creature, who can't speak up for itself, to suffer a worn shoe or a trapped pebble. I take pleasure in clipping an overgrown hoof or paring the residue of a prior journey from the tender part of a foot. A well-applied shoe is like a new beginning.

Outside the shed, our dog barks excitedly, with his black head lowered and his tail wagging. Someone has arrived in the yard.

I continue filing and wait for the visitor to find me. When I finally look up, I'm surprised to see a black-haired girl about four years old standing in the doorway. She's wearing a pale-blue dress with a bow sewn at her throat and hugging a homemade doll. The dog noses her chest and licks her chin. Her giggles bring a smile to my face; it's not often we see children here. She reminds me of someone, although at the moment, I cannot say who.

I lower the horse's hoof to the ground and wipe my hands on the front of my leather apron. "Well, hello there," I say, walking toward the child.

She bunches the doll against her face and watches me from over the top of its head. Her eyes are an arresting shade of blue. When I kneel in front of her, she shyly turns away and scoots off, calling, "Mam! Da!"

I follow her into the sunlight. She's running toward a newly arrived wagon. My eyes squint against the brightness to see who's there. I register the outline of possessions mounded in the back—trunks, a crate of hens, the legs of several upturned chairs.

A man hops off the wagon, and a woman, his wife I presume, gathers her skirt around her calves and climbs down to join him. They join hands with their child and make their way toward me. The woman slides the bonnet from her head to reveal raven-black hair and a sharp chin. When my hand flies to my mouth, the child's father removes his hat and presses it against his chest. His eyes are blue and earnest.

My knees go weak and he runs to catch me.

AUTHOR'S NOTE

This story's genesis hearkens back to a desperate moment between my fourth great-grandparents, John and Martha Lindsay. In 1832, they left County Cavan, Ireland, for a new life in Bytown, Upper Canada. One winter's night, when fire claimed their shanty, John gathered his children and ailing wife into a nearby shed and blanketed them with hay. As Martha's sickness deepened, John drizzled whiskey on her lips and pled, "Martha, my darling, don't leave me."

Mariah Lindsay, Thomas and the O'Doughertys are born of my imagination. Their family friends Patrick and Roweena are a nod to the Newell family who emigrated with my ancestors. My belated writing friend Jay Stewart is commemorated through Brother James Stewart, who reflects but a fraction of his goodness.

In nineteenth-century pioneering communities, single women like Mariah often forewent marriage to aid female relatives and their families. Women were responsible for child rearing, nursing the sick, laundering, sewing and mending clothes, caring for the dairy and chickens, gardening, food preservation, maintaining the hearth fire, and cooking three meals each day. Without assistance during pregnancy or periods of illness, Biddy's household would have floundered. The Home for Friendless Women that sheltered Mariah did exist, although in Uppertown and not until 1882.

Bytown, known today as Ottawa, is located on the traditional unceded lands of the Anishinaabe Algonquin Nation. For millennia, Victoria Island in the Ottawa River was a significant meeting place for Algonquin trade, ceremonies and burials. In the early 1800s, the island was absorbed by Bytown settlers. Before European contact in 1613, Algonquin peoples had lived, hunted, fished and harvested freely throughout the Ottawa Valley; increasingly, government land purchases and colonization now severely hindered their self-sustaining way of life. During this story's time frame, Algonquin people of the Ottawa River Valley continued to suffer the Crown's disregard for their shrinking access to hunting lands. In Bytown, their presence was met largely with contempt.

By 1836, Bytown was home to one thousand permanent citizens, fifteen licensed drinking establishments, plus a large number of illegal groggeries. With ample distilleries and breweries to supply them and the seasonal influx of timber workers, drunkenness plagued the town. Men frequented inns and taverns to imbibe, glean local news, and discuss politics. Such locations also served as recruitment centres for labourers.

The Irish who partook in construction of the Rideau Canal (1826–1832) had fled poverty, famine and self-serving British landlords. They lived on drained swampland along the excavation site in shanties or caves dug in the canal banks. One thousand Irish canal workers and colleagues died of accidents or diseases like malaria transmitted by mosquitoes. The Rideau Canal Celtic Cross stands today at the edge of the first canal lock to honour their sacrifice.

In the three years following completion of the canal, Bytown's Irish community suffered two cholera epidemics, food scarcity and economic depression. Just as Seamus did each winter, men throughout the Ottawa Valley supplemented their income by working at timber camps. Irish timber workers provided cheap labour, but their inexperience led to injuries often caused by their own axe swings. Falling trees crushed men to death, as did logs rolling from atop piles stacked up to seven deep on bobsleds along the ice roads. In *Unrest*'s era, timber bosses prohibited alcohol, gambling and the presence of women to minimize distractions that may precipitate conflict or injury. Circuit-riding Methodist preachers like the fictional Eli Bagwell visited timber camps to minister the gospel and, in the belief that literacy was the path to social reform, taught men to read.

Irish workers' attempts to secure timber jobs brought them to blows with French Canadians, the labour force that timber bosses preferred over the Irish, who were stereotyped as belligerent drunkards. Discriminatory practices stemmed back from England, where the Irish were regarded as an inferior class whose laziness and inferior intellect accounted for their misfortunes. Uppertown residents placed the blame for both cholera outbreaks squarely on Irish immigrant shoulders.

Meanwhile, Bytown's gentry, living comfortably on the Uppertown side of the canal, flaunted their prestige by creating social organizations whose rules made it impossible for the Irish to participate. They established authority through township governance, then used these opportunities to enrich their own class while the poor Irish lived unaided in misery. The Irish, having crossed the Atlantic to find equality and opportunity, were frustrated at being denied both in their new homeland.

The time was perfect for a leader capable of derailing the gentry and muscling the Irish into timber jobs. Real-life Peter Aylen assumed the role with vigour. He attracted disenfranchised men from across the Ottawa Valley, quickly growing his gang of Shiners to roughly two hundred strong.

GWEN TUINMAN

His climb to power had begun years earlier. In 1815, sailor Peter
Vallely jumped ship in Quebec and changed his name to Peter Aylen.
A year later, involvement in the timber trade brought him great wealth.
Throughout the Ottawa Valley, he owned properties and timber con-
cerns at which he hired only Irish workers. By 1835 he'd won leadership
of the Irish raftsmen after promising to establish job security by oust-
ing French Canadians. He also plied the men with extravagant feasts
and alcohol.

Aylen isn't the only Shiner character drawn from the pages of history.
I've also fictionalized his associates: Andrew Leamy, his right-hand
man; Hairy Barney, who truly did blow up buildings and eventually
himself; and John Gleeson, who did cut off horses' ears during the
February 1837 assault on pregnant Mrs. Hobbs, then suffered his own
ears being severed by her outraged husband. The Hobbs daughters'
frostbitten toes are my own invention.

As happened to Peg and her colleague, Shiners did intoxicate and
stage half-dressed prostitutes on Uppertown sidewalks to offend the
gentry. Aylen also hosted spectacular orgies featuring Montreal har-
lots. His stone house remains on Richmond Road in Ottawa, but I
took creative licence and placed his residence along the same road
as a farm inspired by another of his holdings, a sprawling acreage in
Horton County near the Ottawa River.

Ease of escape from Perth Gaol and Bytown's lack of a policing force
fuelled Shiner brazenness. In the spring of 1836, a citizen's group called
the Bytown Association for the Preservation of the Peace authorized
Magistrate George W. Baker, previously a captain in the British Army's
Royal Artillery, to form a group of volunteer constables called the
Bytown Rifles. Around that time, Aylen became a representative for the
newly formed Ottawa Lumber Association, which vowed to end violence in the timber trade. Its initial venture, which Aylen was in charge
of, directly benefited his timber operation on the Madawaska River.

The Orange Order was a social institution that fostered the interests of Protestants and promoted Britishness. Many upper- and middle-class Irish became members to align themselves with Bytown's British and Scottish ruling class. In doing so, they inflamed resentments for poor Irish like Thomas, and even more so for Irish Catholics.

Real-life figure James Johnston was an Irish Orangeman with political aspirations and publisher of the *Bytown Independent*. His anti-Shiner commentaries provoked the gang to burn his home and newspaper office to the ground. In 1835 he erected a new stone house, which they attempted but failed to raze two years later. This second home, at a fictionalized location, is where Thomas meets Clara. Following the January 1837 riot at the Nepean Township council meeting, gang members clubbed the real-life Johnston nearly to death.

As in the novel, by the spring of 1837, the Shiner grip on Bytown had weakened. Aylen sold his Upper Canada properties, expanded his timber landholdings north of the Ottawa River, and resituated in Aylmer, Quebec. His marriage into a prominent timbering family opened doors to rooms of power and opportunity; his three sons would become doctors and lawyers.

Aylen himself went on to serve many years in public office, taking on roles such as property assessor, superintendent of roads and township councilman, all while enriching his bottom line. In 1848, he was awarded the title of Justice of the Peace.

ACKNOWLEDGEMENTS

I've come to realize that writing acknowledgements is no small feat. How does one adequately express gratitude for each kindness and precious inspiration gleaned over the years-long gestation period of this novel? I shall endeavour to do so here.

Heartfelt thanks go to my Random House Canada family, particularly Anne Collins and Lauren Park, whose artful editorial guidance helped me to hew squarely the story that lives in my mind. Thank you so much to my dynamic agent Marilyn Biderman for believing in me and recognizing *Unrest*'s potential. I'm also grateful to editor Heather Sangster for her bolstering comments about the first-draft manuscript.

Thank you to author Jennifer Robson and poet Shannon Webb-Campbell for conversations that led to gold-plated brass and a black dog in the middle of the road. Thank you to Wes Peel for his cyanotype photomontage *Horse Tamer* and to Angela Durante for asking if I'd rather be the tamer, the rearing horse or the girl watching from a distance. Many thanks to my invaluable writing friends Cryssa Bazos, Connie Di Pietro, Tom Taylor, Andrew Varga and the late

Jay Stewart for their support of my *Unrest* journey. Thanks also to Donna Gould and Jo-Anne Green for their thoughtful feedback.

For so generously sharing his time and knowledge, I'm for-ever grateful to William Dick, a member of the Algonquins of Pikwakanagan First Nation and also the Culture Resource Officer of The Algonquin Way Cultural Centre.

For the inspiration of historic maps, sketches and artifacts, my thanks to Library and Archives Canada; Champlain Trail Museum; Bytown Museum; Museum of Civilization; Perth Museum and Matheson House; Algonquin Park Museum and their Logger's Day historical interpreters; and to the stewards of old-growth forest Shaw Woods. Thanks also to Julie Oakes and Eamon McNeely of Pickering Museum Village; Fire Prevention Officer Kristy-Lynn Pankhurst; Lois Thomson of the *Madawaska Highlander*; Ed Campbell; Larry and Karen Aiken; Annie O'Neill-Kahn and Dali.

I'm indebted to Michael Cross for his essay "The Shiner's War: Social Violence in the Ottawa Valley." These books helped shape my understanding of the past: *Whiskey and Wickedness: The Rideau Military Settlements 1875* by Larry D. Cotton; *The Camboose Shanty: Home to the Shantymen of the 19th Century* by Roderick MacKay; *Great Forests and Mighty Men: Early Years in Canada's Vast Woodlands* and *Lumber Kings and Shantymen: Logging and Lumbering in the Ottawa Valley* by David Lee; *The Blacksmith's Craft: A Primer of Tools and Methods* by Charles McRaven; *The White Chief of the Ottawa* by Bertha Carr-Harris; *The Foxfire Book* edited by Eliot Wigginton; *Early Life in Upper Canada* by Edwin C. Guillet; *Algonquin Traditional Culture* by Kirby J. Whiteduck; and *Anishnabe 101* by The Circle of Turtle Lodge.

Thank you to anyone who ever asked how the story was going. Most of all and always, thank you to Eric for walking this road alongside me (and the *Unrest* characters) and to our children for their unwavering support.

And thank *you*, dear reader. I hold you in my heart.

CREDITS

Gwen Tuinman extends her thanks to everyone at Penguin Random House Canada who worked on *Unrest*.

EDITORIAL
Lauren Park
Anne Collins
Sue Kuruvilla
Deirdre Molina
Catherine Abes
Danielle Gerritse
Liz Lee

COPY EDITOR
Tilman Lewis

PROOFREADER
Sophie Weiler

DESIGN
Talia Abramson
Keight MacLean
Noah Kahansky

PRODUCTION
Trina Kehoe
Erin Cooper
Elyse Martin
Asher Nehring

SALES
Evan Klein

MARKETING
Anaïs Loewen-Young
Danya Elsayed
Megan Costa
Paola Gonzalez
Polly Beel

PUBLICITY
Sharon Klein

AUDIO
Sonia Vaillant
Katherine Kvellestad
Ankanee Lagunarajan

CONTRACTS
Samantha North
Jamie Steep
Naomi Pinn

EDITORIAL ACQUISITION BOARD
Kristin Cochrane
Barry Gallant
Marion Garner
Scott Sellers

GWEN TUINMAN is descended from Irish tenant farmers and English Quakers. Her storytelling influences include soul searching, an interest in bygone days, and the complexities of living a life. Fascinated by the landscape of human tenacity, she writes about women navigating the social restrictions of their era. Gwen lives with her husband on a small rural homestead in Ontario's Kawartha Lakes region.